RS   11.50

P9-CQB-249

Praise for th

JAN COFFEY

"Coffey's trademark elements are here: a fast pace, complex plot and interesting characters. What makes this story so intriguing are the questions it raises about ethics— or lack of them—behind closed doors everywhere."
—*Romantic Times BOOKreviews* on *The Puppet Master*

"Timely subject matter, explosive action and quirky characters make it a splendid read...Coffey weaves a swift, absorbing tale."
—*Publishers Weekly* on *Triple Threat*

"Jan Coffey...skillfully balances small-town scandal and sexual intrigue with lively plotting and vivid characterizations."
—*Publishers Weekly* on *Twice Burned*

"An all-consuming, passionate, and gripping story!... Make a note to yourself to pick this one up. You'll really be sorry if you miss it."
—*Romance Reviews Today* on *Twice Burned*

"Well paced, suspenseful, and sometimes startling, Coffey's latest unexpectedly pairs a mystery filled with graphic violence and explicit sex with a sensitive love story....An intense, compelling story that will keep most readers guessing until the very end."
—*Library Journal* on *Twice Burned*

"Fantastic...a nail-biting, page-turning thriller! Definitely a keeper!"
—*Philadelphia Inquirer* on *Trust Me Once*

"A fast-paced, impeccably plotted story with a terrifyingly credible premise."
—*Romantic Times BOOKreviews* on *The Deadliest Strain*

"Lightning-paced and gripping, with a cast of intriguing characters."
—*Romantic Times BOOKreviews* on *The Project*

Also by

JAN COFFEY

THE PUPPET MASTER
THE DEADLIEST STRAIN
THE PROJECT
SILENT WATERS
FIVE IN A ROW
FOURTH VICTIM
TRIPLE THREAT
TWICE BURNED
TRUST ME ONCE

JAN COFFEY

BLIND
EYE

MIRA®

If you purchased this book without a cover you should be aware that this book is stolen property. It was reported as "unsold and destroyed" to the publisher, and neither the author nor the publisher has received any payment for this "stripped book."

Recycling programs for this product may not exist in your area.

ISBN-13: 978-0-7783-2673-1

BLIND EYE

Copyright © 2009 by Nikoo K. and James A. McGoldrick.

All rights reserved. Except for use in any review, the reproduction or utilization of this work in whole or in part in any form by any electronic, mechanical or other means, now known or hereafter invented, including xerography, photocopying and recording, or in any information storage or retrieval system, is forbidden without the written permission of the publisher, MIRA Books, 225 Duncan Mill Road, Don Mills, Ontario, Canada M3B 3K9.

This is a work of fiction. Names, characters, places and incidents are either the product of the author's imagination or are used fictitiously, and any resemblance to actual persons, living or dead, business establishments, events or locales is entirely coincidental.

MIRA and the Star Colophon are trademarks used under license and registered in Australia, New Zealand, Philippines, United States Patent and Trademark Office and in other countries.

www.MIRABooks.com

Printed in U.S.A.

To Lisa and John Lombard

No one could ask for better friends
than the two of you.

and

To Miranda Stecyk Indrigo—Our Editor and Friend

We have been partners together from the first days
of our journey into the world of suspense fiction,
and we've been so grateful for your insight and your
continuing encouragement, and for your belief in our
storytelling abilities.

As you cross this new threshold in life, we wish you
and your beautiful family the blessings of health and
happiness...and of nights filled with sleep.

1

St. Vincent's Hospital
Santa Fe, New Mexico

"You're awake."

Lying on his side, Fred Adrian became aware of the sensation of movement before knowing where he was. The starched white pillowcase was cool against his cheek. The smell of plastic registered in his brain.

The gentle roll of the bed along a smooth floor, the blink of the lights overhead, the words on the intercom that he couldn't exactly make sense of, they all made him want to go to sleep.

"You were a trouper during the procedure," the same woman's voice said cheerfully.

Then he began to remember. The hospital. He was in for the procedure. He was lying on a hospital gurney. Fred's mind was slow to catch up, but things were starting to make sense. He was in to have a routine colonoscopy.

"I'm nervous about it."

"No reason to be nervous. It's over."

"When do you start?" he asked.

She chuckled. "It's all over. You're done."

He wasn't hearing her right. He wanted to go to sleep. "What time is it?"

"It's ten past eleven," the same voice, pushing the gurney along the corridor, told him.

Eleven. Last time he'd looked at the clock it was a few minutes past eight. He couldn't remember anything after that. He lifted his wrist to check his watch. He wasn't wearing it. Fred held his hand up against the passing lights on the ceiling. They were so bright.

"Easy now. You're still hooked up."

He squinted at the IV hanging from a shiny chrome hook near his head. The tube snaking down from it disappeared and then reappeared before terminating under some tape on the back of his hand. His first time under anesthesia. He'd put off having the colonoscopy for a very long time.

"I made it. It's over," he said to the voice, as if that should be news to her.

"You made it through with flying colors," the woman said in an entertained tone.

She slowed down to negotiate a turn.

"I'll be fifty-nine next week," Fred said to her.

"Happy birthday."

The bed bumped its way through a door. Fred didn't mind. The residual mellowness from the anesthesia was taking the edge off of every sensation. His hand flopped onto the pillow and he slipped it under his head. He looked up at the ceiling. He couldn't quite focus yet.

"I'm the first one of us to reach the age of fifty-nine," he told her.

"The first one?" she asked.

They made it through the door, and the nurse parked him. He wanted to talk, to tell her how special this was. His mind was slow to keep up, though. He didn't know if she'd asked the question now or at eight o'clock this morning. He decided to say it, anyway. He had to share the news.

"I'm the first male in my family…" He chuckled, remembering how nervous he'd been before today. He was sure this would be it. Today, he'd die. "I'm the first one to reach the age of fifty-nine. My father…he was forty-two when he died. Brother…fifty. Now maybe I'll live to be sixty. My daughter is getting married next year…and I'll be sixty."

There were two other patients in the room. Fred looked over. Another bed was rolled in after him. Or maybe he was there before him. He was an old man, sound asleep. Fred was tired. Maybe he should sleep, too.

"You're just starting to wake up, but there's no hurry," she told him. "Do you have someone waiting for you in the reception area?"

For the first time he saw his nurse. She was moving the IV from a hook on the gurney to some stand next to it. She was young, not too pretty. She could be, he thought.

"I need a date for my daughter's wedding," he told her.

"Do you have someone in the waiting area, Mr. Adrian?" she asked again. She wasn't smiling now.

"Yeah…she should be out there."

"She?" The nurse picked up a chart and read something on it before putting it back down. "Why don't you rest, and I'll go and get Mrs. Adrian? But don't try to get up or move until I come back to take out the IV, okay?"

"Rest…" he whispered under his breath. His throat was dry. He wanted something to drink. He stared at the table with rolling wheels beside his bed. There was a cup sitting on top. He wondered if there was something in it to drink. The nurse had said not to move.

The guy next to him was snoring. Fred wondered if he'd been snoring while under anesthesia. He'd made it. Made it.

Five minutes later…or three hours. He didn't know. Fred opened his eyes and saw her coming into the room.

"I made it," he said, yawning and closing his eyes.

"You did," the woman said in a low voice. "Your nurse said as soon as you're awake, they'll bring you some coffee and a piece of toast."

"I'm thirsty. Hand me that cup of water." His hand hung in the air.

He heard a soft plastic-sounding snap near his head. She was standing too close to the bed. Fred could smell her perfume. He opened his eyes and saw her take something out of the tube going into his arm.

"What was that?" he asked.

Her hand moved to his forehead and she covered his eyes. "Why don't you get some rest until it's time to take you home?"

The other patient was still snoring. He didn't want to sleep. Fred felt his limbs getting heavy.

"Take me home…I can sleep there."

"Shh…soon."

His heartbeat started drumming in his ears. Suddenly, he didn't feel right. There was something different. The right side of his face felt numb, like he'd been slapped.

"Is he ready for coffee?" Fred heard the familiar voice of the nurse coming back into the room.

Coffee…yes. He wanted to wake up. He wanted to get out of here. He wanted to answer for himself. His tongue felt swollen in his mouth. His eyelids were too heavy to lift. He opened his mouth but he could push no sound out.

Something wasn't right. She'd put something in the tube in his arm.

Then, in a moment of clarity, he thought of Cynthia, and the box he'd shipped his daughter.

"I think he's fallen back to sleep. Should we give him some time?"

"That's fine. Come and get me when he's awake."

No. He wanted to wake up now. He wanted to live. He'd be fifty-nine next week. He needed to walk his daughter down the aisle at her wedding. Fred lifted his hand off the bed to tell the nurse to stop, but cold fingers took hold of his and pressed them down into the sheet.

The kick of his foot at the table was a feeble effort, at best. Like a last gasp for air before drowning.

"Is he okay?" he heard the nurse's voice from far away.

"Yes, he's fine. I'm the klutz. I just leaned against the table."

Vaguely, he heard the sound of footsteps moving into the distance. Hope slipped away like a lifeline through his fingers and was gone.

2

New Mexico Nuclear Fusion Test Facility

More than halfway home.

Even at forty-eight days into the project, Marion Kagan didn't mind working seven days a week, sixteen hours a day. She didn't have time to think about sun and clouds and trees. Sometimes, lying in her bunk, she did have to shake from her mind how much she missed the sting of the wind on her face as she whipped along on her scooter back and forth from her apartment to the UC Davis campus. Down here, there was no sunrise, no sunset. But no commuter traffic, either.

Buried in the underground research facility with eight other scientists, Marion only considered the passage of day and night when she made her journal entry at the end of a shift. The group worked in shifts around the clock. Eating and sleeping happened between shifts, and everyone reported for duty when it was time.

She was fine with all of this. They were over the hump. Only forty-two days left. And anytime she got too restless, she simply reminded herself what a boost it was in her curriculum vitae to be the only graduate assistant chosen for this highly selective project. A project that was already producing groundbreaking results. In the scientific world, the eight academics in her group were already stars; this project would make them superstars. As for Marion, after this she didn't believe she'd have any difficulty finding a job once she had her Ph.D.

Everything was great except for one thing. She just couldn't get used to the ongoing surveillance. The cameras were everywhere, mounted in the hallways, the laboratories, the control room. Marion couldn't see them in the bunk room or the bathroom she shared with Eileen Arrington, the only other female researcher on the team, but that didn't mean that they weren't there.

Truth be told, the cameras made her self-conscious. They recorded everything. Of course, the only camera with a live feed to the world above was by the elevator. Connected to the security station on the ground floor, that hookup provided a quick way to communicate with the outside world in case of emergency.

The rest of the cameras were for documentation, she'd been told. It eliminated a lot of the paperwork that otherwise Marion would have to do. That thought helped to make the surveillance bearable, at least. It had taken only a couple of hours on the first day of the project for her to realize that, as the only member of the team lacking a doctoral degree, she was expected to be servant, gofer, slave, chief cook, dishwasher and, of course, lab assistant for the other eight making up the team.

Marion made a face at the camera in the hallway before punching in the security code on a pad to get into the control room. Hearing the click of the lock, she pulled open the door.

Five of the researchers were already in there, gathered around a rectangular conference table in the center of the room for the morning update. Dozens of computer screens and accompanying electronic apparatuses were scattered around the spacious room. This was the place where most of them spent the day. They worked in overlapping shifts, but each had their own workstation. At any given time, six researchers were on duty and three were off. Glancing around the room, she realized she never ceased to be amazed at the way the personal peculiarities of each individual were so clearly demonstrated by the condition of their personal work space.

Robert Eaton, the project manager, stopped what he was saying and looked up at Marion.

She nodded. "The nine containers are in the test fixtures and set to go," she told him, going around the table and taking her customary seat.

Marion was part of the team, but she wasn't one of them. The hierarchy was clear. The rest sat in their personal faux-leather rolling office chairs with the comfortable cushions. She sat on the single folding metal chair placed at the corner of the conference table. That was her chair and God forbid she should sit in anyone else's.

Eaton motioned to the man sitting to his right. "Arin, why don't you start the countdown?"

Arin Bose had an aversion to walking, due in part to his three-hundred-plus pounds. Holding his omnipresent Cal Tech coffee mug steady on his belly, he wheeled his chair backward to his station and began tapping on one of his keypads to start the sequencing.

Marion looked up at the three-dimensional fracture-mechanics analysis on the projector screen. They'd been looking at a rotating image of a pressurized nuclear-reactor container ring. Currently, the smallest commercially mass-produced reactors were between ten feet and fifteen feet in diameter and were used on smaller naval ships. In the team's experiments, however, size was a major factor. The difference with their ring was that its diameter was about the same as a one-gallon paint can.

"Here are the characteristics of the nine identical test samples," Eaton continued, reading the file, journal number, date and time for the sake of the cameras before motioning to Marvin Sheehan, the metallurgist at the other end of the table.

Sheehan's thin frame straightened in the chair, looking like a runner ready to sprint. The man adjusted his spectacles, his excitement shining through the thick lenses.

"The objective is to test to the point of failure," he told them. "For the record, the material used for the container is Alpha 300-series stainless steel with a threaded lid closure equipped with the specialized HEPA filter vent. The vent allows for the controlled release of explosive gases, including hydrogen."

Dr. Bose had already started his countdown for the sample, but no one seemed to be paying particular attention to the test start-up times, which were imminent. Marion knew the computers monitored and documented those events more closely than any of them could. Besides, this had all become part of their daily routine.

Daily routine or not, there was nothing humdrum about the successes they had already achieved. Their work was part of a series of experiments aimed at the construction of a fast transportable reactor.

Power plants already in existence currently burned only three percent of the fuel they created. The other ninety-seven percent was rejected as "spent" and fit only for disposal. In the ambitious project Marion was a part of, the ultimate goal was to create a process that would achieve an efficiency burn rate of ninety-nine-point-nine percent of the fuel. Once this level was achieved, only one tenth of one percent of the plutonium and the other "ium" products would need long-term storage. At that efficiency level, most of the waste was simply the residue of the fission process, and that nuclear waste had a half-life not of ten thousand years, but only three hundred years.

Already, the project had surpassed the fifty-percent efficiency rate—far better than anything currently available for military or commercial use.

In short, their work would change energy production forever.

In one offshoot of the overall project, the metallurgists in the group had identified a unique alloy of stainless steel suitable for plutonium storage. The revolutionary process required revolutionary housings to go along with it, so the find was a huge accomplishment. That success alone could lead to the development of containers for very small nuclear reactors. With this, progress in energy sources could be as rapid as anything that the electronics industry had been going through in the past two decades. In the same way that computers which had been the size of a room were now palm-size and smaller, nuclear energy production would become transportable. With reduction in nuclear waste and the corresponding decrease in the need for long-term storage, it was clear where energy technology would be heading.

Marion had been told by Robert Eaton that they had already surpassed every expectation for this stage of the project. Now they were all in it to see how far they could push the envelope. She could imagine more than a few of them had started jotting down notes for their Nobel Prize acceptance speeches. She had a feeling Eaton may have already started rehearsing his.

"Each sample container is packed with plutonium-bearing solid material," Dr. Sheehan added, before reading the specifications of the material in each container.

Marion preferred not to think too much about the specifics—and the lethal qualities—of the radioactive material she handled in this facility. They were conducting their testing in an underground facility to minimize the contamination of the geological medium, in case of any accidents. Of course, she kept telling herself, there were not going to be any accidents. Choosing this location was only a matter of convenience and security. As a team, they were following safety guidelines that were stricter than those used in any military or commercial nuclear laboratory in the country. There would be no contamination. Dr. Eugene Lee, Marion's advisor at UC Davis, had promised her when recruiting her for this project that, at twenty-five years old, she had a better chance of getting run down by a garbage truck than dying of radiation poisoning.

She looked up at her advisor as Dr. Lee started articulating his contribution to the testing.

"Two containers will undergo crash analysis in a drop test to an unyielding target. Two others will undergo collision tests. The leak test is the most critical feature of the NRC requirement, so we are dedicating five containers to that testing. The pressurized environment is temperature-controlled to plus or minus one degree Fahrenheit."

Dr. Lee summarized what Marion already had on her clipboard as far as raw numbers. She was well-read on the Nuclear Regulatory Commission's requirements. There were minimum standards they had to adhere to. Unfortunately, she knew that some of the standards were forty years old and pretty much obsolete. But their device would be a first. A major outcome of this research project was the creation of specifications for future manufacturers.

Robert Eaton interrupted the scientist. "A delivery? Now?"

They all looked at the wall-mounted monitor that the project manager was staring at. The large computer screen dedicated to facilities data indicated that the elevator was descending from ground level.

"*Are* we expecting a delivery?" Lee asked.

"Not that I know of," their leader answered. He looked at Marion. "Did we receive any communications from the power company this morning?"

"I'll check," Marion replied, pushing to her feet and moving to her station. She was surprised that the landline phone connected directly to the ground floor hadn't sounded. The security above always gave them a heads-up before the elevator was sent down.

"It has to be a food delivery," Arin Bose commented from his corner. "Maybe a cake or a dozen doughnuts for a little celebration."

"We don't have any delivery on the schedule for today," Marion replied. Technically, the nine scientists weren't *sealed* in this facility for the duration. Still, food and any other special requests were delivered according to a preset schedule by way of the elevator. There was to be no human contact to further minimize the risk of disruption…or contamination.

Andrew Bonn, a physicist from Texas, broke in. "I requested some antibiotics."

Marion already knew the man to be a total hypochondriac. While the rest of them went through standard testing for radiation on a biweekly basis, Bonn insisted on daily testing. But that was nothing compared to the dozen or so imaginary illnesses that he'd claimed to contract since they'd arrived here.

"I didn't know you were sick again," Lee said, unable to keep the skepticism out of his tone.

Bonn snorted. Nobody in this group would survive as a politician out in the real world. Each scientist was too outspoken when it came to anything that might inconvenience them personally. They were treated like celebrities in their own university surroundings, and they brought that expectation into this situation. The Texas physicist rolled his chair back from the table and stood up. A pressurized button on the wall by each door released the lock from inside. Everyone needed to type in a sequence of numbers to get into the control room. Leaving was no problem.

Andrew Bonn left the control room through the door to the hall where the elevators were located.

"They subtract five thousand dollars a shot from our budget for decontamination every time that stinking elevator comes down here," the project manager complained as the door closed behind Bonn.

Everyone in the room had his and her own opinion on the topic and was not shy about contributing it now. Marion, however, made a point of staying out of it. These academics were a peculiar bunch, and she'd decided on day one that she wasn't going to get involved in their little dramas and power plays.

"I'm sorry to mention it," Eaton said over the voices of the cackling flock. "Let's keep on schedule."

As silence gradually settled over the control room, however, a strange popping sound could be heard from the outside.

"What the hell was that?" the project leader asked.

"I'll check," Dr Lee responded, getting up and

pressing the automated button. As the door opened, the stunned team watched two men wearing black ski masks sweep into the control room.

Lee went down as a bullet was fired at his head.

Marion's scream caught in her throat. Suddenly, everything seemed to move in slow motion. She saw the blue eyes of the assailant moving in her direction. The overhead light shone on the top of knit ski mask. She stared at the light gray maintenance coveralls and the name of the power company embroidered on the pocket.

"Hold on a second," Eaton snapped, starting to stand. "What do you think you're doing here? This is a secure research facility for—"

He never finished. The other intruder opened fire, starting with the project manager and then shooting each person around the table in turn.

Amid the popping of the weapons, the last thing Marion heard was the high-pitched shriek that she realized had finally burst from her own throat. As she tried to back away from the table, her metal chair tipped.

She did not see or hear or feel anything more, however. All consciousness exploded in a molten sea of light as a pair of bullets struck her in the head, sending her flying off the chair. Spinning as she fell, Marion's body hit the floor. And when she came to rest, a crimson pool quickly spread over the beige tiles around her head.

3

York, Pennsylvania

Mark Shaw killed the engine of his old Chevy pickup and sat for a moment, looking at the pink neon lettering on the sign above the Silver Diner. Even in the morning sunlight, he could see the *ner* in the name flickering. Those letters had been threatening to go out since he was in high school. Some things never changed.

There was a time when the thought might have been comforting.

Through the windows, he could see the faces of guys he'd grown up knowing. Lucille came into view with an armful of breakfast plates. As he watched, she slung the food onto the cracked Formica of one of the booths as she had been doing since the ark landed. Her husband Abel was visible through the little window in the kitchen behind the counter, looking at the chrome carousel of paper order slips. Mounted on the wall at the end of the counter, the TV was tuned in to CNN.

With a sigh, Mark hauled himself out of the truck. The smell of bacon and onions greeted him before he even went up the three concrete steps to the diner door. He knew Lucille would have a cup of coffee on the counter for him before he sat down.

Inside, a few of the regulars were missing, but there was no one he didn't know. He was surprised to see old Mrs. Swartley sitting at a booth down at the end with two other retired teachers he remembered from junior high. He didn't realize she was still living in York. The three women were wearing matching gold bowling shirts. The short, permed white hair of the trio could have been part of their uniforms. A Thursday morning league, no doubt. She smiled at him but kept talking to her companions.

Joe Moyer and Andy Alderfer were at the counter, and Mark took his place a seat down from them. Joe and Andy had graduated from high school with him and been working for the town's public works department ever since. The bone-colored mug appeared, steam rising from the black liquid.

"Hi, hon," Lucille said. "Let me guess…three eggs over easy with sausage, home fries and wheat toast, with a side of raisin toast."

"No, let's try something different this morning," Mark answered, looking up at the Specials board. "How about bacon instead of sausage?"

"Oh, be still, my heart," she responded dramatically.

"Lucille thought she had a live one on the line," Joe said to Mark with a laugh.

"I think I saw Abel start to dance in the kitchen," Andy added.

"Whadya say?" the cook asked suspiciously through the window.

"Nothin'," Andy replied innocently. "Our boy Mark was just thinking of having some Eggs Benedictine."

"Eggs *Benedict,* you idiot," Abel grumbled. "Jeez, we need a better class of clientele."

"Hey, I'm really hurt here," Andy responded wryly. "Aren't you hurt, Joe?"

"Don't drag me into this," his friend said, sipping his coffee.

Lucille grinned at Mark and stuck his order up on the carousel.

"So," Joe said, changing the subject. "Did you decide what you're gonna do?"

Mark stirred the coffee thoughtfully. He couldn't get away from it. Anywhere he went, whoever he spoke to, that was what they wanted to know. He couldn't just be.

"Hey," Andy said. "My cousin Brian would give his left nut for that spot on the police force."

"Don't rush him," Lucille said, planting a hip against the counter. "He just got back from Iraq. And watch your language."

"Sorry," Andy said contritely. "I meant left testicle."

"Oh, much better."

"How long do you have before you have to decide?" Joe asked.

"The chief said he can give me till the end of the month," Mark said. *If only the rest of them could be as patient.*

"Well, that's fair," Andy said. "Do you know which way you're leaning?"

Mark shook his head. He wasn't being a hard-ass. He really didn't know. Before his reserve unit had been deployed overseas, he would have said he would be a member of York's finest until he retired, but now…

York was home, but it just didn't seem the same. Fifteen months on the ground in Baghdad and Falluja had left him feeling…what? He wasn't sure what the right word was. *Disconnected. Hollow. Restless.* Some word that incorporated all of that.

He wanted to reconnect with things here, but something didn't feel right. Just before he'd shipped out, his father had found a job in Erie, and he and Mark's mother had rented out their old house and moved. The garage and the little apartment above it were saved for him. That was where he was staying…for now. Pretty damn depressing for a twenty-eight-year-old.

Mark had no siblings, and the only relative he had left in York was his grandmother, who had been in an assisted-living home for the past five years. She didn't recognize him at all and had even become agitated when he went to visit her upon arriving home. And his relationship with Leslie had simply petered out a few months before he went to Iraq.

Two girls from the car dealership up the road came in, drawing Joe and Andy's attention, and Lucille went in back to help Abel put together the take-out order.

Mark was glad to be off the hook. He glanced up at the TV on the wall. Lucille never had the sound on, but the aerial images on the screen showed a spectacular fire on what looked like an offshore oil platform. From the text scrolling across the bottom, he realized it was some kind of research facility on a converted monitoring station in the Gulf of Mexico. As he watched, a huge explosion blasted flames and debris in every direction, causing the helicopter doing the filming to shudder.

Whoever was on that thing, he thought, was a goner.

4

Waterbury Long-Term Care Facility
Connecticut

Jennifer Sullivan moved into the room with the practiced quickness that her twenty-six years as a nurse had instilled.

"Hey, what's going on in here?" she said brusquely. She was barely five feet tall, brown eyes, short dark no-nonsense hair, average weight. She considered herself nondescript, plain. But people told her she had a certain presence. She was impossible to ignore. Jennifer knew it was her confidence—and her insistence on providing the best care to her patients. She focused right now on the patient thrashing in the bed. "Come on, sweetheart. What are you doing to yourself?"

Pat Minicucci was already there, trying to hold JD down. Jennifer could see the feeding tube was detached from the abdominal port and lay on the floor.

"I can't hold her much longer," the nurse's aide said, a note of urgency in her voice. "Have you ever seen her like this?"

"Never," Jennifer admitted. Glancing at her watch as she stuck her head into the hallway, she called to a passing dietary aide to get the doctor. Luckily, Dr. Baer wouldn't have left the facility yet to see to his own practice. She moved to the other side of the bed and put a hand on JD's shoulder.

"Did something bite her or sting her?" Jennifer asked, glancing around in the bedding for a spider.

"I don't know," Pat replied breathlessly.

"Well, did she fall? Where did you find her?"

The patient's brown eyes were open wide, and she was looking about the room, continuing to fight against the arms holding her. With each heave of her body, JD emitted gasps of breath from between clenched teeth.

"I heard her as I was walking past the room. When I looked in, she'd already slid down to where the bed strap was up almost to her throat. She'd lost the tube." Pat leaned more heavily on JD's arms as Jennifer checked the bed for anything that might be poking into her. "As soon as I unhooked the strap, she went wild."

JD couldn't have been a hundred pounds soaking wet, but she continued to put up a fight against the hold on her arms.

"Be gentle with her," Jennifer found herself saying. Pat was young and close to twice the weight of the patient. She was also new and didn't know much about JD.

"I thought she was in a coma."

"No, she's an MCS patient. She's in a minimally conscious state," Jennifer added as clarification.

"What's the difference?"

"MCS patients, like JD here, can be visibly awake or asleep. There have been times over the past few years when I've seen her reach for things, even hold them. I've noticed her follow with her eyes people moving about in the room. Sometimes there is even gesturing or verbalization that is intelligible…at least to me." Jennifer caressed the young patient's brow. "The important thing to remember is that she's really fragile."

There was no denying it. All the old-time nurses had a soft spot in their hearts for her. JD had been here a little over five years now, and she was the easiest of the traumatic brain injury patients to take care of.

"Slide her up the bed a little."

Together, the two women moved the patient enough for Jennifer to reclip the bed strap. Sitting against the edge of the bed, Jennifer leaned over JD and put her hands on either side of the young woman's face to check the skin of her neck for any bites or scratches.

Immediately, the patient stopped fighting.

"Jesus, Mary and Joseph," Pat exclaimed softly, "you have the touch."

Jennifer saw the young patient's eyes focus on hers. "Hi, JD. Do you see me, honey?"

JD's arms now lay limp on the rumpled bed sheets. The noise she had been making in her throat stopped. Jennifer motioned for Pat to let go, and the younger nurse cautiously released her grip on JD's arm. Jennifer leaned her head slightly to check her scalp. The eyes followed her.

"What's bothering you, sweetheart?" she asked, accustomed to talking to JD, even though the other nurses were sure she didn't understand.

A male voice came from the doorway. "I hear there's been some trouble here?"

Both women turned to see the physician who had just come in. Dr. Ahmad Baer spent three days a week, a couple of hours of each day, at the nursing facility. Baer was new to them, less than six months. But so far, Jennifer thought, he was doing okay. He had his own practice over by the hospital and saw patients at a re-

tirement home in Woodbury, as well. Jennifer had heard
last week that Baer was also teaching a course at
UCONN Medical School every other semester. The staff
here had already labeled him as workaholic, which was
a nice change as far as Jennifer was concerned.

"We were having some trouble with her…until a
couple of seconds ago," Pat said, staring in amazement
at the calm patient. "She was fighting us like crazy."

The doctor walked toward the bed and picked up the
feeding tube off the floor. He handed it to Pat.

"I can see that." He took a small flashlight out of his
pocket and moved to the head of the bed.

Jennifer stepped away to give the physician room.
She noticed JD's eyes following her.

"She maintains a visual fixation on you," Baer commented. "Is this usual?"

"I spend a lot of time with her," Jennifer admitted.
"I'm one of the few who've been here from the first day
they moved her in. I've thought she might recognize me.
But Dr. Parker, who retired before you got here, always
said it was wishful thinking on my part."

Jennifer had spent more than half of her life doing
this. She was forty-nine, turning fifty in January. Understanding her patients was second nature to her, like
eating or breathing. Still, she recalled one piece of
advice she'd been given early on in her career—to not
get attached to patients. And she hadn't, until JD. There
was something about the young woman that tugged at
Jennifer's heartstrings. It was more than the helplessness. Most of the patients she dealt with were in some
kind of vegetative or minimally conscious state. This
one she somehow connected with. She was certain that
the young woman understood her words more than
anyone believed. JD was just a little older than her own

daughters, and Jen frankly didn't give two shakes what anyone else thought of the way she fussed over her. Seniority had its privileges. She could be extra attentive to a patient if she wanted.

The doctor held JD's chin steady as he checked the movement of the eyes.

"I'm not as well-read as I'd like to be on this patient, Jennifer. What can you tell me about her?"

Who was he kidding? she thought silently. He didn't know *anything* about JD. The young patient was on the same medication and feeding schedule that she'd been on for years. There had been nothing new tried since the first year that JD was here. No rehab efforts, no new treatments. Standard physical therapy and that's it. She'd hoped that Baer would see her sometime soon. But there'd been no reason for it before now.

"Her chart is right here," Pat Minicucci offered, pulling the clipboard from the holder at the foot of the bed. "But it won't help much."

They were grossly shorthanded, and there were a dozen things that Jennifer thought Pat could be doing right now, but the young nurse's aide was apparently curious about what was going to happen, too.

"I'll look at it later. Jennifer, what can you tell me?" Dr. Baer asked again.

There were things that were written every day on a patient's chart, like the medications or nutrients the patient should get, as well as vitals and therapy session records and such. But there were other things that weren't there.

"This January will be six years since her accident," Jennifer told him. "She was pushed out of a moving vehicle one night on the highway, on I-84 in Cheshire. No one saw it happen…or at least no one ever came forward. She was taken to St. Mary's Hospital, the closest level-two trauma center. There were multiple head injuries and a broken arm, as well as a lot of road burn. The trauma team attended her immediately and the acute-care unit at the hospital saw to the minor stuff. She never recovered from the head trauma, though."

"Everyone calls her JD for Jane Doe," the physician assumed.

"There was no ID on her when they took her to the hospital," Jennifer said, nodding. "From what we were told, the police fingerprinted and photographed her that very first night, but there were no matches. Nothing ever came of any investigation, as far as I know."

"Is she a ward of the state?"

Jennifer nodded again. "Title 19 Medicaid patient. The probate court assigned a local lawyer to act as conservator. I can't remember his name right now. But he has power of attorney."

Dr. Baer straightened from the bed, and JD's eyes focused on her again. Jennifer reached over and took the young woman's hand. She was certain JD appreciated the touch. Everyone needed kindness and human contact.

"She's an absolute sweetheart. She's never given any of us a lick of trouble in all the time she's been here. I'm wondering if something wasn't poking into her. It's not like her to get worked up like this."

"How long has she been here exactly?" the physician asked, taking the chart from Pat.

Jennifer knew the answer. "She got bounced around to a couple of different facilities during the first few months after the accident. Then she was moved here. It was in August. So it's been five years and three months."

"What a great memory!" Pat blurted.

Jennifer shrugged. "I remember because my family and I always go to the Cape at the end of July. And JD was brought in right after I came back from vacation."

"Has she been in a minimally conscious state since she's been here?"

"Yes. She came in as an MCS patient."

"Anything done to wean her off the feeding tube?" Baer wanted to know, quickly paging through the chart.

"No." Jennifer wished she could say more. But she wouldn't bad-mouth their former attending physician. Dr. Parker should have retired ten years before he did, as he had no interest in doing anything different. She had made recommendations as far as exercises or little things they could do to work with JD, but he wouldn't have it. Standard maintenance treatment was all he would allow.

"Is it too late now?" she asked. "If there's anything extra we have to do, it'd be okay. We'd really like to help her, if there's a way." She realized it wasn't right to talk for everyone else. "I'll put in some extra hours myself."

Jennifer saw JD close her eyes. She wasn't sleeping, only shutting them out. It was so sad. The young woman did communicate with them. Jen was sure of it.

"Do we have any idea how old she is?" the physician asked.

"The file said early twenties when she arrived here, so we celebrated her twenty-seventh birthday on Christmas Eve."

The physician looked up and a smile tugged at the corner of his mouth. Jennifer thought this was the first time she'd seen him do that.

"Does this mean she'll be twenty-eight this coming Christmas?" he asked.

"Yes. We'll have a big party for her right here and you're invited."

If he was amused by that, he gave no indication of it. He flipped through the most recent pages. "Has she had any epileptic fits in the past that you remember?"

"No," Jennifer said with certainty. "That's not what this was."

She wanted JD to get better, not to be diagnosed with another disorder. With this doctor, she thought there might be a chance. There were a lot of new things that would be tried out if there were family around.

Baer wrote down some notes on the clipboard. "I'm writing a prescription for some sedatives, in case she becomes agitated again."

Disappointment poured through her. "Is that all we're going to do?"

He looked at her with surprise.

Jennifer bit her tongue. She didn't want an enemy but an ally. "I was wondering if you could review her files…perhaps see if there's anything that needs to be changed on her meds…or other things. Treatment that might trigger more responses."

The physician looked down at the clipboard again. "Okay. Put her on my schedule for tomorrow. We'll see if there's anything that needs to be changed."

This was a start.

"I'm impressed," Pat said after Baer left the room. "You really care about her, don't you?"

Jennifer looked over at the bed. JD's eyes were once again open and watching her.

"Yes, I do."

5

Santa Fe, New Mexico

Living in three cities certainly did nothing to cut the size of the crowd.

Cynthia Adrian had planned a luncheon for two hundred after the funeral service. Looking out the small window of the chapel at the packed parking lot, she feared they might have twice as many guests as she'd counted on.

She glanced at her watch and smoothed back her shoulder-length blond hair. Unbelievable. Ten minutes until the service was to start and her mother still hadn't arrived. She took her cell phone out of her purse and considered calling her to see where she was.

Cynthia had been forced to take over the planning of her father's funeral arrangements. Everything—from deciding on the minister to arranging for speakers, even sending a driver to the house to bring her mother here. All Helen had to do was be there.

But being there had always been her mother's problem.

The minister knocked lightly and looked into the room. "Will we be starting on time, Ms. Adrian?"

Could they start this funeral without Fred Adrian's wife of thirty-five years?

"I'm calling my mother right now. I'll let you know—" She snapped the phone shut. "Never mind, here she is."

Cynthia watched the black sedan pull up in the front of the church. "We're starting on time."

She went out the side door to meet Helen in the parking lot. The driver stepped out and opened the back door. Out of nowhere, a reporter and a photographer materialized by the car. The camera was clicking away at her mother as she stepped out.

"Sorry about your loss, Mrs. Adrian," the reporter said, holding up a small tape recorder. "Could we just ask you a question or two?"

Helen Adrian stared at them unsteadily for a moment and then shrugged. "Why not? It's just my husband's funeral."

"Mrs. Adrian, could you tell us how your husband, as director of research at New Mexico Power, would react if he knew about the accident in the Gulf of Mexico today?" the reporter asked. "Wasn't that specific research program a pet project of his?"

"Yes, my husband loved those pet projects of his. They became more important to him than his family."

Cynthia noticed how her mother, using her years of drinking experience, was holding on to the car door to keep her balance.

"If he were alive, do you think he'd agree with the power company's decision to let the fire burn and assume that there are no survivors?" the reporter asked.

"If he were alive," Helen replied coolly. "I know what he'd be doing if he were alive. But he's not, is he?"

She tried to step up onto the sidewalk and stumbled. Cynthia was quick to catch her. "Are you okay?"

"Okay? Okay?" Her breath reeked of alcohol. "How do you think I am? He's dead."

"I know that."

"As a matter of fact, I'm more than okay. I'm fine. I'm great."

Cynthia glanced nervously at the reporter and photographer. They were getting everything.

6

Nuclear Fusion Test Facility

Blackness.

Marion blinked her eyes. She could feel her eyelids move, but there was nothing for her to focus on. Nothing but blackness.

Trying not to panic, she wondered for a moment if she was even alive. The flashes of incredible pain shooting from the side of her head to the back of her brain told her that she was, but the blackness threw her. She wondered if she'd gone blind. She realized she was very cold.

She tried to move her lips, her jaw. The skin on her cheekbone and her temple was stuck to something. The pounding pain in her head was excruciating and became worse when she tried to move her face.

She waited for a few moments…she didn't know how long. Tentatively, she flexed the fingers of her right hand. Every joint was stiff, and she realized she was lying on something hard. She moved her hand, feeling and recognizing the cold tile of the floor. Whatever her face was stuck to had a strange, familiar odor.

And then she remembered.

Cold fear washed through her. Killers. They'd come into the control room. Shooting.

She felt her chest start to heave, her body trying to get air. *Be calm,* she told herself. *Keep it together. You're alive!*

Marion was lying on her left side. She couldn't feel her left hand or arm. She tried to move her legs. They were cramped and stiff, but she was able to straighten one…and then the other. As she did, she automatically rolled onto her back, peeling the skin of her forehead and cheek from the tile floor.

Her head rolled also, and when the back of her skull came in contact with the floor, she felt her brain about to explode.

And then she felt nothing.

7

Joseph Ricker looked out at the half-dozen middle-aged men and the two hunting guides crouched behind portable blinds at the edge of the salt marsh. He shook his head.

Who were they fooling, calling themselves hunters? This wasn't hunting. It wasn't even sport. It was a narcissistic exercise in time- and money-wasting.

In no hurry to leave the limousine, Joseph Ricker watched them a moment longer. He hated the fresh air, the mud, the bad weather, the inconvenience of wearing ridiculously ugly clothes for the excuse of looking the part. But beside all of that, he hated the idea of killing another living thing, unless there was some valid return on the investment of one's time or energy.

Cook them. Give them away. Stuff them. When it was over, you had to do *something* with the kill. In the case of these particular men, however, nothing would be done with the handful of geese they managed to gun down. In the eight years he'd worked directly for Martin Durr, his boss had never bothered with the dead birds. Shoot them down and leave them. The others would do the same. Because none of these men were licensed to hunt in Maryland, not even the guides would send their beautiful retrievers out for them. None of this made sense to him.

Joseph opened the back door of the black sedan and buttoned up his trench coat as he stepped out.

"What time should I come back, sir?" the driver asked.

"You'll wait here for me," he ordered. "I'm not staying."

Joseph flipped up the collar of his coat and stood next to the car for a couple of minutes. A light drizzle was falling from the gray October sky. He considered asking the driver to get an umbrella for him from the trunk but he decided against it. He hoped he wouldn't be out here long.

As he watched, two long Vs of geese appeared in the distance. As the flocks passed within range overhead, Martin Durr and his guests began firing. They were shooting senselessly, like children at a carnival booth. Despite all the fine weaponry they were sporting, only two geese dropped with a splash into the marsh. Joseph was certain that at least one of the birds belonged to his boss. Probably both.

Martin Durr turned and saw the car. Joseph assumed his boss saw him, too, but Durr didn't bother to return the discreet wave. The older man handed his gun to the guide standing near him. He said something to one of his guests and started toward the car.

Joseph knew this was his cue to start walking, too. If he didn't meet Durr at least halfway, he'd hear about it.

He looked down at his four-hundred-dollar wingtips and at the muddy path straight ahead. There was no dry route to take. He reluctantly stepped into the mud and felt his shoes sink in.

Martin Durr didn't believe in cell phones or e-mail or even sending a trustworthy messenger when it came to taking care of business this sensitive. And Joseph was too smart to question the older man's judgment. Durr not only had survived but thrived in a very tough and dirty business for over thirty years. There were still a few things that Joseph could learn from the man.

"Well?" Durr asked when they reached each other.

As he knew he was expected to do, Joseph took one quick look around to make sure he was out of earshot of everyone and that no surveillance equipment was anywhere in sight.

He turned back to his boss. "There was a plane crash this morning. Or rather, a charter plane exploded in midair before crashing."

"And?"

"Five R & D staff scientists from the New Mexico Power Company, along with two *key* administrators and the pilot and copilot, were killed. They were coming back early from a seminar because of the problem in the Gulf. It was a charter flight. They were the only passengers."

Joseph watched as Durr took off one glove and vacantly stroked the fat of his double chin. The nearly translucent skin on his doughy face was normally pale. But now, with the cheeks red from the cold, Joseph thought Durr was looking more and more like an old woman. The thought disappeared, however, when his boss's steely blue eyes focused directly on his face.

"The cause of the accident?"

"The unofficial reports from the airport and from an unidentified source in the NTSB South Central field office are that the pilot radioed in just before they exploded, saying that they were experiencing a malfunction in the fuel system," Joseph told him. "The official reports won't get released for at least a month… but they will confirm the early findings."

The older man looked off into the distance. He reached one hand into a pocket, took out a handkerchief and blew his nose loudly. Joseph refrained from saying anything. He knew he was expected to be silent.

"Where does this leave us?" Durr finally asked.

"I believe it would be safe to say, clean."

"No loose ends remaining? You're certain."

"I'm certain. There are no loose ends, sir."

8

University of Connecticut Health Center
Department of Neurology

"It's absolutely ridiculous to lose the funding on a program this important just because we can't get enough test subjects," Sid Conway complained.

"What happened to the two patients you had ready to go?" Ahmad Baer asked.

"The families backed out. They wouldn't sign the papers at the last minute."

Ahmad moved down the cafeteria line with the young man on his heels. He wouldn't say it out loud, but he wasn't surprised.

Sid was in his first year of residency at UCONN Health Center. For a couple of days each week, he shadowed Ahmad on patient visits at the hospital. Smart, energetic, idealistic and dedicated, Sid was destined for great things as a neurologist. Of that, Ahmad was certain. But there were a few issues regarding how Sid dealt with people that the young man needed some work on. Legal aspects of research work clearly frustrated him, and the psychology of dealing with patients' families also seemed to elude him. There was also a touch of arrogance Baer had noticed, in terms of how Sid dealt with staff, that needed some taming. There was a lot, however, in the young doctor that was workable.

"You won't lose the funding," Ahmad assured. "All you need to do is to go before the committee and they'll renew it."

"I don't *want* to go before the committee. Next year, it'll be only more difficult than this year," Sid told him. "I still can't see what these families have against us doing the testing on the two patients. I mean, it's not going to cost them anything, and it will definitely not make the individuals' conditions worse. These patients are already in a coma."

Reaching the cashier, Ahmad stopped the young man from taking his wallet out and paid for both of their drinks.

Sid was part of a team working on a new brain "reading" device. His work went beyond previous studies, which used MRIs to read a person's possible intentions by focusing on changes in the medial prefrontal cortex of the subject's brain. Sid's research team had already made great advances. Instead of bulky MRI equipment, they now could use portable electronic scanning devices to read the brain's activity. They were actually cracking the mind's internal code to deduce what a person was thinking.

The concern was that the researchers had no way of targeting specific thoughts. Whatever was going through the mind of the subject was what the instruments picked up. And there was no way to determine what was memory, what was real or what was imagined. Still, they were making tremendous strides in understanding how the brain functioned.

"I know one of the lawyers who's involved with this,"

Ahmad told him. "Last time I spoke to him, he was reading up on the results that the neuroscience team at Berkeley published last year. Based on that study, the researchers were able to tap into the patient's secret intentions and memories. Private stuff."

"You know that we have no interest in the specific content of an individual, per se."

Ahmad shrugged. "I know that, but think of what the families are going through. They're dealing with loved ones who have become paralyzed or have suffered mental impairment or have become comatose. They don't know how long before these husbands or wives or brothers or sisters or parents will regain something of who they were…or if they ever will. This is as sticky as a living will. Decisions are difficult. There are privacy issues involved. There is always the chance that the patient might wake up tomorrow. What if your findings include revelations that are not particularly flattering…or are even criminal? Ethically and personally, the families have a problem with doing this. You can understand that."

They stopped by the elevators.

"You're supposed to be on my side, Dr. Baer," Sid complained, half in jest.

"And I am. I understand the positive uses this program can have in the future for people who have become impaired," Ahmad told the young man. "You are making important early steps here. What I'm saying is that you should take your time and not set your mind on the first good candidates you find in this hospital. I know that would have been very convenient. But taking the easy road is giving you the most trouble."

The elevator doors opened and the two men stepped in. Ahmad pressed the button for their floor.

"Well, I have to come up with someone in the next couple of weeks, or I rewrite the grant to get it extended," Sid told him, accepting the advice but obviously disappointed. "Do you have any suggestions where I should be looking for subjects?"

They stepped out at their floor.

"As a matter of fact, I do. One of my patients at the extended-care facility in Waterbury is a ward of the state. A Jane Doe with no known family to have an objection to what you're going to do or what information you're going to abstract."

"What kind of okay do we need to include her?"

"Just the permission of the conservator, who is an attorney in Waterbury, I understand. I'll get the name and phone number," Ahmad offered. "In her case, I doubt there will be any objection. If anything, you can help them to identify her, and it would be a very good thing."

"When can I see her?" Sid asked, perking up.

"You can come with me tomorrow to the nursing facility. We'll put in the call to the attorney's office when we're down there."

9

Mark Shaw had a busier social schedule now than any time before going to Iraq. It had to be a plot.

The next-door neighbors, who were always friendly with his family, have a cookout and he's invited. The police chief's wife throws a birthday party for their eight-year-old daughter…and he's invited. York College's Criminal Justice department is having a retirement party for one of the professors Mark had while he was at school there…and he's invited. Lucille and Abel from the diner have some reasonably attractive female friend over for supper on Friday night…and he's invited. And there had to be a dozen more.

Between the people who knew him or his family, he had yet to go two days without being invited to one event or other. If things got any busier, he'd need to buy a calendar.

Mark appreciated all the invitations he was getting. He knew why he was getting them, too. Some forty thousand people lived in York, and between the tourists and the college kids, the population could swell by an extra ten thousand. As a result, York had some big-city problems. That was why the police force needed nearly a hundred officers. Despite all of that, though, York still had small-town attitudes and values…and folks who cared about servicemen and women just back from overseas with no family around.

Mark knew it was a plot, but not a sinister one. It just didn't help him figure out what he wanted to do with his life.

Thursday night, he was at another get-together. John Landis, a young police officer who was also the younger brother of Mark's first partner on the force, was moving into a new apartment with his girlfriend. Mark had known John for a long time, so he and a couple of other guys had stopped in during the afternoon to help them move. Now everyone was staying for beer and pizza.

The conversation at dinner turned to the politics of the department. Mark went into the kitchen to get another beer. A small TV on the counter was on and tuned to a local station with the volume turned down. As he raised the bottle to his lips, a picture flashed on the screen, stopping him dead. He knew that face.

"Wait!" he murmured as the news story moved on. "Come on. What was that about?"

He searched on the counter for the remote to turn up the volume or change the channel.

"Everything okay?" John asked, toting a handful of empties into the kitchen.

"I just saw…somebody I knew on the news. But it passed on. Do you get another news station? Where's the TV remote?"

John reached under a phone book and handed him the remote. "Was it someone from here?"

"No," he replied, occupied with finding another channel that might show the same clip.

"Was it local or national news?" the young policeman wanted to know.

"I don't know. I walked in and it was there, on the screen…and then it was gone."

"Man or a woman?"

"A woman," Mark said under his breath. The other news stations were covering the fire on the offshore platform he'd seen that morning. A related news story reported that the same company that had been funding research at the site had also suffered another loss today. A separate group from their research and development department had been killed in a plane crash. There had been no survivors.

"Anyone I know?" John persisted.

"No."

"It's really fun playing twenty questions." John slapped him on the shoulder. "Who is she?"

The news channel he'd turned to put a grid of nine faces on the screen.

"Christ. It was her." Mark pointed with the remote as he turned up the volume. "That's her."

"An unidentified source within the New Mexico Power Company has told the local Eyewitness News station that these nine scientists were members of a research team conducting studies in a subterranean facility beneath the converted monitoring station in the Gulf of Mexico. At this point, the company has yet to officially admit or deny the identity of the victims." A split screen showed the burning platform and a photo of a man with the name Dr. Robert Eaton beneath the scientist's smiling face.

"How could they put pictures of people up when there's no official confirmation?" John muttered. "Who is she? Where did you meet her?"

The picture split into four images, showing the photos of the team with the person's name and university affiliation beneath each one.

"Marion Kagan, UC Davis, California," Mark said softly. "Last time I was on leave, I got stranded in the Boston airport because of bad weather. Her flight was canceled, too. We ended up talking."

"Sorry, man," John said, putting a hand on Mark's shoulder. "You okay?"

Mark leaned against the counter and stared at the dark shoulder-length hair, the large eyes, the beautiful face. And then the image switched back to an aerial shot of the fire.

He barely knew her, really. But he remembered how something about her shone from the inside, especially when she smiled. How often had he thought about her over the past year? He ran a hand down his face.

"Marion Kagan. I can't believe she's dead."

10

"I still can't believe how simple it was to get the conservator's okay," Sid Conway admitted as he read the papers the attorney had faxed to the office of the nursing home.

"You are doing clinical research, supported by the UCONN Health Center," Ahmad Baer reminded him. "This patient's care is provided by the State of Connecticut, and I am her attending physician. The testing is noninvasive and cannot harm the patient physically. I am on the advisory committee for this grant, so I am familiar with everything about the situation. Considering all these facts, this can only be a win-win situation, especially if the results help us find out who she is. Why wouldn't the conservator go along?"

"We don't know if we can find anything about her identity or not. We don't have any control over what kind of information we can pick up on the readings."

"That's fine," Ahmad replied. "The bottom line is that you have another subject."

"Can I see her today?" Sid asked.

"Of course." Baer looked at the schedule of patients

he had to see today. Jennifer Sullivan had put JD down as his first visit.

"When can we move her to the medical center?" Sid wanted to know.

Ahmad stopped and looked at the resident. "You can't move her. She is getting the right care here, and I don't want to disturb a good working arrangement for this patient."

With the shortage of beds, nurses and even doctors in the hospitals and nursing facilities across the state, there was no way Ahmad was going to risk having a Title 19 patient lose her bed here while the study was being done. Besides, he liked the idea that there were nurses here who kept a close eye on JD. No, Sid and his research partners could move their equipment down here.

"The nursing home can give you a place where you can set up your equipment. You and the other guys will have to do some commuting. But we're going to keep the patient's welfare at the top of the priority list."

"Sure," Sid said, seeming embarrassed for even suggesting it. "I understand. That's no problem at all."

Ahmad knew this was all part of the learning curve new doctors had to go through. Classroom and textbooks didn't teach you the reality of how institutions functioned.

"Also, despite having all the right signatures, you and your group will need to be sensitive to any questions or concern voiced by the staff at this facility. One complaint by them and the conservator will shut you down," Ahmad told the young man. "One specific nurse in particular is like a watchdog with JD. I want you to treat her as you would if she were family to the patient. Explain what you can, and be sensitive. She only has the welfare of the patient in mind."

Sid nodded again, more agreeable than Ahmad had ever seen him. He figured the young resident was too excited at the prospect of starting the study to object to anything.

As he looked at the clock on the wall, there was a knock on his open office door.

"Here she is…the person I was just warning you about," Baer said, loud enough for Jennifer to hear.

"Warning?" she said, stepping in. "I like the sound of that."

"Sid Conway, Jennifer Sullivan," he made the introduction, intentionally dropping titles. "Sid is doing his residency in neurology at UCONN Health Center."

Ahmad guessed Jennifer was in her forties. She was small built, attractive, but one wouldn't call her beautiful. One thing she did have going for her was intensity. When she spoke, she had that mother voice which was impossible to ignore.

"I'm running a little late, but I haven't forgotten JD. She's the first one I see today," Ahmad said. He figured he'd tell her about Sid's study once they were done examining the patient.

She nodded. "I didn't mean to rush you, but the third-shift nurse told me that JD had another episode about four-thirty this morning. They gave her the sedatives you prescribed."

"How is she doing now?" he asked, picking up the clipboard with the list of patients he was seeing today.

"She's still sleeping and I don't like it. We've never had to give her sedatives to keep her calm. There's something more going on right now. She wasn't like this before." Jennifer held up a thick folder she was carrying. "I double-checked her files. Yesterday was the first episode."

Ahmad took the folder and handed it to Sid. "This will bring you up-to-date with everything else that I might not have mentioned this morning."

Jennifer looked at them in surprise.

"Sid is going to get involved with JD," Ahmad told her before leading her out the door and down the corridor. As the three walked, he asked whether there might have been any changes in JD's routines, in her medications, in the personnel seeing to the young woman's care.

Jennifer had already checked into all of those things. Nothing had changed.

"She lost her roommate about ten days ago. We hadn't needed to put another patient in there, yet. Her treatment has been exactly the same for the past five years…almost six years. Now she has these episodes." Jennifer frowned. "Have you ever seen something like this with another patient?"

"Head injuries and patient response continue to be unpredictable." He motioned over his shoulder at Sid, walking a step behind them as he paged through the folder. "That's why we have to be nice to new doctors like him. Maybe they can open the door for the rest of us."

Friday mornings were traditionally popular for visiting. There were more people around, in the patients' rooms as well as in the glass solarium, than any other day of the week.

Running interference like a lineman, Jennifer moved a half step in front of them, warding off anyone who showed any intention of stepping into their path and speaking to Ahmad.

"The wing where JD is located is used primarily for patients in vegetative or minimally conscious states,"

Jennifer told Sid as they went through a double set of doors. The noise level dropped considerably in this section.

"Is there a way we can set up our equipment in JD's room or somewhere close to her?" Sid asked her.

"What equipment?" Jennifer asked immediately.

"Dr. Conway is leading a research team from UCONN Health Center. It involves vegetative or MCS patients." Ahmad figured this was where formality mattered. "I was able to get approvals this morning from JD's conservator to add her to the study."

"What's the object of the study?" she asked, stopping outside of JD's room.

"The first step of the study involves brain scanning," Sid explained. "The tests are noninvasive. We're recording the raw noise of neurons firing in the brain and feeding them through highly complex computer models to construct visual images of what might be happening at a particular moment in patient's brain."

"You can read her thoughts?" she asked, surprise in her voice.

"That's partly what we're hoping for. The ultimate goal is to develop a means of communication for people in her situation."

"This is great," Jennifer said excitedly. She gave Ahmad a soft tap on the arm. "I…I was hoping that there'd be something you could do for her. It's about time."

Ahmad and Sid exchanged a look as Jennifer stepped into the room ahead of them.

"You are on your way," Ahmad told the young doctor.

Inside, the patient's face was turned toward the window. The shades were open. Sun poured in.

"Good news. My girl is awake," Jennifer said cheerfully, moving to the head of the bed.

The nurse caressed the young woman's short hair and whispered something to her. Ahmad looked at Sid. Standing no more than a step into the room, he was staring at JD.

"Do you want to make some calls to Farmington and get the equipment ready to come down here?"

It took a second or two before the question registered. He turned to Baer. "I…I will. After we go through the examination."

"Everything okay?"

"Sure. It just didn't sink in that she's so young."

As a doctor, Ahmad tried to not differentiate between old and young or men and women. There was still something especially tragic, though, when you had to treat a person who was so young and in this condition. He reached for her chart from last night at the foot of the bed. There was a newspaper on a tray table next to it.

"Someone forgot their paper," he commented.

"No. That was Pat Minicucci, the nurse you met yesterday. She brought it in this morning." Jennifer picked up the paper, opened it to page four and held up an article and photo.

"The accident in the Gulf of Mexico," Ahmad said. "I caught bits and pieces of it on the news."

Jennifer spread the page out on JD's legs on the bed. "The pictures of the scientist who died in the facility. This one." She put on her reading glasses and read the name. "Marion Kagan. Pat thinks our JD looks awfully similar to this young woman."

Ahmad saw Sid lean over the paper, too. JD's face was turned toward them. The eyes were focused on Jennifer's face. He walked to her.

"Maybe," he admitted. Six years in a minimally conscious state had taken its toll on the young woman. She was pale and extremely thin. Her hair was kept short for the purpose of hygiene. "There are similarities, I suppose. In the cheekbones...maybe around the eyes. What do you think?" he asked Jennifer.

She shrugged. "I've heard that every one of us has a double out there."

Ahmad noticed Sid had moved next to the bed, too. JD's eyes were now focused on the young doctor's face.

"Are you any relation to Marion Kagan?" Sid asked.

The patient's right hand lifted off the mattress for a few brief seconds before dropping back down onto the sheet.

11

Nuclear Fusion Test Facility

When Marion opened her eyes, everything was still pitch-black and silent. The only sound was her own breathing.

She closed her eyes again and waited a moment. She was lying on her back and her head was turned to the side. The pain continued to shoot along the side of her head into the back of her brain.

She remembered what had happened. Careful not to roll her head, she flexed her fingers gingerly. She realized that she now had feeling in both hands and arms. She tried her feet; her ankles were stiff, but everything was moving. Bracing herself with one hand, she lifted the other above her, feeling in the blackness for anything above her. There was nothing.

The effort nearly exhausted her, and Marion let her hand drop onto her chest. Her shirt was stiff, and she guessed it was dried blood, the same blood that her face had been lying in.

She had been there long enough for the blood to coagulate and dry.

When she rolled back onto her side, the pain in her head increased again, but she moved slowly and didn't pass out. A feeling of nausea swept through her, but she did not become sick. At the same time, she was unbelievably thirsty. The thought of sitting up panicked her, but she knew she could not lie on the cold tile floor forever.

Resting her chin on her chest, she pushed herself up slowly. The total absence of light added to the disorientation she was feeling. Her head began to spin and she had nothing to focus on. Keeping her eyes closed, she tried to steady her breathing. When she felt she could trust herself, Marion lifted her head.

She had no idea where she was. This could be the control room, but she had no way of knowing. There was no sound of computers, no ventilation, nothing. She could be anywhere…and not just in the research facility.

Carefully, she pushed herself backward, feeling behind her with her hand. She paused once, feeling lightheaded, but then continued on as the feeling subsided.

Her outstretched hand touched something solid. Running her fingers along the smooth edge, she realized it was a desk. Marion pulled herself to it and reached on top. A keypad. Paper. A pencil. A mug tipped over, spilling cold liquid onto her shirt. She could smell orange spice tea.

It was her desk.

Pulling herself up onto her knees, she felt for the monitor and pressed the on button. Nothing. Of course, nothing. Power had been shut off at the facility; otherwise, there would be lights and some sound. Not even the emergency lights were functioning, she realized.

A thought struck her. Pulling open the top drawer, she fumbled inside for a moment until she found it. As her fingers closed around the smooth metal, she sat back onto the floor.

She flipped open the phone and pressed the on button. Because there was no service underground, she hadn't used it since the start of the project. In a second, the screen lit up, startling her with its intensity. She wasn't blind, at least. Turning the illuminated screen toward the room around her, she used the phone like a flashlight.

Looking around the control room, Marion felt the nausea rise again within her.

Nothing was moving. They were all dead.

She sat there staring. Numbness spread through her limbs. She waited for someone to wake her up. This couldn't be happening. It wasn't real. Her face was wet. She tasted the saltiness of tears reaching her lips.

The sound of sobbing startled her. It took a moment, but Marion realized she was the one making the sound. The scene before her remained unchanged. No one else was moving. It was only she who could act. But the thought was terrifying.

Marion was a scientist, not a Girl Scout. As a child, she'd been a bookworm. Her family didn't take vacations—her mother couldn't afford it. Going camping was something the kids who had two parents talked about. As an adult, roughing it on vacation was staying at a two-star motel. She just wasn't built that way. Even watching television, she'd never been able to get through a single episode of those survivor reality shows. She knew if she were ever in a situation like the ones they described, she'd be the one eliminated in the first hour.

She was allergic to nature. She didn't know CPR. The most complicated first aid she'd ever been able to handle was applying a Band-Aid. The sight of blood made her woozy.

And now her worst fears had become a reality.

Her thoughts were in a jumble, bordering on panic. She couldn't figure out what she should do first. If anything.

What about rescue efforts? she thought. The people at the power company who were sponsoring the research *had* to know by now that something had happened to their group. Where were they?

Perhaps all she needed to do was wait and someone would arrive to rescue her.

The light in the cell phone in her hand went off. The absolute darkness gave her a sharp jolt. She pressed the power button again to bring it back to life. The battery had only half a charge left.

"Hello…" she called softly into the room. Perhaps not everyone in the room was dead. What if someone was wounded and needed her help?

Another thought struck her. Not everyone in the team had been in the control room when the shooters arrived. Eileen Arrington, Neil Gregory and Steven Huang were out there. Maybe hiding.

"Dr. Lee," she called. She remembered her advisor had been the one by the door when the gunmen had stepped in.

There was no response. She remembered the gun pointed at his head. The shot being fired. Dr. Lee falling.

She struggled to her feet. What little she could see of the room danced in her vision. Marion had to lean against the desk to stop from going facedown. The phone went off on her again.

"Please don't do this to me." She pressed the on button. She glanced around. "Flashlights. Someone has to have a flashlight."

Hearing a voice, albeit her own, was a comfort. Marion didn't bother to check her desk. She already knew what she had or didn't have there. She stepped toward the conference table. The sharp pain in her head had returned. She touched the back of her head. It hurt. Her hair was matted and crusty against her skin.

Marion didn't want to know the source of the blood. Whether it was a cut or a bullet wound, she didn't need to know right now. She could move around. That was what mattered.

She saw a body stretched out facedown on the conference table. A dried black pool of blood spread over the papers around him. She didn't have to get closer to recognize Robert Eaton. Her stomach churned and tears burned her throat.

"Calm…stay calm."

Her head continued to pound. Moving made it worse. She tried to think clearly. Of all of them, Andrew Bonn would be the one to keep some kind of painkillers in his desk. The physicist had gone out to the elevators and not returned. She moved toward his workstation, but she tripped over something. She knew even as she fell that it was a body. Landing on her knees, Marion somehow managed to hold on to her phone. The screen flipped shut, though, leaving her in darkness again. She rolled and backed away on her bottom. Taking a deep breath, she flipped the phone open again.

The open eyes of Marvin Sheehan were staring straight into hers. She gasped and edged farther away. The metallurgist's shirt had ridden up on his body and she could see the bullet holes black and raw in the scientist's flesh. Blood had congealed around his body like a mat.

Marion's hand shook as she reached over and covered the scientist's eyes with her hand. His face was cold. She closed the eyes.

She made a mental note to keep track of those whom she'd seen so far. She held on to the nearest chair and pushed herself to her feet. Holding her phone up, she saw a body propping the door toward the elevators partially open. She guessed that had to be her advisor.

She was certain Andrew Bonn would be outside of this room. He'd been the one who had assumed the delivery was for him. The only one she hadn't seen here was Arin Bose. She turned around, holding the phone up again. His huge body was slumped over the desk. She didn't need to go any closer to the dead scientist.

Bile rose again in her throat. The air carried the scent of blood and death. Marion realized she couldn't stay here. She had to find out where the other three people in their group were. She made her way to Bonn's desk. She didn't have to search the drawers. An economy-size bottle of Tylenol sat beside his computer monitor. She struggled to open the top. The light on her phone went off again. Working in the dark, she finally was able to open the bottle and pop some pills into her mouth. They stuck in her throat. She felt in the darkness across the top of the desk and found a mug. She stuck her finger into it and found some liquid. She didn't hesitate, fearful of changing her mind, and swallowed the liquid to wash down the pills. Thankfully, it was water. As she drank it, she realized how thirsty she was. She turned on the phone one more time. The charge was quickly dwindling.

She pulled open the drawers. "Thank you…thank you, Dr. Bonn."

The penlight she found there was a godsend. She turned off her phone and used her new light to search the drawers. A pocketknife, another penlight. A small bottle of ibuprofen, some Band-Aids, antibiotic cream, hand-sanitizer bottle. Bonn's desk was like a first-aid station. Marion stuffed everything she could find into her pockets.

She recalled Eaton telling everyone when they first arrived at this station about facility emergency booklets…just in case. She used the light and quickly scanned through the books and notebooks and binders on the bookshelves above his desk. "Please, let it be you who kept them."

On the second shelf down she found what she was looking for. She tucked the three-ring binder under one arm.

She turned around and shone the light in the direction of the partially open door where her advisor lay. She didn't want to go out into the corridor in the direction of the elevators. Not yet. Those elevators were the only way in or out of the facility that she knew of.

She was afraid. It seemed unlikely, but what if the killers were still out there?

Marion glanced down at the notebook under her arm, racking her brain for any more information they'd been given about an emergency exit. Visions of climbing up the elevator shaft flashed in her head but, without power, she didn't know how she could even open the doors.

Perhaps if any of the others were still alive, she thought, they could work together to get out.

She looked at the other exit from the control room. That door led to the research labs, but she could get to the living quarters through there. She had to see if any of the others were still alive.

Access doors into various sectors of the facility were controlled by a security system. A password was needed on the outside, and a push button on a wall opened them from inside. She wondered if she'd be able to open any of them without any electricity.

Marion made her way around the table toward the door leading to the labs and living quarters, one hand pressing against the walls, the furniture, anything that would give her support. As she went, she tried not to look at the bodies of her dead colleagues.

Reaching the door, she pressed the button and pulled the door handle. It didn't budge.

"Please." She pressed the button again and tried to pull harder, but her brain suddenly felt as if it would split from the exertion.

Marion leaned back against the door until the pain lessened. She looked across the room at the other door…where Dr. Lee's body lay.

Nausea swept through her again, and she fought to hold it down. The odor in the room did not help, and suddenly she felt the clutch of claustrophobia. She could feel her heart racing. Grabbing hold of desks as she went, Marion tried to stay as far away from the conference-room table as she could. As much as she told herself to stay calm, panic had a grip on her now. She had to get out of here. She had to get out of this room.

Her advisor lay facedown in the doorway. The upper part of his body was in the control room, one leg holding the door partly ajar. Marion pushed the door farther open. It was extremely heavy but it swung open. Suddenly, she wasn't afraid of the attackers being by the elevators anymore. She had to get out.

She tried not to look down at the blood that surrounded Dr. Lee.

As Marion stepped carefully over the man, the other penlight she'd stuffed in her pocket fell to the floor. She considered leaving it, but the idea of abandoning any source of light didn't seem like a smart decision. She wouldn't be coming back into this room if she could help it.

She crouched and reached back over the body to get the light. It lay next to Eugene Lee's pale, outstretched hand.

The binder under her arm slipped. As Marion maneuvered to hold on to it, her fingers accidentally touched her advisor's cold hand. She recoiled involuntarily, but then gathered herself and reached again for the light.

As she picked it up, however, Dr. Lee's fingers closed around her wrist…and Marion's scream pierced the silence of the facility.

12

Waterbury Long-Term Care Facility
Connecticut

Friday night.

Jennifer Sullivan's shift had ended two and half hours ago, but she'd already decided she was staying right here in JD's room for as long as it took these three doctors to finish whatever they were doing tonight.

JD had again become agitated right after lunch, but the duration of the episode had been brief. This time Dr. Baer was around and no sedatives had been given to her.

Baer had left at his regular time this afternoon. The neurologist, Sid Conway, was joined by two other doctors from UCONN who looked even younger than he. The doctors were residents in neurology, as well. One of them, a young black man named Desmond Beruti, was extremely serious and focused on what he was doing. He struck Jennifer as a man of very few words. The other was a short, squarely built man named Nat Rosen. He looked like an ex-wrestler and talked nonstop. Most of what he said, however, was needling trash talk that his coworkers ignored. Still, when he gave his input on the task at hand, the others listened.

If she hadn't been introduced to them by Dr. Baer,

she could have mistaken all three of them as college kids. They were way too young to be so knowledgeable.

Jen shook her head, watching them work. They were so young. Of course, she thought, it could be that she herself was getting old. Impossible, she decided.

The reason she had ended up staying so long after her shift wasn't because she had anything against young doctors. But the three physicians had managed to fill JD's room with all kinds of electronics and equipment. Jennifer imagined how terrified her own daughters would be if they were suddenly surrounded by this.

With her own kids grown up and on their own, Jennifer had only herself and her husband to worry about, and Ed was good about doing things for himself. Tonight, when she'd called home, he was in the basement, working on a wine cabinet he was building for their oldest daughter for Christmas. Jennifer talked about work a lot at home, so tonight all she had to say to him was that she needed to stay with JD. He understood.

"I'm opening the files," Desmond told the other two.

If there was any doubt that the young patient understood a great deal of what was going on around her, tonight dispelled it in Jen's mind. From the moment all the strange faces and equipment arrived in her room, JD hadn't closed her eyes. She was awake. Mostly, she kept eye contact with Jennifer. But every now and then she would also watch Sid Conway.

"It's curious, but I think she already recognizes me," the young neurologist said.

Jennifer knew exactly how he felt. There was something extremely rewarding in having JD focus on you.

"Tell me if I'm in your way. I can move," Jennifer told him. Nat Rosen had started taping electrodes to JD's forehead.

"No, you're fine."

"Ideally, the readings should be done when the patient is awake," Sid told her. "Of course, that's not possible when we're dealing with comatose patients. As you know, patients classified as being in a minimally conscious state demonstrate a wide variety of behaviors pertaining to awareness. JD's situation right now is ideal…if we can keep her like this."

"Right now she seems almost entertained with all this activity around her," Jennifer told them. "How long does the testing take, anyway?"

"We'll be doing a number of readings over the next couple of weeks," Sid explained to her. "As far as the duration of the test, we'll go as long as she can tolerate it."

"I thought you said before that the testing was non-invasive," Jennifer reminded him, frowning.

"It is," Sid said quickly. "By tolerating it, I mean that she doesn't get tired of it and go to sleep, or she doesn't get agitated by the equipment or the electrodes being attached to her. Like what I said before, we'd like to get the images while she's in this situation."

Jennifer looked at the young woman. She was watching Conway.

"This is kind of daunting," Nat Rosen commented, moving to a chair behind the computers. "She looks… so…fully conscious. Are you sure we have the right patient?"

"Yes," Jennifer said with emphasis.

Everyone was doing something. Jen felt like a fifth wheel, but she wasn't going anywhere anytime soon. She turned to Sid, who had taken over from Nat and was positioning the last electrodes. "Can you explain to me how this testing works?"

He nodded. "Sure. We start with a workable model for

healthy and cognizant individuals. In the past, the way this model was established was to use functional magnetic resonance imaging to measure activity in the visual cortices of participants' brains as they looked at photographs of animals, food, people, and other common objects."

She found it interesting that Sid was not only directing his explanations to Jennifer but to JD, as well. "Wait. I read something about this. You're using computers to try to learn the language of the human brain."

"Well, yes. But we're moving beyond previous studies with our work. Using our own computer formulas, we're actually 'reading' images in the subject's brain using this scanning equipment."

"How?"

"Well, it's complicated, but we do that, partly, by measuring changes in the brain's blood-oxygen level, which have strong links to neural activity," he explained. "So just like you said, the collected data is used to teach a computer program to associate certain blood-flow patterns with particular kinds of images."

"What happens in the case of images that the patient has not seen initially?" she asked.

"That's the second part of the study," Conway explained. "The same participants are shown a second set of images they have never encountered before. Now the model is programmed to take what it learned from the previous pairings and figure out what is being shown in the new set."

"What's the accuracy level of a test like this?"

Sid looked over at Desmond, who was watching Jennifer intently.

"In our last trial," he said, "we were at ninety-five-percent accuracy."

"But you said the test was done on patients who were cognizant. Is this the same sequence that will be done on JD?" Jennifer asked.

Nat Rosen came around from his computer and smiled at her as he readjusted an electrode and went back to his seat. "What the heck are you doing working here? You ask more intelligent questions than our advisory committee."

"You'll go far brownnosing me like that," she told the young man.

Sid double-checked the connections for JD's wiring. "We'll try to follow the same sequence. But there's no guarantee that JD sees or processes anything that we put in front of her. So, at the same time, we try to use data from another test group and compare the second set of readings."

"I'm ready," Desmond told them.

Nat handed Sid a folder. Jennifer assumed these were the initial images. She moved to the foot of the bed, guessing the neurologist needed JD's full attention.

"What do you hope for with the first run?" she asked.

"Anything," Sid told her, opening the folder. "We'll be happy with anything she's willing to show us."

Jennifer watched the young neurologist take a stack of photographs from the folder. He held them one by one in front of the patient. Everything was timed. The other two physicians operated behind the computers. JD's eyes were open. She seemed to be staring at the images.

The answers this test would provide were both exciting and terrifying. Jennifer was glad for the young woman. JD's family had to be out there somewhere, wondering what had become of her. At the same time, Jen feared for JD. Someone had pushed her out of a moving car on the dark highway on a winter night. That person had intended to kill her.

"We have visuals," Desmond announced.

"I haven't shown her the second set of images yet," Sid replied.

"The other model has established a match. It's already giving us visuals."

The other two physicians joined Desmond behind the computer. Jennifer didn't think it was right for her to join them. So far they hadn't minded her sticking around. She hoped they'd retain that attitude.

"What's that?" Nat asked suddenly. "What happened?"

"Nothing happened," Desmond responded. "It's another visual."

"Are you sure it's not a malfunction?" Nat asked.

"No, it's a visual," Desmond said adamantly. "Look."

"Have you seen anything like this?" Nat asked Sid.

"No…it has to be that we don't have the right model match for her."

The curiosity was killing her. Jennifer looked at JD. The young woman's eyes were still open. She was now looking at her.

"Is something wrong?" Jennifer asked finally.

Sid looked up surprised, as if he'd forgotten that she was there.

"You're not happy with the readings?" she asked, too worried to refrain from asking.

"Well, we should be getting images of what she's thinking…or of a memory…anything. But instead, we're getting a black screen. It has to be a malfunction of the computers."

"It's *not* a malfunction of the computers," Desmond Beruti said again. "That's what she's showing us."

"A black wall?" Nat asked.

"Perhaps night?" Jennifer recalled the circumstances of her accident. "Could it be darkness? Could this be a memory image?"

"Maybe," Desmond said. "She's definitely some-where else right now."

13

Nuclear Fusion Test Facility

It wasn't her imagination. He'd moved. He'd taken hold of her wrist.

"Dr. Lee," Marion said softly, crouching down beside her advisor. She shone the light on the hand that she'd seen move. It lay motionless. She directed the beam toward the man's head. There was blood everywhere she looked. A raw wound to the side of his skull was visible. Beyond that, she had no idea how many times the older man was shot or where. She didn't know what she could do to help him.

"Please…Dr. Lee," she whispered again. She put her fingers on his wrist, hoping to feel the pulse. She couldn't find anything. She touched his neck, searching for any sign of life. The blood was sticky on her hand. Whatever she'd thought her aversion was to the sight of blood, it didn't matter right now. She couldn't move away if there was any chance he was alive.

Marion could barely feel it, but there was a weak pulse. She shone the light on the man's face again. His lips were moving.

"Dr. Lee. Please tell me what to do."

He was lying facedown, his face turned to the side. She didn't know if she should try to move him.

"Sa…sa…"

Marion crouched low to the ground, bringing her ear closer to his mouth. She pushed her hair behind her ear. Her hand came away with fresh blood.

"Please…say it again…what do you want me to do?"

"Samp…samp…."

"Samp…?" she repeated. "Samples? The test samples." She remembered the nine containers in the test chambers.

"L…leak…po…power…off. Leak…"

"The power," she said aloud, realizing what he was telling her. With the power turned off, the samples would leak. Without power, the cooling cycles would be disrupted. No controlled atmosphere for the tests. The sequencing had already started. A number of the tests might already be in catastrophic stages if the containers had failed. Or if not, it'd be simply a matter of time before they did. Marion flipped open her phone and looked at the time.

"Is there any way I can stop the tests?" she asked.

"…Ceme…cemen…"

"Cementation," she said aloud.

She knew what he was telling her. There was no ventilation in the test chambers. The containers would eventually generate and release hydrogen. When that happened, a flammable mixture of hydrogen and oxygen would form. The result was a fire or a possible explosion. With the lab hundreds of feet underground, whoever was left down here would be dead.

The facility's power had shut down at approximately the same time that the tests had started. She could calculate the time and figure out the worst-case scenarios of when the first leaks could take place.

The scientist was saying *cementation*. It was a way of sealing the containers so no gases could escape. She started to shake her head and then stopped, as the pain rocketed through her skull.

"There's no power in the facility," she told him. "I can't get the mixes going without it. Dr. Lee, is there a backup system that you know of? A generator?"

There was no answer.

Marion shone the light on her advisor's face. His eyes were open, but he wasn't moving. She pressed her fingers to his neck, where she'd felt a pulse before.

There was nothing. He was gone.

14

The reference librarian wrote down the information Mark Shaw wanted before disappearing behind her wall of computers.

Mark was obsessed with finding whatever he could about Marion. The accident, her family, anything.

Newspapers, television, the Internet and now the library. He reminded himself repeatedly that spending some twelve hours chatting with someone in a crowded airport didn't really constitute knowing the person. But he couldn't stop.

He opened that morning's *New York Times* on one of the library's oversize tables. There were no pictures of the scientists in today's edition, but there was an article on page two. He scanned it quickly. The gist of it was that the group, funded by a grant from New Mexico Power Company, had been working on developing portable nuclear devices. The power company had confirmed that no live radioactive material had been involved in the research program. Mark looked down at the names again. Marion Kagan was the last name listed.

Mark remembered the first moment he'd laid eyes on her. Logan Airport had been packed with stranded passengers. There were no empty seats, and people sat huddled along any available wall and on the wet, muddy floors. Everyone had been miserable. There were long lines at each of the eating establishments. No flights were taking off or landing, and there was no information by the airlines or the airport on how long the storm was going to last. From Philadelphia to Maine, the East Coast was essentially shut down. Marion was sitting at the end of a row of seats, a carry-on suitcase propped up next to her. She seemed oblivious to the complaining around her.

A cell phone was tucked between one ear and her shoulder. An iPod was plugged into the other ear. A foot kept beat with whatever music she was listening to. Her laptop was open, and her fingers were flying on the keyboard. She could just as well have been sitting in a park on her lunch hour on a beautiful summer day.

A four-by-four piece of real estate on the floor opened up next to her. Mark headed toward it, but as he got there her suitcase fell on its side, covering the space.

She looked down at the suitcase, up at him, then at the suitcase again. He stood there, thinking she'd move it. She ended the conversation on her cell and lowered the display of her laptop.

"Can I sit here?" he'd asked her.

She'd looked up at his uniform. "Are you going or coming back?"

People were curious. He had no doubt she was asking about the service. "I'm going back," he'd said. "I was on leave for a few weeks."

"Iraq?"

He nodded.

"I have to tell you I'm against it. I hate our dependency on oil. I believe it's wrong for so many people to die for a foreign policy based on oil. And I'm talking about Iraqis *and* Americans."

He'd stared at her raised chin and the defiance in her dark eyes. Mark thought she was beautiful.

"Do we have to have this conversation while I'm standing up?" he asked.

"Conversation and not an argument?"

"Conversation…argument…debate…whatever."

"I like debates," she'd said with a smile, reaching for the suitcase and pulling it out of his way. "Have a seat."

"Officer Shaw?" The librarian's voice broke into Mark's thoughts. He looked up from the newspaper he had open before him. It took him a moment to wipe Marion's image from his mind's eye. He stood up.

"Were you able to find anything?"

"There are no obituaries for any of the victims, as yet. Not even the universities have posted items. Perhaps tomorrow. I do see that the fire is hampering the investigators from even reaching the accident site."

The fire was still burning. From what Mark had read, the experts were saying that, because of the high temperatures, nothing would be left. No remains. They might not get down into the research facility beneath the platform for months. If then.

"I was hoping to find an address for Marion Kagan's family to send some flowers," he told her. He knew she was originally from Deer Lodge, Montana, but there was no one by the last name of Kagan listed in the phone book when he'd checked.

"You might want to check with the university she was affiliated with," the librarian offered.

"I have…I did. They're too overwhelmed right now and are only answering questions of the immediate family. Their suggestion was to wait for the service arrangements."

"I'll keep an eye open for it. If you want to check back with us, maybe Monday," the woman offered. A thought struck her. "Don't you have access to driver's license records through the police department?"

"Yes, I could go that route…" Mark said. The Department of Motor Vehicle records were traceable to when someone first got their license. In Marion's case, he could most likely get her address in Montana and when first she'd applied. "But this is personal, not professional."

"I see. Well, it just has to be a matter of time before the information starts getting posted."

Mark nodded, pretending to be satisfied, and the librarian returned to her desk. He closed the newspaper and put it back on the rack where he'd gotten it.

He needed to find something to do. He had too much time on his hands. The librarian had addressed him as Officer Shaw. Everyone expected that he would go back to the old job. In his conversation with his parents last night on the phone, it was clear they expected the same thing.

Now he could admit that part of his reluctance had to do with her. Somewhere in the back of his mind, he'd imagined that he'd take a trip to California and possibly meet up with Marion Kagan. Two weeks he'd been back, though, and he hadn't called her. And now she was dead.

What a waste, he thought, leaving the library.

15

Nuclear Fusion Test Facility

The sight of Eileen Arrington's dead body on the bunk in the room they'd shared was the last straw. She'd been shot in the forehead and her eyes were fixed on some spot above the door.

Marion's stomach turned. She grabbed a wastebasket next to her bed and bent over. Her body shook with dry heaves.

She pushed herself to walk out into the hallway. Once in the narrow passage, she crouched down and leaned against the paneled wall, hugging her knees to her chest. She laid the penlight on the floor. A sense of helplessness overwhelmed her. The tears she'd been trying to hold back finally let loose. Sobs rose in her throat. For a while, she had a hard time getting enough air into her lungs.

Neil Gregory's and Steven Huang's bodies had been in the kitchen area. Both men had been shot as they sat at the large table the group used for their meals. She knew it was useless to check for any vital signs in the two, but she forced herself.

Turning away from them, Marion's gaze fell on the door of a facilities room off the kitchen. The door was slightly ajar and, pushing it open, she found what looked like a generator in the corner beside a water heater and an HVAC unit. The generator had been disabled. The people sent down here to kill them had known to do even that.

Eileen had been her last hope. But she was dead, too. Marion alone had survived the attack.

She sat for a long time with her back against the wall and her knees gathered to her chest. The air in the facility was becoming dank. A familiar odor hung in the air. She realized what it was. It was the Monday-morning smell in the meat department at the grocery store where she had worked during the summer when she was in high school. It was the smell of death.

Whether she sat there for ten minutes or an hour, Marion didn't know. Time had lost all significance. She stared up into the darkness around her. The penlight she'd placed on the floor was growing dimmer. She patted her pocket for the other one she'd taken from Andrew Bonn's desk. It wasn't there. She guessed it had dropped out of her pocket when she'd gotten sick inside the room. That was where the facility emergency notebook had fallen, too, along with the clipboard she'd gone back into the control room to get.

Marion recalled what her advisor had told her as he'd taken his last breath. The samples—the contamination. He'd asked her to seal the containers. She'd tried to get into the lab as she'd made her way from the control room. She hadn't been able to open the door. Perhaps there was another emergency generator in the facility that she didn't know about. Even a backup battery source. There had to be something, she thought.

She had yet to calculate the hours before that time

bomb would go off. She needed to know how much time she had left.

Marion realized she needed to go back inside the sleeping quarters and get the things she had dropped.

She was angry with herself for not paying attention to details. She'd had other things to focus on and had decided early on that among the experts in the facility, they'd take care of any possible emergencies. She'd been wrong. They were all dead.

It was now up to her. She didn't know how to get inside the lab, but she had to find a way. But then, even if she did get in, the cementation procedure wasn't something she could do in the dark, without the proper apparatus. There was a long and complicated set of steps to follow to effectively seal the containers. Marion didn't know how she could accomplish any of that. Not by herself. Certainly, not without power.

Her head was pounding fiercely again. The darkness all around was disorienting. She took the phone from her pocket and turned it on. The sunny beach wallpaper on the display made her pause. This was it. This was the end of her life as she knew it.

She stared at the time on the display. No one had come after them. There had been no rescue. She couldn't fathom what the people at the power company's R & D group were doing. It didn't make sense for them not to respond after so many hours. They communicated with them via e-mail on an hourly basis. It just didn't make sense.

Her fingers moved of their own accord and pressed the address book on her cell. Marion wondered if any of the people she had listed there would know that something had happened to her. Most importantly, how many of them would care, or do something about it?

There weren't too many names in the address book. There were even fewer people that she called on any regular basis. Since the start of the project, she'd been incommunicado anyway. Looking at the dearth of names, she realized she'd been incommunicado her entire life.

Her world had been studying, school, trying to make something special out of her future. She'd wanted to prove her mother wrong. There was life outside of Deer Lodge, Montana. She could make a life somewhere else. She wouldn't return as Kim had.

Disappearing with some eight older scientists for three months had been no problem for Marion. She had no boyfriends, no social life, no family that she visited or that visited her on regular basis.

Her fingers scrolled down the list. She stared at the name that came up.

"Mark Shaw," she whispered under her breath.

There had been more than a few times she'd hoped that he'd call. Marion had even tried to call him. Four times. But it was always voice mail, and she never left a message.

He had been heading to Iraq when they met. He was probably still there.

She stared at his phone number and smiled sadly. It's funny how sometimes you can know a person right away, she thought. Mark was the kind of person who would be worrying about her. He'd care.

16

"Same numbers."

Sid Conway looked down at the printout his partner Desmond handed him. "And not just any numbers," he replied. "Ten digits. These must be a phone number."

They'd quit last night around ten. It didn't matter how they'd played with the parameters, they still couldn't get any readings on JD's scans that made sense. This morning, despite being a Saturday, both Sid and Desmond had shown up at the facility around seven. Nat Rosen was supposed to get there at ten; he had to make a stop at the UCONN Health Center first. Like last night, there was only one output for each reading. Not darkness or a black screen this time, but one set of numbers, showing up again and again.

"What do we do with it?" Desmond asked.

Sid wondered if he should call Dr. Baer to ask his opinion. They had set up no guidelines as far as what they should do with the content that was extracted from JD's mind. He assumed that the conservator would be notified if they found anything. But he knew that no one outside of the team expected anything as concrete as a series of numbers to be decoded.

Last night, they had nothing. This morning, they had a number. Tomorrow, they could have her real name. Wouldn't that be something!

When Jennifer walked into the room, Sid wasn't surprised. She'd been there when they left last night.

He smiled at her, appreciating her dedication. "Do you have a home?"

"Do you?" she asked him.

He nodded. He was certain the nurse that had escorted them in this morning had contacted her. He figured Jennifer Sullivan must have left specific instructions about being called at home whenever they got here.

He noticed that she wasn't in uniform. "We get grant money for this. Do you get paid?"

"I'm scheduled to work second shift today."

He glanced at his watch. "Aren't you a bit early?"

"I hope you won't wait until you get to be my age before figuring out that money isn't everything."

It had been only a day, but Sid thought they were getting along. He noticed even Desmond was a little more talkative with her around. His coworker answered her polite greeting.

"You got something this morning?" she asked, looking at the paper in his hand.

"Numbers. Could be a phone number. And that's the only thing she's giving us. Repeated readings and we keep getting the same numbers." He showed her what was printed on the paper. "It's like she's seeing these numbers and running them through her head over and over again."

"Did you call the number?" she asked.

"What?" He looked up, surprised. "No."

"Why not?"

"What do I say if someone answers?"

"Ask for their name."

"And you think they'll tell me that?" Sid asked.

"I don't know." She reached for the paper. "Can I see it?"

He handed it over.

"I guess another alternative would be to contact the police," she told him. "But considering her accident took place six years ago, I don't even know if anyone is still assigned to the case. I could be long retired before we hear anything back from them. I say we call the number."

Desmond cleared his voice. They both looked in his direction. "I just checked the reverse lookup. No name comes up. It's either unlisted or a cell number…or it's not a phone number at all."

Sid thought about this. He was still riding on a cloud that they hadn't lost their funding for the project. He wanted to succeed. At the same time, he knew that people were keeping a close eye on them. They had to dot every *i* and cross every *t,* especially in the gray areas of ethical behavior. Dr. Baer had told him that in so many words, and Sid intended to follow the rules, whatever they were, all the way.

His gaze fell on JD. Her eyes were open. She was watching him. Only him. This was the first time today she'd done that.

But first and foremost, he was a doctor. There was the *project*…and there was the *patient*.

"Do you two mind if I called the number?" Jennifer asked.

Sid realized Desmond was waiting for him to make the decision for both of them. He looked at JD again.

"Exactly what will you say if anyone answers?" he asked Jennifer.

"I'll tell them who I am and ask them who they are," she said. "If someone answers, they don't have to know all the specifics. But if it sounds like family…say, a middle-aged woman…then I'll tell her that we have a patient that we are trying to identify."

JD's pale skin in the morning light made her look like a porcelain angel. The dark eyes seemed to speak to him. Not even twenty-four hours had passed, but Sid already understood the nurse's protectiveness of her. He felt it. He wanted to do what was right for this young woman.

"Yesterday, you said that she was pushed out of a moving car," Sid reminded her. "What happens if this number doesn't belong to a family member or a friend? What if it belongs to the people who think they got rid of her?"

"That's true." Jennifer stared down at the number for a long moment. She glanced up at JD before turning to Sid. "We have to try. We have to be careful. You didn't imagine this. This phone number is in her brain. She wanted us to have it."

There was no security in this facility to speak of, Sid thought, just a young woman who sat at a receptionist's desk in front. She called for one of the nurses to escort anyone who came in outside of visiting hours.

"I don't want to put her in any danger," he said. "She's vulnerable here."

"Put yourself in her position. No, put yourself in her family's position," she challenged. "She's been gone for six years. Don't you think they have the right to know what happened to her?"

Sid shrugged. "Yes, I do."

"Look, I won't give them any specifics unless I sense everything is on the up-and-up at the other end."

Sid ran a hand through his hair. He moved beside the bed. JD's eyes followed him.

"Is this what you want?" he asked her.

"She talks to you, too?" Jennifer asked from her corner.

"She might not be using words, but I get a feeling that she's definitely communicating with us." Her hand lay palm down on the blanket next to where Sid stood. He reached down and placed his on top of hers.

"Is this what you want?" he asked again.

There was the briefest movement. He withdrew his hand and looked down at her fingers. They were curled around the edge of the blanket.

"Okay." He turned to Jennifer. "You make the call and I'll contact Dr. Baer and give him the number. I'll tell him what steps we've taken and he can pass that on to the conservator to do whatever he wants with it."

17

New York City

The car pulled into the West 30th Street Heliport and the two men got out.

As his boss pulled on leather gloves, Joseph Ricker stood silently beside him and looked across the tarmac to the helicopter waiting to take them to LaGuardia airport for their flight back to Washington. The aircraft's engine was already warmed and ready.

There were details that Joseph had followed up on while Martin Durr had been in his meeting, but Durr had not wanted to discuss them in the building or on the short ride over. Joseph knew that his superior's concern for security was not paranoia. Cars and offices were often bugged. They started toward the chopper, where the pilot and an assistant were waiting. But halfway there, Durr stopped and held up his hand for the pilot to wait.

"Okay. Tell me."

Joseph looked up at the helicopter and back to his boss. The noise from the chopper would block any possibility of their conversation getting picked up by a listening device. He covered his mouth with his hand when he spoke.

"The facility is completely shut down. Nellie Johnson assures me that all references to it have been erased from the power company's files. There are no ties between the New Mexico bunker and the power company. For those who look at the records, all of the funded research experiments were being carried out at the lab on the Gulf of Mexico."

"Nothing in any file will send anyone to it?" Durr asked. "Nothing?"

Joseph understood his boss required absolute perfection.

"Nothing, sir," he answered confidently. "This testing lab falls into the same classification as hundreds of other deserted subterranean facilities in New Mexico and Nevada."

"How about TMC Corporation files?"

TMC was a private contractor that ran a number of laboratory and nuclear-waste-station facilities for the government. Martin Durr's connections and influence in the corporation ran deep, but none of that information was public record. Even Joseph didn't know exactly what the arrangements and the degree of ownership were between Durr and this company. From his first day on the job, he'd been told that he was to trust them.

TMC was a crucial part of executing the top-secret, last-minute switch of the facilities.

"I am told that they don't acknowledge even knowing about the attached laboratory in their files. As far as their records, they only manage the Waste Isolation Pilot Plan next door to the research lab. TMC took over the subterranean lots. They didn't build them."

Durr took a handkerchief out of his pocket and blew his nose. "What about the demolition arrangements?"

"Having been down there, our consultant's advice

has been against demolition at present, sir. They have assured me that the personnel have been terminated and the facility adequately sealed. They firmly believe that an explosion is unnecessary and will only generate unwanted attention, due to its proximity to the adjoining Waste Isolation Pilot Plan site. They recommend arranging for a final cleanup, including the removal of everyone and everything from the facility, in three or four months' time."

"How about the offshore platform?" Martin Durr asked. "Will there be questions as to why no bodies are recovered?"

"No, sir. It has already been determined that the subterranean facility beneath the platform imploded after the fire. Essentially, the explosions caused a cave-in. There is no way to reach any remains."

Durr nodded and headed toward the chopper. Nothing more needed to be said. Joseph understood that his superior was satisfied.

18

As he got into his truck in the library's parking lot, Mark Shaw looked down at his cell phone. There were two voice mails, four text messages and three missed calls.

He needed a social secretary these days to keep track of his schedule. He read the text messages first. Three of them were invitations. One was from Leslie. It was short and to the point.

"Let's do dinner."

He was surprised, but then again, he shouldn't have been. This morning at the diner he'd heard from a couple of the regulars that Leslie had split with her boyfriend. He should have figured that it was only a matter of time before she'd call. She was such a creature of habit. She'd always been most comfortable with the known— with someone she'd been with before. She shopped in the same stores, insisted on going to the same place for vacation every year. Established routines were what made her happy. Before they'd broken up, she'd been ready to get married, have three children and move onto the same street where her parents lived.

Mark had no doubt that was still the grand plan.

"Been there, done that." His thumb hovered over the delete button for a couple of seconds. He tried to think of anything positive that could come out of getting back together with her.

No, there was too much baggage between them. He pressed the delete button.

Mark listened to the voice mail messages next. Another invitation, this one to a christening party for a grandson of one of his parents' old friends. The second voice mail consisted of a click as someone hung up without leaving a message. He wondered if that was Leslie again. She did have a single-track mind. When she made a decision, she'd move the earth to make it happen. He checked the number. Leslie.

He glanced down at the missed calls. Three of them, all from the same number. A 203 area code. Off the top of his head, he didn't know what state that was. Not that it had any significance these days. People kept their cell phone numbers even after they moved. The thought occurred to him that it could have been from any number of people he'd served with in Iraq.

Sitting in the driver's seat of his pickup, Mark called the number and looked out at the yellow leaves swirling about the nearly empty parking lot.

"Waterbury Long-Term Care. How may I direct your call?"

For a couple of seconds, Mark was tongue-tied. He thought of his parents first and whether they were okay. He'd talked to them a couple of days ago and they were both fine.

His mind searched for possibilities of anyone he knew who might be staying at any kind of long-term care facility. His grandmother was the only one, but this wasn't the name of the place where she was staying. He considered the people he had served with in Iraq. There was a possibility of someone being hurt and taken to a facility like that.

"My name is Mark Shaw. I'm calling from Pennsylvania. Someone tried to call my cell number three times over the past hour from your number. Is there any way you can help me?"

"I'm the receptionist. I'm afraid I don't keep track of calls out of the facility," the woman explained. "I can write the information down and give it to the head of the nursing staff to see if she knows anything about it."

"And you're in…Waterbury?"

"Connecticut," the woman offered.

They'd tried to reach him three times. It had to be something important. He left his name and cell phone number.

Mark tried to remember what he had on the agenda for the morning. As he roughed out the rest of his day, his thoughts kept wandering back to the mystery phone call from Connecticut. Very strange. Starting the pickup, he pulled out of the parking lot.

He hadn't driven two blocks from the library when his cell phone rang. He looked at the incoming call. It was the same 203 area code. He pulled to the side of the road and answered the phone.

"Mr. Shaw?"

"Yes, this is Mark Shaw."

"Hello. My name is Jennifer Sullivan. I'm a member of the senior nursing staff at the Waterbury Long-Term Care Facility." The woman paused. "We have an unusual situation here, and we were wondering if you might be able to help us."

He'd become a cop because he was one of those crazy people who believed in helping people. Right now, he wasn't a police officer, but the impulse was the same.

"How can I help you, Mrs. Sullivan?" he asked.

"We have a patient with severe head injuries who was transferred to our facility with no form of identification on her. She's currently in a minimally conscious state."

"I assume your local police department has been involved."

"Yes, they have." She paused again, as if thinking about how much she should say. "For as long as she's been here, this phone number is the first piece of information she's revealed."

"How long has she been there?" he asked.

Again, there was a pause before she spoke. "Actually, I need to tell you I'm feeling very uncomfortable making this call. Other than your name, I don't know anything else about you. Perhaps I should pass on this information to our local police department and let them handle it."

Mark's curiosity was piqued. He'd had this cell phone number for at least seven or eight years. At the same time, he agreed with the nurse's reaction. "I believe that's the right way to go. I don't know anyone from Connecticut, but I've just gotten out of the service, so if this patient was recently admitted…"

"I really don't want to discuss any specifics."

"Okay. Then why did you call me, Mrs. Sullivan?" he asked.

"Well, I thought that if you had a family member that was missing, perhaps you could help us."

"Thankfully, I don't. I'm sorry."

The disappointment coming through the line was palpable. "Well, thanks anyway. Do you mind telling me where you're located?"

"Not at all. I'm in York, Pennsylvania."

"Have you ever been to Connecticut, Mr. Shaw?"

Mark had to think about that for a moment. "No, I don't think I have."

The nurse was silent.

"Listen, Mrs. Sullivan," Mark continued. "I'd like to help, but it sounds as if you're in a bind. I can understand that."

"Thank you," she replied.

"Like I said, I think giving the police my name and number is the way to go. The investigating officers can always contact me if they need me."

19

Waterbury Long-Term Care Facility
Connecticut

"His name is Mark Shaw. And he agreed when I suggested giving his name to the local police."

Sid and Desmond both looked at the doorway where Jennifer stood, telling them what she'd learned.

"Okay then," Sid said with a shrug. "Why don't we do that?"

"And wait another six years until someone gets motivated to help her?" she asked, walking into the room. "He wouldn't be telling me to contact the police if he was up to no good."

She moved behind Desmond, where she could see the screens. "Anything new?"

"Nothing," Desmond answered.

"I'm just thinking that maybe I should have told him a little bit more," Jennifer said, continuing her thought.

Sid stared at his monitor, pretending he didn't hear her. He was not about to change his position. Still, he intended to tread lightly with Jennifer. He'd left a voice mail for Dr. Baer with the information, but he had heard nothing back. He figured it might be Monday before he talked to the physician. At the same time, Sid wasn't going to stop Jennifer if she decided to be more aggressive with the information they were turning up.

Jennifer answered her own suggestion. "Great idea, Mrs. Sullivan. You should definitely tell him more. He might just hold the key to JD's identity."

Sid looked up, and he and Desmond exchanged a look. Nat Rosen had called from the hospital. He had been delayed in a meeting and was going to skip coming down here today. Sid decided that was a good thing. Between Nat and Jennifer talking all the time—and now answering their own questions—he and Desmond would be in straitjackets in no time.

"Would you mind if I called from here, so you two could make sure I'm getting it right?"

Sid gave a noncommittal shrug. "Whatever you want to do."

"She's asleep," Desmond said, looking at his monitor.

Sid got up and walked to the bed. JD had indeed fallen sleep.

"I think we should pack it in for today," Desmond told him.

His partner was right. Sid started gently removing the electrodes. They didn't want to push her too much, especially not at the beginning of the experiment. At the same time, Sid didn't want to leave. He understood how Jennifer felt. JD was sleeping peacefully. He could just stand there and watch her.

The electrodes had left red welts on the skin of her forehead. "She might be allergic to the adhesive on these tapes. Let's use the hypoallergenic tape next time."

Desmond made a note of it in the files he still had open.

"Hello, Mr. Shaw?" Jennifer started speaking on the

phone next to JD's bed. "This is Jennifer Sullivan again. From…yes…of course, you remember. Being that today is Saturday, and I have two of the physicians seeing to the patient's care here…and the fact that you sounded like a trustworthy individual…I thought…"

Sid looked up at Jennifer. She pulled a chair next to the bed and sat down. She was listening intently to something Mark Shaw was saying on the phone. She looked around as she pulled a pen from her pocket and gestured for paper. Desmond handed her a pad. She started scribbling something down. In a couple of minutes, there was a noticeable transformation in her face. She gave them a thumbs-up sign.

"Okay. Let me first explain some of what you told me to the physicians here."

She covered the mouthpiece. "He's an ex-cop, just back from Iraq. He gave me the name of the chief of police in York, Pennsylvania, where we can check his references. He still believes we should go through the local law enforcement to get help with the case, but he's willing to help us if there's any way he can."

"Does he know anyone who's been missing for six years?" Desmond asked.

Jennifer removed her hand from the mouthpiece of the phone. "You asked me before how long this patient has been here," she told him. "Well, she's been in this facility for six years. This is the first time we were able to get any information from her."

Jennifer's gaze rested on JD's face. "Yes, you heard me correctly, it's been six years. We call her JD…for Jane Doe." She paused, listening. "Yes, that's why we were excited about trying to get any information we could from this number." Pause. "It really just happened and we haven't called the police yet.

We don't even know if there's an active file on her at this point."

Listening to the conversation, Sid picked up a tube of anti-inflammatory cream and put dabs of it on where JD's face had reacted to the adhesive.

"Connecticut. Yes, it's a pretty good drive from Pennsylvania," Jennifer said into the phone. "Picture? E-mail you a picture of her?" She looked at them.

"Do you have a digital camera at the facility?" Desmond asked.

Sid found himself becoming less enthused by the minute. He told himself he was being cautious. They still didn't know much about this guy.

"Yes, give me your e-mail address. We'll send it off to you in a few minutes. Sure thing."

She wrote down more information and ended the call before looking at them. "So what do you think?"

Sid shook his head. "I think it's a mistake," he told her.

"Why do you think it's a mistake?" she asked him.

"This is the first piece of information she's given us. By the end of the weekend, she might give us so much detail that we won't need the help of some stranger like him."

"A stranger who's been giving us all kinds of references," she reminded him.

"Still, why can't we wait until Monday?"

"I learned long ago to jump at the chances we are given in life. Waiting is just about all we do around here. Patients are brought to this wing and this is where they stay…waiting until the end," she said quietly. "Look at her. She's been waiting for six years. Why don't you tell her we're not going to do anything about what she's given us until Monday? *You* tell her to wait."

Sid looked at JD. She seemed to be having a nightmare. A slight frown on her forehead deepened and her body jumped. Her eyes immediately opened. She looked at him.

Aside from some nurse's kindheartedness, JD had had no one to sit beside her, hold her hand, fight for the treatments she should get. Sid didn't know where this sudden awareness in him of a patient's needs was coming from. But he understood what Jennifer was fighting for.

"Okay."

"Okay, what?" she asked.

"Okay, do what you need to do. Take her picture. E-mail it to this Mark Shaw."

She stood on the other side of bed and stared at him for a long moment. Then she smiled.

"Don't worry," she said finally. "You can bring a barricade and a tent and set yourself up in the front lobby."

"You mean, set my tent up next to yours," Sid responded.

"Exactly." She headed for the door. "I'll be right back with the digital camera."

20

Nuclear Fusion Test Facility

At first glance, the facility handbook offered a lot less than Marion had hoped for. She was looking for a reference to the emergency exit, but could find nothing listed in the index. Great handbook. She double-checked the facility identification. Every page was labeled with NMURL, New Mexico Underground Research Lab. The publication seemed to be put together in a pretty haphazard manner. A lot of information was missing.

She thumbed through the index. There was no mention of an auxiliary power source that she could find, either.

The schematic of the laboratory layout at least offered something, she thought, looking closely at the page as she held the penlight that she'd retrieved from the floor of her quarters. Operating information regarding ventilation, power, water and sanitation were also covered in depth.

Studying the layout diagram for the entire facility, Marion couldn't even see the generator she'd found in the room off the kitchen. She didn't know whether that was a good thing or a bad thing. Maybe there were pages missing. Maybe there was another power source.

She put the penlight down on the open book and pressed her fingers to her eyes. Her head still had a dull ache, and her eyes were so tired.

"Toughen up," she chided herself. "No time for that."

Returning to the facility diagram, she decided her first stop had to be the maintenance closet. She needed a much more powerful source of light than what she was operating with. During the past few weeks down here, she'd poked her head into that room a number of times for cleaning supplies. She remembered seeing a box of oversize flashlights. She hoped the batteries were still good.

There were other things she knew she had to see to immediately after that. Checking out the walk-in freezer in the kitchen for space was part of one grim task. The temperature in the facility seemed to have remained constant, but it would only be a matter of time before the bodies of her coworkers began to decompose. Marion wondered if she was strong enough, mentally and physically, to drag them to the freezer.

Whether anyone was coming after her…ever…was something she didn't want to think about.

The pounding in her head was coming back. She moved down the hall, trying to ignore the pain. Her throat was parched, and she couldn't imagine trying to swallow any more pills without something to drink.

The maintenance closet was near the living quarters. Reaching it, Marion tried the door handle. It was locked.

"No…no," she said aloud, pushing on the handle again.

The door wouldn't open.

She shoved the handle down harder, but it didn't budge. She kicked the door, then leaned a shoulder into it. The jarring sensation caused sudden light-headedness.

Nothing. It wouldn't give. She wanted to put her head on the floor and close her eyes.

She tried to remember whether the room had been locked the other times she'd come to get supplies. She didn't think so. She remembered a conversation between Eileen and Eugene Lee about Andrew Bonn taking most of the extra toilet paper rolls back to his bunk only a couple of days ago.

Marion hadn't paid much attention. They must have decided to lock up the supplies. She had no idea where she should look for the key. Perhaps Robert Eaton, the team leader, kept it.

She leaned against the door. Her heart was racing, and the light spilling from the penlight in her hand was shaking. Her body trembled. Her breath was choppy. She wondered if these were signs of a panic attack.

She put her back against the door and leaned over, putting her forehead between her knees. She tried to take deep breaths. She had to think of something else. Somewhere else. Anyplace but here. She remembered reading in a yoga book about the positive influence of maintaining one's calm. She even recalled the line beneath an ancient Mogul miniature depicting a man looking into a stream from a bridge. *Only when the water is still can you see through it.*

Marion wished she'd read more. She chided herself for not taking a real yoga class. Serenity was a distant concept for her. She was a busy woman. She overbooked her schedule. She was proud of her ability to multitask. Coming down here and working as an assistant to eight scientists was part of it. Dr. Lee knew she was one of very few research assistants at UC Davis capable of doing the job.

Marion tried to empty her mind of this place, of the

other people she'd been working with. She focused on her breathing. But it wasn't enough. She tried to remember a saying she'd stumbled on while searching online for something completely different. It was one of the Dalai Lama's meditation techniques. Something about breathing out the bad, breathing in the good, and holding it while the healing properties spread throughout the body. Breathing out, breathing in, holding. Breathing out, breathing in...and then suddenly, she was thinking of Mark Shaw.

They were so different, the two of them. She knew it from the moment he sat down on the floor next to her at the airport. She hadn't been very nice to him, arguing her points on oil, on military recruitment, even her disenchantment with the system of justice in America today. She'd probably come across more strongly than she really felt about all of those things, but by then he'd told her that he was a cop, and Marion was probably a little tired of sitting around in the airport.

He explained to her about the world he'd seen in Iraq. The people, the tribal feuds, the sectarian violence. He told her about people who had forgotten what living peacefully was about. He knew his history. He told her about the region and not once did he try to paint a rosy picture of any of it. There were good people, and there were those who intended to profit from the misfortunes of others. It was obvious on every level and on every side of the conflict. The complexity of human nature was what set people apart...not ethnicity or nationality.

Marion's steam over politics had fizzled out soon enough. She found herself enjoying her time with Mark Shaw, and it didn't matter if they were talking about politics or if he was making fun of her for her lack of interest in classes that provided practical skills. He'd really laughed at the fact that she lived in California but had never learned to swim. What was the purpose of living there, he'd asked, when you couldn't go surfing? They'd also spent a good amount of time arguing over which fast-food restaurants had the shortest lines.

She'd never known herself to have so many opinions. She hadn't realized she could talk so much, or become so animated.

She'd never been attracted so much to anyone so quickly.

The pull she'd felt toward him had brought with it a wave of openness she rarely felt. She'd told him about her childhood, growing up in Deer Lodge, Montana. He'd told her stories of being raised near the Amish Country. Marion shared memories of her family, something that she never did.

They'd both been actually sorry when the weather cleared enough for the airport to open again. They'd each left with the promise of calling the other at some point down the road.

Why hadn't it happened? she wondered.

Marion lifted her head and looked at the faint ray of light left by the penlight. She realized that she was sitting. Her breathing was back to normal. The headache had eased somewhat. A bud of hope was forming in her. She pushed herself to her feet and pointed the light along the wall. A glass cabinet with an ax and a fire hose was a few feet down the corridor.

She walked to it. The cabinet was locked. Without hesitating, Marion slammed the corner of the notebook into it. Shards of glass showered onto the floor. She reached inside for the ax, took it out and walked back to the maintenance closet.

"Mark, you'd be proud of me," she said aloud into the silence before bringing the ax down like a hammer on the brushed nickel doorknob.

21

York, Pennsylvania

Mark generally went home to his apartment above the garage only to sleep. Today, he made an exception. He was anxious. He needed to be by a computer to check his e-mail.

He pulled into the driveway and got out of his pickup. The air was fresh and crisp outside. A perfect fall day.

"Everything okay, Mark?" Ryan asked.

The husband and wife who were renting the main house were outside, raking the yard. From what Mark could see, Dora was pretty far along in her pregnancy, but nothing seemed to slow her down. He knew this was their first child and they were both very excited about it. Mark told his parents, anytime he talked to them on the phone, that the renters took as good care of the house and yard as they had when they were still living here. In fact, Ryan had mentioned a couple of times that if and when Mark's parents decided to sell the house, they'd be interested, although right now they couldn't afford it.

The two were eyeing him curiously. They knew he rarely came home during the day. He waved them off.

"Everything's fine," he told them. "I'm expecting

some e-mail, so I figured I'd come home and check on it." Cable TV and Internet service were two amenities that he'd run out to his garage apartment as soon as he'd gotten home from Iraq.

"We're having some friends in tonight. Why don't you come over?" Dora asked.

Mark figured these two had joined the "let's feed Mark" team.

"We want to get all of our socializing with adults in before the baby comes," Ryan added.

"You'll probably know some of the people," Dora said.

"Thanks, but…" He couldn't think of an excuse. He appreciated the offer, but somehow the wires in his head were all twisted up. He couldn't remember what he had planned for the day, or for tonight. There was only one thing that he could think of. That e-mail.

Mark pointed to the garage and the stairs on the side. "I have some work to do now but I might poke my head in later. Please don't wait for me, though."

He made some comment about Dora taking it easy and headed up the stairs, taking them two at a time.

Maybe his life was too boring. Maybe it was the lack of having a day-to-day routine. Mark couldn't remember being this wound up about anything since he'd arrived back in York.

Going into the apartment, he left the door open and walked straight to the computer.

Waiting for it to boot up, he checked out the fridge. Four beers and a quart of orange juice he couldn't remember buying were the only things on the shelves. He shut the fridge door and looked back to the living space. He wasn't regressing, he told himself. His bed was made, and there were no piles of dirty laundry lying around. The apartment looked neat. He just always ate out. No harm in that.

He went to the kitchen cabinet and took down a can of coffee. Thanks to his mother, the cabinet was still full of soups and canned foods and other nonperishables. Looking at them, he felt a sense of comfort, knowing he could still manage here if he needed to.

He started a pot of coffee and sat down at the computer.

Mark opened his e-mail. He'd checked it last night. Since then, he had a dozen messages. He found the one from Jennifer Sullivan at the top of the list. The e-mail had an attachment.

He opened it, anxious and not knowing why.

There was a brief message from the nurse, summarizing pretty much what they had said on the phone. He scrolled down. The computer was taking its time to load the picture.

Mark looked over his shoulder at the coffeepot. It was ready. He turned back to the computer to see if he still had to wait.

He felt a sharp kick in the gut in response to the picture on the screen. He stared at the face for a long moment.

Mark reached for his cell phone and dialed the last called number. The operator at the long-term care facility in Connecticut answered.

"Jennifer Sullivan, please," he told her. "Please tell her it's Mark Shaw."

He didn't have to wait long before Jennifer was on the line.

"I know her," he said into the phone.

The shock was transferred to the other side of the line. It seemed a few long seconds before the nurse found her voice.

"You do?" Jennifer asked. "Who is she?"

"Have you been watching the news about the accident and those researchers on the Gulf of Mexico?"

"I've read a little about it."

"Well, I believe the name of the person in the photo is Amelia Kagan. She's the twin sister of Marion Kagan. The scientist who died in the research facility yesterday."

22

Nuclear Fusion Test Facility

Marion aimed the ax at the door handle, but she was tiring quickly and missed. The blade hit the tile floor and glanced off, just missing her foot. Raising the ax with an effort, she took more careful aim and swung it again.

Two total strangers meeting in an airport, and yet Marion had revealed things to Mark that she'd never told to people she considered her closest friends in California.

She'd talked about the town where she was from. Deer Lodge, Montana. This was the one place she never discussed, almost never allowed herself to think about, if she could help it. Even in her mind, she liked to pretend that it never existed.

Most importantly, though, she'd told him about her sister, Amelia. People she'd met after leaving Montana never even knew Marion had an identical twin.

She'd told Mark how, even as children, they were like one person divided into two bodies. What set them apart, though, was their reaction to life—their distinctly different way of handling their emotions. Amelia reacted, pouring hers out and showing everything; Marion repressed every uncomfortable feeling.

Marion leaned against the door to catch her breath. She was determined to get it open, and she knew she was almost there. Her mind wandered to her past again.

Deer Lodge. Her mother had returned to the home of Marion's grandparents with the twins after their father took off with another woman. As soon as she got her feet under her, Kim Kagan had immediately changed her last name back to her maiden name. She was Kim Brown to everyone who knew her. The twins were only three, and neither of them remembered much about the man who'd fathered them. In the years that followed, they never saw him or heard from him.

Deer Lodge was not much to speak of. Except for the fact that some big NBA coach had come from there, the tattered gray town was famous for just one thing. The prison. The biggest employer in town. That was where Marion's grandfather had worked his whole life, and that's where her mother had gotten a job as a secretary after returning home with the twins.

Living with a mother who always worked overtime to make ends meet and elderly grandparents who had their own lives, Marion and her sister did not have an ideal childhood.

There was so much Marion had never liked about her life. The house was always overshadowed by a black cloud of tension, guilt and sadness. That cloud emanated from their mother. She was unhappy and let everyone know it, feel it. Marion hid her misery and buried herself in her books and her studying. She erected walls out of the knowledge she found in those pages and hid behind them.

Amelia, on the other hand, took the brunt of their mother's unhappiness. Sensitive and caring as a child, she felt it all deeply and eventually rebelled against it.

Their grandfather had a soft spot in his heart for Amelia. But that bit of attention made Kim only angrier. She constantly complained that the old man was meddling in the way she was raising her daughters.

The girls' mother made sure they knew that to be vulnerable was to be weak. Because of Kim, a person needed thick skin to survive in their home.

As an adult Marion often thought back over those years and came to realize that Amelia never had stood a chance. Kim was of the school of parenting that allowed choosing favorites. And in her eyes her daughters, though identical, were each a model of one parent. Marion was like Kim and Amelia was like their father. She was one bad egg.

Amelia became more miserable as she grew older, and her actions reflected it. She ran away at twelve, but was caught and returned three weeks later. For the next four years, she was constantly in trouble at school and at home, and spent as much time on the streets as she could. The grandparents took sides, as well. The girls' grandmother had as little patience for Amelia as her daughter did. Their grandfather continually sided with Amelia. It didn't matter much, however. He didn't have any say in the way things ran in the house.

At seventeen, Amelia ran away for good. To this day, Marion believed that her mother was relieved. Kim had clearly been expecting it. Like father, like daughter. Good riddance.

After that, no one was allowed to talk about Amelia at home, just as no one was ever allowed to mention the name of the man who had fathered them. Even at school, no one mentioned Amelia. Everyone who knew them pretended that she had never existed.

Marion picked up the ax and swung it hard, slamming it against the door.

"But not me," she said out loud.

For Marion, her sister had never died. She *knew* Amelia was alive. There had been times long ago when she could feel her sister's pain, her feeling of restlessness. But for a long time now, there'd been a sense of peace. Not death, but a calmness that made Marion believe that perhaps her sister had finally found the happiness she'd been searching for.

She lifted the ax again and let it drop.

With the sound of cracking wood, the entire handle separated from the door, and it was open.

23

There was a slight movement of the fingers. Sid looked down and realized he had laid his hand on JD's hand as he listened to Jennifer on the telephone.

JD looked up into his face. She was watching him.

"Are you listening to this, too?" he whispered.

He didn't know exactly what was said on the other end of the line, but one thing was clear. Mark Shaw knew who JD was. Sid was aware of an anxiety that he knew he had no right to be feeling. He'd only started working with her yesterday.

The possibility of having to stop the experiment wasn't what concerned him now. This acceptance alone was a transformation in who he was and how he worked. But there was something more, and he couldn't put his fingers on it.

Science wasn't the only thing in this equation here. He felt that there was more JD wanted to convey to them. This phone number was only the beginning.

Jennifer was writing things down speedily. Sid looked over at Desmond. He hadn't done anything more with shutting down their equipment for the day.

He seemed as interested in what the nurse was able to find out as Sid was.

"I never expected this when we started. Did you?" Desmond asked.

Sid shook his head. He told himself that this was the point, the purpose behind what he was studying, what he wanted to do. The theory of how many pictures of cats and dogs the computer could guess correctly from the readings was only a stepping stone to this. To actually help someone. To help find out who this young woman was.

"Okay, I'll be here," Jennifer said before ending the call.

Desmond came around the computers. "What do you have?"

The nurse stood on the other side of the bed and looked down at JD. The patient's eyes remained on Sid.

"Amelia?" she called softly.

There was no movement. Sid kept his hand on hers, testing for any reaction.

"Amelia Kagan," she repeated.

Sid looked into her dark eyes, wishing he could see what it was going through her mind right now. They'd removed the electrodes.

"Is that her name?" Desmond asked.

Jennifer nodded. "Mark Shaw believes she is Amelia Kagan, the twin sister of the scientist who just died in that explosion in the Gulf of Mexico." She looked around the room. She moved to where a stack of papers had been left on a table. "Wasn't there a newspaper here from yesterday with the article and pictures? Here it is."

As Jennifer flipped through the paper, Sid couldn't bring himself to look away from JD. The intensity of the young woman's stare rooted him to the same spot. He felt there was a change from what he'd seen before.

"Amelia Kagan," he repeated the name. "Next time we connect her to the computer, I want to see if anything shows up when we mention her name."

"Do you think they'll let us continue?" Desmond asked.

"We have all the signatures that we need for right now. I'll only stop when someone comes in and tells me to stop."

"So who is this guy…Mark Shaw?" Desmond asked. "Family?"

"No, only a friend to JD—*Amelia's* sister," Jennifer said. "He's decided to drive to Connecticut. He's offering to help out with whatever the conservator or the police might need from him. I got the feeling there was something between him and Marion Kagan."

Sid felt the movement again. The fingers shifted beneath the weight of his hand.

"Here's her picture. Marion Kagan, age twenty-five…"

Amelia's fingers moved. She tried to raise her hand.

"Say her name again," Sid told Jennifer.

She lowered the newspaper. "Amelia?"

"No, her sister's."

"Marion. Marion Kagan."

"She's responding to it," Sid said excitedly. "She's responding to that name, but not to her own."

"Should we hook her up again?" Desmond wanted to know.

"I believe there are some phone calls that you or I should be making first," Jennifer reminded Sid. "Dr. Baer, the conservator. They should be ready to meet with Mark Shaw when he gets here."

Sid knew how bureaucracy worked. Things took time. He hoped there would be no problem meeting

Shaw today, considering he was coming here all the way from Pennsylvania. He'd leave the information for Baer with his answering service. They'd get the message to him. And the physician knew how to reach the conservator.

There was no reason to rush Amelia, to put her under any undue stress.

"She's right." He turned to Desmond. "You should pack up for the day."

"And the calls?" Jennifer asked.

"I'll make them," he told the nurse. "At the same time, I'm not going anywhere. This Mark Shaw doesn't see her unless I'm in the room."

"Just like I told you before, that makes two of us." She laughed. "I'll have the staff set up your tent."

24

"Stop apologizing, Shawn," Cynthia Adrian spoke into her cell phone. As she talked, she looked out at the familiar streets. They were only minutes from her house now. "I know how these things are. I'm not mad at you, at all. It wasn't like you were next door and decided not to come to my father's funeral. You're not even in the country."

"I never realized you had to do everything on your own," Shawn said from the other end. "Your mother's a beauty."

"It's fine, love. Helen was being Helen. She was upset. If I'd left it to her, she probably wouldn't have even collected my father's body from the hospital." Cynthia wasn't exaggerating. "Somehow I managed to survive the week. It's over. I'm home."

She had arrived at the San Diego airport only a couple of hours earlier. There'd been a driver and a bouquet of flowers waiting for her, both from her fiancé, Shawn Dunlap, who was wrapping up a business deal in Botswana. Shawn had just left for the trip when she'd heard from the hospital about her father's death. Complications from the anesthetic after a routine colonoscopy. It wasn't right.

Cynthia motioned to the driver which driveway to pull into.

"I'll see you when you get back next week," she told him.

"I hope you're going to take a couple of days off and not go back to work right away," Shawn encouraged.

"I'll see how I feel Sunday night," she said. She pointed to her condo unit. "Got to go. Love you."

The driver had the luggage out and to the steps by the time Cynthia found her keys and wallet. The young man wouldn't even accept a tip, saying that all the arrangements had been taken care of by Mr. Dunlap. She told the driver that she could take care of things from here and sent him on his way.

Cynthia wished Shawn could have been in New Mexico, but she knew that was impossible. She knew what she was getting into when she'd accepted his proposal to marry next year. Shawn was a very successful attorney. But he was also a workaholic, similar in many ways to her father. Still, Cynthia had walked into this relationship with her eyes open. And she was certainly not her mother.

She'd asked one of the neighbor's teenagers to come over and check on the cat and bring in the mail while she was gone. The Newmans lived only two doors down, and they'd bought their place around the same time that she had bought hers.

As Cynthia opened her front door, the large pile of mail on an end table was the first thing that greeted her. There was also a package leaning against one leg of the table.

There was no sign of her cat.

"Shadow," she called, making kissing noises. "I'm home, puss."

Putting down the flowers, she went out and brought in her suitcase.

The thirteen-hundred-square-foot, three-story condo had been an early investment she'd made after landing her first real job out of college. Her parents had helped with the down payment and, after six years of living here, she was in the position where she'd make a pretty good profit when she sold it.

Shawn was after her to put the unit on the market and move in with him, but Cynthia wasn't ready. That wasn't because she was old-fashioned or because she had any doubts about her future with him. It was all about her independence.

She wasn't marrying to have someone else take care of her. She wanted a partner, someone with whom she could share her life. The real estate market wasn't the best right now, to say the least. In another year, the condo's value could only improve. Or at least, that's what she told herself. In the meantime, she enjoyed her own space.

"Shadow," she called out again, kicking her shoes off.

Sometimes, the family who watched the cat took her over to their house. Cynthia figured that must be the case, for the black cat was more focused on anyone coming through the front door than most guard dogs.

She considered walking over right now and getting her pet. But she was too curious about the package even to take the luggage upstairs to her bedroom or check the phone messages.

Picking up the box, she looked at the sender's name. A gray cloud immediately spread a shadow over her spirit.

The package had been sent by her father the day before he'd gone in for his procedure. She shook the box. Nothing moved inside that would give her a clue. Cynthia sat down on the edge of the sofa and considered what might be in the box.

Her father's legal issues were certain to be taken care of by the attorneys. Cynthia wasn't exactly clueless about what had been happening to her parents' marriage the past few years. They had been spiraling downward toward divorce when he died. Her mother had been living outside of Houston for months. Fred had a girlfriend or two, and from what Cynthia heard, he wasn't altogether shy about showing them off. She tried to stay out of it. Out of both of her parents' lives.

Cynthia had heard Helen complaining this past week about how Fred had been threatening not to give her what was due to her in any divorce settlement. She had even implied that if there was any "funny business" in the will, she'd contest the estate settlement.

Cynthia didn't care about any of that. She was an only child, and as far as she was concerned, her mother could have it all. She relied on herself and her future with Shawn. Nothing else.

She ripped open the top of the box and peeked in. It was packed with what looked to be documents.

"Great," she muttered, pulling everything out.

Two large manila envelopes and a smaller white business envelope, held together by a large elastic band, dropped onto her lap. A folded note was on top.

Pulling off the elastic band, she opened the note and read her father's distinctive scrawl:

Cynthia,
Hope you never have to open this or do anything about the stuff inside. I have every intention of

calling you as soon as I get home from the hospital tomorrow and asking you to put this box aside for me.

But you know the Adrian men. We don't have such a good survival record. So here we go. You're smart. You'll know what to do with what's inside if you need to. But again, let's hope you don't have to.
Dad

No greetings. No endearments. No closings. This was her father. Worried about dying when he was just going in for a routine test he'd put off for years.

He would have been just fifty-nine this week.

She shook her head in disappointment. She loved him very much. She already missed him terribly. But there were more than a few things she hoped she and Shawn would do differently once they had their own children.

She laid the note aside and opened the small white envelope first. In it, she found another folded note and a safe-deposit key. The note contained only the safe-deposit box number and the bank's name and address in Santa Fe.

Cynthia stared at the key and frowned. She hoped her father didn't plan on pitting her against her mother. Helen had a lot of problems, most of them stemming from being an alcoholic, but she was still Cynthia's mother.

She put the key back in the envelope and laid it on the folded note beside her. She'd simply send it to her father's attorney.

Cynthia opened the first of the large manila envelopes. "This isn't much better."

Inside, there was a thick, folded blue document. "Of course," she murmured. "Your will."

Taking one look at the date, Cynthia knew she wasn't ready to see more of it now. The will had been revised the week before her father had gone in for his colonoscopy.

"Why are you doing this to me?"

She was suddenly very weary. She slipped the will back into the envelope and dropped it onto the pile beside her. Maybe tomorrow she could read it and try to figure out the logic in what he was doing.

She looked at the last envelope, wondering what more he could be putting on her. This one appeared to be packed with more papers. Cynthia thought about not opening it.

"Okay, Dad," she said finally with a sigh. "What other surprises do you have for me?"

She tore open the flap of the last envelope and pulled out the stack of paper. A large black clip held together what had to be two hundred pages.

No explanatory note. She fanned through them.

The packet seemed to consist of technical documents, information about testing and test sites. The first dozen pages were an extensive report on a nuclear test facility in New Mexico. Some of the pages were stamped as classified.

Naturally, he would send backup data about projects he had in the works. Her father was an engineer by education and training. He always said he was the "belt and suspenders" type. Detail-oriented to the last. He believed Cynthia was cut from the same cloth and had pushed her to get her engineering degree, too. She'd gotten the degree but had never worked in the field; she'd been working in management from day one.

She put the bundle beside her, too, making a mental note to call Nellie Johnson, her father's assistant, on Monday to see what she wanted done with the stuff. Certainly, she had no use for information about any research projects.

With a sigh, Cynthia got up and slipped her shoes back on. Standing by the small mirror inside the front door, she pulled her blond hair back into a short ponytail and fastened it with a black elastic from her pocket. As she scrutinized her face, she realized she looked as tired as she felt.

She would look at the will tomorrow, she thought. What she really wanted right now was to go and get her cat back from the neighbors.

25

In the thirty-five years that he'd been practicing law, Juan Viera could count on one hand the number of days that he had worked on a Saturday. The decision to maintain a five-day workweek had been a conscious one. He'd had many offers to work for prestigious law firms in Manhattan, as well as opportunities to participate in state politics, but he'd turned his back on it all.

Attorney Viera liked his profession, but he also had a life that included his wife and grandchildren and golf and travel. It was a life that he enjoyed very much.

Of course, the business with the patient at the Waterbury facility could have waited until Monday. Dr. Baer had been the one who'd called him, and the physician had given him the option of putting off the meeting until whenever was convenient for him. Viera had decided to call the facility first, though, and speak directly with the researchers who were doing the testing.

The contact name he'd been given was Dr. Sid Conway, and the young man had answered right away. The excitement of finding Jane Doe's name had been palpable in the young man's voice. The people at the facility clearly were more than doing their job. Viera appreciated the effort. Because of that, he made this exception of his Saturday rule. He could do his part, too.

He'd agreed to meet with Dr. Baer and a person named Mark Shaw at the facility this afternoon. Shaw was coming up from Pennsylvania. The other staff who were involved with the testing he'd approved yesterday would be on hand, as well. The earliest Mark Shaw could get to Connecticut, however, was six o'clock, so Viera had put in a call to the Waterbury PD. They were sending one of the detectives with the old files from the case to the meeting.

This was a very sensitive situation. Attorney Viera wanted to have as many facts as possible before he contacted the patient's next of kin. He could imagine the shock. For six years, these people must have been living with the worst-case scenario. The young woman had been completely off the radar. Now, once he contacted them, there would be thousands of questions. He needed to be prepared.

He arrived at the facility half an hour before the scheduled meeting time. The receptionist at the front desk directed him to the conference room, but he asked to see the patient first. After making a call, she told him the nurse in charge would be down in a moment to escort him to the room.

Viera had been assigned as conservator by the state one other time in his career. That had been a case involving a minor with a terminal disease and unfit parents. Viera had visited the young boy a number of times over the years before he'd passed away at the age of sixteen. In this case, he'd only seen this young woman twice during the six years…once at the beginning and another time, two years later, when he'd made a surprise stop at this facility to check on the care the patient was receiving. Everything had been fine.

He looked around the lobby. The place had changed since his last visit. A pang of guilt nagged at him that perhaps he should have come and checked on her more often. But the periodic reports appeared to be complete and satisfactory, the facility was reputable, the physicians in charge kept him in the loop when there were changes, and the fact that she was an MCS patient made his own laissez-faire attitude more excusable in his mind.

"Attorney Viera."

He turned to the double doors leading into the facility. A woman in her forties, dressed in a sweatshirt and khakis, greeted him. She was not wearing a name tag.

She extended her hand. "Jennifer Sullivan."

"Yes, Mrs. Sullivan," he said, shaking her hand. "I've heard a great deal about you."

She gave him a curious glance. "You have?"

He nodded. "From Dr. Parker and Dr. Baer. You appear to be JD's leading advocate."

"Her name is Amelia Kagan," she told him.

He nodded, not bothering to argue the point that it was still premature to call her by that name. They needed something more concrete as far as identity.

"You want to see her?" she asked.

"Yes, I do." He nodded again. "I'm early for the meeting, so there should be time."

She motioned for him to come with her. "Dr. Baer is already here, and the neurologist from UCONN, Dr. Conway, has been here all day. His research is what helped us to come up with the phone number."

"Yes, I spoke to him on the phone."

The administrator in charge of the facility wasn't here today, but Attorney Viera had spoken to her on the phone this afternoon. He had been told that Jennifer Sullivan was qualified to provide him with any kind of information he needed from the patient's files.

"We're waiting for someone from the police department, and for Mark Shaw," she added.

"You spoke to him on the phone."

"I talked to him several times. Hope that was okay."

The attorney shrugged. "I can't see why not."

There were many times when Viera knew it was important to be a stickler about following procedure, but this was not one of those times. In this case, it was obvious the nurse and everyone else involved had only the patient's best interests in mind.

The hallways were quiet, with the exception of the aides who were delivering trays of food to some of the rooms. The wing of the facility where JD's room was located, however, lacked that little bit of distraction.

Jennifer knocked on the open door before they walked in.

Attorney Viera's gaze first fell on the patient. She seemed thinner than he remembered, much more fragile. She was lying on the hospital bed with a safety strap around her middle. Her eyes were closed. She was facing away from where two physicians were standing before a group of computers. He tried to imagine how someone related to this young woman would feel, seeing her like this. Six years was a long time.

"Attorney Viera," the older of the two men said politely, stepping toward him. "We've been speaking on the phone."

"Dr. Baer," he said, shaking the man's hand. He'd done a bit of research on Baer after he had been made the visiting physician for this facility. Of German and Persian descent, the man had impressive credentials right down the line.

Introductions were made to the younger doctor. Viera was glad that he'd looked over the curriculum vitae that had come with Sid Conway's research documentation papers. It was surprising to see someone so young in such a critical position. Conway was dressed in jeans and a T-shirt, but the expression on his angular, handsome face was all business. About medium height, lean yet muscular, the young man had a head of curly brown hair that was in desperate need of cutting. There was a deep shadow on his face that said it might have been at least a couple of days since the last time he'd shaved. He looked pretty casual for a neurologist, the attorney thought.

Viera had to remind himself that it was Saturday, though, and he himself was only wearing a polo shirt and sport jacket. When they'd spoken earlier on the phone, Viera had gotten a clear sense of the neurologist's confidence in his own abilities. He'd come across as a man who knew his business.

"You must be excited to see your project producing practical results so soon after getting started," he told Conway.

"I am, but I'm glad we're getting this chance to speak face-to-face at this point," the young man told him. His voice was anxious. "Do you know how quickly Amelia's family will be contacted?"

"It all depends," Viera answered noncommittally. "Why do you ask?"

"I believe what we were able to capture is only the beginning. She has a lot more to tell us. And, given the circumstances of her accident, I think it would be beneficial to continue with the study."

Viera considered the neurologist's words. Dr. Baer had been forthright telling the conservator about the objections to the study by family members of other patients at the health center. He'd been thorough in explaining the pros and cons of what could be discovered and of the limited control they had over the type of information the patient would give them.

Before signing the documents giving Conway authorization for testing, Viera had asked Baer's opinion on JD's prognosis as to recovery. The physician had told him that his best estimate was that she had less than a five-percent chance of progressing beyond her current state, and that was being optimistic.

"I'll tell you this," Viera told Conway. "You already have my authorization with regard to her being a subject in your study. We still don't have any definitive, admissible proof that she is Amelia Kagan. You can continue with the study until we have court authorization to transfer decisions about this young woman's care to her next of kin."

Sid Conway seemed visibly relieved.

"So what's next in your testing? What's your schedule?" Viera asked.

"I work with two other resident neurologists at the UCONN Health Center, and so far we plan to have a set of readings done every morning for a week, starting Monday," Conway explained. "Meanwhile, I intend to be here as much as I can over the weekend, as the patient has had a number of episodes of agitation this past week. I hope to be able to capture a reading if that occurs again."

Jennifer Sullivan said something under her breath to Conway that Viera didn't quite get. But it was obvious it had something to do with spending too much time there.

"Is this schedule of testing okay with you?" Viera asked Baer.

"Absolutely."

A nurse poked her head into the room. "There's a Mr. Shaw in the lobby."

Attorney Viera glanced at his watch. The man was fifteen minutes early.

"You mentioned that he's never met this young woman?" he asked Jennifer Sullivan.

"That's correct. He's an acquaintance of the twin sister," she said. "I'm sorry. He *was* an acquaintance of Marion Kagan."

If JD was in fact Amelia Kagan, the twin sister to the dead scientist, Viera dreaded the conversation he was going to have with the parents. After losing one daughter, the condition of the other one simply meant more bad news on top of all they were undoubtedly trying to deal with already.

"How about if we ask Mr. Shaw to take a look at the patient in person?" he asked.

"I'll go and bring him in," Mrs. Sullivan offered, heading for the door.

Viera turned his gaze toward the bed.

"She's awake," he said, shocked.

"Yes, so she is," Baer said quietly.

"She looks like she's aware of what's going on," the attorney said. The two times he'd seen her, she'd been asleep. "Does she understand us? Hear us? Does she know what's going on around her?" Viera felt like a fool, asking the questions. He should know all of this. "Sorry…it's strange to actually see her awake," he continued before either doctor could make any explanations. "I didn't expect this. I mean, she *is* considered to be in a minimally conscious state, no?"

"That's no problem, Mr. Viera," Baer replied. "You're correct. Her condition is MCS, but that classification covers a rather broad range of clinical features, and those features can change for each individual patient, for better or worse, over the course of time."

"I guess I half expected her to be…well, comatose." Viera, realizing he was whispering, recovered his composure. He couldn't recall the last time he'd been caught so off guard.

"That would put her in a different medical classification," Baer replied. "If she were classified as being in a coma, her condition would entail a lack of consciousness, her motor functions would be reflex action only, and she would demonstrate no auditory, visual or emotional functioning. And, of course, she wouldn't be able to communicate."

"But that's clearly not her condition," the attorney said, remembering that this would be part of the explanation he had to make to her family when he spoke to them later.

"Not now," Baer responded. "She was in a coma for a time after the accident, but that condition changed before she was transferred here."

"So, being in a minimally conscious state, she has different…what did you call them? Clinical features?"

"That's correct." Baer looked at Amelia. "MCS patients can appear to be awake. At different times, they might demonstrate the ability to reach for an object or even hold an object that requires making accommodations for its size or shape. Like Amelia, they might localize a sound's origin, show sustained visual location or even follow an object with their eyes."

Viera thought he should be taking notes. At one time or the other he'd heard all of this, but it hadn't sunk in until now.

"Also, there might be gesturing or verbalization that is intelligible. An MCS patient might even smile or cry appropriately in response to stimuli."

"She can do all that?" Viera asked, happy for this information.

"No, she can't. Not all of that. And not all the time," the doctor replied. "These features constitute a range of functions that MCS patients *might* demonstrate, depending on their condition and their recovery. One patient might be able to hold an object one day, but be unable to sustain visual pursuit. And that can change the next day."

"It must be frustrating for the family," the attorney said, looking at the patient.

"It is hard for everyone, especially her," Baer put in.

"Of course," Viera said.

Sid Conway spoke up, directing his words to Dr. Baer. "I noticed this morning that she reacts to hearing her sister's name. Even just now, she was asleep until Jennifer mentioned Marion's name."

It was impossible to miss. All of them saw it. The patient's gaze moved until she located Conway.

"I'd like to get a reading as she meets Mark Shaw," the young neurologist said hurriedly.

"How much time do you need to set up?" Baer asked.

Juan Viera sensed that there was something in the air of this room. It was obviously related to the patient. You wanted to help her, wanted her to improve. The pang of guilt was back again, but he pushed it away. Conway and his gadgets hadn't been available during the past six years. The research was cutting-edge.

"Five minutes," Conway told him, already starting to boot up his equipment. "Ten, tops."

Ahmad Baer glanced over at the attorney.

"Okay by me," Viera said. "I'll talk to him in the hallway. Call us in when you're ready."

As he stepped out into the corridor, he heard Baer asking Conway what he could do to help.

Viera went out past the double doors leading to Amelia's…JD's hall. He didn't have long to wait, for Jennifer and their visitor from Pennsylvania were coming down the hall. The introductions were made, but he gave no indication that he was ready to let Shaw in.

"I appreciate you making the long drive," he told the young man. Shaw was tall and physically fit. He was clean-cut with pleasant looks. The short haircut indicated his recent tour of duty. Viera had made a call to the York Police Department this afternoon and checked the young man's references. The captain on duty had spoken very highly of Mark Shaw.

"More than once along the way I almost turned around and went back," Shaw admitted. "I kept asking myself what was the point of coming all this way, when I've told Mrs. Sullivan here everything I know about Marion's sister."

"So you never met Amelia?" Viera asked what he already knew.

"Never. I never met their family, either," Shaw said. "The whole thing is perplexing. Marion and I only met once this past winter and exchanged numbers. I don't know how Amelia would know that phone number. Marion told me her sister had been missing for more than eight years."

"Eight years?" Viera asked.

"I'm pretty certain that's what she said. She told me they're identical twins and that her sister was never found by the police. Still, Marion knew that Amelia was out there, that she was alive, and that she planned to one day hire some detectives and actively look for her."

"How would she know that her sister was alive?" the attorney asked.

"She said they always had a…I don't know…a connection between them."

The situation was becoming more complicated by the minute. Viera couldn't even guess what some of the explanation might be. He was relieved when Dr. Baer came to find them. Mrs. Sullivan made a quick introduction, and Baer explained to Shaw about the brain scan they intended to do when Amelia met him.

Mark Shaw seemed wary and the attorney didn't blame him. This whole thing was obviously more involved than the young man had bargained on.

Viera let Baer and Shaw lead the way. He followed behind with Mrs. Sullivan.

"What do you think of all this?" he asked her.

"It's about time," she said. "No one deserves to be ignored the way she's been."

Ignored. Lost. Forgotten. There was nothing he could have done about that, Viera told himself. She'd been imprisoned in her mind for all this time. The attorney wondered if there was an end in sight to that, as well.

As they neared the room, Baer indicated that Viera and the nurse should go in first. Mrs. Sullivan remained by the door, but Viera moved across the room to the windows behind the computers, where Conway was standing with his fingers on the keyboard. He was trying to work several computers at once. Where Viera stood, he could see one of the monitors. It contained what looked like a multicolored cross section of a brain. The colors were changing constantly.

Viera looked at the patient. While he was gone, they

had taped electrodes to a dozen places, from her temple and forehead to the base of her skull. The wires led from them to a console on a table beside the bed. Conway stood behind the computers. He was speaking in a low voice to the patient. Her gaze remained on him.

Baer was standing inside the door. On Conway's signal, he gestured for Mark Shaw to enter.

Shaw appeared in the doorway, staring at the bed.

"Do you still think she's Amelia Kagan?" Baer asked quietly.

"No question," Mark Shaw answered without a pause.

Viera thought the young man looked pale, disturbed. If this woman was an identical twin to someone he knew and possibly cared for, that was understandable.

"We have visitors, Amelia," Conway said, glancing at the doorway. "Jennifer, why don't you bring Mr. Shaw closer and introduce him to Amelia?"

Viera realized what they were trying to do. The use of the nurse, perhaps the one person present that the patient knew best, limited the attention to the new visitor.

Jennifer touched Shaw on the arm and nodded to him to follow.

"We believe she is maintaining a partial level of consciousness right now," Conway explained to Mark Shaw. "She's had visual fixation on certain people in the past. But today we noticed she localizes sound origin, particularly when she hears her sister's name."

"Her sister's name and not her own?" Shaw asked.

"That's right," Conway answered.

"Can she speak?" Shaw asked.

"We call it vocalizing. It's not really speaking. At this point, she only vocalizes when she's anxious or in distress. She's had a number of episodes of that this past week."

The two were standing next to bed. Jennifer reached down and caressed the patient's hand. "You have a visitor, sweetheart. Someone who's come all the way from Pennsylvania to see you."

She stepped aside, encouraging Mark Shaw to move in to where she'd stood. He did as he was directed. Amelia's attention remained on Sid Conway.

"You can talk to her," Sid encouraged. "A guaranteed response is the mention of her sister's name."

"Hi, Amelia," Shaw said in a tense voice.

The attorney realized he was holding his breath, trying not to be a distraction. The patient didn't respond to the man's voice.

"I'm a friend of your sister, Marion…Marion Kagan."

The response was immediate. The gaze moved to Mark.

"Keep going. Keep going. Talk to her," Sid encouraged, sitting down behind one of the computers.

"I…my name is Mark Shaw," he said. He cleared his voice. It was obvious he was trying to relax. "Your sister and I only met once. In an airport in Boston. We were stranded there quite a while. I believe we became good friends. She talked about you a lot. She told me how she missed you and…"

Her right hand lifted from the bed.

"Has she ever done that before?" Baer asked.

"Never intentionally." Jennifer answered.

"Keep going," Sid encouraged. "I'm recording everything."

"Somehow, you knew about me…about Marion and me."

The hand reached for Mark's.

He took it, held it…and she smiled.

26

Nuclear Fusion Test Facility

He was there. She held his hand. She could feel the warm strength of his grip. She wasn't alone.

Marion opened her eyes, startled and disoriented in the total darkness. Fighting back a wave of panic, she realized she was on the floor, leaning against a wall. She felt around her in the darkness, and her fingers brushed against a hard edge. It was a door, and it moved with the pressure of her hand.

The maintenance closet door. She'd broken the lock and opened it. After that, she'd been exhausted and had sat down to rest. That was the last thing she remembered. She must have slept, she thought, or passed out. Her head was aching.

She'd been dreaming. But it was so real. Mark was there. He'd come after her. She was saved. She closed her eyes, wishing the dream would return. She wanted to go back to where she'd been.

A feeling of hollow despair was all she could muster. That and darkness.

"Please," she sobbed.

She searched around on the floor for the penlight she must have dropped. She couldn't find it.

Her head hurt so badly that she couldn't keep her eyes open. She reached into her pockets and found the pills she'd taken out of Andrew Bonn's desk.

Why was no one coming after her? They *had* to know something had happened to them.

"Mark?" she called into the darkness. He was the only one that she'd seen. He knew there was something wrong with her. Reality and imagination had woven a tight strand in her head. She couldn't distinguish between the two.

She put her hands on either side of her forehead.

Marion was in too much pain. She didn't bother counting pills. She had to stop the pain in the back of her head. She popped whatever was in her hand into her mouth. They stuck in her throat, and she started gagging. They wouldn't go down. The bitter taste filled her mouth.

She rolled onto her hands and knees, trying to cough the pills out.

27

"**W**hat is she doing?" Mark asked as he saw Amelia start to struggle.

Jennifer Sullivan pushed him aside. "She can't catch her breath."

The two doctors were beside the bed in a second. Mark moved back to a place near the door. The attorney came and stood next to him. Viera seemed as stunned as Mark was at the turn of events. One second she'd been holding his hand, smiling. The next second, she'd stopped breathing.

There was something uncanny about the whole thing. Mark knew the two women were identical twins, but for a second he thought he might have been looking into Marion's face, the eyes he remembered so vividly.

"There's something stuck in her throat," Conway said to the other doctor.

"She's on a feeding tube," Dr. Baer answered. "There should be nothing. Maybe mucous. Make sure her air passage is clear." He started firing directions at the nurse.

"You two will have to wait outside." Jennifer ushered

them both to the door as she went to get whatever they would need.

Mark looked over his shoulder at Amelia. She was gasping for breath. And she was crying. Right before he was pushed out of the room, he saw her lift her hand in his direction and look at him.

Jennifer closed the door behind them and called to one of the nurses as she moved quickly across the hall to an emergency station.

"You can find your way back to the front lobby," she said over her shoulder to the attorney. "The receptionist will take you to the conference room. They'll join you when they can."

She disappeared back inside the room.

Mark was stunned. He looked at the door, wishing he could go in. Amelia needed him; he'd seen that in her look. But he didn't know how he could help.

"I wish I knew what happened in there," Attorney Viera said quietly. "From all the reports I've received over the past six years, she's never been like this. Something has happened."

He preceded Mark through the double doors leading toward the front of the building.

Mark looked over his shoulder through the small windows of the door as a nurse rolled a piece of equipment into Amelia's room.

"Has it been just this week?" he asked. "The changes in her…have they all happened this past week?"

The attorney looked at him curiously. "I believe so."

Mark remembered some of the conversation he'd had with Marion. She had talked a lot about her twin sister. She believed that there was a special connection between them. Being an only child, he hadn't been able to identify with any of what she'd been saying at the time. But she'd been adamant about one thing…she knew her sister was alive, despite the fact that she hadn't seen or heard from her for so many years.

"Has something occurred to you?" Attorney Viera asked.

Mark didn't want to sound crazy. There was a great deal he didn't know about what was science and what was myth.

"Just something about twins. Something Marion said to me," he replied finally. "That young woman back there lost her twin sister this week. Maybe that loss has something to do with the sudden change in her condition. I don't know. Even if the events are connected, maybe it doesn't matter."

If the lawyer thought Mark was crazy, he didn't give any indication of it.

The detective from the Waterbury PD was standing at the receptionist's desk when they walked into the front lobby. Mark knew she was a cop before they were within ten feet.

Attorney Viera recognized her and introduced her as Rita Ricci.

"Officer Shaw," she said. Ricci had obviously done her homework on his background.

"Just a civilian at the moment, Detective."

She smiled. "From what we hear, not for long, if your chief has his way."

Attorney Viera showed them the way to the conference room. He and the detective carried on some small talk as they walked. Mark's mind was still on Amelia Kagan, though, and what had happened in her room. He tried to think of why his cell phone number was the one Amelia knew. And why it was that she seemed to know him.

Mark followed the other two people inside the conference room. Attorney Viera closed the door.

"We really appreciate the long drive from Pennsylvania on such a short notice," the detective started right away. "Perhaps if I could get a statement from you, then you won't have to stay around longer than you need to."

"No problem." Mark looked at the attorney. "Before I go, though, I'd like to see her again. Dr. Conway was doing a brain scan when I introduced myself to Amelia. I'd be interested to know if something showed up. She seemed to recognize me."

The attorney sat down on the same side of the table. "I have no problem with that. You stay as long as you want. I assume you feel the same way, Detective Ricci?"

"Happy to have him in town," the detective said as she sat herself across from them and took out a pad and a small tape recorder.

Viera looked thoughtful as he turned to Mark. "This has all become twenty-second century to me. We'll talk to Baer and Conway after this. I'm certain they'll let you know to what extent your visit might be beneficial to the patient."

Mark nodded.

"I'd still like to begin taking down your statement," Ricci commented. "Also, any information you might have as far as next of kin, Officer…Mr. Shaw, would be helpful."

"Sure. And *Mark* is fine."

"All right."

Mark actually had very little to share. He told them what he knew of their last name and the town and state where Marion had said they were from. Beyond that, though, he could only suggest that Ricci contact the university where Marion was a grad student. They would have information on file.

"Were you able to go back in the files and see if a missing-person's report was ever filed on Amelia Kagan?" the attorney asked Detective Ricci.

She leafed through a folder she was carrying and took out a sheet. She slid it across the table to the two of them.

"Yes. She was reported missing eight years ago in Deer Lodge, Montana. That matches what Mark has just said. And the descriptions match the patient identified as Jane Doe."

The photo on the page really wasn't a good copy. The description was vague and included physical appearance and where she was last seen.

"Do we have fingerprints, anything more concrete as far as identifying her?" the attorney wanted to know.

"She had no records at the time she went missing. No fingerprints. But we do have a much better photo."

She took an eight-by-ten black-and-white copy of a photograph from her file and slid that in front of them. The face of a teenager smiled up at them.

"We're pretty certain that the Jane Doe is Amelia Kagan."

Amelia or Marion, Mark thought. It could have been either one of them.

28

Attorney Viera decided if he were the parent, waiting even one extra hour would be too long a delay. It wouldn't matter how many years had gone by. He'd want to know. So he decided to make the call tonight.

By the time he got home, it was 9:55 p.m. He double-checked the time difference for Deer Lodge, Montana. They were two hours behind Connecticut. Just about eight o'clock on Saturday night. The time was right, but he wasn't looking forward to making this call.

Mark Shaw didn't have a phone number for the family, but he had been able to tell them that Amelia's mother lived with the girls' elderly grandfather in Deer Lodge. The old man was a widower, Mark thought Marion had said. As far as finding the last name of the family, Detective Ricci had all the information on the missing-person's report filed on Amelia eight years back.

The phone number was listed under the name Kim Brown. He assumed she'd gone back to her maiden name sometime after the divorce. Detective Ricci was also able to double-check with the University of California for confirmation of next of kin for Marion. Their record listed Kim Brown, as well. No one else's name was on file.

Prior to going to the long-term care facility tonight, Viera had pulled Amelia's files from his office. He'd read over everything. There was very little there. He knew it all by heart.

"Wish me luck," he told his wife.

"Good luck, sweetheart," Ellen said, handing him the cup of decaffeinated coffee she'd brewed after he'd arrived home. She knew JD's history. He'd told her everything that had happened over the past couple of days. Ellen wasn't only his wife, friend and the mother of his children. She was also his most trusted sounding board for his law practice in issues like this. Arriving home tonight, she'd agreed wholeheartedly that Juan should make the call to the mother in Montana tonight.

Viera gathered everything he needed and closed the door to his study. He dialed the number.

He wondered if he should leave a message if an answering machine picked up. There was no way he could leave a coherent message conveying the kind of news he had to share. At the same time, he wanted to make contact with the family.

The decision was made for him. After the third ring, the tired voice of a woman answered the phone. He gave his name, a quick summary of what he did and where he was calling from. He asked to speak with Kim Brown.

The tone immediately became cautious. "You *are* speaking to her."

"Ms. Brown, I'm calling with news of your daughter Amelia."

There was no sound from the other end of the line. Absolute silence. He remembered the other call she must have received this week about the death of Marion. He made a point of being quick and to the point.

"My understanding is that Amelia has been missing for a number of years. It has just come to our attention that a patient who has been in a minimally conscious state in a long-term care facility here for the past six years is your daughter."

"Who are you again?" she asked, a hard edge creeping into the tone.

"My name is Juan Viera. I'm an attorney here in Waterbury, Connecticut. I have been serving as the court-appointed conservator for Amelia since her accident. Until today, we had no idea of her identity or where she might be from."

The heavy silence continued for a few more moments before the mother spoke again. "Six years, you say, she's been in that hospital?"

"Yes. She was—"

"She's legal age. I hope you don't expect me to be paying for nothing you people have done for her."

This time it was the attorney's turn to be struck dumb. He'd expected questions regarding Amelia's health or how she'd arrived there or even how they had been able to connect her to her family.

"No…no…" he answered when he'd regained his composure. "The purpose of this phone call is not to recover any expenses from you. She's a Title 19 Medicaid patient. All the expenses have been taken care of by the State of Connecticut. I don't see that changing in the future."

"Good," she said, the tired tone returning. "It's been a hard week."

"I understand," he said. "Please accept my sympathy on the loss of your other daughter."

"So you heard?"

"Yes, it's been in all our papers," he replied.

"Look, Attorney…"

"Viera."

"Right, Viera. I've been bombarded with calls since it happened," she told him. "Newspaper and TV people. Lawyers. The people from the university. *Good Morning America* wants to interview me. First I said no. But the lawyer I finally decided on says I should do it. The TV crews will come to Deer Lodge, so I don't have to go nowhere, and he says it'll be really good publicity for the lawsuit he's filing."

Viera stayed silent, trying to not make any judgment based on what she was saying. He told himself people grieved differently.

"I didn't know just how outrageous the rates are you lawyers charge. I never needed one before. Not even for my divorce," she said. "Good news is that I don't have to pay up front. This one will get a percentage of the settlement. A good percentage, but he thinks it'll be a darn good settlement, too. He really thinks this is the way it will go. I—"

"About Amelia…" he interrupted.

"Yeah, Amelia. She was always trouble, that girl. Nothing like her sister," Kim Brown's tone conveyed irritation, annoyance, but not grief. "You raise identical twins, you think there should be some similarity in the temperament. But no. Amelia, she's like her father. Every step of the way. Eight years since she's been gone. But I knew I wasn't done with her."

"I'm sure it's been very difficult for you." Viera tried to keep any hint of sarcasm out of his voice.

There was a long pause at the other end of the line. He could almost see her lighting a cigarette. He hadn't smoked in thirty years, and he suddenly felt like lighting up.

Her voice was flat when she continued. "So what did you say is wrong with her?"

Viera had to fight the urge to defend Amelia. "She has been in a minimally conscious state."

"What does that mean? Is she a vegetable?"

"No, she's not in a vegetative state. She has some visual and motor functions," he explained. Most people didn't know the difference. Until today, the specifics hadn't been entirely clear to him, in spite of the documentation sent to him when he'd been assigned as her conservator.

"She can't take care of herself, can she?" Kim asked.

"No. She's on a feeding tube and needs full-time nursing care."

Silence again. Viera waited for her to get her thoughts together. There wasn't much more that he wanted to tell her. He wasn't a doctor. Ahmad Baer had already offered tonight to talk to her on the phone, if need be.

Viera figured there was no point in even mentioning the clinical trial the neurologists were running. He didn't want to stop anything that might be helping Amelia. From a legal standpoint, the young patient's mother had not expressed any interest in being involved.

"Okay, what do you want from me?" Kim Brown finally asked.

She had a blunt way of speaking that Viera found repellant, but he forced himself not to take offence. The woman had to be pitied, in spite of her response to everything.

"It would help if we can have you confirm her identity."

"Sounds like you've already done it," she told him.

"As far as we can. But, of course, you're her next of kin," he replied. "If it is inconvenient for you to come to Connecticut, we can send you an overnight packet with photos and any other information we have."

"What's the rush?" she asked, sounding suspicious again. "You're not moving her from where she is, are you?"

"No, not until you identify the facility you wish to have her moved to. If you'd like to have her closer t—"

"Do I have to?" she broke in. "Legally, I mean. Do I have to get involved at all?"

Viera paused. He had dealt with all kinds of people before. He knew men and women like this one, to be sure. Based on the missing-person's files, Amelia was now twenty-five years old. In the eyes of many parents, she was an adult. He also tried to imagine this woman receiving the kinds of news she'd received this week. Any sane person could flip unexpectedly and say things that might not make sense when put on the spot.

"Ms. Brown, you have no legal obligation," he told her. "And you don't have to make any decisions right now. With regard to your daughter—if it is actually Amelia—I will continue to act as conservator until you decide what level of involvement you'd like to take on. But perhaps I could leave you my name and phone number and address. I'll call you again on Monday. Perhaps by then, you'll have had a better chance to think about any concerns and questions you might have."

"Well…" she replied doubtfully. "Give it to me."

The attorney gave her all the pertinent information about himself. But he also gave her the name and phone number of the facility, including Jennifer Sullivan and Dr. Baer as contacts there.

"Then I'll call you on Monday," he told her.

"No. Don't call me," she told him. "I'll either have my attorney contact you or I'll call you myself, when I'm ready to. That girl doesn't seem like she's going anywhere anytime soon. Is she?"

"No, she isn't."

"I have too much on my plate right now with arrangements I've gotta make for Marion to be thinking about the other one. There's Marion's apartment near the university. I don't know how much stuff she's collected since she left home. I have to move her things out of there and back to Deer Lodge. Then, there are memorial services they set up for her and the advisor fellow at Davis. I don't know if I'm going to get there for them in time or not. But I have to set up some kind of service here, too. People around town have known my father for years. And Marion was always a favorite. Maybe a full Mass…it's tough without a body. It's gotta be done, though, my lawyer says." She paused. "No. That other one will have to wait."

He forced himself to try to understand all her concerns. Amelia wasn't in any immediate danger. She wasn't acting out of negligence.

"I'll get back to you sometime," she told him before ending the call.

Viera dropped the handset on his desk and stared at the copy of the missing-person police report he'd gotten from Detective Ricci.

"No wonder you ran away."

29

Waterbury, Connecticut

The all-night diner was supposedly near the Mall View movie theaters. Mark Shaw found the eating establishment, despite the fact that there was no mall in view.

Both doctors he'd met and the nurse, Mrs. Sullivan, had been too busy with Amelia to join them in the conference room by the time Attorney Viera and the detective had finished up with their business. There was no telling when or if Mark would be able to see the patient tonight.

On his way out, Mark had left a message—including his cell phone number—for Sid Conway. He'd chosen the neurologist, as he seemed to be the one in charge of the experiment they were running on Amelia. Also, he figured Conway was about the same age as him, so there was more chance of the young man not having a family to go home to. Mark was hoping the doctor might meet him for some coffee or food after he left the facility.

He'd also struck Mark as a guy who might share information about the patient, despite privacy issues, if he thought it would help Amelia.

Sid Conway had called him back and suggested this place.

It was almost eleven o'clock at night when Mark walked into the diner. He'd already checked into a Hampton Inn near the interstate highway in Waterbury. He'd packed an overnight bag leaving York. That had to get him through until he was ready to go back.

The diner was big on neon lights. Booths lined the windows looking out onto a busy strip. The smell of fries and onions hung in the air. A handful of the booths were occupied, mostly by a young moviegoing crowd. A few third-shift types—clearly regulars—were sitting at the counter, coffee mugs and egg dishes in front of them. Mark figured this was the kind of place that probably got really busy once the bars in the area shut down.

A waitress told him to sit wherever he wanted. Mark moved into one of the booths. He took the seat facing the door. He ordered coffee. The waitress returned not a minute later and put a large plastic coffeepot and a mug down in front of him. She pulled a handful of creamers from a pocket in her gold uniform and dropped them without ceremony next to the cup.

"Anything to eat?"

"Not yet. I'm meeting someone," he told her.

Mark didn't have long to wait. The waitress hadn't even walked behind the counter when Sid Conway came through the door. The young doctor came right over.

"Hey, thanks so much for meeting me this late," Mark said as the other man took the seat across from him.

"That's fine. I know how it works. You meet Amelia and immediately become consumed by what's going on in her head. She's certainly not the kind of patient that you read about in med-school textbooks."

The waitress was back at the table. Conway ordered coffee, too. He took a quick glance at the menu and ordered toast. Mark ordered apple pie.

"Is she okay now?" Mark asked.

"It was strange. She was choking, but there were no obstructions. We think it might have been spasms. She is also suffering from pain that we can't find any reason for. We had to sedate her for the night."

"What kind of pain?"

"Acute pain in the occipital lobe."

"In the head?"

Sid glanced up at him quickly. "Yeah. In the back of her brain, just above the spinal cord."

"And how do you know that?"

"The readings pinpoint where she's feeling pain," Sid told him. "She was still connected to the computers during the entire episode. There was a lot that we could see tonight. Depending on the position of the response, we are starting to get an idea of where patients are experiencing pain in their body, but Amelia's pain seemed to originate right there in her brain. It's complicated."

"What else do the readings show?" Mark asked.

"You know…" The neurologist paused and looked him square in the face. "You arrived today. You'll probably be gone by Monday. Why do you want to know everything that she's telling us?"

The waitress was too fast. She was back with their orders.

Mark pushed the pie aside and decided to be honest with the physician.

"The reason I wanted to meet with you tonight is that there is something I can't explain going on here. Jennifer Sullivan told me that there's no possible way that

Amelia could have had contact with her sister in the past six years," Mark told him. "Well, Marion and I met for the first time this past winter. The hours that we were together were brief, but there was a connection made. Something clicked for us. And here, months later, Amelia gives my cell phone number to you people. And then, when I see her tonight, she seems to know me, recognize me. I want to know why."

"And if you get the answers?" the neurologist asked. "You're not family. What are you going to do about it?"

Mark thought of the restlessness he'd felt since he'd been back from Iraq. For the first time in his life, he didn't seem to have purpose. He didn't get excited about tomorrow or the next day or what he was going to do a week or a month from now.

"I don't know," he said truthfully. "Marion and Amelia's family were torn up. Things weren't all that happy in Deer Lodge with their mother. Maybe, somehow, Marion wants me to help her sister. I know that sounds screwy."

Sid was looking intently at him.

Mark held the other man's gaze. "I'm not a nutcase. I'm a pretty serious guy. All I can say is that I'd like to help. I don't know how I can help yet…but I'll try to figure it out."

Sid looked down, taking his time stirring two packs of sugar into his coffee. He spread jelly on his toast and took a bite of it.

Finally, he broke the silence. "You can't quote me on this."

"All right." Mark was relieved that the neurologist had decided to talk to him.

Sid did not look up as he talked. "I think what we are seeing in her brain scans might have something to do with being an identical twin."

"I thought so," Mark replied. "I'm a cop. My training and experience has taught me to believe pretty much only in facts—in things that are concrete. But I said the same thing to Attorney Viera. Somehow, these two sisters were communicating with each other."

"Or…they *are* communicating."

"The only problem is that one of the sisters is dead."

"I know," Sid said.

"That doesn't sound very scientific."

"I told you that you can't quote me."

Mark nodded. "So what do you think is happening?"

"I don't know." Sid leaned forward. "Somehow, before the sister died, she passed information to the twin. I don't know how or why. I have to go and read up on the studies involving twins. I know that a lot of work has been done…and if I remember correctly, most of that work raises more questions than it answers. Scientists don't have much faith in mental telepathy or things like that, but somehow, Marion transferred your phone number to her sister. I think the sister was trying to help Amelia."

Sid Conway sat back, picked up his mug and took a healthy sip.

"Trying to help her," Mark repeated, staring at him. "Your conclusion has big holes in it."

"True, if you think like a cop."

"Or a scientist," Mark replied. "But look at what we know. Assuming that Marion didn't find her sister in the past year, and it doesn't appear she did, then she didn't know that Amelia even needs help. That aside, if Marion's intention is only to help her sister, then why not give her the phone number to their house in Montana? Or why not mention Amelia's name, or the family name, or a dozen other things that would be more useful than my number?"

"Maybe she did, but we didn't pick up on it. Our capabilities are cutting-edge, but we are still limited. And remember that we were taking the readings for very brief periods of time. There could have been a lot there that we missed."

Mark wasn't satisfied. "I'd like to stick around until Amelia's family shows up. Attorney Viera doesn't seem to have a problem with me being involved. I agree with you that the two communicated, but I'd like to know *why* Marion wanted me involved. Maybe this does sound screwy, but I have a gut feeling that there's something more that she wants me to do. Something I'm *supposed* to do."

The neurologist topped off the coffee in his mug. He grabbed another two packs of sugar. "Okay. I'll buy that."

"Does this mean you're going to share anything else you pick up on your readings?" Mark asked.

"Everything I say has to be off the record," Sid told him. "I think we might be bending some serious rules when it comes to patient care or even law enforcement, so I want you to agree to that."

"I absolutely agree," Mark promised. "This is bordering on voodoo stuff for me, so there's no way I'm going to share any of it with anyone."

"Look at it from my position. On one hand, it could offer breakthrough data for studies on twins, never mind what we originally started out to study. But on the other hand, my credibility as a researcher goes right in the toilet if the scientific community even gets a whiff of what you call *voodoo*."

Mark had always assumed doctors ate healthy. This one was a sugarholic. He saw Sid top up another half a mug of coffee and grab two more sugar packs.

"Tell me something," Sid asked. "Did you and Marion meet in some kind of train or bus station? A place with a lot of people around?"

"We met in an airport," Mark told him. "Logan Airport in Boston. Why?"

"When you first met Amelia, she raised her hand and smiled," Sid said. "We picked up an image that could have been a terminal…I guess it could have been the airport that flashed through her mind."

Every piece of information was confirming what he'd already come to accept. "So the two sisters *were* communicating."

Sid shrugged and then nodded, moving his focus to the toast and putting more jelly on it. He ate in silence for a few moments.

"The terminal was the easy part of deciphering the readings," the neurologist finally said. "Our computer programs are tremendously complex, matching and combining literally millions of tiny images, but after working over all the computations, there are still unexplainable readings."

"But you expect that," Mark said, guessing.

"Of course. But take the choking, for instance. While Amelia was choking, her brain was telling her that she had pills stuck in her throat."

"Pills?" Mark asked.

Sid nodded. "We know for a fact that for the past six years, she's been fed through a feeding tube that passes directly into her stomach wall. This has to be a long-term memory or…"

"Or?" Mark prompted.

"Or it is something she is picking up…well, possibly from her sister."

Mark wished he knew more about how the communication between identical twins worked. "This happened right after Amelia met me."

"When you and Marion were at the airport, did she pop pills?"

"No," Mark said. "I don't think so."

Sid frowned. "Then there is the pain in her head that I told you about," he continued. "There's more to it than I told you before. Her brain is telling her that she's sustained a serious head injury. A blow to the back of the head, or something."

"How about her own accident, six years ago?" Mark suggested. "Could this be memory of the pain she felt after that injury?"

The neurologist dismissed the idea immediately. "No, the memory function originates in a different location."

"Could she be imagining these things?"

"Aside from recognizing you, do you think she imagined your cell phone number? I'm not much of a believer in coincidences...and certainly not ten-digit ones."

"Is there anyone you know who might be able to tell us something about this stuff?"

"You mean at the university?" Sid replied. "I don't know, but I wouldn't be surprised. I'm going to make a couple of phone calls in the morning."

"Can I come by and see Amelia tomorrow morning?" Mark asked.

"Sure. But I suggest not showing up until noon. Guard dog number one—that being Jennifer Sullivan— told the guard dog number two—that being me—not to arrive at the facility before noon."

"What happens if she wakes up or is in distress again?" Mark wanted to know.

"They know to call me."

Mark's life had been in decision limbo since he'd come back from Iraq. Now he had a purpose, but things weren't moving fast enough for him.

Patience was a virtue, he remembered his mother telling him.

He'd never considered himself particularly virtuous, though.

30

Nuclear Fusion Test Facility

Not one pill had made it down her throat, but somehow the pain in the back of her skull was lessening.

Marion moved slowly, lethargically. Fear was somehow pushing off to a distant plane in her mind. She knew what she had to do but she suddenly felt no rush to get things done. There was tightness in her stomach and weakness in her limbs that she associated with hunger. Her body craved food and water. But those needs were not as distinct, either.

She didn't bother to find the penlight or open her cell phone for the illuminating glow. Marion left the door open and felt her way to where the shelves of the supply closet were. Different-shaped objects were stacked in front of her. She closed her eyes, trying to discern solely through her sense of touch what she was feeling.

She handled cardboard boxes and the soft packs of plastic-wrapped towels. She racked her memory for where in the closet she had seen unopened packs of batteries. She tried to remember the last time she'd been here and relive the cursory glance she'd given all the shelves looking for whatever it was she'd come looking for. Lightbulbs. That was it.

"Top shelf…next to the lightbulbs," she whispered, remembering and reaching up. Her fingers barely brushed against the bottom of the shelf. She remembered using a three-step ladder to reach the bulbs. She felt to the left, where the ladder had been hanging.

It was there. She carefully opened it and climbed to the top step. She held one hand on the shelves to keep her balance as her fingers moved over the section of the top shelf. The lightbulbs…in a cardboard box with one side cut away. Beside it was another box, the front also cut away. Reaching in, she felt her hands sweep over a row of bulky items. Her fingers closed on a hard plastic handle.

"Flashlight," she cried out exultantly, yanking it out of the box.

Marion's thumb immediately found the on/off button, and she turned it on. The flood of light felt as good as a breath of fresh air. She directed the beam around the closet, across the shelves, taking an inventory of what was there. Fearing that the light might fail, she looked around with an irrational sense of urgency. Like a blind woman given just a few moments of sight by the gods, she frantically tried to imprint everything she saw on her memory.

There were more flashlights in that box on the top shelf. Packs of batteries were on the shelf beneath them. That was a relief. Cases of bottled water, paper products, cleaning solutions. There was even a small, open box of granola bars. She thought of the hulking corpse of Arin Bose in the control room. Oats 'N Honey. She knew who had stashed the box of granola bars here.

Even as Marion took mental inventory, she greedily pulled a bottle of water free of the plastic wrap holding the case together. Tucking the light under her arm, she struggled to twist off the top, but she finally managed. She drank down half of it without stopping. Her parched throat, dry as the high desert, couldn't open wide enough. She was on the second bottle when the cramping in her stomach told her to slow down. She took a large swig of water and held it in her mouth. Twisting the cap back on the bottle, she put it on a shelf.

She reached for one of the granola bars but didn't open it. She stood on that ladder for a full minute, not moving, feeling the water in her mouth, holding the flashlight in one hand and the power bar in the other. She could not remember having a better feeling than this for a long time.

Tearing open the green foil wrapper with her teeth, Marion took a bite of the granola bar. Dinner in the finest restaurant in L.A. would not have tasted better than that first bite.

She carefully leaned against the wall and looked again at the contents of the closet as she finished the bar and took another drink of water. She considered using this room as her base. It was a little surprising to think that she'd already accepted the terrifying fact that she might be stuck down here long-term.

Wanting to know how many lights were left in the box, she shone the flashlight back up at the top shelf. As she did, something on top of the box of lights caught her eye. Pushing the box, she felt it shift. Pulling it forward, the box angled slightly toward her and a half-dozen notebooks avalanched down on top of her.

Pushing the box back up onto the shelf, Marion directed the light down at the mess around the base of the ladder.

One of the notebooks lying open on top made her

heart jump, and she scrambled down the stepladder. Andrew Bonn must not have had all of them.

Snatching up the notebook, she read the words on the cover sheet out loud.

"Emergency Exits and Procedure."

31

Rancho Bernardo, California

The clock alarm was buzzing. No, the phone was ringing.

Disoriented, Cynthia Adrian lifted her head off the pillow and stared around the darkened room. The curtains were drawn. The shades behind them were closed. She was home, in her own bed.

The phone stopped ringing. Cynthia's head dropped back onto the pillow. After a moment she stretched, feeling strangely well rested. She turned her head to the bedside clock—10:45 a.m. She panicked for a moment, trying to recall why she wasn't at work already. Appointments. She must have missed some appointment. It took her a long moment before she sorted out in her mind what day of the week it was. Sunday. She'd stayed up until dawn last night going through all the mail, answering the zillion e-mail messages that had piled up while she was gone, spending some quality time with her cat. She'd been too wound up to go to bed.

"Shadow," she called softly, searching the bed for the black cat. She wasn't here. She saw the door to her bedroom was ajar. The cat had to be downstairs.

The phone started ringing again. Cynthia picked up

the handset and looked at the number on the display. Someone from New Mexico Power Company. Still somewhat groggy from sleep, she wondered why people at her father's company were working on a Sunday morning.

She answered the call.

"Did I wake you up, Cynthia?"

No introductions were necessary. She recognized the voice. Her father's administrative assistant.

"Nellie. What are you doing working on the weekend?"

"I only poked my head in for a couple of hours. To catch up and…well, clean up a few things."

"Did you just try to call me a couple of minutes ago?"

There was a slight pause. "I did, but I didn't leave a message. I didn't want to play phone tag," the other woman said in a sheepish tone.

Cynthia draped her legs over the side of the bed and sat up. "He ruined you, didn't he? You've become a workaholic."

"No…maybe…" The young woman hesitated. "This place is going to be so different without him. I already miss him."

Cynthia did, too. And *her* life was going to be different, as well. She had always considered herself an independent person. But taking care of just herself was no longer an option with Fred Adrian gone. Like it or not, her mother, Helen, and everything else her father had left behind would be her responsibility now.

"…hard to justify." Nellie was talking, and Cynthia realized she hadn't been paying attention to her. "You know how this place operates. Without your father, New Mexico Power has no soul. They've already sent a memo down from corporate saying they're naming the new vice president of R & D this week."

"You're not worrying about your job, are you?"

"I don't honestly know. I don't think so. I imagine they must be promoting someone from inside. They haven't had time to do any interviewing."

"Nellie, you do a great job and everyone knows it. I'm sure you'll be fine."

"I'm hoping, but to tell the truth, I haven't had time to think about it too much," the woman admitted. "Right now, I'm trying to tie up all the loose ends before the new person starts. Your father made life so easy. If the new vice president is only half as organized as he was, then there should be no problem."

Cynthia appreciated the comment. Her mind had cleared enough, though, that she was wondering about the reason for the call. She'd seen Nellie at the funeral last week, but with all the people there, they hadn't said more than couple of words to each other. The two of them got along. Her father had always sung his assistant's praises, claiming that she was the real brain that held the office and projects together.

Early on, when Nellie first started working for her father, Helen was constantly on the phone to Cynthia, complaining bitterly that Fred was having an affair with his smart, attractive young assistant. Cynthia had never been much of an audience, though, when her mother climbed on that soapbox. Helen's legendary escapades while drinking had been a source of embarrassment to Cynthia since junior high. Eventually the complaining stopped. If Fred and Nellie ever had something between them or not, Cynthia just didn't want to know.

She got up from the bed and walked to the windows,

starting to open the shades. Another beautiful Southern California day was unfolding outside.

Shadow came through the bedroom door and raced across the room to Cynthia, weaving herself between her owner's legs. As the young woman leaned down to pet the cat, Shadow slithered through Cynthia's fingers and ran out again. She knew her cat enough to realize the animal had come in because she wanted something.

Standing up again, she suddenly remembered why Nellie would be calling her Sunday morning.

"So you got my e-mail," Cynthia said.

"Yes, I did."

"It was so late when I wrote it. I didn't know if I made any sense," she said apologetically.

"In your e-mail, you mentioned that a package was waiting for you from Fred when you got home," Nellie replied. "Some of it was personal, but that you also had copies of files from work. Is that right?"

"Right."

"Do you know what the files pertain to? Have you gone through them?"

"No, I only glanced at the first page. They have something to do with test facilities."

There was a long pause.

"I'm so relieved," Nellie finally whispered.

"About what?"

"I've been turning your father's office upside down looking for the folder on a project we have coming up, but I couldn't find it," she said hurriedly. "Fred was the last person who had the files out. He must have sent you the originals."

"That's not a problem, is it."

"No." Another pause. "No, not now. I'm glad you let us know."

"Me, too." Cynthia shifted the phone to her other ear. "Why do you think he sent me that stuff?"

"Honestly, I can't even guess," Nellie said vaguely. "But you know better than anyone how nervous he was about going under anesthesia."

"Well, I'll get the files back to you."

"Great! Are you going to be home today?"

Cynthia walked out of the bedroom, phone to her ear, looking for Shadow. "Yeah. I think so. Wait, I do have to go to the grocery store. Never mind milk and bread, I'm almost out of cat food."

"Okay. I'll get a courier service to your house this afternoon," Nellie told her.

"If you can wait one day, I can overnight it to you tomorrow," she offered.

"It's no problem. The company can afford it. Cynthia…I'm sorry. Can you hold on a moment?"

"Sure."

Nellie seemed to be checking on something at the other end. Cynthia spotted her cat, sitting on the small table by the window in the hall. The window overlooked the street and Shadow was focused on something outside. She approached the animal and reached out to gather it in her arms. The cat slipped through her fingers and moved to the other side of the table, still looking out the window.

Surprised, Cynthia looked carefully at the cat. The feline's ears were back, her eyes fixed on something on the street. She wondered if there was a new cat in the neighborhood.

She reached out to pet Shadow, but the cat made a sound somewhere between a cry and a meow. Cynthia moved around and tried to see what was bothering her pet.

There were no other animals that she could see. But

there was a dark sedan parked along the curb, partly blocking her driveway. She couldn't see the driver.

"Okay." Nellie came back on the line. "Will you be home from the store by noon?"

"That's…so fast. Sure. I'll just go to the store after they pick up the package," Cynthia told her. "I put it back in the same box it arrived in. Should I address it to you?"

"That would be great," Nellie said. "I've given the courier company all the information, regarding address and charge-to accounts, so just give the package to the driver when he shows up at your door."

"It's good to know that there are courier services that work this promptly, even on Sundays. What company did you use?"

"It's a private company here. I'll e-mail you the contacts, if you want to use them in the future."

Nellie thanked her again for saving her and sending the documents back. Cynthia ended the call.

Shadow was still perched on the table, but turned and looked at her. She suddenly didn't seem as stressed. Cynthia looked at the street.

The car blocking her driveway was gone.

32

Waterbury Long-Term Care Facility
Connecticut

The clarity of science had now descended into chaos. There was no defined line separating order from anarchy. Facts were muddled together with assumptions. And the assumptions didn't correspond with anything they could refer to as a precedent.

Sid Conway didn't think he'd ever been so confused. He didn't like the feeling.

"I think we might be violating the fire codes for this room," Jennifer Sullivan announced to the three physicians as she walked in with Mark Shaw. "There are too many people and too much equipment in here."

Sid looked up from the stack of paper that had spit out of the printer, relieved to see Mark—the one person he could talk to about the information showing up on these pages.

"I asked the head nurse this morning if there was a way they could move all of us to a larger room. She looked at me like I had two heads," he told Jennifer.

"You do have two heads if you think we have that kind of flexibility in this place," she said good-naturedly.

"We're fortunate that they haven't already moved another patient in here. We're running at full capacity."

Sid introduced Mark to the other two doctors.

"The receptionist at the front desk told me you got here before eight this morning," Jennifer continued, giving Sid a narrow glare. "Didn't I say not before noon?"

"These two arrived only an hour ago," Sid pointed to the other doctors in the room. "I didn't think you really meant me."

She shook her head and smiled, walking to the bed.

Actually, Sid had arrived before the Sunday-morning receptionist. The night-shift security attendant, after seeing his ID, had let him in. Sid couldn't sleep last night. And he couldn't explain what was going on in his own mind, either. It was a crazy mix of worry, bewilderment, fascination. Things that he preferred not to voice, for they confused the hell out of him. The only thing that soothed him was being here.

"Did she recognize you when you came in this morning?" Jennifer wanted to know.

"No. She woke up early but made no eye contact. She's been facing that direction all morning. No response to any stimuli." Sid had even tried mentioning the sister's name. There'd been no response to it, at all. He figured it might be because of what was going on in her mind—if the printouts that he held in his hand were correct.

"I see you have her all connected already. Anything good?" Jennifer asked, fussing over the young woman's bed and blanket. She touched the patient's hand and Sid watched carefully. There was no reaction.

"I don't know. I don't know if what we have is good or bad. I can't really understand it." Sid looked at Mark.

He was still standing by the doorway watching Amelia. He knew how the other man felt. She had a hypnotic effect on you.

"Maybe this," Sid said to him, "is something *you* can make some sense out of."

Mark walked over. "What do you have?"

"Pages of technical information." Sid handed the papers to the other man. "But the very fact that we're picking up the readings makes no sense."

"What do you mean?"

"Well, do you see where she's looking?"

"At the wall."

"Right." Sid knew he had to simplify the issues he was grappling with, if Shaw was to understand it at all. "Okay. None of us—Amelia included—becomes aware of visual information, or rather, what we're seeing, until that information reaches the frontal area of the visual cortex—"

"Like a chain reaction?" Mark interrupted.

"More or less. Let me give you a streamlined version of the way we see something." Sid thought for a moment. "The image our eye takes in bounces along the retina, which consists of three layers of neurons. Those neurons are responsible for detecting the light from the image and then causing impulses to be sent to the brain along the optic nerve. The brain eventually decodes these images into information that we know as vision, but that happens after the impulses pass through the visual cortex at the rear of the cerebellum and reach the cortex neurons at the frontal area of the visual cortex."

Mark was holding his hands out to Sid to stop. "Hold on. Let me get this straight. The image comes through the eye along the optical nerve to the rear of the…the…"

"The cerebellum, a section of the brain."

"And then the image passes to the frontal area of the…visual cortex?"

"Right. It's there that the impulses are decoded as an image."

"Okay," Mark said. "I've got that part."

"Well, we're picking up our readings—intercepting messages—from the frontal part of the visual cortex."

"So?"

"That indicates that what we're intercepting is an instant visual experience."

"What do you mean by instant visual experience?"

Sid rubbed the back of his neck.

"The initial brain-reading device used by researchers was a master predictor," Sid finally said. "They showed patients photographs of different things, and at that very instant, the equipment captured the same image in the visual cortex of the participant's brain. You showed them a picture of a dog, and in an instant you captured the picture of the same dog."

Mark nodded.

"Well, we can see what Amelia is looking at. It doesn't match the images that she is decoding. It's as if she is *not* seeing what she is looking at. She's seeing something else."

"And that 'something else' is on these sheets of paper?"

"Exactly. She's looking at the blank wall, but she's *seeing* what amounts to pages of technical data."

Jennifer was staring at Sid. The other doctors were now leaning over Desmond's shoulder.

"Could it be memory?" Mark asked.

"No. If memory were involved, we'd be seeing other areas of the brain lighting up on our equipment. Besides, in my opinion, there is no way Amelia could memorize detail this specific in this kind of volume. Everything points to the conclusion that what we've captured on these pages is some kind of instant visual experience."

"But not the same visual experience that Amelia is having at this instant," Mark said in a low voice. "There are no pages of data in her line of vision."

Sid nodded.

"And this is what she was seeing." Mark was looking at the sheets.

"There seems to be a very logical order in what she is showing us," Desmond added. "This is a sequence of material. Pages. And I have a lot more data that we haven't printed yet."

"Some of this looks like hieroglyphics."

"A lot of it is garbled, but more of it is not. The garbled portions are due to the limitations of our computer programs."

"We're operating the most advanced programs on a huge system of linked computers," Sid said. "But we're still no match for the human brain."

"She makes me feel stupid," Nat Rosen commented from his computer.

It was tempting to tell Nat to go with the feeling, but Sid decided this was probably not the right moment for humor.

Mark paged quickly through the sheets of paper. "It seems to be a manual—a facilities manual of some kind."

Sid put his hand on Mark's arm. "Remember our discussion last night?"

"About twins?"

Sid nodded. "Look at this…" He took a page that Desmond had printed and handed it to Mark. "Read this out loud."

Mark took the page and read it. "'Such a multidisciplinary approach was also followed for the characterization of fracture zones at the GTS, especially by attempting to relate seismological parameters to mechanical and hydrogeological properties of fractures.'" He stopped.

"This is not a phone number that she's memorized," Sid said.

"You think Marion would have known or read this kind of material."

"Except that Marion is dead," Sid said bluntly. "And there's no way anyone, no matter how bright, could have memorized all of this. We're talking about word by word."

Jennifer broke in. "Some people have a photographic memory."

"*This* precise?" Sid asked, shaking his head. "Maybe, but as I told you before, this is not memory."

"What are you saying?" Mark asked.

"I don't know. I have no clue." With the back of one hand, Sid rapped the stack of papers that continued to spill out of the printer. "I don't know what this stuff is. I don't know how she's doing it."

Silence fell across the room. Mark had been struck speechless, too. Sid looked over at Jennifer. She had moved to the other side of the bed, where Amelia's face was directed. She was sitting on the edge of the bed, watching the young woman.

"She starts with a phone number," Nat said, breaking the silence. "The next day she's feeding us some kind of technical manual. I can't wait for tomorrow."

They all looked at him.

He shrugged. "It looks to me like she's getting ready to teach us how to build an atomic bomb."

"Do something useful," Desmond snapped at the other man, "and go get me a cup of coffee."

As the two young physicians started bickering, Sid watched Mark move to where Jennifer was sitting. He followed him.

Amelia was looking at an empty space on the wall. This was the most detached from her surroundings Sid had seen her when she was awake. The printer continued its rhythmic production of paper.

"Speaking plainly," Jennifer started hesitantly in a quiet voice, "you're saying that telepathy between the two sisters is the only way to explain this. Amelia is seeing everything that Marion is reading right now."

Sid and Mark both looked at the nurse. No one needed to say it. They all knew what every news media outlet was reporting. Marion couldn't be reading anything if she was dead.

"They haven't found the bodies. They're assuming that they are all dead," Jennifer said, frowning. "If you're right, this is the reason for the changes in Amelia. For six years, there was no progress at all in her condition. And then last week, even before you arrived, she started having episodes. She's trying to tell us something."

The nurse looked in the direction of the medical charts at the foot of the bed. Sid grabbed the clipboard and flipped the pages back to last week.

"Thursday. Both you and Dr. Baer made notes in here."

"The explosion in the Gulf of Mexico was last Thursday morning," Mark told them. "My cell phone number. The way she looked at me when I first met her yesterday, like she knew me. The response to Marion's name. And now the facility handbooks. This is important. She *is* trying to tell us that there are survivors in the research facilities." He looked up at them urgently. "We have to notify the authorities. Tell them all of this."

"Mark…" Sid started to object. He knew how bureaucracy worked. They wouldn't take their findings seriously. What they were doing wasn't an established and approved method. Not yet. And the telepathic communication between twins added a whole additional level of implausibly to it. "Everything we have is hypothetical. What we have here is a lot of assumptions."

"All the information is lining up so much better in my head," Mark told them. "Clearer. Now I know why Amelia would give you my number and not a friend in California or someone in her family. And as far as not having exact facts, I come with the training that says you respond to *every* 911 call."

"Do you really think you can get whoever is in charge down at the Gulf of Mexico to believe that there's been a call?" Sid asked.

"I have to try," Mark said. "I have to."

33

Nuclear Fusion Test Facility

"Two facility names. Two sets of books. Two different locations."

Marion's words cut through the darkness and the silence. It was comforting to hear her own voice, especially when things were getting worse than she'd ever thought possible. She turned on another flashlight and propped it on the floor of the maintenance room.

She sat with her back against the wall. Empty bottles of water and a couple of green granola bar wrappers indicated that she'd met some of her basic needs of survival. But the two separate piles of the documents sitting by her feet on the floor made her wonder why she'd bothered.

Marion had looked through hundreds of pages in the manuals.

"NMURL and WIPP."

Two separate sets of books. She had thought their group was stationed in the New Mexico Underground Research Lab. The documentation she'd grabbed off Andrew Bonn's shelves confirmed it. But the books sitting on the top shelf of this room identified this facility as the Waste Isolation Pilot Plan.

There was a complete layout of the facility in WIPP booklets. Room by room, the drawings matched this facility, the one she'd been working and living in from day one. The WIPP booklets appeared to be complete, professionally done. But she'd been told they were in NMURL.

She closed her eyes and took a deep breath, trying to calm the feeling of panic that once again lay like an icy snake between her shoulder blades. She tried to think back to the first days, to the information she'd been given.

They were operating under a grant funded by the New Mexico Power Company. Originally, they were to be working at an underground research facility by the Gulf of Mexico. She knew her salary, the duration of the project and the medical benefits. There were pages and pages of confidentiality agreements that she'd had to sign. Though the principal researchers probably had separate contractual agreements, hers stated that anything she discovered would belong to the power company. For her to even refer to this project in any scientific papers she wanted to publish, she needed their permission. Dr. Lee had told her those kinds of restrictions were fairly standard.

As far as the facility itself, she hadn't been given much detail up front. And she hadn't asked many questions, either. It didn't matter, she'd thought.

"Stupid."

Too excited about what she considered an amazing opportunity, she'd followed like a sheep in the flock. She'd left her future in the hands of people she considered experts.

Marion wondered how many of the other scientists in this group had been clueless. How many of them had

had no idea where they were? And what about the people at the power company? The heading used in their daily communications was NMURL. The liaisons up top had even been sending them weather reports for the Gulf.

Only once during their time down here had Marion suspected that they weren't being told all the details. It was during their first week working at the lab. The quantity of live nuclear test lots on hand was higher than research labs were normally allowed. The safety precautions were the same, however, so she hadn't lost any sleep over it.

She thought back to when they'd first reached the site. She had been somewhat surprised that so few people had been involved in the actual transportation here. They'd arrived at the lab by helicopter in the middle of the moonless night. Beneath them, everything had been nearly black, and for some time before landing, she had seen only an occasional flicker of lights in the distance. She remembered being surprised that the Gulf coast was so deserted, but she hadn't thought anything more of it. It was not until they were hovering directly over the facility that she'd said something to Dr. Lee about it. The lights along a perimeter fence and a square patch of tarmac had lit up. At the center sat a two-story concrete building with a line of garage doors along the side facing the landing pad. On the roof, she saw what appeared to be a small crane. There was nothing to indicate that a research facility was housed beneath the building.

She hadn't smelled the salt air she'd been expecting. That's the only thing Marion remembered thinking was at all odd. But her mentor had only shrugged. He wasn't much on flying, and his gaze was riveted to the landing area. So she'd shrugged it off, as well. She didn't know how close exactly to the Gulf the underground research lab was supposed to be located. And once they were on the ground, she'd been completely focused on making sure all the equipment they'd carried was moved into the building and loaded onto the elevator.

"Idiot."

She dug her fists into her eyes, forcing them to stay open. Too late.

They'd dropped beneath the radar, clearly. Why, though? What were they doing that would cause anyone to have a group of killers come down that elevator and eliminate them all?

She thought of all the online chatter about conspiracy theories. Ever since the fifties, it seemed, television and movies teemed with tales of UFOs, government cover-ups, and major corporations in league with everyone from Satanists to Freemasons. She'd always had a more than passing interest in such stories, but she had never thought any of it might actually touch her own life. As far as she could tell, not one of the scientists in her group had considered even for an instant that some harm might befall them.

She didn't know if she was on the right track, but nibbling along the edge of her consciousness was the nagging thought that someone might not have wanted the research they were doing to surface. Why else come down and kill them?

Their project goal was to design and build portable nuclear energy devices without the fear of leakage or accidents. Because of the demands of the world energy market, it was just a matter of time before size could no longer be a limiting factor. The unique alloy of stainless steel for plutonium storage they'd discovered was not only the answer to applications like factories or apartment buildings, but could lead to storage devices for individual homes, or even transportation vehicles. Because of the work they were doing, the possibility actually existed that an automobile would only have to be fueled one time for its entire life, or that any building could be self-sufficient in meeting its heating, cooling and electrical needs for decades.

There was, of course, a lot of money to be made. And their work would add huge gains in the effort to break the world's dependence on oil. That was the most worthy outcome, as far as Marion was concerned.

The power company. The New Mexico Power Company. She racked her throbbing brain, trying to come up with a reason why the power company would "kill" the project. The irony of the term didn't escape her. If it weren't for the dead bodies of people she knew, lying not forty yards from where she was sitting, she might be amused. Robert Eaton. Arin Bose. Steven Huang. Eileen Arrington. Dr. Lee…

If the power company was somehow behind it, she tried to imagine how they could possibly get away with this. They couldn't. They'd made the grant very public. There'd been so many press releases in science magazines and in technical journals about what the group was on the verge of accomplishing. Naturally, the specific technical details were to be published once the study was over. In fact, now that she thought about it, Marion realized that the importance of the project had to be the reason behind all the security regarding the location.

Another thought in defense of the New Mexico Power Company popped into Marion's head. They were the ones set to make the most money in the production of the portable reactors and energy devices.

It couldn't be them. It had to be someone else.

The word *conspiracy* was again burning a hole in her brain.

"No one is coming for me," Marion said out loud, her voice cracking as she suddenly felt the crushing sensation of the nearly half mile of rock and dirt between her and the world above.

34

Rancho Bernardo, California

There wasn't enough time for a shower. Cynthia hastily yanked on a pair of sweatpants and a sweatshirt, and pulled her hair into a ponytail. Casting a cursory glance in the mirror, she frowned and ran downstairs.

"Blame it on the engineer in me," she told Shadow. The animal, sitting on a kitchen chair, shot Cynthia the cool look that she used anytime she was not the center of her human's attention. "Besides, I have twenty minutes to get to the copy store and back."

Cynthia didn't want to say anything to Nellie, but she was stunned that her father would take the only copy of any important document and send it outside of the company. Even to his daughter. She agreed that Fred had been exceptionally nervous before the procedure the week before. Still, she doubted he'd do that. At least, it bothered her to think that he might.

Cynthia decided that there was no point in arguing the issue with Nellie. Her father was dead.

When it came right down to returning it, though, she *was* her father's daughter. She would never send the only copy of anything so important via courier. Things got lost all the time.

The black cat hopped off the chair and trotted over. As Cynthia tried to find her car key amid the piles of half-sorted mail on the kitchen counter, the animal rubbed up against her calves.

As Cynthia thought about it more, she knew she was doing the right thing…even if she wouldn't say anything about it to Nellie. There was always a method to her father's madness. Cynthia was the same way herself. It was genetic. Outsiders might not see the rationale for their decisions right off the bat, but a rationale existed nonetheless.

Fred wanted his daughter to have those documents, and Cynthia wasn't going to send off the only copy. Maybe not today or tomorrow, but sometime soon, she would go over them.

She grabbed the thick folder off the counter and found her car keys. Glancing at the clock on the kitchen wall, Cynthia knew she was cutting it close. She didn't wait around until second thoughts had a chance to surface. Instead, she ran for the garage.

Though her car hadn't been started for a week, it roared to life as the garage door began to rise on its tracks. Backing up, she heard the twang of the antenna clipping the door on the way out.

As she emerged into the sunlight, she caught sight of a young boy on a bike behind her. His parents were walking briskly behind him, and Cynthia waited in her driveway for them to pass.

She'd already decided which stationery supply super-store was the closest. She looked up at her condo as the garage door closed. Shadow was back in the window upstairs, scratching on the glass.

"What is it with you?" she asked under her breath. "You act like you're still dealing with separation anxiety. I told you I'd be right back."

She turned around to back the car out of the driveway. A dark sedan was blocking her in. Cynthia's fingers immediately reached for the lock button. Hearing the distinctive sound, she quickly double-checked the windows. They were closed. This looked like the same car that had been in front of her condo before.

Cynthia glanced up and down the street. She could only see the backs of the couple with the son on the bicycle. She reached in her purse and grabbed her cell phone. She wasn't one to overreact, but an uncomfortable feeling was clutching at her stomach.

Her neighborhood was safe. Still, she hated people who acted stupid in dangerous situations. There was no reason for these people to be here. She didn't know them.

She considered who to call. Shawn was on the other side of the world. Calling her mother would be useless. It was embarrassing to call the police. What would she say? She wasn't some college coed who needed an escort to get somewhere.

She checked the directory of her phone and saw the number for the neighbors who'd watched Shadow. It was a long shot for the Newmans to be home on Sunday, with the boys involved in so many different sports. Even so, she called them.

She watched in the mirror as the passenger door of the black sedan opened and a burly man in a navy-blue Windbreaker stepped out. He was wearing sunglasses and quickly pulled a baseball hat on. For the second or two that the door was open, she only caught a glimpse of the driver who remained in the car.

Her neighbor's answering machine clicked on. The large man started toward her door.

"Hi, this is Cynthia…Adrian. Please pick up if you're home."

He was standing next to her car door, looking in.

Cynthia left the car running and looked up. The mirrored aviator glasses blocked her view of the man's eyes. The Windbreaker was zipped up. No company logo or name tag. The baseball cap, also devoid of any identifying logo, shaded the face.

"Ms. Adrian," he said through the window, tapping the glass with his knuckles as he bent down slightly.

The phone buzzed into her ear. The answering machine had timed out. Cynthia continued to hold the phone against her ear.

"Hold on a second," she said to no one on the other end. She lowered her window a fraction of an inch. "Can I help you?"

"Yes, ma'am. I'm here to pick up a package for New Mexico Power Company."

The thick folder sat on the passenger seat.

"I wasn't expecting you until noon," she told him.

"It just so happened that I was in your neighborhood when the call came in."

He'd been sitting in front of her condo when Cynthia had been speaking to Nellie on the phone. Suddenly, she felt a greater sense of urgency about not sending the only copy of whatever this file was.

Nellie had been her father's right hand for four years. The young woman was trusted with everything. She took care of all the details, large and small. To copy and mail anything, Fred would normally have asked his assistant to take care of it. Cynthia should have questioned sooner why Nellie didn't know anything about these documents.

"Well, I have to run out for a quick errand. You can pick it up at noon." She rolled up the window, dismissing him.

He glanced at his watch. "That's only fifteen minutes from now."

"I'll see you in fifteen."

"Ms. Adrian, I have other pickups and deliveries scheduled. We won't be able to come back later today."

"That's fine. I'll ship the package tomorrow, then," she told him. "Please move your car. I really need to be going."

The man straightened up, and Cynthia no longer could see his face. She thought he motioned toward the car blocking the driveway.

She didn't trust them, and she was fighting back her fear. She looked around the car. There wasn't enough room to turn or go around the sedan. The next driveway, separated from hers by shrubbery and a curb, sat a foot lower.

"Yes, I'm back," she said, pretending to be talking on the phone and looking over her shoulder as she inched the car backward.

The man continued to stand beside her door. She saw the driver's door of the sedan open and another man step out. She shut the phone and dumped it on the seat, holding on to the wheel with both hands.

The little boy on the bicycle and his parents were coming back. She jammed her hand on the horn and rolled her window down an inch again. "I'm running late. Would you please move your car?"

She had the attention of the family. Cynthia saw the driver get back into the car. The man standing by her door backed up a step and stared into the window for a moment before slowly walking back toward the sedan.

She waved to the couple, though she'd never seen them before. She knew everyone in the condos around her, but it didn't matter that they weren't neighbors. They waved back, and the husband was looking hard at the sedan blocking her in.

Cynthia was relieved when the two men drove off. She quickly backed the car out of the driveway and onto the street.

The boy had stopped the bike and was standing with one foot on the curb. The parents were standing next to him.

"Beautiful day to learn to ride a bike," she told them, rolling down the window.

She didn't pay attention to what they said in return. Her mind was focused solely on seeing if the sedan was still hanging around. She saw the car take a left at the end of the street and then disappear from view.

Suddenly, she didn't want to send this package back to New Mexico at all. She didn't know of any private couriers who made deliveries in black sedans. And those men frightened her.

This was more complicated than she had imagined. There was a reason her father had sent the files to her. She wanted to go back inside the house and read what was in there. She had a strong suspicion, though, that the two men would be back. Her mind was racing. She again considered calling the police, but what would she say?

Her cell phone started ringing. She looked on the display. It was a New Mexico number. She didn't have to answer to know it would be Nellie Johnson. She ignored the ringing phone, grabbed the thick folder and got out of the car. Hurrying to where the condo sections mailboxes were situated, she stuffed the package into the Newmans' box and closed the door.

The young family was looking at her curiously. She simply nodded to them, jumped behind the wheel and drove off.

People didn't check their mailboxes on Sundays. And even if her neighbors did, Fred's note was in the folder. They would know whom it belonged to.

Cynthia still didn't know what she was going to do. She had no clue what was written in the pages of those files or why Nellie wanted them back. There was, of course, a strong possibility that she was overreacting to everything. After all, she'd just buried her father.

Nonetheless, she knew there was safety in numbers. She glanced at the clock on the dashboard. There was a noon yoga class every day at the community center not five miles away. Normally, she went three times a week, and she was friends with a number of the people who took the class. She could go there and invite a couple of them back to her condo for lunch. They all knew she'd lost her father last week. They'd be sensitive to her feelings. She could get the file out of the mailbox when she got back and go over it.

Cynthia took a right on Pomerado Road. It was difficult to imagine Nellie being part of some conspiracy. Fred was a good judge of character, and he'd trusted her for many years. Right up to the very end.

She didn't know where the other car came from, striking her vehicle with the force of a cannon. Cynthia felt as much as heard the loud crunch, and watched in a stunned helplessness as her own car, pushed by the impact, shot across the center line into oncoming traffic.

The telephone pole loomed straight ahead. Cars were coming straight at her, the horns blasting.

Cynthia jerked the wheel once, then lost her bearings as the car spun and flipped over. The sound of screeching metal drowned out every other sense, but as she dangled upside down, she thought vaguely that she was going to survive this.

Without warning, another wrenching blow hammered at her...and then there was nothing.

35

The quickest Mark Shaw could get to the accident site in the Gulf of Mexico would be tomorrow morning. But even if by some miracle he could get there sooner, he had enough experience with the red tape of investigations to know that getting somebody to talk to him or even listen to what he had to say was pretty unlikely. The television news was reporting that the fires enveloping the facility continued to burn. Mark wondered how long it would be before Marion ran out of air or the lab blew up.

He made three calls from the extended-care facility. The first one was to Attorney Viera, but he only got his answering machine. He left a message, asking the conservator to call Sid Conway. The neurologist needed to talk to Viera and explain the latest developments with Amelia.

The second call he made was to his police chief back in York. He reached him at home.

"You're not going to take a job in Connecticut and leave my ass hanging in the breeze here, are you?" Lucas Faber wanted to know when Mark called to confirm he could use the chief as a reference.

"No, Chief. I'm not. And I won't even start looking without talking to you first."

Mark mentioned Marion's name and the accident in the Gulf of Mexico. He only went as far as explaining that he'd gone to Connecticut because of Marion's twin sister. Mark wasn't ready to offer any more detail than necessary, but he needed the chief's help.

"Can you tell me how I can get in touch with whoever is in charge of the rescue operation—or whoever's running the investigation at the accident site in the Gulf?"

"Why, Mark? What do you have?"

"The doctors working with Marion's sister have come up with some information that could be critical for the people working the case."

Mark knew there were a lot of questions that Faber could have asked, but he must have sensed the urgency in Mark's voice.

"Let me see what I can do. I'll call you back."

Mark called Rita Ricci next. The detective had left her cell phone number with Mark and offered her help if he needed it.

There wasn't too much to explain to Rita. She had all the background information from their meeting with the conservator last night.

"The neurologists have come up with information," Mark said, "that suggests there might be survivors at the lab facility."

The detective was silent for a long moment. "You know it's gonna be pretty damn difficult getting the right person's attention."

"I know," Mark agreed. "I've already left a message for Attorney Viera. I'm hoping he can suggest something."

"Look, I'm working today. Why don't you come in, and I'll try to find out what I can here."

She gave him directions to the police station.

Mark checked again with Sid before leaving the facility. They were still recording pieces of information from Amelia, but the output now was scattered and often incoherent.

The Sunday-afternoon streets of Waterbury were nearly empty as he drove to the station, and Mark had no trouble finding his way. Rita Ricci met him at the dispatcher's desk and escorted him back to her cubicle.

"I have some bad news."

"What is it?" he asked.

"My deputy chief was able to get a copy of the report from the fire rescue group submitted to the New Mexico Power Company this morning. The report will be all over the six-o'clock news tonight."

She handed him a fax from her desk.

Mark looked down the page, skipping past the background information he already knew.

"Second paragraph," she told him. "There were a number of fuel storage tanks on the platform, even though the platform itself was not being used for production."

Mark looked where she pointed and read aloud.

"'…gas condensate leaked from the two blind flanges. At around twenty-three-hundred hours, the gas ignited and exploded, causing damage to other areas with the further release of gas and oil. Some twenty minutes later, a third major explosion occurred, followed by widespread fire. Further explosions then ensued, followed by the eventual structural collapse of a significant proportion of the installation.'"

"It's clear to them, based on what's here, there's no way there could be any survivors," Rita told him.

"I understand that, Detective, but Amelia is telling us her sister is alive," he said adamantly. "I'm not imagining this. Dr. Conway has substantial data that points to that conclusion. There has to be something more they could be doing. What about sonar searches? If the underground platform has imploded, has anything there been recovered? Body parts, pieces of clothing? Is anyone pushing these people to do more?"

"You're asking the wrong person," she said softly.

"I'm sorry. I just…"

"I understand. I was there last night myself. But it's hard to explain what those doctors are doing if you haven't been there. When I was trying to get my deputy chief to help out, I realized I sounded a little wacko with what I was telling him." She paused and looked him in the face. "Word of advice. If you're thinking about demanding anything more than what those rescuers are already doing…"

"I know. I don't have much to push them with."

She paused and thumbed through the folder on her desk, pulling out a page. "You need next of kin. Get Marion Kagan's mother on your side. With her doing the asking, you might have more leverage."

She handed him a paper with the woman's name and phone number on it.

"I suggest you call her and see what she says."

36

Nuclear Fusion Test Facility

Finally figuring out the name of the facility she was sitting in was a huge help. Now, she had pages and pages of information and drawings right in front of her.

Marion carefully pored over the folded maps that displayed a detailed view of the Waste Isolation Pilot Plan facility. The first drawings showed the building above ground as well as the small rooftop crane she'd seen when first arriving here. The elevator shaft was directly beneath the crane.

Curiously enough, the underground lab they were using was only a small fraction of the total footage of the facility. According to the drawings, on the far side of the elevator, a long series of sealed tunnels led to another entire wing. From the sketches, it appeared that the elevator had doors that could open into either facility.

Marion tried to remember those doors now. She'd only traveled down the shaft once. Unfortunately she had paid little attention to that kind of detail, but it was on the plans.

She adjusted the light and opened another folded section of the drawings.

The main tunnel running to the other underground section was labeled Test Drift. The tunnel opened out onto acres of subterranean vaults and storage areas. Though she could see scores of separate chambers, the entire facility was clearly connected by one continuous hallway.

She unfolded another section and her heart jumped. At the extreme end of the Test Drift, a second shaft appeared on the drawing. The shaft was circled and marked as a revision. They'd added another means of access for the other area.

Marion looked closer on the revision block. The change had been signed off in 1999.

"They have to have built it," she said loudly. "And that means there's another way out of here."

But she had to get there. The elevator wouldn't work without power and a half-mile climb, feeling the way she was, seemed impossible. But maybe she could get out through the Test Drift tunnel.

She thought about what the facility on the far side of the elevator shaft might have been used for. It certainly didn't appear to be an underground lab. There was nothing on the drawings that indicated living quarters…only storage areas and machinery spaces.

Marion thumbed through the pages again, this time searching for anything she could find on Test Drift.

The index at the back of one of the books directed her right to the answer. As she read it, though, her heart sank. She felt a chill run down her spine.

Waste Isolation Pilot Plan.

Test Drift accessed a disposal area for high-level radioactive waste. Her worst nightmare was now a reality. The pictures she'd seen over the years of past nuclear disasters paraded through her mind. The victims, the long-term effects, were no longer just vague statistical references.

Dr. Lee's last words rushed back into Marion's mind. He'd told her to activate cementation procedures in their lab.

He *knew* what lay next to them down those long tunnels. She looked down at the pages again. Waste Isolation Pilot Plan, located 2,150 feet beneath the surface, was designed to house radioactive waste material.

Dr. Lee knew that an explosion in their lab could easily start a chain reaction that would lead directly into the Test Drift. With all the potential fuel there, the resulting nuclear explosion would be powerful, so horrifically devastating, that the Chernobyl blast, in comparison, would look like a firecracker in a can.

She could no longer worry about just her own life. The number of casualties would be in the tens of thousands. And there'd be no warning. No chance to get away. Not that anyone *could* get away.

Real people would die. Real babies would be born with birth defects so horrifically debilitating that parents would give them up to special facilities built specifically to care for them. Never had something like this ever happened in the United States. Never.

Now, more than ever, it was critical to know how much time was left before the first test containers would start leaking hydrogen. Marion still didn't know how to stop the accident from happening. But she had to know when the end would be.

She had her notes with her on the clipboard. It took some adjustment to shift her mind back into the scientific mode. It felt like ages ago that she'd been doing these kinds of calculations. Normally, they would be done on a computer. The answer wasn't something that stared her in the face, either. There were variables. She had to estimate how advanced each container had been in the testing cycle when the power had gone off.

Her mind still worked. She was happy to know that at least she remembered the basics of what she'd been studying for so many years.

The numbers began to accumulate beneath the tip of her pencil. Calculating, checking, rechecking. She changed the results to days, hours, minutes.

"Five days, sixteen hours, thirty-two seconds."

Marion didn't know where she was in the countdown. She searched for her cell phone and turned it on. It took a long time for the device to come to life. The red bar warned her that there was practically no charge left. She looked at the date and time on the screen and wrote it down.

"Forty-two hours," she said aloud. Only forty-two hours remained before so many lives would change forever.

37

Deer Lodge, Montana

Kim Brown was overwhelmed by the words of sorrow and respect she received during the Sunday-morning service. People whom she'd never spoken to in her life stopped her in the parking lot of the church to convey their condolences. The minister even paused after his sermon, leading the congregation in prayer for the Brown family during this difficult time. A women's ministry had already set up meals they were planning to deliver during the coming week. There were offers by people to come and stay with Kim's elderly house-bound father when she had to go to California to make the final arrangements for Marion's things.

It changed things…all of this.

Kim had always considered herself an outsider after the divorce. There had been plenty of talk, too, after Amelia's disappearance, and not much of it good. Still, this was her hometown; it was where she belonged. She worked at the prison forty to fifty hours a week. She attended church every Sunday. She volunteered her talents, baking or sewing, anytime they were doing any kind of fund-raiser at church. She never socialized because whatever free time she had was spent looking after her father.

The past couple of years, especially, she'd felt about as special as flowers on faded wallpaper. She was hardly, if ever, noticed. But these people were now treating her differently.

For the first time, Kim walked down the stairs to the social hall after the service and had a cup of coffee with the other parishioners. Everyone had questions about Marion. They wanted to know what Kim had been told about what had happened to the scientists. None seemed too happy about what they'd been watching on the news.

Kim didn't have many answers, but whatever she said was accepted as absolute gospel truth. She mentioned that she had a lawyer. And there would be lawsuits filed. Someone's negligence had to have caused the tragedy. She told them how she was supposed to be interviewed by Katie Couric...maybe even Oprah.

Everyone was impressed. For the first time in her life, Kim felt important.

As a result of all the hoopla, she was a couple of hours late getting back home that Sunday. She didn't think her father would even notice it, so she didn't call to let him know.

Ed Brown was only seventy-two but he looked ninety. Two strokes and the loss of his wife to lung cancer—all in the past two years—had left Ed unable to leave the house. He needed a walker to get around, and he occasionally needed help just to move from the bed to the chair or the bathroom. He had partial paralysis of his left side, and he'd developed difficulty speaking after the second stroke.

The doctors at the hospital recommended physical and speech therapy, as they thought Ed could make improvements if he worked at it. But that meant he would have to travel to Butte, thirty miles away, for treatment. Kim worked every day, but there were vans for the elderly that traveled the route from Deer Lodge to Butte almost daily. Ed just didn't want to bother with it.

The living arrangements for her father suited them both. A bathroom had been added to a bedroom off the kitchen after her mother was diagnosed with cancer and the stairs had become too much for her. Ed had stayed there after she died, and now he simply lived between that bedroom and the living room…with occasional stops at the kitchen and bathroom. Kim lived upstairs.

Kim wasn't surprised to find her father in the living room, sitting in his worn brown faux-leather recliner when she got home. The walker lay on its side next to the chair. She'd moved most of the furniture out of the room to make it easy for him to get around.

She *was* surprised, though, to find the television off.

"Are you okay, Dad?" she asked.

She stared at him. The TV, with the volume cranked up high, was constantly on. So often, when Kim was working in the kitchen or doing laundry in the basement, she could hear Ed having full conversations with whatever show happened to be on at that time. In fact, she was the only one who ever turned the TV *off* in the house.

His color seemed good. The lunch dishes sat empty on the TV tray next to the chair, so she figured he'd eaten. He was just staring at the gray screen.

"Are you okay?" she asked again.

He didn't say anything. His gaze never wavered from the screen.

"Fine. Be that way." She took off her jacket and hung it in the closet near the front door. There were more and more days lately when he was in too sour a mood to deal with at all.

She decided his mood might improve if she told him about church. It was the same parish that he and her mother had belonged to.

"After the service, I went downstairs for cof—"

"Why din…you…tell…me?"

"Why didn't I tell you what?" she asked, alert to the sharp tone.

"About daughter…my gran…daughter."

Kim looked at the phone sitting on the floor next to the food tray. Somebody from their church must have called home to pass on their condolences directly to Ed.

"I did tell you about it. And you've been watching the news on TV every minute of the day since it happened." She shook her head and walked over to pick up the tray. "Dad, you're forgetting things."

"Not…for…forget." He managed to get the words out. "You…never…"

Kim wasn't going to argue. She picked up the tray and started for the kitchen.

"A…melia…" he shouted at her.

Kim froze with her back to him in the doorway.

"You…di…din…tell…about…A…melia."

She gathered herself and walked into the kitchen.

"Kim!" he shouted.

She hadn't told him about Amelia. There was no point. She was mad as hell at that lawyer. He must have called back and talked to Ed when she was at church. That was the only way her father could have found out. She'd told him not to call.

"*Kim!*" he shouted louder.

He was going to have another stroke if he kept this

up. She put the dishes in the kitchen sink and decided to go back and face it.

In the living room, her father was already on his feet, the walker in front of him. He was coming after her.

She stopped and leaned against the doorway. "Who called?"

"Why?" he asked, letting go of the walker and sitting back heavily in the chair.

"There was nothing to tell. I didn't think you needed to hear more bad news."

"Bad…news?" he asked, shaking his head and looking at her with hurt in his eyes.

"Yes, bad news," she told him. "I don't know who the big mouth was that called you today, but the news is just bad. The only way news about Amelia *could* be. If you really want to know, Amelia is a vegetable. She's been that way for six years now. She doesn't talk. She can't move. She can't take care of herself. She can't even eat on her own. A vegetable, Dad. Are you hearing me?"

Kim looked past him at the window. She could see the tears that immediately gathered in the old man's eyes. She tried to remember the last time she'd seen him do that. It certainly hadn't happened when they'd received the phone call about Marion's death.

What was the use? she asked herself. Each of them had their favorite. That was the way it had always been. Kim and her mother had doted on Marion, and Dad had always supported Amelia, no matter how much trouble she caused. To this day, Kim believed that her father was responsible for how Amelia behaved. She didn't have to listen to her mother. There was always a higher authority in the house to go to.

Kim remembered her father had been the most upset of any of them when Amelia had run away, except maybe for Marion. The old bastard had gone looking for her, for all the good finding her would have done. Amelia would have just run away again.

"Tell…me," he said.

Kim crossed her arms. Still looking out the window at the leafless gray tree in the side yard, she forced herself to push aside the hard feelings she had kept hidden inside over the years. He was her father. She loved him, she supposed. It made her sad to see him like this. He was the only family she had left. The two of them were it.

"I've already told you most of what I know. A lawyer called me yesterday. He says Amelia was in an accident a couple of years after she left here. Bad head injury that left her a vegetable. She had nothing on her so they didn't know who she was. She's been kept in some kind of nursing place in Connecticut."

He seemed to be processing everything. His gaze turned to her. "They…fo…found us. Th…this number. She must be…be…better."

"I don't think so. The lawyer who called me had a name for her condition. I can't remember it exactly. But it was definitely a vegetable. She needs constant care. He said that. He also said the state would keep taking care of her there."

The conversation with the lawyer was all a haze in her mind. When he'd phoned and first told her the reason for calling, Kim felt like she'd been kicked. There was no end to the bad news. She couldn't deal with it. She didn't want to think about it at that moment. She didn't really want to think about it now. Last night, she couldn't wait to get off the phone. She couldn't remember exactly what she'd said. Thinking about it now, she'd probably sounded heartless. Cold.

With an effort, she shrugged off the thought. She didn't care what that lawyer thought of her.

"Who called this morning?" she asked. "What did they say?"

"A…melia…an…Marion…"

"You're not making sense, Dad. What about Marion?"

"He…called to say…" Ed touched his forehead. "A…melia…hears…Ma…Marion."

Kim came into the room. She understood what he was trying to tell her now. She sat down on the edge of her mother's chair and stared at her father. She hadn't thought about this for years. But there'd always been a connection between the girls. From the time they were infants. One cried when the other one got a bee sting. Earaches were a joint illness, even though only one of them had the infection. Accidents, bumps and bruises. Never one experiencing anything without the other feeling it.

There were dozens of instances, probably more, when they were growing up. Kim couldn't recall all of them. But she'd stopped doubting what they had between them a long time ago. Kim's parents had witnessed it all, too. They all knew.

When Amelia ran away, Kim feared that the police would find the teenager's body in some ditch, raped and murdered. She knew what animals men were. Marion kept telling her, though, that her sister was okay.

"Mark…Mark…Sh…aw," Ed Brown said. "He… he's fr…friend of Marion. He…called."

She looked up at her father. "Where is he? Where was he calling from?"

"Con…Conn…"

"Connecticut?" she asked.

He nodded. "With…A…melia."

There were important questions that Kim had forgotten to ask the attorney last night. Things like what had changed and why was it that they now knew who Amelia was. Kim had never heard of this Mark Shaw. But that didn't really surprise her. Marion never shared anything personal like that when they talked on the phone.

Kim noticed her heart was racing. She didn't know what the phone call meant. What did it mean that Amelia hears Marion? Did it mean that the twins were in contact? Marion was dead. How could that be? And how was Amelia telling anyone?

Kim jumped up, started for the kitchen, then came back.

"Did he leave a number for me to call him back?"

Ed nodded, reaching for the pad of paper sitting on the end table next to the chair. He slowly picked it up and she snatched it out of his hand.

Her father's handwriting was nearly illegible from the stroke. Kim read the number out loud to make sure she had it right. She started for the kitchen again. That was where she'd left the lawyer's number from last night. She planned to call both men.

"Kim."

Her father's voice turned her around.

"A…melia…com…coming home?"

"I don't know. They're giving her good care where she is. And if she's improving, then it's best to keep her where the best hospitals and doctors are."

He looked away. Kim looked at him suspiciously. He was a stubborn, cagey old bastard. He wasn't arguing. This would certainly be a first when it came to Amelia.

Ed fixed his gaze on her again, forming his words carefully. "Then…wi…will you take m…me…to her?"

Her father didn't want to leave the house. The last time, when he just had to go downtown for a blood test, it'd been war…and Kim had lost *that* one even. She'd needed to get a lab technician to come to the house to draw blood.

"I'll try." She couldn't help but smile. "Maybe we can both go and see her."

38

The food at the facility had already gotten to Desmond and Nat. The two men had left around half an hour ago to get a decent lunch somewhere in Waterbury. Sid had no appetite.

First sleep, now food. He didn't want to leave the room. He wanted to stay by Amelia. Jennifer was already teasing him, suggesting that a feeding tube should be put in so he wouldn't get sick himself.

His partners were having too much fun with that. To stop the harassment, he'd asked them to pick up a sandwich while they were out. Somebody had to catch up with the documentation they needed to be keeping for the study. Everything was moving at light speed. On top of everything, Sid had to keep Attorney Viera and Dr. Baer in the loop about what was happening. E-mail seemed to be the most logical method.

Jennifer had to leave for a couple of hours, too, as she was supposed to have an early Sunday dinner at the house of one of her daughters. So Sid pulled two chairs together, facing each other, and put his feet up with the laptop open. He started writing.

Despite it being a Sunday afternoon and the parking lot full of visitors' cars, the care facility's wing where Amelia's room was located was very quiet. Sid listened to her calm breathing as he worked. She was asleep. They'd left the headpiece and the electrodes on her to minimize the skin irritation. They were planning to take more readings when everyone returned.

Sid's fingers flew over the keyboard as he explained the latest changes in Amelia today. The e-mails weren't much different from the journals and logs he kept for the study. He started with the journal. He covered every detail from the time he'd arrived this morning. He mentioned the change in her. She wasn't responding to the stimuli that had worked the day before. Then he started writing about the extensive manuals that she was sharing with them. Sid tried not to make any assumptions. He didn't include what he and Mark had talked about, regarding Marion being the likeliest candidate to have access to that kind of information.

Hard, concrete, scientific data was documented, but the rest of what was going on...

His fingers paused and hovered over the keyboard. He believed a dead sister was communicating with his patient. How could he write that? He didn't want to be the laughingstock of the neurology community at the start of his career. He believed what was happening, but there was too much that still lay in the realm of the unknown. He searched for the right way to document the data they were accumulating.

"Report the facts," he said aloud. "Just the plain data. Let the reader come to his or her own conclusions."

Sid's gaze wandered to the bed. He was startled to find Amelia's eyes open. She was watching him. She seemed so aware, right there with him. He recalled the first moment that he'd seen her. He'd thought the same thing then.

"I thought I'd be used to this by now," he told her. "You still manage to surprise me."

She was so pale. Sid wondered if the nurses ever took her out into the sun. It was a beautiful sunny fall day outside. He was tempted.

"I have to finish these reports," he told her. "And I have to send the e-mail."

He glanced out the window for a moment.

"Do you remember Mark Shaw?" he asked, looking back at her.

She didn't answer.

"You met him yesterday. You obviously know him. Well…actually, I believe Marion knows him. *Marion,* your *sister.*"

Sid watched her, looking for any change at the mention of her sister's name. There was none. She continued to watch him.

"No patterns of recognition whatsoever," he typed.

"I was telling you about Mark Shaw," Sid said, looking up again. "He called me a few minutes ago. He's calling your mother in Montana. He's hoping for some cooperation about Marion. I only hope she doesn't object to what we're doing with you."

Attorney Viera had been reassuring about the study continuing. Still, Sid was a little anxious.

"Through the grapevine, I hear that you didn't have too great a relationship with your mother," he commented. "The same goes with me…not my mother, though. She died of brain cancer when I was a teenager. It's my father that I don't get along with too well."

Last time he went home was last New Year's. He flew

to Tampa on New Year's Eve and flew out twenty-four hours later.

"He got married again. Three children…three teenagers, now. They adore him. Neither of us really needs the other."

Sid looked at the screen, trying to start where he'd left off. He couldn't concentrate. He turned back to Amelia.

"That's right. I wanted to study the human brain because of her. I considered oncology for a while, but…" He shrugged.

"You're talking to yourself."

Sid hadn't heard Desmond come in. He shot his friend a guilty look over his shoulder. "Caught me."

Desmond handed him a brown paper bag that was still warm. "Meatball grinder. And you must eat it, my friend, or I shall tell Jennifer when she gets back."

"Okay, okay." Sid put the bag on the floor next to his chair.

"I mean it."

"I have to send these e-mail messages first. Five minutes. Where's Nat?"

"Outside in the parking lot, making a call," Desmond told him. He moved to the bed and started adjusting the electrodes connected to Amelia's forehead. "I think there's a new girlfriend in the picture. I bet as soon as he comes in he'll be asking what time we're going to finish up."

Sid had no problem letting the other two men leave early. Both of them had put in a lot of hours this weekend.

"My God. She's looking at me," Desmond said, a note of excitement in his voice.

Sid glanced at Amelia and saw her gaze focused on Desmond's face.

"This is the first time she's noticed me."

Sid smiled at his friend's genuine excitement. He knew exactly how the other man felt. "You've joined the land of living as far as Amelia is concerned. Congratulations."

Nat walked into the room. He saw the brown bag sitting on the floor.

"Eat that." He turned to Sid. "What time are we going to wrap it up around here?"

Desmond shook his head and laughed, moving to his station behind the computer.

"What's so funny?" Nat wanted to know.

"What's her name?" Sid asked.

Nat stared at him a moment and then grinned. "We're not at the point of introductions, yet."

"You don't know her name?" Sid asked.

"We're not at the point of introducing each other to people we know."

"I didn't ask for an introduction. I just wanted to know her name," Sid said, happy to return some of Nat's teasing.

"I can't believe this."

Desmond's tone quieted both men. He was staring at the screen before him in astonishment.

"What have you got?" Nat asked, moving behind the computers, too. "Holy shit."

Sid put the laptop down and jumped to his feet. He noticed that Amelia was now watching him.

"She is watching you," Nat said in awe.

"She's in the room with us," Desmond followed. "She's present…conscious…awake."

39

Joseph Ricker wasn't on the guest list for the black-tie dinner party his boss was throwing for the Arizona senator. But the handlers at the front door of the mansion were already expecting him when Joseph got there.

A young waitress, carrying a tray with glasses of champagne, approached him as soon as he stepped into the front hall. Joseph knew the guest list was around two hundred. And he'd seen the itinerary and the menus for tonight's party.

Tempted but knowing better, Joseph shook his head at the waitress, declining the drink. It would have been nice to be here as one of the invited guests, but unfortunately this wasn't the case.

One of Joseph's assets was the fact that he was a decision maker. At the same time, a greater asset was that he recognized the danger of drowning, even in shallow water. He'd relax later…when he was firmly on high ground.

He'd made a number of decisions in the past twenty-four hours that Martin Durr would have been proud of. Cynthia Adrian's case was a no-brainer. No one could have anticipated that Fred Adrian would leave a trail with his daughter. Not even Nellie Johnson, his assistant, despite all her claims that she knew him like the back of her own hand. Nellie had been smart enough to call Joseph right away. Thankfully, they hadn't lost any time.

The idiot, Joseph thought. It wasn't enough that he had to die himself. Now he'd made sure his daughter wouldn't have a chance, either.

Cynthia was in an intensive care unit at a hospital in San Diego. The problem was that there was no sign of the files in her car or her condo. Joseph knew better than to order his people to finish her. They had to wait until she came around and find out what she'd done with them. Loose ends were not tolerated in the organization.

Any communication he could convey to Durr on this topic had to be face-to-face. That was why Joseph knew it was time to share the latest developments with his boss.

"Mr. Ricker," a soft voice called to him.

He turned to the young woman who'd called his name. She was dressed in the same black-and-white outfit as the rest of the waitstaff. She was a pretty little thing, and Joseph had never seen her. Of course, there were not too many times that he was invited to Martin Durr's house. He didn't know who worked here and who was with the caterer.

"Mr. Durr is expecting you," she said, extending a hand toward a set of double doors that were closed to the rest of the guests.

Martin Durr led two lives, and he was a master at keeping them separate. Most people were only allowed access into one life or the other. The personal side of Martin Durr was that of the kindly philanthropist. A family man who donated enormous amounts of money to charities and schools and political causes. On the business side, Martin ran his ventures with an iron fist and zero tolerance for failure or for lost capital. He planned far ahead and he always succeeded.

Joseph had seen Durr's cunning in operation when he'd maneuvered his way into being elected a board member on the New Mexico Power Company.

Of course, Joseph was privy to only a scant portion of his boss's extensive investments. His position was… special. But he did know of Durr's interests in a number of oil companies. Those investments were well hidden through the use of offshore covers and dummy holding companies. Still, Durr had made a great deal of money in the past in oil, and Joseph was amazed that no one currently seated on the board at New Mexico Power had called him out for a possible conflict of interest. New Mexico Power was well-known for its efforts in developing alternative means of energy. That is, in anything but oil.

Well, they were now paying a very high price for their stupidity.

The young woman closed the door once they were inside. Joseph looked around the spacious room, knowing he wouldn't find his boss here. Library, reading room, study, a place for casual business. Of the rooms that Joseph had seen in the house, he thought this was the classiest. Dark walnut, leather and Persian carpets, the room was fit to receive royalty. It probably had done just that on occasion.

"Mr. Durr is expecting you downstairs," she told him, moving to a wall panel and pressing a concealed button.

"I know the way, thank you," Joseph told her.

The wall moved to the side and an elevator door appeared. She waited until the second set of doors opened and Joseph stepped inside.

Ricker had visited his boss in his private office three other times since he'd started working for him. There were only two buttons on the paneled wall of the elevator. Up and down. He pressed the down button.

The young woman's pretty face disappeared as the door slid shut. The descent was silent and smooth. There was no elevator music, no mirrors where Joseph could adjust his bow tie or check his tuxedo. Only dark paneling surrounded him in the suffocatingly small, two-person lift. As pleasing as the dark walnut paneling was in the room above, here it gave the feeling of a coffin. He touched a brass plaque beneath the buttons bearing the name Otis. His toe tapped the smooth marble floor. An expensive antique facade covering brand-new machinery, no doubt.

Everything he had to say and ask, Joseph had organized in his mind. With a hundred guests above, he knew Durr's time was precious. He was pleased that his boss had given him an audience at such short notice.

The doors to the elevator began to slide open just as the cab reached its destination. Joseph waited until the floors lined up before he stepped out into the dimly lit hallway.

He didn't know if he was twenty feet below, or twenty-five hundred. He remembered being quite nervous the first time he came down here. Not anymore.

Durr kept some valuable pieces of art in a gallery down here. Most of the pieces' origins were questionable, but Martin Durr had two "connected" people who bought for him on a full-time basis. Acquiring rare art was really not difficult, if a person was willing to pay for it. As a result, this special collection was kept only for Martin and for the private enjoyment of his close friends.

Joseph strode quickly along the hallway to his boss's private office. The door was open. He went in, but then stopped, surprised to find no one inside. Durr must be on his way, Joseph realized. He wouldn't leave his guests and come down here unless he knew his assistant had arrived.

The bright light of the office was somewhat shocking, compared to the dim light of the hallway. As he glanced around, Joseph realized this was the first time he had ever been alone in the office. The space was comfortable, not overly large. Bookcases lined the walls. Many of the shelves were stuffed with folders and stacks of paper. Most likely copies of investment information. Durr was very old-fashioned in that regard. He liked hard copies of almost everything.

Joseph looked on the desk. No computer. He tried to recall if there'd been one the last time he was here. He didn't remember. The other visits had been in and out— no chance to let his attention wander from what the man in charge was ordering him to do.

He heard footsteps coming down the hall. This time wasn't going to be much different. Joseph moved to the center of the room, to a spot he hoped Martin Durr would consider a neutral space.

Like a white-faced old bulldog dressed in a black tuxedo, Durr stalked into the room.

Joseph knew he had to be quick and to the point. "Thanks for seeing me on such a short notice, sir. An urgent matter has come up regarding Cynthia Adrian."

"I know. She's in the intensive care unit. And you haven't found the copies of the documents that Fred sent her."

Joseph felt like someone had blown a hole in his sail. He wasn't going to ask how Durr knew. Nellie Johnson was the nervous type. She must have contacted Martin Durr right after she'd called Joseph with the news. Well, so much for his boss's preferences when it came to discretion in channels of communication. Clearly, Nellie didn't care and Durr let her connect with him directly.

Martin Durr moved behind the desk. He didn't sit down but planted his meaty hands on the smooth wood surface. The overhead light accentuated the patches of red on the pale, bald head. There was no question that he was angry.

"Here are a few things that you don't know," Durr said in a thin voice, shifting his weight forward on his palms. "Marion Kagan, the only graduate student in the research group, has a twin sister who has been practically comatose in some care facility in Waterbury, Connecticut, for six years."

In spite of the growing sharpness in Durr's tone, Joseph reminded himself that he hadn't done anything wrong. He had not been tasked with eliminating every family member of every researcher. There was no reason for Joseph to have known about this twin sister. And even Nellie wouldn't have known this. He relaxed his shoulders, trying to concentrate on what this sister had to do with anything.

"Suddenly, after six or eight years, this twin wakes up and starts talking to the people around her." Durr stood up straight. "And—are you listening to me? She's saying that her sister is alive."

"Mr. Durr, we know that's impossible," Joseph asserted. "We are certain Marion Kagan is dead. Our people went in, completed that phase of this task, and now that facility is sealed. Besides, who is going to believe something as bogus as that? This is just a family member trying to get some publicity."

"Another error," Durr barked, pointing a fat finger at the door. "There is a two-bit cop on leave from Pennsylvania who is asking questions. I'm told that he's got a bunch of neurologists from the University of Connecticut who are backing this bullshit. They say the identical twins *are* communicating."

Joseph wanted to reiterate how ridiculous this all sounded. Durr was overreacting. But he knew his boss too well to say anything. He didn't want to have his own head handed to him. The patches of red now covered the skin on Durr's neck and throat.

"This is what you will do. Step by step. No deviation, no going on some tangent of your own devising."

Joseph nodded.

"Number one. You will take care of Cynthia Adrian." He straightened from the desk. "Bug her hospital room, her phone, her cell phone. Access her e-mail. Post people in the hospital to watch her around the clock. I have heard nothing about those documents showing up with someone else. But it's still early. Also, have those two goons of yours retrace her steps. A neighbor, maybe, that she could have stopped at before leaving the development."

Joseph wished he could take notes. Remembering the orders wasn't the problem. He didn't like having nothing to look at but Martin Durr's cold eyes.

"When the report shows up, finish her."

"Yes, sir." That was already in the works.

"Number two. I want that crew to go back down into the WIPP facility."

"Sir, that's impossible," Joseph objected. "They sealed the facility."

"You're not listening to me," Durr snapped. "No lame excuses. No deviation. I know perfectly well what is impossible and what isn't. They will restore the power and go back down there."

"The group that went down there might object, sir. There was live nuclear testing, and with the power down for so many days…there might be…"

"Then find someone else to do it," Durr interrupted. "I want an accurate body count of everyone down there. Especially, I want proof that Marion Kagan is dead."

Joseph wondered if a head on a platter would be proof enough for his boss. He kept the comment to himself. So long as Joseph didn't have to go down there himself, what did he care?

"The bodies will have already started to decompose, sir. What do you want for proof?" he asked, knowing he had only one chance to get it right and satisfy the man standing behind that desk.

"I don't want a souvenir. Nothing that could incriminate me," Durr said in a mocking tone, as if Joseph were an idiot.

"A total body count and verification that they see Kagan's dead body." He jabbed a finger at Joseph. "If I find they've made a mistake down the road, it's *your* head. Do you understand me?"

"Yes, sir," Joseph muttered.

"Number three."

A shudder ran down Joseph Ricker's spine. Things were complicated enough already.

"The sister. The one in Connecticut. Eliminate her."

40

Sid Conway wasn't going to leave Amelia's room until he was certain no one would disturb his patient. He was told everyone was waiting for him at the conference room. They could wait.

Word had gone around like lightning. Amelia was awake. Six years in a minimally conscious state and now she was awake. Right in the middle of his study. He'd already sent the other two neurologists to the conference room to meet with the conservator and Dr. Baer. Sid was told Mark Shaw was waiting there, too.

Amelia was awake, but she was scared. They had connected monitors to keep track of her vitals. Anytime someone else poked their head into the room, Sid saw her heartbeat accelerate. And there were plenty of people who were doing that. Nurses. Aides. Family members of other patients who claimed they had walked into the wrong room.

This was where science and faith fought to explain and take the credit, depending on a person's beliefs. He'd already overheard some of the nurses in the hall say that this was a miracle. Sid had a scientific explanation for what had happened. He wasn't going to debate anyone, though. Healing was the ultimate goal. How someone believed they got there was not the point.

"Please tell me this is real."

Sid was glad to see Jennifer as she sailed into the room. Before he could say anything, the nurse moved to the side of the bed and took Amelia's hand.

"She looks the same to me."

He noticed that some of the staff were already gathered in the doorway. He walked to the door and closed it.

"Talk to her. Ask a question," he encouraged, moving to the other side of the bed.

Amelia's dark gaze moved from Sid to the nurse. She looked tired. There were shadowy circles under her eyes. Amelia hadn't gone back to sleep since she'd opened her eyes early this afternoon. Sid refused to sedate her, even if it might be for her own good. He wanted to give her body a chance to start taking charge.

"Honey. I'm Jennifer. You and I have known each other for a long time. Do you remember me?"

Sid checked Amelia's vitals. She wasn't stressed by having Jennifer here.

"She can't speak yet. But she'll give you a sign."

There was the slow blink of her eyes. Jennifer's cheeks were wet with tears.

Sid always kept a tight lid on his emotions, but he found his own throat tightening up. From what Dr. Baer had told him, Jennifer had been fighting for improving Amelia's care for a long time. For that reason alone, he was relieved that the young patient gave the indication that she was familiar with the nurse.

A knock on the door. Another one of the nurses poked her head in.

"They're waiting for you, Dr. Conway," she reminded him.

"Will you guard her?" he asked Jennifer.

"With my life."

He had no doubt that she meant it. "I'll be in the conference room."

"There are no plans to move her, are there?" she asked anxiously.

"We don't know yet. I can only make a recommendation. Dr. Baer and Attorney Viera will make the decision."

"And your recommendation?"

Sid shrugged and looked away. "She should be moved to a rehabilitation center. Six years is a long time. She needs to learn to talk and eat and get intensive physical and speech therapy. It's going to take a lot of work for her to get over years of immobility and tendon contracture. You know that type of rehab care doesn't travel. We have to go to them."

Sid looked back at her and Jennifer nodded.

"What do you think will be the extent of her recovery?"

"It's too early to tell. But she's already beaten all of the odds. There's no paralysis that was ever identified. So I think she has a shot of going pretty far physically. I don't know about speech or auditory processing."

"Is there a possibility of relapse?"

That was always a possibility. There were many cases of MCS or coma patients waking up only to go back to sleep, minutes or even days later. "We'll think of the positives. We're planning a recovery."

Jennifer nodded, obviously agreeing. "Can I raise her bed?"

"Try it. But go easy. She has to learn to do everything again."

"Baby steps." Jennifer smiled and turned her attention back to Amelia.

Sid picked up his notes and headed for the door. Before leaving, he glanced back at Amelia. She was watching him.

"I'll be back," he said.

"I won't leave her," Jennifer assured him.

There was a buzz in the hallway as Sid passed through. People were looking at him, nodding to him. He felt extremely self-conscious. He wished he could stop and explain that Amelia had done this. It was not his work or that of his group.

As he entered the conference room, an immediate hush fell over everyone. Sid closed the door behind him, and when he turned toward the table, Ahmad Baer gave him a half salute.

He figured this was as good a time as any to explain. "Listen, I hope you all know this wasn't me or my partners here. We can't take credit for what's happening to Amelia."

He took a seat at the table. He didn't want the families of MCS patients out there demanding he throw some electrodes on their loved ones' heads, thinking their sons or daughters or parents would miraculously wake up.

"What do you think caused the change?" Dr. Baer asked.

He pushed a couple of articles he'd printed this afternoon across the table. "There have been a few published cases…a thirty-nine-year-old male named Wallis in Arkansas. At age nineteen, he was in a bad car accident. Severe head trauma. After twenty years in a nursing home in a minimally conscious state, he wakes up and asks the nurse who the other woman in his room is. The nurse tells him it's his mother."

He looked around the room. Terry Wallis's story had been front-page news back in 2003. A lot of doctors were divided on that case. Some wanted to use it as a foundation of hope for other cases and learn from it. Others considered it an anomaly.

"Some researchers hypothesize that Wallis's recovery was caused by slow regeneration of essential neuron networks over time. It's early to tell, but it's possible the same thing could have happened with Amelia."

Baer glanced down at the papers for a couple of moments and shook his head. Sid decided he must fall into the second group of doctors.

"Could it be the magnetic field from your devices might have produced a kind of DBS with this patient?" Baer finally asked.

Juan Viera sat back and Sid glanced at him and Mark Shaw. They both looked confused.

"Dr. Baer is referring to an FDA-approved procedure called deep brain stimulation, DBS, that has produced similar results in cases involving MCS patients," Desmond explained. "But nothing we've done in this case has any similarity to that procedure."

"Wait a moment," Viera said. "What does deep brain stimulation involve and why wasn't it done on Amelia before?"

"DBS is a surgical procedure where electrodes are implanted in the brain to deliver electrical impulses," Sid told them. "The ten-hour surgery has only been found effective for patients with Parkinson's disease, and it's still considered something new. There are a number of studies being conducted using MCS patients. Nothing conclusive."

"I see," the attorney said.

"And the magnetic field our device radiates," Sid

continued, addressing Dr. Baer's suggestion, "is nothing more than a person experiences using a cell phone or a hair dryer."

"How communicative is she now?" Mark Shaw asked. Sid realized it was the first time he'd spoken.

Ahmad Baer had examined Amelia as soon as he'd arrived at the facility tonight. Sid looked at him to see if he wanted to answer the question. He nodded and tapped the table twice with his pencil before speaking.

"I ran a classic battery of tests. She used blinking to respond to questions. She isn't using her vocal cords. At this point we don't know if it's by choice or not. My belief is that she is cognizant of her surroundings. She is capable of exercising her short-term memory. *Some* language use may return with speech and physical therapy."

"So what's the next step?" the conservator asked.

Sid spoke up immediately. He wanted the right decisions made for Amelia before her mother arrived from Montana and muddied the waters.

"My recommendation is to move her to Gaylord Hospital in Wallingford. They have one of the top ten brain-injury rehabilitation centers in the country."

Viera looked at Baer, who nodded in agreement.

"The only question is if Medicaid will cover it."

"It will," Viera told them. "I'll check on the exact number of weeks that the benefits will cover and get the court to order an extension, if necessary. To start, though, so long as the primary physician recommends it, there shouldn't be a problem."

"I can make the referral," Ahmad said, looking at Sid. "I believe it's essential that you continue your study with her, even after she's been moved to Gaylord. We don't have all the answers yet as to why she came around at this moment."

Nothing could make Sid happier.

"Can we also keep this off the front pages of newspapers?" he asked. "Any kind of traffic would only be stressful for her. And my group is certainly not anywhere close to making any public statements."

Viera nodded. "I was already planning to speak to the head of the facility here to instruct the staff. We have medical confidentiality issues in play that need to be observed."

"I will speak to staff myself," Dr. Baer told him.

Viera turned to Mark. "I spoke to Amelia's mother after you talked to her this afternoon. Ms. Brown told me that she and her father are making arrangements to travel East. Now, as far as any publicity after she arrives, that will be largely out of my hands. The first time I spoke to her, she mentioned she was scheduled to be interviewed on television about Marion."

A momentary silence fell over the room. It was obvious everyone had their doubts about the impending visit.

Mark Shaw broke the silence. "Can I see Amelia and ask her some questions about Marion?"

Sid frowned. He knew what Mark wanted, but it was so much easier to concentrate on one thing—Amelia's recovery.

"I haven't been able to get any cooperation from the people fighting the blaze on the rig. Everyone is convinced that there are no survivors," Mark told them. "They're treating it as an environmental issue now, rather than as a rescue."

He pushed a thick folder across the table toward the conservator. Everyone in the room knew it was the printouts from Sid's readings. Viera had already been told how unlikely it was that it could have come from Amelia's memory.

"I believe everything that's happened is related," Mark continued. "Maybe even Amelia becoming conscious now is connected. Maybe she's trying to help her sister."

A week ago, in a similar situation, Sid would have said the idea was ridiculous. In the middle of the table, however, lay copies of the manuals that they'd produced from Amelia's brain readings. He'd be a fool to say there could be no relation.

"We have quantifiable results with one sister. She's awake," Viera said. "Then, we have a…a notion regarding the other. I've tried, but at this point no one outside this room is taking what's happening here seriously. And there's no reason they should. We have to let the people in charge of that operation make their own decisions…just as we would not allow some firefighter in the Gulf of Mexico to tell us how to care for Amelia. We can't tell them how to do their jobs."

"I know that. But that gives us even *more* reason to talk to Amelia," Mark persisted. "Before, we were relying on computers and formulas and electronics and brain science I couldn't begin to understand. Now we can ask her directly."

Sid understood the other man's struggle. If there was even the slightest possibility that Marion was still alive, Mark Shaw wasn't about to give up.

"Maybe you and I could pursue that possibility after this meeting," he said.

Attorney Viera and Dr. Baer looked at him for a long moment, and then the two men shrugged. It was clear they didn't want to be involved with this part of the situation.

41

Nuclear Fusion Test Facility

The door to the test lab was sealed and no amount of force that Marion could possibly exert was going to budge it.

Dr. Lee's words kept repeating over and over in her head.

Somehow, she had to get power restored to the facility. The clock was ticking. Her course of action was simple and clear. She had to get out and get help.

Marion had two choices. She could either force her way into the elevator shaft and try to somehow climb the two thousand feet to the surface...and hope the killers were not waiting at the top. Or, she could find a way to gain access through the elevator shaft to the Test Drift area and hope that the elevator at the opposite end of the facility was working.

She didn't want to dwell on the magnitude of the disaster that was brewing here. But not even taking into account the loss of human life—hers being the first—random numbers she'd studied in graduate school continued to bounce in her head. Numbers like peak radioactivity for plutonium 239...240,000 years to subside. The entire Southwestern U.S. and large sections of Mexico could easily be uninhabitable for that many years.

She wondered if there was any chance that the planet would still be around for that long.

Marion forced herself to focus on the books open in front of her. She couldn't allow herself to become overwhelmed.

Based on the schematic of the WIPP that she'd seen, the disposal area operated under a separate power source and transportation system. The chance existed that the people who'd killed her coworkers and shut down the generators could have done the same thing at the neighboring facility. But Marion figured that was unlikely.

Test Drift documentation indicated that it was a one-hundred-percent robotic facility, used as one of the military's disposal sites. The killers wouldn't bring attention to themselves by shutting down someone else's operation.

The added incentive that she might see sunshine and breathe the fresh air once more before she died gave her the final push.

Marion looked at the diagrams one more time. The only way she could get to the Test Drift was through the elevator doors. She had to somehow pry them open and climb inside the first shaft. Once she was in the elevator shaft, she would have to pry open the next set of doors...if the doors still existed. In any event, she needed to get into the elevator shaft before she could decide what was the best exit route.

A burst of energy ran through her at the thought of getting out. The piercing headache had turned into a dull throbbing pain that she was able to ignore. She gathered bottles of water and power bars and stuffed them into a shoulder bag she'd found in the room.

From the maintenance room she took a crowbar, and

two screwdrivers and a hammer that she packed into the shoulder bag. In a box containing an assortment of batteries, she found a small timer, which she set to her calculations. It tortured her to see the seconds clicking silently along, but she needed it. She stuffed the timer deep in her front pocket.

She gathered everything that she thought she might need, including extra batteries for her flashlights. Her eyes scanned the closet for anything else. On the floor, a large box with a radiation sticker caught her attention, and she pulled it out. Inside, she found protective rubber clothing, from booties to lightweight overalls to gloves to bonnets. There were no particle masks for airborne contaminants, however.

She knew that radioactive poison could enter the body by way of inhalation, ingestion, absorption or through a break in the skin. She seemed to have some serious gashes, especially on one side of her head. She could do no more about that than she could do about airborne particles, though. About the latter, she'd just have to stop breathing.

"Ready to go," she said aloud, double-checking what she had.

Then she remembered the bodies of her coworkers that she would have to face on her way to the elevator.

It was probably the least important thing she had to do, but somehow it mattered to her. Marion grabbed a roll of clear plastic bags off the shelves. She told herself she wouldn't go out of her way to cover everyone, but she would cover the colleagues that she had to pass by.

Marion put the bags with the rest of the things she needed. There was too much to carry in the shoulder bag. She remembered the duffel bag that she had in her room.

Marion peeled one of the plastic bags from the roll and headed that way.

There was a strong smell of rotting meat before she even reached the doorway. She covered her nose and mouth and shone the light inside the room.

She shouldn't have looked but her gaze was drawn uncontrollably to the body of Eileen Arrington. Her face and neck were a greenish-blue color. Her features were already unrecognizable

Marion shook the plastic sheet open. Trying to hold her breath, she rushed in and practically threw the bag at the corpse. The plastic only covered the head and upper body of the scientist.

She quickly reached inside the closet and found her duffel bag. On the way out of the room, the light in her hand flashed on a framed picture of her and Amelia. They were eleven in the photo. She remembered the day so clearly. Their mother had taken the picture at a picnic the warden threw each summer for the families of the prison employees. She always kept the picture at her bedside wherever she went.

Marion grabbed it and darted out. In the hallway, she felt her head suddenly about to explode. Pain so intense hit her so hard that she could not keep her eyes open or even turn her head. She thought she was about to pass out and grabbed for a wall. Quick flashes of light blinded her in the darkness.

Her brain was playing games with her. Suddenly, she was in a hospital room somewhere, an array of equipment spread out around her. A dark-haired woman was watching her. She could smell the scent of the woman's shampoo. There were others she couldn't see. Only voices. Then she was back in the research facility. She stumbled toward the direction of the maintenance closet. After only a few steps, though, her legs stopped moving entirely, as if every muscle and tendon had become rigid.

Marion banged hard against the wall and slid to the floor. She could hear voices again. Someone was asking her questions. One voice was familiar. A man's voice. She looked down at the picture frame she was holding.

"Amelia," she said aloud. "Tell them where I am, Amelia."

But where was she? Marion's mind was caught between two worlds. She'd become a soul divided.

There was that familiar voice again. Marion closed her eyes and she could see him. *Mark.*

"WIPP…" she said aloud. "Waste Isolation Pilot Plan. Tell him, Amelia. Tell him where I am."

Marion opened her eyes. She was back in the dark hallway. The flashlight lay on the floor by her knees, its beam reflecting on the tools and shoulder bag she'd left by the maintenance-room door.

Unsure if she even could, she pushed herself to her feet. Her legs were once again working. There was a sense of fear lying like acid in the pit of her stomach. This was much different than how she'd felt an hour before.

She knew what it was. It had to do with Amelia. She only got this sensation when she knew her sister was in trouble.

Marion moved quickly. She had to get out of here.

42

University of California, San Diego Medical Center

"I just finished talking to the doctors, Shawn," Helen Adrian said into the phone. "I think you should take the next flight home."

She was relieved when her future son-in-law assured her that he was already in the airport, and he'd be in San Diego by early afternoon tomorrow. Shawn was saying something else, but Helen couldn't concentrate. She hadn't had anything to drink since the flight over from Santa Fe. She needed a drink badly.

She looked up at the signs hanging from the ceiling and wondered if they sold any kind of liquor in the gift shop.

"Yes, I'm here," she said into the phone, realizing that Shawn was asking something. "What did you say?"

"The extent of Cynthia's injuries," he repeated. "How bad are they, Helen?"

"They're very bad. They say she's in critical condition."

He wanted to know exact details, but Helen couldn't remember everything. It wasn't supposed to happen like this. Cynthia was her rock. The responsible adult in her life. She had to make it through.

Her head hurt. Helen sat down on the nearest bench. "I don't know, Shawn. I just know they're doing everything they can for her here. You can call the hospital directly yourself."

He asked for the name of the doctor in charge. Helen couldn't remember. Everything was moving so fast. Nothing was being given to her in writing. No help for her, really. No consideration. Just that young doctor, talking a mile a minute, and Helen having a hard time picking up even every third word he was saying.

"It's not like he's her personal doctor or anything," she said weakly. "Just call the hospital. They'll connect you to whomever is in charge of her care."

Helen wanted to hang up and go to Cynthia's condo. She needed to sleep. Shawn needed to be here, taking care of this, she told herself. Cynthia and Helen both needed him. Somebody had to take charge of things.

He was asking something else. "Say that again. I don't have good cell service here," she lied.

"Did you see her?"

"Yes, I saw her. They would only allow me to be in there for a few minutes. She's hooked up to all kinds of equipment. She's out of it…totally. Still unconscious. She's so broken up. It's so sad." Helen was overwhelmed with so many emotions. She wished she could remember more of what that young doctor had told her about what was wrong with Cynthia. But she couldn't.

She asked him to wait as she grabbed a tissue and wiped her face and blew her nose. She came back on the line.

"When did you say you'll get here?" she asked, not remembering if he'd told her or not.

He told her he'd be in tomorrow afternoon.

Helen wanted to ask him why so late, but she remembered that he was somewhere in Africa. She'd never been there and had no idea if that was making good time or not.

"I have to go, Shawn," she told him. "There's no reason for me to stay here. I'm staying at Cynthia's condo. They can get hold of me there if they need to. No one tells you anything here, anyway, and the waiting areas are so…public. There is no privacy…."

Helen stopped making excuses when she realized Shawn wasn't trying to get her to stay at the hospital. She was glad they understood each other.

She ended the call and looked around for one of the nurses to tell them she was leaving. There was a man standing very close to her, a cell phone pressed to his ear. Helen hadn't seen him before and she hadn't heard him saying anything. She was sure he'd been eavesdropping.

He turned his back to her when she glared at him.

"Goddamn press," she muttered under her breath, walking to the nurses' station.

43

Waterbury Long-Term Care Facility
Connecticut

Mark Shaw and Sid Conway sat next to the computers and other electronic equipment that had been pushed to the side in Amelia's room. Everything was turned off, and all the equipment was ready to be moved with the patient to the rehabilitation hospital tomorrow afternoon. Between the calls Dr. Baer and Attorney Viera had been making and their insistence on immediate action, Amelia did not have to wait before being transferred.

They both looked at the door at the sound of someone's footsteps going past. As the sound receded, Sid stifled a yawn and rubbed the back of his neck. It was sometime after midnight. They'd been quietly talking in the semidarkened room for a long time.

"When was the last time you slept?" Mark asked.

Sid shrugged. "I haven't kept track. I'm not really tired." Another yawn belied his words.

"Well, you look tired," Mark told him. He understood, though. Neither one of them wanted to miss anything that might happen next with Amelia. "I'll stay here if you want to go and at least take a shower."

The neurologist glanced at the bed and the patient. He seemed to be considering the offer.

Amelia had been sleeping when they came back from the meeting in the conference room. Jennifer went home soon after; she had to work first shift tomorrow. Sid had mentioned that Amelia's sleep patterns would very likely follow no schedule. She could wake up after a short nap…or sleep for another six years. Both men were hoping for a few short naps and then something more "normal."

Mark hadn't seen Amelia since the change from her minimally conscious state early Sunday afternoon. He didn't know if she would still recognize him when she woke up. But he believed what he'd said to everyone in the conference room. He was convinced that some kind of communication between the two sisters had been going on and was the *cause* of this sudden development in Amelia's case. After talking to Sid tonight, he saw no reason to change his mind about anything he'd said.

"Jennifer mentioned there's a shower off the staff's kitchen area that I can use," Sid told him. "You'll stay with her until I get back?"

"I have nowhere else to go," Mark reassured him.

The neurologist picked up a shoulder bag that was slung over one of the chairs and left the room.

Mark meant what he said. This was where he needed to be right now. The phone calls from the police station in Waterbury and from his chief in Pennsylvania had given him nothing new. No one at the Gulf of Mexico site was doing anything different because of their inquiry. As far as those rescuers were concerned, there were no survivors.

He didn't know where to go or whom else to call. Kim Brown had told him that she and her father were coming

East. She was uncommitted, though, as far as the exact timing of her trip. Mark didn't know how much of a difference the mother's presence and involvement would make in terms of anyone believing that Marion could be alive.

Mark looked at the sleeping woman. He remembered his talk with Marion so vividly. He thought how happy she'd be if she knew she'd been right all these years…if she knew that her sister was alive.

Amelia knew things, too. And she'd try to tell them. Mark believed there were a lot more answers that lay with her.

There was a soft knock on the door and a young nurse poked her head in. She looked at the bed and her gaze searched the room until it fell on him.

"Officer Shaw?" she whispered.

Mark got up and walked to the door.

The nurse had moved to the hallway and was standing next to a two-level pushcart with different prescriptions and medications lined up along the top.

"Yes."

"Someone's waiting for you at the front desk."

Mark stood still, staring in the direction of the double doors that led to the front entryway.

"Are you sure they're waiting for *me?*"

The woman reached inside the front pocket of the flowered scrub top she was wearing and handed him a pink slip of paper with the message on it.

"This was at my station when I came back from down the hall."

Mark looked down at the note and then at his watch. The time on message was only a couple of minutes ago. He tried to think who could possibly be waiting at the front desk for him at twenty minutes past midnight.

"I can stay with JD if you want to go and check it out," she offered.

Mark realized that, to a lot of these people, Amelia would always be JD.

He'd seen this nurse a number of times before. The name tag read Pat. There was no receptionist at the front desk at this hour of the night, so the night security person must have been the one who called.

"I think I'll call the front desk first," he told her.

She motioned to a phone on the hallway wall. "You can use that one. Dial zero and it will ring at the front desk."

The door to Amelia's room was wide-open. Mark walked to the phone and dialed the number. No one answered the first or second ring. He turned around toward the door in time to see the nurse who'd been speaking to him walk into Amelia's room with two syringes and her clipboard.

He dropped the phone on the cradle and ran across the hall into Amelia's room. The woman was setting up whatever injections she was going to give her on the table next to the bed.

"What are you doing?" he asked.

She looked back at him, surprised. "I'm giving JD her meds."

"What kind of meds?" he asked.

"The meds Dr. Baer has prescribed. Is there a problem with that?" Her tone had turned defensive. She motioned to the rolling table next to the bed and the clipboard next to one of the syringes. "See for yourself."

"Is this something new or medication she's been getting all along?" he asked.

"Something new," she said flatly. "I was told by second-shift nurses that JD woke up this afternoon, and that Dr. Baer was here and examined her. He changed her medication. Now, I have a lot of patients to attend to, so if you don't mind…"

She held up one of the syringes and tapped it, ready to insert it into the IV that they had hooked Amelia up to tonight.

"Wait," Mark barked.

The nurse jumped. Amelia's eyes opened. She looked startled. She looked up at the nurse and at the needles she was holding.

"You scared me. Scared her," she complained, glaring at Mark before her attention shifted back to the patient. "She's looking at me. She never did that before. Does she understand us? Is she really conscious now?"

"What's going on?"

Mark breathed a sigh of relief seeing Sid coming back into the room. Maybe he was overreacting, but somehow his cop instincts were on full alert tonight.

The night nurse quickly complained that Mark was interfering. "I'm trying to do my job and I don't appreciate being pushed around by people who have no business even being here after visiting hours. The system for distributing meds works perfectly fine. Just because a patient has a new scrip—"

"What new scrip, Pat?" Sid asked. It was obvious he knew her, too. The water still dripped from his hair. "Dr. Baer prescribed nothing for Amelia that I know of."

Frowning, she pushed up the paper with the list of patients and their medications, and nodded to the prescription slip on the clipboard. "Right there."

The neurologist pulled the piece of paper from under the clip and looked at the writing.

"Where did you find this?" he said immediately, looking and sounding alarmed.

The young woman backed away from the patient. As she did, she dropped the syringe on the table as if it were hot coal. "The scrip was clipped to JD's folder at my station. Dr. Baer's name is on top and there's a signature on it."

"Do you *know* Dr. Baer's signature?" Sid asked accusingly. "This could be anyone's."

Mark reached into his pocket and took out the message she'd given him before. He handed it to Sid. "Does the handwriting match this note?"

"They could be the same," Sid said.

"And it's not Dr. Baer's handwriting, is it?" It was not a question.

Sid was glaring at the nurse. "No, I guarantee you it isn't."

"What were they trying to give Amelia?"

"A muscle relaxant called vecuronium," Sid said. "At this dosage, with the sedatives still in her system, Amelia would have been dead in minutes."

44

Nuclear Fusion Test Facility

Marion had no idea the elevator doors could be so heavy.

Prying the doors open with the four-foot-long crowbar she'd brought from the maintenance closet, she pulled until she could get her shoulder and then her body wedged between them. As she did, the crowbar fell with a loud clang that reverberated in diminishing echoes along the corridor.

Marion stopped. She had to rest. The doors were crushing the breath out of her and her head was about to explode. The two corpses lying not twenty feet from her made breathing very difficult. She had to do something before she became sick yet again.

She looked around, desperately hoping to find something that would help take some of the pressure off her body. Seeing the duffel bag on the floor, she slid downward to a sitting position, straddling the door with one leg and one arm on either side, and reached for it.

She couldn't reach it. Not even close.

Terrified that she might not have the strength to open the doors again if she let them close, Marion paused, forcing herself to think clearly. Now was not the time to panic.

The crowbar. On the floor in the dark, outside the beam of the flashlight that lay beside the duffel bag, she spotted it. Reaching with her foot, she was able to pull it closer until her fingers encircled the cool metal bar. It was heavy, but Marion was able to maneuver it well enough to pull the duffel bag over to her.

Quickly taking the hammer from the bag, she laid it on the floor next to her. She took a deep breath and pushed the doors open a few more inches, enough to stuff the hammer beneath her on the track between the two elevator doors. Still holding the doors with all her strength, she gently eased them back to the point where they rested against the two ends of the hammer.

It was a little more than a foot, but it was all she needed.

Backing out of the elevator entry, she picked up the duffel bag and the shoulder bag and pushed them through the partially opened doors. They hit the floor, dropping three or four feet beneath the research lab's floor level to the bottom of the elevator shaft. She picked up the flashlight and the crowbar, and shot one last look at the bodies of the two scientists she'd covered with plastic bags. Pushing the crowbar through the opening, she stepped over the hammer, dropped the light onto the bag and climbed carefully down into the shaft.

The cement at the bottom was rough and the bumpers for the elevator took up most of the space. The drop was more than she'd thought. Standing upright, Marion looked just over the top of the hammer at floor level. She shone the light down on the unfinished cement surface and gathered up her bag. The air was moist and warm and heavy and unmoving.

Marion looked around. The double doors to Test Drift facility were directly across from the doors for the lab.

Opening the first set of doors had taken a lot out of her. She sat down on the duffel bag and directed the light at the rungs of ladder that went up the side of the shaft and disappeared into the pitch blackness overhead.

She wondered if the ladder went all the way up to the hoist on the roof. From the looks of it, though, she didn't think there was much room between the ladder and the track for the elevator car. She realized there must be an emergency access door in the floor of the car itself. The WIPP facility manual identified the distance from the lab floor to the surface at 2,150 feet.

"I might as well be climbing Mount Everest," she muttered in the murky air.

Marion considered for a moment if climbing the ladder—assuming she had the strength—was the best way to go. It was unlikely the killers were hanging around up there after all this time, but there was nothing to say that the building at the top of the shaft hadn't been destroyed.

She had to make up her mind.

Marion reached inside the shoulder bag and took out a bottle of water. She drank half of it, then shone the light up the metal rungs again. It still seemed like the better choice. Going up, she wouldn't have to think about the imminent risk of radiation poisoning in the Test Drift storage area. At least, not more risk than she'd already taken. There was a reason the adjacent facility was run by robots.

The booklet identified the radiation levels in the sealed chambers as topping at four hundred rem, about equivalent to forty thousand or so chest X-rays. That amount of radiation would kill half the people receiving it. Marion's estimation was that the actual numbers would probably be a lot higher than that.

Having talked herself into climbing the elevator shaft, she went through the two bags. There was no way she would make it carrying both of these bags. She separated what she thought she might absolutely need as far as food and drink. If she survived the climb, she might also have to survive a walk through the desert, and she didn't know how far that trek would be. She took extra batteries for the flashlight. The tools were heavy, but she decided she might need something to help her open the doors at the top once she got there. She couldn't carry the crowbar; it was just too heavy. The best choice seemed to be the hammer.

As she yanked the hammer free, the doors slid shut with a dull thud.

Marion took a couple of deep breaths to fight the momentary feeling of panic. The walls instantly seemed to grow closer. Her lungs couldn't draw in enough air.

She leaned down and hurriedly put all the things she'd decided to bring into the shoulder bag. She laid the flashlight and the coil of rope she'd found in the maintenance closet on the ground at her feet and hoisted the bag across her shoulders. She couldn't think too much about where she was, how little her chances were. She couldn't defeat herself before she tried. There was still the question of where the elevator was physically in the tunnel and if she could get around it or through it. She decided she'd just have to face that hurdle when she got to it.

Marion pushed her head and one arm through the coil of rope and hooked the flashlight to it.

"Okay. Let's do it," she whispered, looking up.

45

Someone wanted to kill Amelia.

The written message, intended to draw Mark Shaw away from the patient's room, sealed it. This wasn't some tired night-shift nurse's mix-up. There had been no one at the front lobby waiting for Mark.

Someone inside the care facility had planned the murder.

Sid stepped into Amelia's room and closed the door. Three Waterbury police cars had responded immediately, racing to the facility when they'd called it in. Mark and a couple of detectives were interviewing the nurse. She claimed that she was following what was on the prescription slip, and she didn't even know what the medication was for. Sid believed her and he thought Mark did, as well.

The rest of the police officers were combing the building, questioning everyone else who was working tonight. They were also searching for any unauthorized people who might be inside. There was no security to speak of in this place. Sid guessed there had never been much need for it.

The flashing lights from the police cars outside reflected off the walls of Amelia's room. Sid walked toward the windows. He could see two officers outside walking the perimeter of the building grounds. Dawn was about to break; the sky was just starting to grow lighter. He closed the shades.

Sid wondered how much Amelia had understood of what had happened, and he worried how much more helpless she might feel now because of it. He turned to her. She was awake, watching his every move.

Sid hadn't left the room since the chaos erupted following the attempt to give her the wrong medication. Still, police detectives and the night security man and Mark had been in and out of the room. The entire time, Amelia had observed everything going on around her. He wondered if perhaps…just perhaps…she knew exactly what was going on.

"Why would anyone try to hurt you?" Sid asked, walking to her bedside.

He remembered what Jennifer had told them about how they'd found Amelia six years ago. Someone had pushed her out of a moving car onto the highway. They had intended to kill her then. Sid couldn't help but wonder if word had gotten out, and now the same person was back to finish the job. She might recall the details of that night. She might even be able to tell them who was responsible.

He considered the possibility of connecting her to the test equipment again. He didn't know if she would communicate better with them that way. The last time she'd been connected, they'd only been able to record what she was actually seeing at that moment.

Too much was happening too soon. Sid understood there was the possibility that she might slip into a minimally conscious state at anytime, in the same manner that she'd come out of it.

"We're not going to let anything happen to you," he told her. "Tomorrow, we're moving you to a new place where they'll start teaching you how to talk and use those muscles, maybe even walk. You can explain some of what's going on to us then."

Lines that weren't there before creased her brow. He wanted to reach out and smooth them. There were dark circles under her eyes. She blinked as if agreeing to what he was saying. Despite the stress, she had the most beautiful eyes. Sid caught himself and looked at the IV drip hooked into her arm. He picked up her chart.

"There will be all kinds of new people working with you when you arrive at Gaylord Hospital." He felt the need to talk, to let her know what the changes would be. But he had to remind himself that she was his patient. There were ethical lines Sid was willing to toe, but getting inappropriately involved was not one of them. "My team and I are going to stay with you. And Jennifer has already promised to come and see you every day. Gaylord is half an hour away from here, and she tells me it's only a ten-minute drive from her house."

Sid hung the chart back up. That was when he saw her right hand. Her fingers were moving and not just involuntarily. They were repeating a pattern.

"You're going to get all better by yourself, aren't you?" he asked her. "You're not waiting for anyone else to tell you it's time to move your hands or your feet or anything."

He looked at her face. Her gaze was focused now on her right hand. He tried to figure what she was doing.

"Are you tracing letters on the blanket?"

She blinked.

"Do you want a pen and paper?"

She blinked again.

He looked around him and spotted a pad of paper and a pen next to the room telephone. She was trying to communicate with them. She was ready to tell them things.

Sid raised the head of the bed to a forty-five-degree angle, then adjusted a pillow behind her so she had lower-back support. Jennifer had mentioned that Amelia had done well with that before. She was able to support her neck for short periods of time. He placed the pad of paper under her right hand. He positioned the pen between her fingers. She tried to hold it but it slipped through her fingers. He placed it in her fingers again. Her joints were weak and the muscles unresponsive. Finally she wrapped her fingers around the pen and held it.

"Excellent. Take your time. Write down whatever you want," he said, pulling a chair next to the bed.

She stared straight ahead for a minute and then closed her eyes. Her fingers, though, continued to struggle to move the pen. It was obvious she wasn't going back to sleep but concentrating.

"You're doing it," he told her. The ink started to leave a mark on the paper. She made some scratching marks before moving the tip of the pen an inch away. A letter started to form.

"W," Sid said aloud.

She opened her eyes and lifted her neck from the pillow, looking at what she'd done. She blinked, yes. He took her fisted hand and moved the pen to where she could write more.

He tried to think what the letter might signify, but she seemed already intent on the next letter.

This one was only a straight line. *"L?"* he asked.

She only stared at him.

"Is it an *I?*" he asked.

She blinked, yes.

"So far, we have *wi,*" he told her.

She blinked again.

She seemed to be struggling with the next letter. First, Sid thought it was *o,* but she gave no indication that he was right. She drew a line next to it.

"P?" he asked.

She blinked again.

"Wip?" he asked.

She made him understand that he was right. She immediately started writing again. This time Sid picked it up the first time. "*P* again?"

She blinked, and Sid thought he saw the trace of a smile on her features.

"I'm not so dumb after all." He smiled to himself. "So far we have *wipp.*"

Amelia closed her eyes for few moments and opened them again.

"Okay, tell me what's next?"

With an effort, she opened her hand and let the pen drop through her fingers onto the blanket.

She laid her head back on the pillow and turned her face away.

46

Washington, D.C.

Joseph Ricker felt the disposable phone vibrate in the inside pocket of his jacket. Taking it out, he looked at the display. The call was from his contact in Connecticut. Instead of answering, he looked around Nebraska Avenue. The traffic was light.

"Right there," he told the driver, pointing. "Pull over and stop there."

They were very close to the American University campus. The driver did as he was told.

Joseph moved across the back seat and got out of the car. The cell phone had stopped ringing, but he knew it'd be only a matter of minutes before it rang again.

He moved across the sidewalk up onto a lawn. The grass was wet. He didn't like that his shoes were getting wet. The phone in his hand came to life as he'd expected. He checked the number. The same contact.

"I expect good news," he said without greeting.

"Not yet."

Joseph swore under his breath.

"Being discreet is a problem," said the man at the other end.

"What do you mean?"

"We tried it. It was a damn good setup, too. The autopsy would have written the death off as medical staff error. But it didn't work."

"Why not?" Joseph asked, frustrated.

"You didn't tell us she has guard dogs."

"She's a vegetable, practically in a coma. Of course, there are people who look after her."

"I'm not talking about nurses. She's got a cop and an M.D. who burn the midnight oil in her room."

The cop Durr had mentioned. Joseph didn't know the son of a bitch was still hanging around.

"Listen, you're getting paid a lot of money for this. You should be able to handle any kind of complication that comes up. Are you professionals or not?" The best defense was offense.

Joseph immediately looked around, realizing he'd been talking far too loudly. A woman passing by on the sidewalk was staring at him. He felt like giving her the finger but decided against it.

"We *are* professionals," the caller replied coolly. "There's no job that we can't handle—so long as we have all the details. You didn't give us enough information."

Joseph rubbed his neck. He'd given them everything he knew. Martin Durr would not like this. Joseph had to take this woman out of the picture. Simple as that. Durr would never expose himself to criminals like this one, but he wanted the job done.

Joseph would face serious consequences if these men failed. He knew it would not be a matter of decreased salary or diminished perks associated with the job. And there would be no looking for a comparable position anywhere else. Even if he could, there would be no job postings out there for someone with exactly his experience. No, he thought, there would be consequences, but not the kind an ordinary employee faces. Durr would never let him go.

Joseph had never been able to find out anything about his predecessor. He'd been told the position was new when he'd moved into it eight years ago. Joseph hadn't believed it then, and he still didn't. Someone as powerful as Durr needed middlemen to handle the pawns. To manage the dirty work.

The man or the woman who'd been Durr's personal assistant before Joseph had disappeared off the face of the earth. He sure as hell didn't want to go there.

Joseph walked farther away from the sidewalk and softened his tone.

"Okay. You have a suggestion about how you are going to complete this job?" he asked, enunciating every word. He wanted to make sure the man understood he was still expected to finish the contract.

"I have a couple of ideas."

"What are they?"

"The first one is messy."

"How messy?"

"We can blow up the place."

Joseph coughed to hide his shock. "That's bit much, isn't it? Aren't there a lot of people that work there? Aren't there patients?"

"I told you it would be messy. But it would work. They've been working on the gas line in that section of town for a month now. It would be easy to set it up."

"No," Joseph said firmly. There were way too many variables that he couldn't control. They'd have half of the Connecticut State Police *and* the FBI *and* Homeland Security on their tail. "What else?"

"I-84."

"I assume that's a highway," Joseph said.

"Yeah, it is," the man told him. "They're moving her today to some bigger hospital. They'll take I-84 to get there. People die every day in accidents on I-84."

"She'll be in an ambulance," Joseph reminded him.

"My men have taken care of a number of jobs involving transportation. Today's front page of the Waterbury paper has a picture of a jackknifed truck. Three people died as the result of it. On I-84. We've arranged accidents just like it. Taking care of an ambulance will be easy."

Joseph wasn't convinced. Also, Cynthia Adrian's mishap in California had been handled as an automobile accident. He wasn't crazy about patterns. Still, he had no plan of his own to suggest.

"Remember, I don't want any major disasters. No explosions. No mass murder. Nothing that brings in the feds. But the job *has* to get done."

"Even if it isn't discreet? Or accidental?"

"Even if it isn't. She *has* to die."

"How about bodies? Do they have to find her?"

"What are you going to do to her?" Joseph asked.

"Answer the question. I want a backup plan. We might have to change the details depending on how things go."

"Go for it," Joseph told him. At the last minute, he remembered what his boss was having him arrange for in New Mexico. Durr wanted proof that Marion Kagan was dead. "But if the body is going to disappear, I'm going to need proof that you've actually done the job."

"You're a strange bird, man," the caller had the nerve to say.

"You're getting paid a lot of money," Joseph reminded him again.

"No problem. I'll send you an early Christmas package…but don't open it in front of the missus."

47

Nuclear Fusion Test Facility

Rung is definitely a four-letter word, Marion thought without humor.

She didn't know if she was a tenth of the way or half the way to the top. What she did know was that she could no longer ignore the pain in her head, her back, her legs, her arms. Her muscles were screaming and her head was hurting so badly that her vision was beginning to blur. With every metal rung of the ladder she was climbing, she felt the burn on her fingers and palms where blisters had long ago formed, only to be rubbed raw.

At the start of the climb, she'd tried to keep track of the number of rungs as she went up. The climb, though, was harder than she could ever have imagined. The bag she was carrying across her shoulders was so much heavier than it was at the bottom. Before she'd climbed a hundred rungs, the fatigue had begun to set in and her brain lost the ability to keep count. Looping one arm through the metal and resting her feet on another rung below, all she could see was darkness above and below.

The beam of the flashlight shone on electrical cables that ran up along the wall to her right. For a fleeting second, Marion thought she saw a small creature running down it.

She shivered. "Please…no rats."

She turned her back to the cables, thinking how stupid it would be to let go of her hold because of a fear of rats.

Her throat was raw. She moved the flashlight hooked through the rope to the side. Trying to balance her weight on both feet and one arm, she shifted the bag on her shoulder. It was a struggle, but Marion was determined to get a bottle of water.

Feeling like a high-rise construction worker, she pulled the bag around slightly and tugged a plastic water bottle out of the bag. Twisting the top open was another story, but she was finally able to do it with the help of her teeth.

She gulped the water as if she'd been stranded on a desert isle for weeks. She dropped the empty bottle into the hollow darkness below. The bottle disappeared almost instantly, but if there was a sound to the soft plastic hitting the bottom, she didn't hear it.

Since she had access to the shoulder bag, she decided to take another bottle of water out and tuck it into a more convenient spot for later.

Realizing she had nowhere to put it, Marion decided to simply slide it inside her shirt. Holding the top of the bottle in her teeth, she began to unbutton her top buttons with her free hand.

No sooner had she begun, however, than the arm she had hooked around the rung slipped and her body swung outward. The bottle fell, striking the flashlight clipped to the rope. Grabbing for it only made things worse. In an instant, Marion was looking helplessly down the shaft as the flashlight fell end over end to the bottom.

This time she saw and heard it. Unfortunately, the bottom wasn't as far away as she'd hoped. And the flashlight went out when it hit the cement.

Marion was too angry with herself to cry over the loss of the light. She had never been a star athlete in her youngest and brightest days. She considered exercise a punishment. She'd always aspired to be an academic. What was she thinking, to assume she could climb almost three thousand feet…and in the condition she was in now!

She wasn't going to make it.

Marion leaned her forehead against the cool metal of the ladder, trying to rethink her decision. Opening the doors to the Test Drift area now seemed like a vacation. Getting exposed to radioactive waste didn't sound too bad at all. The risk of death suddenly seemed less certain than the death that a fall from this ladder would produce. She reminded herself that people cleaned toxic spills every day in power plants and research facilities. Besides, there was no saying what the radiation levels were in the Test Drift tunnel. And she had protective clothing in her bag to boot. If she'd had the courage to go back to her desk in the control room and get her radiation exposure dosimeter, they'd know exactly how to treat her when she got to the surface.

The ringing in her ears came over her like a wave. Marion knew what it was before she even lifted her head.

"Electricity," she said excitedly.

She looked over her shoulder into the darkness. There was a soft buzzing sound from the wall where the electrical cables ran.

They're powering up the station, she realized.

"I'm down here," she yelled up the elevator shaft without thinking. "Please...*help!*"

And then she stopped cold.

48

Mark Shaw was relieved when Sid sent one of the nurses to get him.

Questioning the night nurse was absolutely useless. The young woman was as upset as everyone else about what could have happened to Amelia if the medication had been administered. Besides, every staff member working that shift—as well as the newly arrived director of the care facility—was defending the woman. She'd been set up. It could have happened to any of them.

The police officers continued to search for intruders. Rita Ricci and another detective were interviewing everyone who had been working during the shift. There had been no visitors at all. No one believed any of the other patients would have been able to come up with anything so elaborate. Certainly, none of them had the requisite knowledge of toxicology to know what medication to prescribe and at what dosage. And what motive would any of them have?

One thing Mark knew, the attempted overdose wasn't a random act. It had been planned, and the plan had focused specifically on Amelia Kagan. What Mark couldn't understand was why. The news of her change of condition was not supposed to leave the facility. But even if word had gotten out, who would want to kill her?

Whoever it was, Mark knew that Amelia was their best lead.

The Waterbury Police Department seemed to have the investigation under control, so Mark followed the nurse who'd been sent to get him.

Amelia was awake when Mark entered the room. Sid had his laptop open and was typing away. She looked right across the room at him, appearing very aware of her surroundings. Mark closed the door behind him.

"She's awake…you're awake," he told her.

He walked toward the bed. "Do you think she remembers me?"

"I think you can talk to Amelia directly," Sid told him. "She understands everything."

"I'm a friend of your sister, Marion," Mark told her. "I was here in your room before. I'm not sure if you remember me."

Amelia gave no indication that she did. She continued to watch him, though, as if trying to make up her mind.

He decided to introduce himself. "My name is Mark Shaw."

She was conscious, but this young woman was very different from the one Mark had met Saturday night when he first arrived. The immediate recognition then was not present now. Mark was convinced that was because of Marion.

Looking into Amelia's eyes, he thought he saw sadness there. Perhaps it was frustration. She wasn't studying him to remember. Behind her steady gaze, it seemed she was trying to communicate something.

Perhaps something about Marion.

Once again, he wished he had a better understanding of how the two sisters could communicate with each other.

Sid clapped his hands together. "This could be it."

"*What* could be it?" Mark asked, looking over at the neurologist.

"The reason I sent for you is that Amelia wrote these letters down."

Mark looked down at the pad of paper Sid handed to him.

"WIPP," Sid told him. "That's what she wrote down."

Mark motioned to the laptop. "Are you checking to see if it's an acronym for something?"

"I am…I did. WIPP stands for Women Impacting Public Policy or Women in Periodical Publishing. They can't be it. But this one makes sense."

"What do you have?"

"Waste Isolation Pilot Plan. Here's their Web site," Sid answered, starting to read from the screen. "It says 'the Waste Isolation Pilot Plan, or WIPP, safely disposes of the nation's defense-related transuranic radioactive waste…'"

Mark moved behind Sid. "Who runs the facility?"

"The Department of Energy."

"Who's doing the actual work?" Mark asked, crouching down so he could have a better view of the laptop screen. "I ran across this once in my police training. Private companies bid on these kinds of situations and the jobs get farmed out. We need a name…someone that I can contact directly."

"So you're thinking what I'm thinking?" Sid asked.

"Somehow, Amelia has picked this information up from Marion," Mark said. His gaze moved to the bed. She was watching them.

He stood up and stepped toward her. The lines on the forehead were gone. Her jaw was relaxed. There was a pronounced softening of her features. The expression on the young woman's face was the same as Mark remembered the twin sister having. Amelia was clearly relieved that they understood.

"Do you think this is where your sister is?" Mark asked. "This WIPP place?"

She blinked.

"She was telling us about WIPP yesterday, too," Sid said. He was going through a copy of the manual they'd printed yesterday. "There are references to a Waste Isolation Pilot Plan in here."

"I feel like an idiot. We should have had someone who understands this stuff go through it," Mark said, shaking his head.

"I've already given a copy to Attorney Viera." Sid put the laptop aside and stood up, too. "He was going to take care of that."

"We've got to do this. We can't count on other people right now."

Sid stared at him but said nothing, and Mark turned back to Amelia.

The recognition and happiness Mark had seen the first time he'd met her was back. But this time it was directed at Sid. Mark watched the neurologist put his hand on top of hers.

"Amelia, is your sister alive?" Mark asked gently.

As he watched her, she turned her gaze to the far wall. Then, unmistakably, a look of uncertainty appeared.

49

Nuclear Fusion Test Facility

She had to go down. Fast.

The realization washed over her with a dread even more powerful than that first wave of excitement. The power was being restored to the elevator shaft. Marion couldn't stay where she was or she would be peeled like a skin off the wall as the elevator descended.

She had no clue about what the clearances might be, but she doubted there was enough for her, even squeezed in against the ladder. In the darkness, she couldn't tell if there were any holes or niches in the wall that she could scramble into. She hadn't seen any while climbing up. Her mind was working at top speed. There would be no time to react if she waited. She started down as quickly as she could.

Marion couldn't hear anything overhead, yet. That was a relief.

Going down should have been a lot easier than going up, but her joints continued to protest. The muscles in her thighs felt like rubber. Within a few rungs, the stinging feeling in her hands grew even more painful...and her palms were starting to slip a little on the rungs. The raw places that had once been blisters were now bleeding, but she couldn't worry about that.

Marion considered dropping the shoulder bag down ahead of her. But she remembered the other flashlights and the bottles of water. They could all be crushed on impact. As quickly as she could, she tugged the coil of rope over her head and dropped it into the darkness below.

She continued moving down one painful rung at a time. This was it. They were coming to rescue her. She didn't need the supplies. Her mind was a jumble. But she *might* need them. What if this was just a maintenance crew up above? In any event, she needed to get down to the bottom quickly, open the doors, and climb back inside the lab before the elevator came down the shaft…if it was coming.

Marion pushed herself to go down faster, but it was so difficult. The last thing she wanted was to lose her grip. That would be the last thing she ever did.

Questions started hammering at her brain. What happened if the elevator came down now? She'd be dead. Who was it that had restored the power to the lab? And why it had taken them so long? Could she trust whoever these people were? She didn't know the answer to any of those questions. How many days had it been since the shooting? She couldn't even remember that.

"Don't trust them," Marion murmured to herself. She'd been fooled before. They'd all been fooled. She wasn't stepping into any traps. If someone came down, she'd have to find out who they were before showing herself…somehow. That meant she had to get back inside the lab before anyone got down here.

Another thing. With the power on, the Internet might be back, too. If she could get down there while the power was up, she could contact…

A whistling sound from far above froze Marion.

"Elevator," she blurted out in panic. It was coming down.

Marion shrugged the bag off her shoulder, and it hit with a loud bang. She was near the bottom.

But the whirring sound of the elevator was getting closer.

She gave up her hold of the rungs and gripped the metal sides of the ladder. She began backing down two and three rungs at the time, her hands sliding down the rough painted metal. The pain in her hands shot like streaks of fire up her arms.

The sound of the elevator was becoming even louder.

She remembered how fast the ride down the elevator had been that first day. Marion looked up in panic. She could see the dim lights that framed the bottom perimeter of the elevator plummeting toward her.

She knew she wasn't going to make it.

As she glanced up, her foot missed a step. She slid, out of control now, clutching the side rails as her feet bounced off the rungs. Her chin hit a metal rung, snapping her head back.

She lost her grip entirely. As she began to fall backward through space, she glimpsed the elevator floor not fifty feet above her.

The fall was quick. She landed on her heels and felt a sharp pain shoot up through her right ankle. She fell onto her backside and immediately rolled to one side.

The elevator was almost on her. She was going to get crushed. She rolled again, pushing herself up against one of the walls. The bag she'd thrown down was right beside her head. She was going to be pressed flat. The enormous metal box continued to drop.

Marion closed her eyes and she heard the whirring

slow as the elevator neared the bottom. She felt the press of air in the shrinking space.

Marion moved her face toward the wall, thinking of her sister, wondering if anything she'd been imagining these past few days was real.

The smell of rubber brakes permeated the air. The pressure in her ears was intense. Marion squeezed shut her eyes, holding her breath.

This is the end, she thought.

50

Rancho Bernardo, California

"Bastard." Helen shredded the pages of the will into hundreds of pieces. "You dirty, conniving, thieving bastard."

Helen hadn't intended to go through Cynthia's mail. But the blue packet containing the will was sitting on the cabinet where her daughter kept the liquor. Seeing Fred's name on the folder and the recent date, she had to open it and see what vindictive little surprise her husband had planned for her after his death.

She poured another glass of vodka and drank it straight down. Three pieces of the will were stuck to the heel of her hand. She shook them off onto the floor and put her glass onto the table.

He was leaving her a beggar. The concept of community property clearly meant nothing when a vicious, two-faced scum of a husband tied up money in blind trusts and overseas investments and God knows what else…with lawyers, accountants and trust managers overseeing and running every investment. Helen was being given living expenses that put her practically on the poverty line.

She barely got past reading the names and numbers. That was enough. She wanted to destroy the document that, actually, was the perfect representation of her wasted time, staying married for nearly thirty-five years.

It didn't matter. She knew this was hardly the only copy. Knowing Fred, there'd be dozens floating around, backups of backups. But it made her feel good to destroy at least one.

She didn't fault Cynthia for having a copy. Helen knew how hard her daughter worked trying to avoid taking sides. Being the only offspring of a horrible marriage wasn't a choice her daughter had made.

Fred and Helen had been wrong for each other from the very start. She wanted a friend, a life partner. He wanted an ornament to run his house and look good in public and raise his children and leave him alone to do his thing, making money. The children ended up being only Cynthia. And being domestic wasn't exactly Helen's forte. Besides, having a marriage where one partner was never around was a sure road to depression. God, he'd driven her right to it.

Fred didn't understand. He didn't want to. Helen never did well with antidepressants. She reacted badly to them. That was when she'd started drinking. Casually at first, here and there, to mask how unhappy she felt. But at some point it had gotten out of control. She'd become dependent on it. To exist she needed alcohol as much as she needed water and air. And the handful of times she'd checked herself into hospitals and rehabs for detox, nothing had helped. She'd be good for days, perhaps a couple of months. But the unhappiness was always there. The roots ran too deep. And the bastard had just kept watering those roots.

Helen looked at the nearly empty bottle of vodka on the kitchen table. She tipped the last of it into the glass and polished it off.

Ladies don't drink out of the bottle.

Staring at it with that crystal clear, yet mildly skewed vision that came with practiced drinking, she couldn't remember how full it had been when she took it out of the cabinet.

This was what it meant to be an alcoholic. She knew that. She blanked out occasionally. So what? So what that she forgot things? Sometimes, she totally forgot what a miserable marriage she had. And that she had no friends. And no life to speak of. Days ran into each other and it didn't matter if it was Monday or Sunday. Christmas was just another day. Worst of all, men barely looked at her anymore.

The glass sitting on the table was empty. Helen pushed herself up out of the chair and stepped carefully over the scraps of papers scattered across the tiled floor. She pulled open the cabinet door.

"Wine. Wine. More wine…" she complained, taking out the bottles that blocked the good stuff in the back. She couldn't see what was back there. Cynthia had to have more vodka hiding in the back. "No civilized person has just one bottle of vodka."

Helen looked around for something to stand on and then moved unsteadily back to the table to pull a chair over. As she put her hand on one, the front doorbell rang.

"No company," she yelled.

The doorbell rang again.

"I'm not answering the door. Go away!"

Another ring.

"Christ," she muttered, going around the table and

looking out the second-floor kitchen window. There was a woman standing at the front door. She looked up and waved at Helen.

"Neighbor...neighbor. What's her name?" She couldn't remember.

She considered not going down. But she recalled this neighbor was the one who took care of the cat whenever Cynthia was away.

"Where *is* the cat?" Helen looked around the kitchen, remembering that she hadn't seen the animal since arriving. She'd never liked cats. She couldn't understand why Cynthia kept one.

A thought occurred to her. Maybe the neighbors were watching the sulky animal. Helen started down the stairs, holding tight to the railing. She should tell them to continue to watch the animal until Cynthia was released from the hospital. Her daughter cared for the nasty creature too much, and Helen didn't want the responsibility of anything happening to it.

Helen cast a cursory glance at her reflection in the mirror downstairs. Her hair was flat. She should have taken a shower when she first came in. There were mascara blotches under her eyes. She grabbed a tissue out of a box, wet it with the tip of her tongue, and used it to wipe away the black marks.

The narrow windows running up and down either side of the front door showed her that the neighbor was still there waiting.

Helen opened the door.

"Hi. I'm Karen Newman, a friend of Cynthia. I live two doors down."

"Yes...yes...I think we've met before. I'm Helen Adrian, Cynthia's mother." She leaned against the open doorway, needing something solid to support her. At the same time, Helen had no intention of inviting the other woman in.

"Yes, I know. My condolences about your husband, Mrs. Adrian."

Helen waved a hand. She was tired of lying about how hard it was. She didn't want to talk about Fred at all. "That's behind us. I have other problems on my plate right now."

"I heard the news. How's Cynthia doing?"

Helen shook her head. "Not too well. The doctors are hopeful, though."

"Do they allow her to have any visitors?" Karen wanted to know.

"Only immediate family. She's still in intensive care and unconscious." Helen straightened up. "I need to get some sleep right now and then get back to the hospital, so if you don't mind…"

"I won't keep you." Karen immediately put a hand out. "Just a couple of things. We have Shadow. She showed up at our door last night."

"The cat was outside?" Helen asked, surprised. "I thought Cynthia always keeps her in the house."

"She does. I don't know how she got out. We'd already heard about Cynthia's accident last night. Anyway, when she showed up, I sent my husband over to check the condo and make sure no doors were left open. He couldn't find any. I don't know how the cat got out."

Helen remembered when the animal had been declawed. Such trauma. She didn't think there was any chance Cynthia would let the cat out.

"Well, however it happened, would you mind holding on to her for now?" she asked. "I know my daughter would appreciate it."

"Sure. No problem." Karen Newman reached inside a canvas bag she had over one shoulder and took out a thick folder. "Also, this morning I went to put our outgoing mail in our mailbox and this was there. I believe it belongs to Cynthia."

Helen took the folder without even looking at it.

A car went slowly by on the street. Helen's gaze was drawn to the dark gray sedan. The dark windows hid the occupants.

"Thank you, Mrs...."

"Newman. But call me Karen. And if there's anything I can do—"

"Thanks, I'll let you know." Helen was tired. She knew she should take a nap. But she wanted a drink first. She waved to the younger woman and stepped back, closing the door.

At the last minute, Helen turned around and slid the security chain into the slotted track. Cynthia always bragged about the safety of this neighborhood. Still, Helen felt exposed. With the exception of this neighbor, she didn't know anyone else here.

The folder slipped from under her arm and fell with a thud to the floor. Pages scattered everywhere on the tiled entry.

"I don't need this," Helen grumbled under her breath, crouching down to pick up the pages. She quickly put a hand out against the wall to steady herself.

More of Fred's things, she could tell. The New Mexico Power Company heading was on all the pages. Some of the pages were stamped at the bottom "Company Classified." Naturally, those were the pages that Helen's attention was drawn to.

Fred had always considered her stupid. Maybe Helen didn't have an IQ of 165 and maybe she hadn't gone to graduate school and maybe she didn't have some advanced egghead degree. Still, Helen always thought she could hold her own when it counted…or when he gave her the chance.

Picking the pages up off the floor and trying to put them back in order, she found herself reading some of the text. The scientific gibberish didn't discourage her. She'd lived with technical journals and publications lying around the house for too long.

Page ten of the report had a listing of names. Helen's gaze was drawn down the page as she realized she knew some of these names.

She slid down onto her knees and looked back up to the top of the page. She wasn't brain-dead, after all. And the phone calls she'd received from the newspaper people was another reminder. The names belonged to the scientists who'd recently died in the explosion on the platform on the Gulf of Mexico.

She understood why this information would be classified, considering the project was experimental. Or at least that's how the media kept describing it. Below the names were the transportation arrangements. The destination was another curiosity. Fred or someone else had underlined in red the acronym WIPP a couple of times.

Helen searched on the floor until she found the next page in the document.

The facility they were taken to… Helen stopped and checked page ten of the document again. The group was being transported to the Waste Isolation Pilot Plan in the Chihuahuan Desert outside of Roswell, New Mexico.

"New Mexico?" she asked aloud. "Not Texas?"

This didn't make sense. The fire was still burning on

the platform in the Gulf. That was where the news said the scientists were.

Suddenly, it was essential for her to know what it was *exactly* that she had in her hands.

Helen reached for the pages that were still scattered on the floor. She hurriedly tried to put them in order, trying to find the first couple of pages. Finding a note from Fred to Cynthia, she scanned it quickly.

You're smart. You know what to do with what's inside if you need to.

She pushed past the note and glanced at the first page of document.

…testing a small, sealed, transportable, autonomous reactor…

Helen pushed past that page, too. There were scientific explanations about the project duration and costs on the next couple of sheets. Certain words on page seven were marked in red. Helen focused on those words.

Dual facility…use of live radioactive material…

The next page had Fred's handwriting on the margin. Helen tilted the page to make out what he'd written down.

Board approved project without knowledge of end run around NRC. Except Martin Durr, Dir came up with WIPP.

Helen knew NRC stood for Nuclear Regulatory Commission. She didn't know who Durr was. But she guessed he or she had to be someone on the board of directors.

A movement through the glass windows adjacent to the door caught her attention. A car had pulled into the driveway.

She leaned forward for a better view and saw the dark

gray sedan. It was the one that she'd seen drive by before.

Events shifted, prioritized, focused in her mind, and suddenly Helen was sober beyond what she'd thought possible.

The news had been packed with lies for days. They were reporting people dead in a place that they hadn't been. Fred's death. And the plane crash of the company R & D directors. Cynthia's accident. And this file being stuffed in a neighbor's mailbox.

It was all related.

Someone was standing at the door. Helen's gaze moved to the glass. They weren't ringing the bell.

The taste of bile rose in her throat. Her legs wouldn't move. She looked around frantically for the phone. She couldn't see one.

She tried to stand up, but lost her balance and fell forward. Still on her knees, she grabbed up the loose pages left. Struggling to her feet, she staggered toward the stairs.

Helen was on the second step when she heard the lock click in the front door. They had keys. The chain stopped the door from opening.

She ran up one flight. When she reached the kitchen, she dropped the pages on the counter and searched frantically for the phone handset again. It was on the kitchen table.

She heard the sound of the chain snap downstairs as she snatched up the phone. Fighting back her panic as she tried to focus on the numbers, Helen racked her mind for whom to call. She sure as hell didn't know the phone number for the police out here.

Nine-one-one. It dawned on her with brilliant clarity. Nine-one-one.

But as she tried desperately to find the three numbers on the keypad, she heard the footsteps on the stairs and realized she was too late.

51

"**I**'m hitching a ride on a military transport. I should be in Roswell, New Mexico, by early afternoon," Mark explained to Sid after getting off his cell phone and walking back into the room.

"That's a long way to go without having…what do they call it on TV? Substantiated evidence," Sid said, looking over his shoulder at Amelia.

She had been lost in a world of her own for a couple of hours now, not paying attention to anyone else in the room. Mark could tell that Sid was already concerned about it. The young doctor had told him that he couldn't wait until she was transferred to a more equipped facility where they could keep a closer eye on her.

"Maybe it's not substantiated for everyone else, but it's good enough for me. She's given us the same information twice. Once with the manual and another time writing down the letters. That's the first thing she's written in…how long? No, I'm going with it."

The neurologist nodded. "I'm just thinking that you might not get any cooperation from anyone once you get there."

"That's a risk I'm willing to take. But I do have a couple of things in the works that might help me."

"You mean about this WIPP facility?"

Mark nodded. "I found out the name of the company that manages the site. TMC Corporation. Detective Ricci was able to get information from the FBI on them. They're a half-billion-dollar company that manages and operates a number of remote nuclear laboratory and disposal sites for the Department of Energy...and for a handful of power companies."

"The New Mexico Power Company one of their clients?" Sid asked.

"You got it. That's why I'm flying out there this morning," Mark said quietly. "Interestingly enough, the facility that's burning on the Gulf of Mexico was also one of their managed sites."

"Have you been able to contact anyone inside the company?"

"No, but I don't know if I want to," Mark admitted. "Too many things have happened this past week. Too many coincidences. The cop in me is asking a lot of questions. I was talking to my chief in York an hour ago. He's using his contacts to get someone from the FBI field office in Albuquerque to meet me in Roswell when I get there. He's trying to stir up some interest at the higher levels."

Sid looked anxious. "What do you mean, there are too many coincidences?"

"A few days before the initial accident in the Gulf, the head of Research and Development at New Mexico Power died after a routine test procedure in the hospital. A colonoscopy. This guy, Fred Adrian, was at the helm of this project. Right after the incident, a charter plane goes down, killing a number of people from New

Mexico Power…people who worked on this specific project. I find it extremely convenient that *everyone* who was closely tied to this research project is gone. So does my chief, and so does the FBI special agent in charge in New Mexico. At least, they both agreed that it's worth checking into."

Sid looked over at Amelia again. "She's been giving us her sister's view of some of the things Marion was involved with. Technical data, even the name of this WIPP location. Do you think the wrong prescription she almost got last night might have something to do with your theory?"

"At this point, anything's possible," Mark told him flatly.

He was relieved when his chief, Lucas Faber, had seen the connections. Lucas was a bit less enthusiastic about Mark's source of the location. He knew a little about some of the odd connections between twins, but he wasn't about to commit to anything coming from Amelia. After all, he'd argued, even though she'd woken up from her minimally conscious state and named a facility twice, there could be an explanation other than the one Mark was suggesting. No one knew where Amelia's travels had taken her, after all.

Mark hadn't argued the point, even though the information was more current than the date Amelia had been injured. The important thing was that the FBI was now involved and he was heading to New Mexico.

If Marion was there, he was going to find her.

Chief Faber had also offered to check nationally for any other homicides or incidents involving New Mexico Power personnel or the TMC Corporation in the past week. Not everything made the headline news.

"So you're saying," Sid said, "Amelia could still be in danger."

He looked over at the patient. Amelia was watching them. He wondered if she'd heard the last question.

"She could very well be," Mark said quietly, glad that the Waterbury PD was on board. "She's revealing things that someone has gone to a lot of trouble to hide. If they tried once to stop her from talking to us, there's no reason to think they won't try again."

52

"There is one tried and true way to kill a project, Martin. You make an offer of an enormous amount of money. You buy it and you bury it."

Martin Durr reined in his anger and remained silent. The caller was breaking two of Martin's basic rules. First, no one told Martin Durr what to do. Second, you didn't talk about sensitive business matters on an unsecured line.

Durr sat in the backseat of the limo, staring in disbelief at the granite buildings lining Constitution Avenue. Here he was, at the heart of D.C. on a cell phone, listening to this idiot come very close to exposing them all. He considered the situation extremely uncomfortable.

"When we talk about killing a project, no one is talking about literally—"

"Look, I can't hear you," Martin said, cutting him off. "This phone connection is not working."

"Martin, my clients are concerned about the events of…"

The lawyer continued to talk, and Martin wanted to stuff something down his throat. He was spouting bullshit and they both knew it. Everyone involved knew exactly how he conducted business. Durr made the decisions and executed them. His fellow investors didn't care about the details. They wanted results. Period. Beyond that, they cared for nothing and no one.

Martin said nothing, though. He wasn't going to give them an inch of solid ground. The lawyer was only a mouthpiece, and a newly hired one at that. He was representing a dozen investors worldwide who had combined their wealth nearly two decades ago for leverage. Now worth over five hundred billion dollars, the group's investments were primarily focused on oil. And to protect that interest, the group kept track of key figures in the automotive and alternative-energy industries to stay on top of developments—or to squash projects if there was a need.

Not that Martin and his group needed to do it all. Those directing the American automobile industry had certainly been doing their part. There was a reason why the fuel efficiency of automobiles had moved at a snail's pace for the past several decades. Even directors of the Japanese auto industry, now well entrenched in oil investments, had bought into the plan.

This project, however, was perhaps the most important breakthrough they'd had to deal with since GM's EV1. This project promised to be the greatest advance in energy since Edison beat out Tesla. The successful development of the portable nuclear container system would crush the demand for fossil fuels in a decade, eventually taking over nearly all commercial applications in a twenty- to thirty-year time frame. No, they had to kill it.

Martin Durr was an investor, a businessman, a political power. Many considered him a genius. He was on the board of directors of half a dozen corporations and universities. Durr would always be the tough son of a tougher West Virginia coal miner. He'd never had time for any bachelor's degree. He'd married twice for money…unsuccessfully. His third marriage had been a success, though, and he had two children to show for it. By the time he'd married the third time, he'd been the one with the bank accounts.

Durr had only a handful of people he did business with. They had all been with him for many years. There was no beginning or end to projects. One thing rolled into the next. Their goals were the same—to make money. There was no bullshit nitpicking about how something got done. The end result was what mattered.

Martin couldn't understand this phone call. There was no reason for it. At first, he figured the lawyer was trying to justify his salary. Then, a suspicion that something else was in play began to creep in.

"My clients want to know how you intend to resolve—"

"Can you hear me?" Martin finally said into the phone, cutting him off again. "Look, we have a bad connection. I didn't hear a word of what you said."

"Mr. Durr…"

"If you can hear me, call my office. Make an appointment with my secretary. I'll assign one of my people to assist you. That is, if we can help you at all."

"Mr. Durr, my clients—"

Martin ended the call. He threw the phone inside his open briefcase. The cell immediately started ringing. He decided it had to be the lawyer again. People like him didn't take too well to being hung up on. Durr shut the briefcase, muffling the sound.

He needed to think through this. Lately, he'd been

spending too much time pursuing politicians and not paying enough attention to the day-to-day details. Not too far down the road, Martin liked to see himself serving as a political advisor for someone in the White House, the way Karl Rove had been to the Bush family. It was certainly within the realm of possibility. He could get things done in a way Rove only dreamed of.

As it was, though, he'd been depending too much on his assistant. Joseph Ricker was smart, ambitious. The problem with him was a lack of follow-through. And the years were starting to add up. Joseph was getting lazy. He wasn't as sharp as he once was. Not as eager to please. There were flaws in the projects he'd been overseeing. Martin found himself double-checking what Joseph was supposed to get done. That wasn't good.

This operation had been particularly sloppy. By the time everything was resolved—as the son of a bitch on the phone said—the body count could very well attract attention. It wouldn't take a genius to start connecting dots and tying everything up in a nice bundle. In a case like that, the legal types wouldn't settle until they had someone to hang.

Everyone would be looking for a fall guy. That was what the phone call on his cell phone was about. They were probably taping that conversation, just in case.

Martin Durr wasn't going to be anyone's fall guy. He always operated with utmost caution. Nothing would ever come back to him. He understood how things worked.

If his business partners wanted him out…fine. That was their problem.

As for him, he'd finish this up and then find his place in those dark back hallways of power. He had enough money.

Politics was the future.

53

Nuclear Fusion Test Facility

The metal frame beneath the elevator floor was barely three inches from her face.

It took a moment for her to grasp the fact that she was not dead. Then she heard the voices.

They were not here to rescue her.

Marion couldn't see them, but she could hear the urgency in the muffled tones. They would know there was a survivor in the facility the moment the elevator door opened. She'd covered Andrew Bonn and Dr. Lee's bodies with plastic.

Inching sideways, she realized the frame forming the base of the elevator was about three feet or so beneath the floor of the elevator car itself. Bundles of wire and cable crisscrossed the space.

As the doors opened, two people left the elevator. The footsteps were heavy. She decided they were wearing boots. She imagined the same masked men, armed with guns, that had begun this nightmare, and a cold feeling of dread washed through her.

Marion couldn't tell if anyone stayed behind or not, but the doors of the elevator remained open. Voices from out in the lab. They'd spotted the bodies. They knew someone had survived. Then, everything became quiet.

The lights along the outer edges of the floor lit the jammed space where Marion lay. It was difficult not to feel claustrophobic, considering her face was only inches away from the heavy metal frame. The air was warming up quickly. She felt droplets of sweat run down to her hairline. She guessed this was what being trapped in a casket alive must feel like.

Marion inched closer to the side near the door. Sheet metal lined the edge of the frame, and some kind of rubber seal beneath the door blocked her view. Working one arm into position, she fit her finger up between the elevator frame and the cement wall. Stretching up as far as she could, Marion could just barely reach the seal. The rubber was soft and pliant, though, and she was able to get one finger around an edge. Very carefully, she tried to peel it downward toward her. If she made any sound, they might find her.

If they found her, she'd be dead.

She struggled to pull the rubber down, without success. She'd almost given up when she realized that her other hand, pressed flat on the floor of the shaft, had brushed away a shard of broken plastic from the fallen flashlight. Carefully feeling for it and then transferring it across her body, she pushed the sharp plastic up into the seal, puncturing it. In a moment, she was able to make enough of hole that she could get a good grip to pull.

A two-inch gap appeared and she stopped. She didn't need to pull the rubber any farther. She could see him.

There was at least a third person. She saw the soles of two boots spanning the small space between the edge of the elevator and the lab floor. The person had to be standing in the open door.

Marion tried to shift her weight to get her head closer to the hole. She pressed one foot against the floor and the shock of pain in her ankle nearly made her cry out. For the first time since falling, she became aware of the throbbing in her ankle.

She gritted her teeth, forcing herself to forget the pain. From her new position, she could see a little more. The man above was wearing the same gray overalls the killers had worn, and there was something hanging from the person's belt. It looked to be some kind of radio device. Marion doubted they could use it to communicate with someone on the ground level. It had to be for communication with the others down here.

She could also see the short, gunmetal-gray machine gun in his hand.

As she watched, the radio vibrated. Marion tilted her head and saw more of the person answering the device. He was wearing a ski mask. She wasn't surprised.

"What do you have?"

A man's voice came through the radio. He was speaking quietly. "He was right. Everyone accounted for but Kagan. We're going to do a thorough sweep and flush her back to you."

Shit. They'd called her by name. Shit. They knew she was missing. They were down here looking for her.

Marion didn't think she could possibly be more afraid.

"I'm ready," the man standing above her answered.

"We're starting the sweep now," the voice said. "She has to be somewhere."

Marion closed her eyes, forcing herself to breathe as she began the countdown until they realized exactly where she was hiding.

54

Deer Lodge, Montana

Kim Brown couldn't recall the last time she'd called in sick to work. This morning she had to.

Last night, she'd had a nightmare. It was like that Scrooge story. She was dead, her body lying on a steel plate in a morgue. It was terrifying. Her soul was hovering over her near the ceiling. She saw both her daughters walking into the dark room. Their hands were connected. They had two bodies but it was as if they were one person. They seemed happy. Then, a man in a white lab coat came in, walked past them and yanked the sheet off her face. Marion and Amelia both shook their heads. They pretended they didn't know her. Without a word, they just turned and walked out.

Kim woke up sobbing. She thought she'd been sleeping for days, but it had only been a couple of hours.

She'd been too afraid to go back to sleep. Sitting in bed, her mind had begun to race. Memories of her girls, when they'd both been around, played again and again in her mind. They had gone everywhere as one. They'd walked through their childhood holding hands.

It was Kim who had tried to separate them, but she'd

been the one who'd lost. In the end, she'd lost both of them.

She thought about her past as she'd never done before. She realized her girls could never have been any less than an extension of each other. They were two halves, one completing the other.

She'd put all the enmity she felt for her husband right onto Amelia. She had been so wrong.

As Kim continued to think of the twins' childhood, memories of those other times began to come back to her. She remembered the girls as two dark-haired angels, racing and shoving each other as they hurried downstairs on Christmas morning. She recalled Amelia giving Marion and herself a haircut when they'd been five. As much as Kim had been angry, she remembered the good time they'd had when the girls had talked her into getting a haircut, too—by them. The three of them had looked like bona fide punk rockers.

Kim had grown increasingly miserable as her daughters were growing up. She knew that. She was still bitter about being deserted by her husband. She felt like a failure for having to go back to the town she'd been so desperate to get away from. But it had never been the girls' fault.

The night of memories ended in tears. Kim sobbed, knowing her own failures had driven Amelia away. She'd cried, realizing how much she missed both of them. How much she loved them. She wanted to…to apologize to Amelia. She wanted to hold her daughter in her arms and tell her how sorry she was for everything that had happened. She wanted to tell her that she would take care of her—stay with her.

She wanted to tell Amelia that she loved her. She always had.

They'd told her Marion was dead. But the young man, Mark Shaw, claimed Amelia was trying to give them clues about the whereabouts of her sister.

Amelia had been injured and confined to a bed for years, but she was still trying to help…while Kim was wallowing in her own self-inflicted misery. She had to do something, anything.

It was half past four when Kim left her bedroom and tiptoed downstairs. Outside the windows, there was no sign of dawn. She went into the kitchen and put on some water for tea. Then she took the phone into the living room, called her work number and left her boss a long message.

Everyone at work knew about the news Kim had received concerning Marion. They all expected she'd take some time off. But Kim had not committed to anything. Until now. On the message, she told them that she was not going to California but to Connecticut…to see her daughter, Amelia. Kim guessed word would get around fast. She figured it was time.

Kim didn't own a computer. She used one at work and knew the systems the prison used, but she'd never bothered to learn her way around the Internet. That was what everyone at work used to plan any trip. She went back into the kitchen and opened the phone book and searched through the Yellow Pages for a travel agent. She wondered if people still used them to make flight arrangements. The only time she'd ever flown in her life was when she'd gone on her honeymoon. Kim hadn't even gone to Marion's college graduation. She'd never been to California to see where her daughter lived.

More tears ran down her cheeks. Kim knew she was not just mourning her daughters. She was mourning all the years she'd lost.

She wrote down the name and phone number of a place in town. No one would be there now, but she'd call first thing in the morning.

She saw her father's bedroom light go on. He never closed his bedroom door completely, but she knew him to be a sound sleeper. Kim wondered if she'd awakened him.

"Kim…" he called.

She wiped the tears with a tissue and went to his door and tapped lightly, opening it. He was sitting on his bed, staring at his bare feet and the floor.

"I'm sorry, Dad. Did I wake you up?"

He shook his head. His breath was unsteady. "Ni… night…night…mare…abo…gi…girls."

"I'm calling a travel agent when they open. I'll try to get us a flight for today or tomorrow. We're going, Dad. I'm not going to put it off," she assured him.

He nodded repeatedly, his gaze remaining on the floor. "You…go…"

"What do you mean?"

He looked up. "It…be…faster. She…needs…you. Am…Amelia."

"Were you having a nightmare about her?"

He nodded again. "Dan…danger. She…needs… you."

A week ago, Kim would have stood there and argued with her father that dreams weren't real and that he was overreacting to a bad night.

Today, she didn't. She understood. She felt it.

"Okay." She thought a moment. "I'll call someone from church to come and look in on you. I'm just going to get dressed, throw some things in a bag, and drive to the airport. I hear people can get on flights standby. I think that would be the fastest. But are you sure you'll be okay?"

"Kim…go," he ordered. "You…n…need her…too."

She did need her, Kim thought as she looked at her father. They needed each other.

55

Waterbury Long-Term Care Facility
Connecticut

The ambulance and the police car to serve as escort were ready. Gaylord Hospital was prepared for Amelia. Sid had arranged for Desmond and Nat to move his car to Wallingford later today. This way, he could travel in the ambulance with Amelia. The two neurologists were taking care of the transfer of equipment, as well.

Amelia's room was bustling with staff. Despite the short notice, Jennifer had managed to throw a going-away party for her patient. Before this morning, Sid thought Amelia's eyes were brown. Today, there seemed to be a greenish tinge to them. As he looked at her, he suspected a small amount of makeup had been applied, as well.

Jennifer had dressed the young woman in a hunter-green sweatshirt and sweatpants, and they'd also put a matching green headband on her. Amelia looked flat-out pretty—still pale, but not like someone who'd been confined to her bed for six years.

They had raised the head of her bed higher than before. Amelia's muscles were becoming stronger every day. She was holding her neck up for longer periods.

Balloons and banners hung from every corner. Sid watched Jennifer make a big production out of reading each of the signs. Some of them were really funny, and he'd seen Amelia smile.

He felt totally out of place in the midst of all these people who were anxious to see and talk to Amelia before she was taken away. She was responding to them. She seemed happy. Jennifer appeared to be serving as the mediator between Amelia and the others. Everyone was having a great time.

Sid hovered by the doorway. He couldn't bring himself to let her out of his sight. The Waterbury police had been unsuccessful in finding the party responsible for the wrong prescription last night. As a result, they were providing a police escort for the ride to Wallingford, three towns over. Once at Gaylord, they'd worked it out with the Wallingford PD to keep an officer on duty outside of Amelia's room for the first week or until there was some explanation as to who was responsible for the attempt on her life.

Sid knew that Attorney Viera had been making a lot of noise to ensure the police would come through with protection for Amelia. It had not been advertised publicly, but it was understood by all who were involved that her safety was directly linked to information she'd revealed through the brain scans. This morning, after Mark left, Viera had called Sid, telling him that the technical information they'd printed yesterday had been passed on to the Dean of the Mechanical Engineering department at UCONN, who in turn was going to pull together some of the faculty of his college and someone from Yale in New Haven to go over the pages today. They were supposed to call him as soon as they knew what these documents were. Sid told the attorney the name of the facility Amelia had given them late last night. Viera was going to pass that information along, too.

At some point in time during this past weekend, Sid had crossed into new territory. He believed everything Amelia was telling them. He believed that her sister was communicating with her.

One of the nurses came into the room to remind Jennifer that the patient needed to be readied for the transfer. Sid was glad he wasn't the one ending the party; there was a lot of moaning and groaning.

As everyone started filing out of the room, Sid made his way to where Jennifer was standing.

"When was the last time you slept?" she asked him.

He couldn't remember. "I'm not tired."

"You're a liar, Dr. Conway." She smiled. "Are you going to stay with her on the trip over?"

"Yeah, I am."

"Good. But then you need to get some rest. This study of yours can wait a day or two, can't it?"

The study. They had barely started this phase of it, and already there were so many aspects that they hadn't planned for. Study goals could always be revised, he told himself. They were making groundbreaking discoveries in the field of neurological science.

The fact of the matter, though, was that professionally and personally he wanted to be nowhere else.

"Seriously, at some point you should go home and take a shower. A change of clothes would be nice, too."

He looked down at the jeans he'd been wearing all weekend. "I'm not too bad. I changed my shirt. And I did take a shower last night, before all hell broke loose."

He frowned, thinking over the events of last night. Actually, the water had barely touched him when he'd gotten a horrible feeling something was wrong. Sid didn't know where the feeling had come from, but he knew he had to get back to Amelia's room. He knew she'd needed him.

Perhaps it was a terrible thing in a doctor—especially in one at the very beginning of his career—to go with gut feelings over scientific data. Maybe it was, but when it came to her, he found he was no longer waiting for the objective results of blind studies. When it came to Amelia, gut feelings seemed to work just fine.

Sid was certain Mark wouldn't have allowed anyone to inject anything into Amelia until he got back. But the prospect of what could have happened was terrifying.

"You do know that night nurse is innocent," Jennifer said, reading his expression. "She'd never do anything to hurt any one of the patients. Especially Amelia."

Sid looked at her. "I know. The woman was *very* upset. I might have leaned on her more than I should have, but I was upset, and they almost got to Amelia. Whoever is behind this went through a lot of planning. Pat just happened to be the one working at the time."

Jennifer glanced at Amelia. "Who *would* do that? Who would want to hurt her?" The nurse paused. "It's a little unnerving to think that this person had access to our files…to our building. They had to be inside to leave the prescription and the note at the nurses' station. If you or Mark weren't here, they could have walked right in and injected her themselves."

Sid shook his head. He didn't want to think how vulnerable Amelia was. Still, he wished he had the answers.

"Mark is working on it. So are Attorney Viera and the police."

Their conversation was cut short as a gurney came

into the room. Sid saw Amelia's attention immediately focus on the rolling bed and the two men pushing it.

Sid found Jennifer checking the men's badges. Clearly, he wasn't the only one who was anxious. He, for one, was happy that the local police department was taking what had happened last night seriously enough to offer the escort.

Jennifer lowered the head of the bed and readied Amelia before allowing the two men near her patient. "I'm going to bring over her bag."

Sid knew of the circumstances under which Amelia had arrived at this facility. He looked at her curiously. "Something you put together for her?"

"I didn't do it alone. Everyone pitched in. Don't forget, she's had a number of birthday parties over the years and there are gifts that we've saved up. Now she'll finally get to use some of the things and hopefully enjoy them."

Sid wasn't going to ask what they were. He was touched, though, by the gesture. Regardless of what the media every now and then presented about substandard care in long-term nursing facilities, he knew there were a hell of a lot of very dedicated people working in them.

Jennifer left the room. Sid double-checked the equipment to make sure everything was packed and ready to go for Desmond and Nat. He pulled on his jacket and zipped it up.

He frowned. That sensation was back. There was a nervous fluttering deep in his stomach. He looked over at Amelia.

The two paramedics had the gurney up against her bed. They were getting ready to shift Amelia.

She was staring at Sid, her gaze unwavering. He saw her hand. Her fingers were barely off the sheet, but they were reaching for him.

"They've told you that I'm coming in the ambulance with her?" he asked one of the men. He moved to the other side of the bed from the gurney.

"No. Nobody said anything about—"

"But that's fine," the other one said, finishing his partner's sentence.

Amelia's head turned and she continued to keep eye contact with Sid.

"Everything will be fine," he said to her gently. He took her hand. Her fingers immediately clutched to his, holding tight. He was surprised by her strength.

"We're ready to move her," the first paramedic said, looking over at their joined hands.

Sid tried to pull back his hand, but Amelia's grip was tight.

"She's nervous," he told them. "This is probably the first time that she's left this place in quite a while."

Both men seemed impatient. They were only interested in getting their job done. No small talk. No friendliness. They hadn't spoken a word to Amelia. She could as well have been a piece of furniture that they were told to move. Sid found himself growing annoyed.

"If you come over to this side of the bed, we can move her," the same one spoke.

As he tried to loosen her grip, she struggled to hold on, a stressed noise rising from deep in her throat. He knew it would only be a matter of time before she discovered her voice and found her ability to talk again.

"I'm right here. I'm only going around to the other side."

She'd been conscious since last night. She'd heard all the conversations going on around her. She knew someone had tried to take her life. But there was nothing she could do to protect herself. She was totally helpless.

Sid felt honored, touched that she'd chosen him as a person to trust. Attorney Viera had told him earlier that he received a call from Kim Brown early this morning. She was flying East today. She planned to go directly to Gaylord Hospital. Viera had said that Kim was suddenly concerned about Amelia. The attorney had decided not to mention anything about the threat last night. The mother could learn the facts when she arrived.

Sid wondered if Amelia would remember her mother. And frankly, he was worried what Kim's plans would be regarding her daughter's future care.

He was honest enough with himself to admit that he was also nervous about what Kim Brown might think about how attached Sid had become to her daughter. The study was no longer his top priority. The welfare of the patient…okay, *Amelia's* welfare now took precedence over everything else, by miles.

He reached over and took her other hand as they hoisted the sheet and shifted her to the gurney.

Amelia's grip was even tighter than before. She watched only Sid. One of the paramedics started putting the straps around her.

"Can one of you guys hand that bag to me?" he asked. Sid wasn't going to try to detach himself from her again.

The shoulder bag was handed to him.

"Where's the ambulance?" he asked.

"In the back of the building," one of them said brusquely.

They were quick. Amelia was strapped on the bed, and they started pushing her out of the room.

"One of the nurses is getting the patient's things," Sid told them.

"She can catch up to us in the parking lot."

Sid considered ordering them to wait, but considering how upset Amelia seemed to be, there were advantages to getting her settled into the ambulance.

A few of the nurses were gathered in the hall, and words of goodbye and good luck were showered on Amelia. Sid told one of them to send Jennifer to the back door.

"You're quite popular," he told Amelia as they moved quickly through the halls.

She refused to look at anyone but him.

"There's nothing to worry about. We're talking maybe a forty-five minute ride, tops."

Soft sounds left her mouth. She was trying to tell him something. Sid couldn't make out the words, but it wasn't long before they'd maneuvered through two sets of doors and emerged from one of the back entrances of the building.

Sid was familiar with this entrance. It was the door they'd used to move in their equipment. A low loading dock of sorts was located right outside the door. Backed up to the building, Sid saw the open doors of the ambulance. Next to it, there was a police car with two officers standing by.

The late October weather was sunny but crisp. A breeze ruffled through dried leaves, sending them up in spirals occasionally and pushing them across the pavement. Sid noticed Amelia take a deep breath as soon as they rolled the gurney out. Her gaze immediately fixed on the trees overhead.

"Hold it," Sid ordered the men. They were ready to push the bed right into the ambulance. "Give her a minute."

She stared at the sky with amazement. He wondered how many times the staff had taken her out of that hospital room for fresh air over the years. If they had, she hadn't been at the level of consciousness where she could enjoy it.

Yellow and red leaves were dancing around his feet. He leaned down and grabbed one and held it up for her before placing it next to her hand. It was a maple leaf, brilliantly red.

"The colors are especially beautiful this year," he said, though he hadn't even noticed until just now.

She let go of his hand and laid her fingers on the leaf with utmost gentleness. She took another deep breath and this time lifted her chin and closed her eyes.

Sid took a deep breath, too. The autumn air felt good in his lungs.

He stared at her. Because of her, he was remembering to look at the simple joys of life.

"We have two more patient transfers today," one of the men grumbled, breaking the serenity of the moment.

"We're not going anywhere until her bag comes," Sid told him in a sharp tone.

Luckily, Jennifer stepped out only a minute later. Sid had every intention of making them wait, though, if it had taken another hour.

The nurse was teary-eyed when she said goodbye to Amelia. She promised to come and see her by midweek. One of the cops gave instructions to the driver regarding the exact route to take to Wallingford. Sid climbed into the ambulance first and the two men moved Amelia in next.

He saw one of the medics was about to climb into the back, too.

"That won't be necessary," Sid told him. "I'm her physician. You can sit in the front with the driver."

The two paramedics looked at each other and then one shrugged. "Sure, Doc. Whatever you want."

One of the cops was standing behind the medic, who was reaching for the door.

"I'll get it," the cop said, taking hold of the door. He was a tall, burly guy with the ruddy face of a guy who spent a lot of time outdoors. He looked at Sid. "What kind of trouble do you expect?"

"I wish I knew. Did anyone tell you what happened last night?"

"Yep. I'm just wondering if we should have arranged for a couple of cruisers."

Sid would have felt better if they had.

"We'll be okay. It's a straightforward stretch of highway, and we're traveling midday." The officer was talking himself out of it. "We can always call for help if we need it."

"That's right," Sid replied. "Just keep an eye open."

"That's what we do," the cop said cheerfully. "We'll see you in Wallingford." He closed the back door of the ambulance.

Sid took his seat on the bench beside the gurney before he looked at Amelia. She was casting anxious glances around the enclosed space. He laid his hand next to hers, and she immediately clutched his fingers. He tried to remember the last time he'd ridden in the back of an ambulance. It had to be when he was an undergraduate student, doing an internship with an EMT corp.

He looked around him, imagining what it would be like to see all of this for the first time. Even more frightening, he supposed, if he were unable to speak or move the way Amelia was now.

The ambulance jerked slightly and they were underway.

"These are just supplies," Sid told her, motioning to the shelves next to her. "Nothing to do with you."

Amelia looked where he'd pointed. A sharp turn caused everything to rattle. Her grip tightened even more.

"Jeez," he said with a smile. "Must be a new driver."

A divider with a cabinet at the bottom and a sliding window at the top separated them from the driver. Sid was tempted to reach over and tap on the glass, reminding them that there were passengers in the back and the patient was stressed enough as it was. To do that, though, he'd have to free himself from Amelia's grasp. He decided against it.

He didn't know how much of her memory Amelia had gained back. Memory recovery in patients covered a wide range. Some never recalled anything of the years they'd been in the MCS state, while others reported details of that gap immediately. What she would remember of the time prior to the accident was also unknown at this point, but Sid knew that she remembered her sister, at least. It wasn't until she regained the use of her voice or improved the motor skills needed to write or type clearly that they could test her on those things.

As far as her involvement in their research study, he knew he needed to proceed very slowly. All of the ethical issues that factored into a patient's family's decision not to participate were now a reality with Amelia. Still, he wasn't going to worry about that for now.

The ambulance was weaving through traffic, with more occasional rattling of equipment. He glared over his shoulder at the driver. The dividing window was closed. Through it, Sid caught a glimpse of the highway. The traffic appeared to be light.

Sid felt Amelia's fingers let go of his. He looked at her hand. She was trying to trace letters on the blanket.

He looked up at her. "Good, I'd much rather carry on

a conversation with you than worry about this crazy driver."

Her fingers continued to move.

He looked around him for something she could write on. Digging into his bag, he took out a pad of paper and a pen. Amelia's left hand was next to Sid. He already knew she was right-handed. He undid his seat belt and stood up, looking over the gurney. The fingers on her right hand were moving, too.

"How about if we make this a little easier?" Reaching over, he carefully placed the pad of paper under her right hand. Holding the pen upright, he wrapped her fingers around it.

Watching her face, he could see she was concentrating very hard, but her motor skills were already improving. The first letter was easy to recognize.

"'*B*,'" Sid repeated.

She blinked. He grabbed hold of an overhead safety bar as the ambulance veered again in the traffic. They were really moving.

"What the heck?" he complained, glancing up at the window. The driver or the other guy had closed the privacy cover on the divider.

Amelia's fingers continued to move on the paper. Trying to maintain his balance, Sid looked over.

"'*Bad*,'" he repeated what she'd written down.

She blinked again and was already writing on the pad again.

"Wait." He repositioned the pad so that she was writing on a clean space. "Okay, go ahead."

Sid focused on the paper as she wrote. She had trouble with these letters but in a matter of seconds what she'd marked became clear.

"'*Gun?*'" he asked.

She blinked. The pencil dropped onto the blanket.

"Bad…gun," he said.

She was staring at him like he was an imbecile.

"Gun…where would you see a gun?" He tried to think why she would think of that word now. "The cops…the police officers by the building. They had guns."

She again just stared. Sid sat down as another weaving movement of the ambulance nearly threw him against the side wall. He couldn't understand the reason for driving like this. He watched Amelia's eyes move upward…toward the front of the ambulance. She tried to lift her head, but she couldn't, lying flat on her back. She succeeded in slightly pulling herself against the straps holding her, and raising her eyes to the window again, before she dropped back down.

"Do *they* have gun?" he asked.

She blinked.

56

After four flight changes and eighteen hours of travel, Shawn Dunlap was bone weary by the time the plane touched down in San Diego International Airport. As soon as the okay came through from the pilot to use electronics, Shawn had his cell phone open and was dialing Helen's number.

She didn't answer.

Shawn dialed the number for Cynthia's condo next. The answering machine picked up there. He didn't leave a message.

He'd tried to take a nap on the last leg of the flight, but he couldn't sleep. He was too worried about Cynthia. He'd spoken to a doctor in the intensive care unit at the hospital while waiting to get on the plane in Gaborone, the capital of Botswana. The information he'd been given then was vague. They didn't have the results back from a number of tests that had been done on her. The prognosis so far was not good. That much was clear.

He'd tried to call Helen from Johannesburg, South Africa, then again from Dakar, Senegal. Each time, there'd been no answer. He'd tried the hospital again at every flight change, as well, but hadn't been able to get any of the doctors on the phone, until his last flight change at Dulles in D.C. Her condition was still touch and go. She had sustained internal bleeding. They were in the process of deciding if they should go ahead with surgery or not.

Shawn knew how Cynthia had always struggled with her mother. Their relationship had reversed at some time when she was in high school. The daughter had become the parent. Helen was definitely the dependent one.

He would have thought that in a situation such as this, Helen would pull herself together and stick by her daughter until he arrived. Maybe she was doing that, Shawn told himself as he followed the line of people leaving the plane. Optimist that he was, he wanted to think that perhaps Helen was back at the hospital, and she had her cell phone off because of hospital regulations.

Shawn didn't wait for his luggage before heading toward customs. Because of the standby status at every leg of the trip, he'd been warned that it might take days before his suitcase arrived in San Diego. He couldn't care less about that now. They'd hold it for him.

He was ahead of the crowd going through customs. A quick swipe of his passport by the immigration officer, and he was heading for the doors to get a cab. Cynthia had dropped him off at the airport when he'd left on this trip.

A line of people stood waiting at the sidewalk for taxis. He decided to call the hospital again. Maybe by now the doctor he'd spoken to would have more definitive answers for him.

He asked for the physician. Shawn was told that the

doctor was gone for the day. He asked for the physician in charge of Cynthia's care at the moment.

"I can connect you to the nurses' station on the floor the patient is located," the operator told him.

"That's fine."

"The name of the patient?"

"Cynthia Adrian," Shawn said. There were two groups before him to get a taxi. There was a traffic jam of cars waiting for travelers, and an airport security officer was directing the traffic in front, allowing only one taxi to pull against the curb at a time.

"Can you spell the name?"

Shawn gave her the spelling. There was a considerable pause on the other side. He figured she was probably transferring the call. He was wrong. The same woman's voice came back on line.

"I'm sorry, sir. But we have no patient under that name at this hospital."

He turned away from people waiting in line. Now he was getting pissed off. "I suggest you check again. My fiancée has been a patient—"

"Mr. Dunlap?"

Shawn turned around and looked at the two men standing a few feet from him. One of them already was holding out a badge.

"Mr. Dunlap?" the man asked again.

"Hold on," Shawn said into the phone before answering. "Yes?"

"Sir, I'm Special Agent Mendoza and this is Special Agent Sirnio. We're with the FBI." The other one took out his badge, too. "Could we have a word with you, sir?"

Shawn could feel the eyes of everyone around them in line.

"Of course."

As an attorney specializing in international law, Shawn had, for most of his career, simply worked on closing foreign business deals. There hadn't been too many times when he'd had to deal with law enforcement officers. He checked their identification.

"Does this have to do with Cynthia?" he asked, guessing.

The one who'd made the introductions nodded.

"She's okay. Isn't she?" he asked. Shawn noticed that his cell phone was still open and the operator was saying something on the other end. He closed it. The agents were not answering, and their faces were serious, giving away nothing.

"Would you come with us, sir? We need to talk privately."

"Why?" he protested. "I want to know what's happened to my fiancée. Is she okay? Where is she?"

"We'll take you to her," Agent Sirnio said quietly.

A minute ago, he'd been told that Cynthia was no longer at the hospital. Shawn shrugged and walked with them to the curb. Immediately, a dark SUV pulled in front and Shawn climbed into the backseat with Sirnio.

The vehicle pulled into traffic.

"What's going on?" Shawn asked impatiently. "Where's Cynthia?"

"We had to move her to another location for her own safety," Agent Mendoza said, turning in the front seat to look at him.

"Her own safety?" Shawn repeated. "What happened to her Sunday morning wasn't an accident, was it?" It wasn't a question.

"We don't believe so." The man turned back in his seat, staring at the traffic.

Shawn waited for either of the agents to say more. Neither did. The driver had said nothing, either, since they'd left the terminal.

"Why Cynthia? And how is it possible that the intensive care unit at a hospital isn't safe?"

More silence.

"Are you going to explain to me what's going on?" Shawn barked. He was too tired to care how they took his tone.

The driver stared at him in the mirror. The agent sitting in front finally turned around.

"We're at a critical stage of a major investigation. No names or events can be released at this time," Mendoza explained. "I can tell you, though, that we had a call from another field office that there could be a possible threat on your fiancée's life. Local law enforcement determined that the details of her 'accident' were suspicious, to say the least. In light of the call we received, we took over this end of the investigation. We set up our own security for the wing of the hospital where she was located. As expected, there was a security breach that could have been part of an attempt on her life. The perpetrators were not apprehended, but we are following leads right now. With regard to your fiancée, the decision was made to move her to a safer location."

Shawn felt he still was in the dark. "The last time I spoke to her doctor, they were contemplating surgery to release some of the pressure building up from internal bleeding in her brain. Was she in any condition to be moved?"

"Yes, she was. And she's already been operated on and our understanding is that a stent was put in. That's all we know."

They were taking Shawn to her. He decided he could

ask his medical questions of the doctor who was looking after Cynthia's care. He rubbed his neck. He was upset, but at least he now felt closer to the situation.

"Helen Adrian," he said, remembering Cynthia's mother. This explained why she hadn't been answering her phone. "I assume she's with her daughter."

"No, she isn't," Sirnio answered. "We've been trying to contact her."

"Did you send someone to Cynthia's condo? She might be there. She can't have just disappeared."

Sirnio shook his head. "She wasn't there. Actually, we were hoping you might know where she is."

57

Connecticut

"Why would they have guns? They're medical personnel."

She blinked. Her fingers started moving again. The pencil was beneath her fingers. He put it back in her fist, and she began to write again.

"Saw?"

She blinked.

"You saw a gun?"

She gave him a long blink and dropped the pencil again.

They had moved her. She had a different view. She thought they were bad. He remembered the pact he'd made with himself to not question her. Sid immediately searched in his case and grabbed his cell phone. She'd been trying to tell him that something was wrong shortly after the two men had walked into the room. He called 911. It took a couple of minutes of rapid explanations before the dispatcher understood the nature of the urgency and agreed to connect him to the police cruiser that was following their ambulance. It seemed to take forever before the officer came on the line.

Sid introduced himself before getting right into it, telling them about what Amelia saw.

"Okay," the officer said. "We'll call for support and stay behind you. As soon as the traffic starts moving freely, we'll have the ambulance pull over."

"What do you mean, when the traffic starts moving?" Sid asked. The ambulance was flying along the highway.

"Just what I said. There's a construction slowdown ahead. So when the traffic opens up—"

"Where are you?"

Pause. "On I-84. The traffic is backed up before the I-691 exit. It shouldn't be too long."

"Well, we're moving. We're not sitting in any traffic jam. Can you see the ambulance?"

"We're right behind it. You're crawling. We don't consider that moving."

The ambulance made another sharp turn. They were off the highway. Sid realized that they'd been off the highway for some time.

"That's not us," Sid told him. "Check for yourself. Look, I just found out that these people are armed. I believe they're trying to kidnap her. Remember what they tried to do last night."

"Where are you?"

"I can't tell. They covered the window to the driver's seat."

The vehicle made another sharp turn, this time to the right. From the sudden rough surface, Sid could tell they had just turned onto an unpaved road.

"We're on some kind of back road. Gravel, I think," he said, guessing from the sound of the tires crunching beneath the vehicle. "Listen, I have to get ready for them if they stop."

"Keep your cell phone on. We'll trace it."

Sid left the phone open and dropped it in his bag. He looked around him for something that he could use as a weapon. His options were limited.

He felt like an idiot for not asking more questions. No one had. Even the cops had assumed these two were legit. And how difficult was it to steal an ambulance? These killers were smart enough to plan out everything last night. How they had got clear of the escort, he had no idea.

The ending would be no surprise. Sid didn't have to wait until the ambulance stopped to know what they were going to do with them. He moved to the back door and tested the handle. It turned. He remembered one of the police officers had been the one to shut the door.

He couldn't jump out of a moving ambulance with Amelia. She could be seriously hurt. Also, the drivers would know as soon as he tried.

Sid felt the adrenaline rushing through him. They could stop anytime. And then it would be too late.

He looked at what he had available. His brain was racing. He looked at Amelia. She was watching him steadily.

"Don't worry. We'll get out of this," he said with as much conviction as he could muster.

She blinked.

Beyond her, strapped to the side wall of the ambulance, two pressurized oxygen bottles caught his eye.

"Oxygen," he whispered to Amelia. "All I need is a match."

58

Nuclear Fusion Test Facility

Staring at the watch gave Marion something to occupy her mind, but it also got her thinking again of what would happen to the region when she was gone. It was a countdown to the end.

The space beneath the elevator was cramped and growing increasingly stuffy. Moving slowly, she could shift from side to side, but she had to be careful not to come too close to the electrical wires. She also wanted to stay out of the light that edged the bottom of the elevator. Her face was inches away from the steel-framed bottom. Listening to every noise, she'd thought that at any minute they'd discover her whereabouts.

She was feeling more and more claustrophobic as the minutes ticked by. She had to take her mind off the tomblike confines. She had to stop thinking about whether there was enough air and worrying what would happen if she had to sneeze or cough.

Pulling the watch from her pocket and staring at the changing digits had given Marion that other horror to think about. The time on the watch was all any of them had left.

The searchers spoke to the man in the elevator above

her every ten or fifteen minutes. They were moving from room to room, carefully going through storage spaces and closets, checking under the beds, and searching above the drop panel ceilings. Opening ventilation ducts.

She stared at the watch face.

Thirteen hours, twenty-five minutes before the first sample leaked.

The man watching the elevator crouched down. He stood. At some point she heard him relieving himself in that same hallway where they had killed two of her colleagues. These men are scum, Marion thought.

Time dragged on.

He was again standing in the elevator door when his radio again beeped. One of the searchers, she heard, was changing into protective clothing and going inside the test lab.

They obviously knew enough that elevated levels of radiation were present inside the lab. Once inside, Marion wondered if they would recognize that there had been a test in progress that needed to be stopped. She doubted it.

She waited, thinking as the time ticked by slowly that perhaps they did know about the test samples and the impending disaster. Perhaps they had come down to find her…but also to secure the radioactive samples.

Eleven hours, seventeen minutes, fifty-seven seconds…fifty-six…fifty-five.

The voice on the radio. No, she had been right in the first place. They had no clue. They were out of the test lab, and approaching the elevator.

And Marion couldn't think of a single place that they hadn't checked.

59

Connecticut

This was no time for second-guessing. No thinking about the fact that he'd been trained to help people and not to hurt them.

Sid checked again to make sure he was ready. He glanced at Amelia, tucked against the back door, the mattress from the gurney wedging her in.

"All set?" he whispered.

Blink.

"I'm going to put the blanket over your face now. Like I said, the glass could go everywhere."

Blink.

Sid gently turned Amelia's face to the door and covered her head, using a box of bandages to create an air passage for her to breathe.

This was it. He'd have only one shot at this.

Standing up and bracing his feet as well as he could, Sid opened the valve on the oxygen bottle, busted the regulator and smashed the head of the tank through the glass separator into the driver's section of the ambulance.

"What the…?" one of the men shouted.

Sid could hear the fast-escaping oxygen and saw the man grabbing the bottle and feeling for the valve.

The driver slammed on the brakes. Throwing Sid up against the divider.

He wasn't going to give them a chance to get out. Straightening up, he lit a match, set fire to the entire book of matches and tossed it through the window at the oxygen tank. He barely had time to duck.

The entire driver's section immediately lit up like a torch, flames shooting into the rear of the ambulance through the window, as well. The two men in the front were screaming.

Ignoring their cries, Sid moved quickly toward Amelia. The sudden stop caused her to slide forward, twisting her on the floor beneath the gurney. He pulled the blanket from her face, and she looked up at him.

Sid shoved the back doors open and leaped over her onto a dirt road. Pulling her toward him, he hoisted her, still wrapped in a blanket, over his shoulder.

They were on a wooded road. He had no idea where. It looked like a fire road. There was no sign of any houses. Just woods on either side. He didn't hesitate or look back. Moving off the road, he ran straight down a slight incline into the woods. He wanted to get as far away from the burning vehicle as possible.

There was no saying that the two might not get out of the burning ambulance. He didn't want to stick around. Also, the odds were that these two had others waiting to meet them. They could be just around the next bend.

Sid was breathing heavily, tiring quickly. Low-hanging branches scratched at them, and he tried to protect Amelia as much as he could by pushing through the thick brush with his free hand. One of her arms had worked free of the blanket, and it was dangling by his butt. No sound came from her.

He didn't know how far they'd traveled when he heard the explosion. A second blast followed immediately after the first.

For the first time, he turned around. Not too far in the distance, he could see smoke rising above the trees.

Sid turned and looked in every direction. There were no buildings that he could see, no paths through the woods. He had no idea what part of the state they were even in. From Waterbury, the highways ran in every direction. His only guide now was the smoke and burning ambulance. He turned his back to it and started again through the woods.

Draped over his shoulder, Amelia had still made no sound. He tried to twist around to get a view of her face. She weighed practically nothing.

"Are you okay, Amelia?" he asked, wondering if he should put her down to at least check on her.

He was relieved when she tapped his hip. She was giving him a sign.

Sid stopped, reached around and held her hand for a moment.

"We're okay," he said. "We're going to be okay."

But they were still not far enough away from the ambulance, and Sid knew it. They were still not far enough away from the people who wanted to kill her.

Taking a deep breath, he plunged deeper into the woods.

60

Nuclear Fusion Test Facility

Ten hours, twenty-seven minutes.

When the searchers all converged at the elevator, Marion learned two things. First, the killers decided that she had made her way into the Test Drift sector of the underground labyrinth. Second, their group was larger than the three men who'd come down to search the facility. The search party had communicated via phone to the security office in the building above. Whoever was up there had told them that the small building sitting atop the elevator shaft leading up from the far end of the WIPP storage facility was being watched. So far, there had been no sign of her.

Terror raced through Marion as she thought about how they would gain access to the Test Drift tunnels. Based on the plans she'd seen, there should have been two doors in the elevator, one to the research lab and the other to Test Drift. But the killers knew that the elevator wouldn't have been available to her. If they decided to follow her steps, then they'd send the elevator up, pry open the doors, climb down the shaft, and climb through into Test Drift.

Except they wouldn't have to go any farther than looking into the shaft. She didn't want to think of that.

An argument had broken out right above her about the safety of going through the Test Drift tunnel. They seemed to know that the subterranean storage facility was operated robotically...and for a reason.

Finally, one of them used the closed-circuit phone in the elevator to communicate with others on the surface. After making the call, they waited for instructions. She could see them through the small hole. One liked to pace, another was impatient to get out of here. The third one, who'd stood guard for the entire time down here, crouched quietly in the door. He said very little, but there was a coldness in the low tenor of his voice that sent chills through her.

Panic once again threatened to overwhelm her mind. The temperature of the air in the confined space had risen. She was sweating. She could feel something crawl on her scalp. She rolled her head from side to side and flinched at the pain shooting through the back of her head. The crawling sensation stopped, but only for a second before starting again.

Marion closed her eyes. She felt as if every inch of her body was hurting. She was exhausted, hungry, thirsty. She wanted to go to sleep and wake up to find this was all a dream. That didn't seem to be a possibility.

Then, Amelia was in her thoughts. Her sister was frightened. Marion wondered if it was her own fear or her twin's she felt. She had to be calm for both of them.

Her eyes opened. She lifted the watch closer to her face.

Nine hours. Thirty-nine minutes. Forty-two seconds. Forty-one. Forty.

The phone in the elevator rang. The man who paced picked it up and listened. "Got it."

Marion heard the other killer approach.

"We go up," the man who'd answered told them. "We're to go up and get the special protective uniforms we need for that side. And dosimeters. And we have to pick up the key that opens the elevator door into the other facility. There are also other keys for doors farther on. We need them."

"She'd have had those keys?"

"She could have. Eaton had a set down here. Let's go."

A surge ran through her. Marion knew exactly what she would do. There was power in the facility. As soon as the elevator went up, she would climb back into the lab. The computers would be back on. She could contact someone, anyone, via the Internet. They wouldn't search the research lab again. They'd go into the Test Drift.

She could contact the outside world for help and then get inside the lab and start the cementation steps.

Nine hours, eighteen minutes. She'd need every minute to secure the test samples.

61

Apparently, there was more to Roswell than UFOs and Area 51.

From the two army pilots who were flying the transport plane, Mark learned a lot about the history of Roswell and what he should see and do. He now knew the location and quality rating of every strip club and live-music bar within a two-hundred-mile radius. The pilots had no idea why he was flying in and he did nothing to enlighten them, either.

Like everyone else who'd ever had even a passing interest in space or in life outside of this solar system, Mark knew about Roswell. He'd read plenty about it as a teenager and even seen the so-called autopsy photos of extraterrestrials. From what he recalled, back in 1947 some rancher had notified the authorities about a crash on his land. Roswell Army Airfield announced, within a few hours, that they had recovered a flying disk. But a few hours after the initial press release, U.S. Army Air Forces officials stated that there was no UFO. They'd simply recovered fragments of a weather balloon.

It wasn't until the 1980s, when the actual reports were released, that Roswell became a focus for conspiracy theorists.

According to the pilots, though, the Roswell UFO incident took place some seventy-five miles away. Actually, the ranch where the crash occurred was closer to Corona, New Mexico…which, in turn, was about thirty miles from the best whorehouse ranch south of the Nevada state line.

Oh, and one of the pilots had nearly been eaten by a three-hundred-pound bear a couple of miles north of Corona. Just in case Mark was going hiking up there.

Fascinating.

Actually, listening to them, Mark thought it peculiar that he was heading to Roswell for what could easily be construed as another conspiracy theory. In this case, though, there were no spokespersons for the event. No online forum to consult. All his information came from a young woman who'd spent six years of her life in a minimally conscious state.

And his own belief that a woman everyone in America thought was dead—a woman he cared about— needed his help.

Mark was glad these guys weren't asking him why he was coming to Roswell.

He had no confirmation that anyone would be meeting him when the plane landed. His chief had made the arrangements from Pennsylvania. But Mark didn't know how successful Chief Faber would be in selling their theory to anyone who could do something about the investigation.

Mark was relieved to see a car waiting near one of the hangars and the two black-suited FBI agents beside it when his feet hit the tarmac. Walking across to them, he shed his jacket in the heat and turned his cell phone on.

A minute later, after seeing their badges, Mark knew his chief had gotten the message across.

"The Waste Isolation Pilot Plan is a government facility, but it's managed by TMC Corp, a private corporation," one of the agents explained. "It might take a day or two before we are able to obtain a search warrant to get inside."

"That might be too late," Mark said, knowing he had nothing more to offer in support of his claim.

The two agents, Botello and Harvey, exchanged a glance.

"We understand the urgency of this situation," Agent Botello told him. "Meanwhile, we are having the layout of the facility faxed to our field office. At the same time, there are agents from the Nuclear Regulatory Commission on their way."

"We can't wait," Mark insisted. "A woman's life is at stake."

"We know how you feel," Agent Harvey said. "We can tell you that we're taking it seriously. We're pulling together a surveillance team right now to watch the WIPP facility. That should happen today."

"Can I be part of the surveillance group?" Mark asked.

"You were recommended to us with all clearances. You can be where you want to be," the other agent told him. "We're glad for the added man power."

They all climbed inside the car. Mark asked the question that had been burning on his tongue. "You mentioned the urgency of the situation. Have there been any other developments since I left Connecticut this morning?"

Agent Botello was behind the wheel, and Harvey turned to answer him.

"Our agents in California have tied an attempt on an individual's life to the death of a director of R & D and to a plane crash that killed a number of other administrators in the New Mexico Power Company. All of that has happened in the past few days. In about an hour, the central offices of the New Mexico Power will be served with subpoenas for their records."

"But the WIPP facility's connection is still a mystery," Mark commented.

"You've had enough aces in the hole that the wheels are turning," Agent Harvey told him. "If you say something is down there, we're ready to jump on it."

Mark's cell phone rang. He glanced at the display. Waterbury Police.

"Hold on," he said to the agents. "This call is from Detective Ricci from Waterbury."

She didn't bother with small talk. "You should know that the ambulance that showed up to transport Amelia to Gaylord was stolen."

"And you discovered that before she got in it," he said hopefully.

"No."

Mark swore profusely under his breath. They'd told him that she'd be watched around the clock. This couldn't be happening.

"So they have her?"

"We believe she might be okay."

"How's that?" A ray of hope sparked in his gut.

"Dr. Conway was in the ambulance with her. He suspected something and called us. That's when he realized that the police escort wasn't behind them."

Mark waited, forcing himself to be patient, allowing her to continue.

"We'd been tracking his cell phone but the signal

stopped. About ten minutes ago, the fire department in Wickfield called the state police. There appears to be a fire burning in the woods at the White Memorial Nature Preserve. We don't know if that has anything to do with the missing ambulance or not. But it's in the same general direction that Dr. Conway's last call came from. We have fire department and state police on their way right now."

Sid was no cop, Mark thought. But he was young and smart. If he'd discovered something was wrong before they got to him, there was hope.

"These guys are persistent," Ricci stressed. "We thought you might want to have an update."

"Please call me back when you find them."

62

Connecticut

Sid wanted to kick himself for leaving his cell phone behind. But there'd been too many things on his mind. His priority had been to get the two of them out of that ambulance.

The woods were quiet. He could still smell the smoke but he could no longer see it. The trees were dense, and walking between them was becoming more difficult. They had yet to cross a path or any buildings. They'd reached a marshy area, forcing them to veer off.

Twenty minutes later, they saw a small dry clearing beneath an ancient oak tree. He had to stop and decided this was as good a place as any.

"Are you still okay, Amelia?" he asked gently. She gave him no sign.

He moved next to the tree and carefully lowered her off his shoulder. Her eyes were wide-open. She was looking at everything around her in awe. From being upside down on his shoulder for so long, her face was flushed with color. She looked healthier than he'd ever seen her. Sitting her down, he tried to lean her back against the tree. She fell to her side, her face sinking into the leaves.

"I'm so sorry," he said, scrambling to help her. "I'm not treating you too well, am I?"

He sat her up again. Sitting down next to her, he propped her weight against his shoulder and the tree. Leaves were stuck in her short hair and on her face and nose. Somewhere along the way she'd lost the headband she'd been wearing. Brushing the leaves off, Sid noticed she was smiling.

"Do you think this is funny?" he said in mock angry tone.

There was no blinking of the eyes. This time she slowly nodded, still smiling.

Sid shook his head. She was amazing. Based on what he'd already seen, he figured her recovery would come in leaps and bounds from here on.

"Are you cold?" he asked, touching her hands. Her fingers were cold. She was wearing only hospital socks and no shoes. He pulled the blanket around her and placed her hand in his.

She traced the word *no* in his palm.

Sid put an arm around her anyway, pulling her closer to his side. His heart was still racing. He couldn't believe how close those people had come to killing them. His mind turned to the two men who'd been sitting in the front seat of the ambulance. Sid wondered if he'd killed them.

He leaned his head against the tree and closed his eyes. He had done the right thing, he told himself.

She was tracing letters in his palm. He looked down.

"OK?" he said aloud. "Me?"

She blinked.

He nodded. "I'm okay now."

A breeze ruffled the leaves and brought with it a whiff of the smoke.

"The police should find us soon. Connecticut isn't a huge state. And that ambulance is still creating a lot of smoke. We'll be okay."

Sid looked down at her. Amelia had her head on his shoulder and her eyes were closed. She'd fallen sleep.

63

Nuclear Fusion Test Facility

Marion heard the footsteps in the elevator. She stared up at the floor, waiting. It seemed like hours, but the doors finally closed. She heard the sound of gears and bearings sliding smoothly into position.

As the elevator started up, the temperature of her prison immediately dropped, and she felt as if she were being sucked off the ground. The elevator moved slowly at first and then, like a rocket being launched, shot upward through the blackness above.

Darkness surrounded her once again.

She knew there wasn't much time. Marion reached into her bag and pulled out a second flashlight that she had stuck in there earlier. She turned it on as she sat up. It worked, in spite of the drop.

Her back hurt. Her joints were stiff. Her arms felt like they'd fall out of their sockets if she moved them too fast. She looked at the watch.

Eight hours, forty-three minutes left.

As she stood up, her right ankle almost buckled under her. She'd forgotten about landing on it when jumping down the ladder. She didn't have time for this now, she thought, putting her weight on the other foot.

Standing there, Marion realized another dilemma faced her. From where she was, the doors to the lab were high, nearly at shoulder level. She had to somehow get them open. She found the same bar she'd used to open the doors from the lab side, but she knew she had very little strength left in her shoulders. Stacking both bags against the wall, she used them as a step to get a better angle to pry open the door.

As she lifted the bar, she realized she'd crossed a point during these past few days. Nothing stopped her. Pain was only a bump in the road. Anxiety was merely a nuisance. Whatever slowed her down or created a barrier, she could get past it.

Marion jammed the bar between the two doors and pulled. The doors started to open a couple of inches but immediately slammed shut again. She needed to wedge something between the doors. She'd used the hammer before. But she didn't know if she could keep the doors open long enough to get something between them.

Determined to succeed, she didn't slow down. She jammed the bar in again. Putting all of her weight behind it, she managed to slide the tip of the bar in farther, opening the door an inch.

"Come on. I don't have a lot of time," she cried softly, pulling the crowbar sideways. "Open."

And then, like magic, it happened. The metal doors slid open. She looked up in surprise.

A boot appeared, holding the door open, and Marion tumbled backward.

The voice was low and cold. "I knew you'd show up sooner or later."

Marion stared up at the killer, the machine gun in his hands, knowing she now faced the one hurdle that she could not get past.

64

There was a time when Joseph Ricker liked being center stage. Not anymore.

Not when he considered the mess he found himself in the middle of. Out of the limelight suited him just fine right now. In fact, Joseph was starting to think it was far better to be an extra, rather than the leading man. That way, he didn't have to hang around and see how everything ended.

As he left the office, he told the driver that he'd get himself home. There weren't too many times that Joseph did that, but tonight was an exception. He didn't trust anyone.

Flagging down a cab, Joseph stopped at an ATM on the way to his condominium apartment and took out the maximum allowable cash withdrawal for the day. The amount was paltry, but he wasn't going to bring any attention to himself. The branch was still open, and he could have gone in and written a check, but he chose not to. He wasn't about to empty his accounts. He regularly moved his funds, so he wasn't worried. He could complete the transfer of what was left anytime.

Long-term planning was Joseph's forte. His passport

was always current. He'd saved up a healthy percentage of his salary over the years, dispersing much of it and keeping a solid chunk of cash in a safe at home. Getting on the next flight and disappearing to any country in South America was always within reach.

Pulling up in front of his building, Joseph considered having the cab wait, but then decided against it. He wasn't going to be home long. He didn't want to feel rushed.

Today had not been a good day. In fact, during the past twenty-four hours, everything he'd touched had gone sour. He was dealing with imbeciles. Suddenly, it seemed nothing could go right. No, he told himself, actually, one thing had gone right. The idiots had managed to recover the document that Fred Adrian had sent his daughter. Nellie Johnson had called to tell him about that.

Still, statistically speaking, he was deep in the hole. The first reports from New Mexico revealed that Marion Kagan's body wasn't in the lab. He'd decided to keep that little detail from his boss. At least for now. That was a preliminary report, he reasoned. There was no saying that they wouldn't find her once they conducted a thorough search of the facility.

He wondered, though, if his boss already knew more than Joseph. While he was still in the office, there'd been a message from Martin Durr. He wanted Joseph to come to the house later tonight.

No way in hell was he going there. He wasn't that stupid. Even Nellie, who always thought she was a favorite of Durr's because she took care of some of his jobs herself, had sounded nervous on the phone. Too many strange people were poking around their offices. And this morning, there'd been a number of meetings behind closed doors at the power company headquarters.

He could feel the ground shaking. It was time to get out.

Joseph didn't stop to get his mail when he walked through the lobby. A sense of urgency had taken hold of him. He planned to be on a plane and in midair by the time Durr figured that he was a no-show tonight.

The elevator was crowded. Joseph didn't socialize with anyone in his building; he recognized no one. The turnover on the leased apartments in the high-rise was frequent, he'd heard. He barely recognized the faces of the people who lived in the units adjacent to his. He pressed the button for his floor and noticed that he was the first stop.

A middle-aged couple was waiting by the elevator doors on the seventh floor when Joseph got out. He ignored them, pulling out his key as he moved down the hallway. His mind was already putting together a list of everything that he needed to do. Despite the fortune he'd spent on his suits and ties and shoes, he knew he couldn't pack a suitcase to take with him. That would be too obvious. After eight years of working for Martin Durr, he knew how deep his network of spies ran in Washington.

A bag with his cash packed into the lining. A few essentials. His passport. That was all he needed.

The phone inside the apartment was ringing as he walked in. He let the answering machine pick up as he went into the hall closet for his shoulder bag. Whoever had been calling his phone didn't leave a message.

Being organized had its rewards. Packing his bathroom supplies took no more than a minute and he stuffed them into the shoulder bag.

Joseph went into his bedroom and dropped the bag next to his bed.

Opening the closet door, he looked wistfully at the tidy line of suits, jackets, dress shirts, slacks, the rack of ties. The shoes were the most difficult to leave behind. He shook his head at the temptation and crouched down on the floor. Removing the two-tier shelf of shoes, he exposed the door of the safe.

He was spinning the knob when the phone started ringing again. Joseph focused on the combination, disregarding the phone.

The door of the safe swung open. He knew exactly how much cash he had, mostly in large bills, five hundreds and thousands. He knew there wasn't enough here to retire on. But there was certainly enough to buy him a year or two of living comfortably and give him a chance to find another line of work.

The voice on the answering machine stopped him dead. He sat back on his heels and listened. In all the years Joseph had worked for him, Martin Durr had never left him a message. But he was leaving one right now. Joseph was stunned.

He stood up and walked out into his bedroom.

"I've tried your cell phone several times, Joseph. This is my second call to your apartment. I know you consider the cell phone an extension of your hand…"

Joseph stared at the machine.

"Anyway, I know I asked you to come over later tonight so that we can get some work done. But I have to postpone that. I totally forgot that my wife wanted me to go with her to the Young Concert Artist Series at the Kennedy Center. You know I'm working from home tomorrow, but call me when you get to the office in the morning. Maybe we can get together tomorrow afternoon."

The call ended.

"Since when are you interested in the performing arts?" Joseph continued to stare at the phone. "*Maybe? Maybe* we can get together tomorrow afternoon?"

His mind was racing. This was not the Martin Durr he knew.

Joseph had turned off his cell phone when he'd left the office. That was stupid, but he'd made up his mind. He was leaving the country and getting as far away as possible from Durr. It didn't matter. He tried to focus on the positive. He didn't have to go to Durr's house tonight. That meant he could take his time packing and getting to the airport.

He dismissed the option as quickly as he considered it. No, there was definitely something wrong. Durr sounded downright civil on the phone. That feeling of urgency again crept in. Hurrying back to the closet, he quickly fit all the cash into the bottom lining of his bag.

Joseph knew his boss better than he got credit for. Durr was covering himself. That call was the kiss of death.

He grabbed a pair of Italian leather loafers that he'd bought only last week and stuffed them on top of the money with the bag of toiletries. On top, he packed a pair of khakis, two shirts, and some underwear and socks. Going out of the bedroom, he zipped the bag shut and swung it up on his shoulder.

Joseph turned off the lights as he went through. By the front door, he turned around and took one last look at his apartment. He wondered what would happen to his things once he was gone. Collecting the furniture and the few modest pieces of art had been a labor of love. He switched off the light and opened the door.

The only family he had left was a younger sister in

Chicago. He hadn't seen her for years. He always regretted not doing his part to stay in touch. She was a good kid, one of those people who had her hand in a dozen things to help her community. She sure had tried to stay in contact with him, but had given up after a while.

He guessed she'd end up with everything. But that was assuming someone would declare him dead. Missing didn't automatically call for an estate settlement. It would be years.

Joseph went out into the hall, thinking that maybe he didn't have to stay away forever, anyway. Stranger things had happened. Durr might end up in jail and Joseph could be a key witness.

That was a possibility he hadn't considered until this moment.

As Joseph slid the key into the dead bolt, he looked up and down the hall. It was empty, but the elevator suddenly seemed miles away. Pocketing his keys, he hurried toward it.

Perhaps, he thought, he should be going to the police instead of going to the airport.

As he reached for the elevator button, he hesitated, startled by the sound of the adjacent utility-room door opening behind him. He turned in time to see the silencer on the handgun appear from the darkness inside.

Two shots were fired, driving Joseph back against the elevator doors. As he slid to the floor, his assailant came toward him, the gun aimed for the kill shot.

Just before he saw the flash, though, Joseph thought of his sister. She'd have no trouble inheriting his things, after all.

65

Connecticut

The change came on like a fast-moving storm. One moment she was sleeping peacefully. The next, Amelia shivered violently. Sid guessed she was having a seizure. He held on to her face. Her eyes were open. Her muscles were tense.

"You're okay, Amelia. We can work this through. Stay with me."

He'd taken his jacket off a while ago, and he quickly folded it now and put it under her head. He laid her down on her side.

She suddenly stopped breathing.

Sid recognized what was happening. Amelia was having a tonic-clonic seizure. During the tonic phase of this seizure, the patient sometimes temporarily stopped breathing. The muscles, including chest muscles, stiffened for a short period of time. He gently touched her face.

"We can get through this. Come on, Amelia."

He kept track of the second hand on his watch. Her face was getting darker. From his experience, this kind of seizure didn't require CPR, as the patient would soon begin to breathe again on her own. He tugged at the neckline of the sweatshirt, making sure it wasn't pressing against her throat.

Forty-five seconds.

"Come on, Amelia."

At the very moment doubt plunged an icy hand into his brain, she took a shallow breath. Then she took another breath. And another.

"You're doing great. Come on."

He continued to keep track of time. She was still shaking. But her eyes now were watching him. Sid reached over and took her hand. She held on to him.

"It's over. You're okay."

She started crying. Tears rushed down her face. He picked her up off the ground and gathered her against his chest. A soft sob escaped her. Her mouth moved. Incoherent sounds escaped her lips.

"You've been under a lot of stress. Also, you might be dealing with a sugar imbalance or mild dehydration. Nothing to be frightened of."

She took his hand and letters started forming on his palm. He was able to decipher what she was writing right away. *M.*

"Marion?"

The slight movement of her head indicated yes.

"You were thinking of your sister."

She stared writing on his palm again. There were more letters this time. At some point, he lost track.

"Start again," he told her.

She started again. He looked down at her fingers tracing letters on his palm. *D...A...N...G...*

"Danger?" he asked.

Another nod.

"Marion is in danger?"

She confirmed by tapping her hand on his before

starting to write again. He knew the next word as soon as she began. *W...I...*

"WIPP?"

She nodded. He shifted his body until he was looking into her face. Tears glistened on her cheeks. He brushed them away.

"I know."

The sun was going down. She was shivering, but he knew this wasn't because of a seizure. She was cold.

"WIPP," she wrote again on his hand.

Amelia wasn't thinking about cold. The concern was for her sister.

"Mark Shaw is on his way there," Sid assured her. "In fact, he might have already arrived."

She didn't seem at all convinced.

Sid considered their options. The smell of smoke had disappeared. He couldn't see any sign that the fire was still burning. Not too long ago, he'd heard a siren in the distance that he'd guessed was a volunteer fire department signal. Whoever had arrived to put out the fires must have succeeded by now. It was only a matter of time before they'd come into the woods looking for them.

Perhaps they had...but didn't know what direction to go.

The breeze was picking up. The temperatures dropped down into the thirties overnight. This past week, there'd even been hard frosts several times. He couldn't have her spending the night outside.

Amelia started tracing letters on his hand again. She wasn't giving up. Still, he had no option. The decision was clear.

"We're going to try to find our way back to the ambulance before it gets too dark," he told her. "That does two things for us. We might find someone to help us, and once we find someone with a phone, we can contact Mark and you can hear his voice yourself."

The look of determination on her face told him that Amelia would stand on her two feet and lead the way herself if her body would cooperate.

Sid just hoped there were no surprises for them along the way. They'd escaped one near-death experience. He was afraid they wouldn't be so lucky the next time.

66

Nuclear Fusion Test Facility

Marion knew she only had seconds before the man pulled the trigger.

"The lab…the samples that are in there…they have to be stopped or the entire Southwest will be destroyed," she said hurriedly, looking up from the bottom of the shaft. It already felt like a grave. "We were in the middle of testing when…when you killed the others. The clock is ticking. The containers are exposed. And we're sitting next to a stockpile of nuclear material."

He raised the weapon, ready to fire.

"That's the only reason I was trying to come back in here. Please, talk to someone. Ask their opinion. This is more than killing one person. You'll be destroying this region for the next thousand years. This will be the largest nuclear disaster in history. You must have family. Think what you'll be doing to them. Think how *their* children will suffer."

Marion was amazed by her own courage. Pleading, reasoning, was the only thing she could do—the only way she could fight him. He wasn't wearing a mask this time. The man pointing the gun at her was of an age that he might have a family. She already knew that asking for compassion for her would never work. Not when she'd seen how brutally they'd killed the other scientists in her group. She had to stress the things that *he* could lose.

"How could you—one person—stop it from happening?"

She was relieved when he spoke. He wasn't a machine following orders. There was hope.

"The cementation technique. I have to seal each container. They started leaking when the power went off."

"The power is now on."

"Yes, but the leakage already started. Some of these samples were intended to fail. The only way to stop everything from going up, including the storage site next door, is to completely seal each container."

"How many containers are you talking about?"

"Nine." She saw no reason to lie. At this point, her only focus was on stopping the nuclear accident.

"How do you know you're not already too late?"

"I did the calculations when the power went off. I've been keeping track of how much time is left before the first containers start releasing hydrogen into the test lab. If that starts to happen, we're all dead."

She held out the watch so he could see it. She glanced down at the numbers.

"We have eight hours and twenty-three minutes left," Marion told him. "This is a lengthy process. I *have* to get started right away." This last bit of information was a lie. But she guessed he wouldn't know that.

He stood there, thinking. Marion knew she'd introduced at least the element of doubt. She was still alive.

Suddenly, he bent down and laid the crowbar in the track. The doors closed until they reached the bar.

"You wait right there," he ordered. "Step back against the far wall and don't move."

Marion did as she was told. She had no place to go. Going up the ladder wasn't a viable option. Neither was trying to open the door to the Test Drift facility.

He backed away from the door and disappeared, but she could tell he wasn't far away. She could hear his voice, talking on the phone.

For the moment, anyway, she was alive.

67

Roswell, New Mexico

Agent Jerry Harvey spread the blueprints on the faded, splintered picnic table and ran a hand through his thinning red hair.

"So what are we looking at?"

Three other agents had met them at the deserted restaurant and filling station five miles from the airport. Everyone's attention was on the drawings they'd brought. One of them spoke up.

"These are the plans of the WIPP storage facility that TMC Corporation faxed to us."

Mark looked carefully at each page as Harvey and the others studied the drawings. Finally, Harvey shook his head.

"There's nothing that resembles a habitable work area anywhere," the agent said. "This supports what we already knew. The facility is a hundred-percent robotic. Actual inspectors go down there only occasionally for short periods of time to monitor the integrity of the containers."

"Did TMC build this facility?" Mark asked.

"I don't believe so," another agent answered. "Right

now, they're in the middle of a ten-year contract. They took over the job from the Department of Energy."

"I'm not a lifer, as far as military service," Mark said, "but I do know that the policy of working with contractors is to give them as little information as they need to know. Is there any way we can get the layout of the facility from the group that actually built it?"

Botello and Harvey exchanged a look that said they'd had this conversation before.

"The DOE is impossible about releasing classified drawings," Botello replied.

"I understand. But I think, given the circumstances, they can at least give us a simple answer." Mark motioned to the blueprints spread on the table. "We need to know if this is the extent of what's there."

"Interesting point," Botello said, looking at Harvey.

"I'll make some calls," Agent Harvey agreed, walking back to their car.

Agent Botello motioned to Mark to follow him. When they were ten feet from the others, he stopped him.

"You strike me as a guy who has a lot at stake here."

Mark looked steadily at him. "A lot? Absolutely. I'll do whatever it takes, including going down there myself and searching through that facility."

68

The Kennedy Center, Washington, D.C.

Nellie Johnson was ambitious. She had guts and presence of mind. She was young. She had expensive tastes. She was hands-on. She knew exactly what was going on and what they had to do.

As far as Martin Durr was concerned, she was just exactly the person to take over for Joseph Ricker…for now.

Communication, though, was an issue. She was in New Mexico. He was in Washington. She had to be able to contact him—especially tonight. Martin would have to break his cardinal rule of not using electronics for sensitive communications. For that reason, he'd brought his BlackBerry with him.

It was only ten minutes into the dance performance when he felt the soft whir of the device vibrating in his pocket.

"I have to get this. I'll be back," he said under his breath.

Despite his wife's obvious disapproval, Martin stood up, worked his way to the end of the row and moved quickly up the aisle to the back of theater.

An attendant closed the door behind him. Durr

looked around the spacious lobby and approached a greeter wearing a name tag. He asked her where the public phones were located.

She pointed out two places in the far corners of the lobby. They were both too public.

"Any others?" he asked.

"Let me see." She thought for a moment. "Oh, yes. There's a public phone on Parking Level A, at the entrance to the lot."

Durr started in that direction, taking the BlackBerry out of his pocket and checking the text message. Just as he'd thought, it was from Nellie. Short and to the point.

Call me.

Martin Durr was breaking his own rules, but he was being extremely careful about it. There'd be nothing incriminating in this call. Nothing for anyone to trap him with. He was still on the board of directors of New Mexico Power, and it was absolutely understandable for Nellie to contact him—especially with all the changes the organization was going through right now.

There was no one on Parking Level A, which suited Martin perfectly.

He dialed the secure number he had for her. She answered immediately.

"Good news. Your missing item has been found."

He knew she was talking about Marion Kagan. This was good news. That only left the twin sister. He hadn't yet heard anything from the group sent to eliminate her.

"I'm good here. You can talk. Did they proceed as they were instructed?"

"Actually…not entirely," she said. "The subject is

claiming that certain objects she was handling need to be sealed or a Level Seven accident will occur."

Martin knew enough about nuclear accidents to know that a Level Seven accident was the most catastrophic. But that didn't affect him. He could care less if that entire state went up in smoke. In fact, something of that magnitude would shift everyone's attention to the cleanup that had to follow. Now that he thought of it, there could be money made in that, as well.

"Finish the job," he instructed.

"Sir, if I may. I know enough about the issue at hand and the location of the objects in question. I strongly recommend that something be done."

"Where were you when the original directives went out?" he asked, not liking to be second-guessed when he gave an order.

"Sir, I was never privy to specific details."

Nellie wasn't stupid. He still didn't like it.

"Are you going to make the call or should I do it?" he asked, letting his anger come through in his voice.

There was a slight pause before she spoke.

"I'll make the call," she said finally. "And then I'm on the next flight out of New Mexico, sir."

Durr had never taken her for a coward. But he guessed everyone had to have a vulnerable spot. He'd found hers.

69

Waterbury, Connecticut

Kim Brown had never expected that she'd feel like this. The sense of loss was crushing.

During the flight from Montana, she'd relived so many memories from Amelia's childhood. She'd gone over everything that she'd done wrong. She got herself ready to tell Amelia what she wanted to do for her now. How she wanted to make things right.

She was asking Amelia for a second chance…to be the mother she'd never been for her before.

But she'd arrived only to find out she might have lost Amelia again.

Kim wasn't told the danger her daughter was in until she arrived at Bradley Airport. There, she was met by police detectives and Attorney Viera, the lawyer she'd spoken to on the phone.

She wanted to be angry at them for keeping her in the dark, but she couldn't. Not when she realized everything they were doing to try to find Amelia. If only she'd insisted on a fraction of this effort the last time her daughter had gone missing…

They'd made a reservation for her at a Courtyard Hotel at Wallingford, but Kim didn't want to be dropped off there to wait. She agreed to be taken to the hospital where Amelia was supposed to go…before the ambulance was stolen. She wanted to be someplace where she'd get news of her daughter. Kim was relieved when Attorney Viera stayed with her.

There was a lot that she seemed not to know about what was going on. Viera hinted that the testing and experiments that were done on Amelia might have been responsible for her coming out of her minimally conscious state. She met two neurologists who arrived at Gaylord with a van full of equipment. They knew her daughter, and they were partners of Dr. Sid Conway, the doctor who had been in the ambulance with Amelia.

Viera waited with Kim in a small conference room that was adjacent to a kitchen used by staff. The attorney's tone with her was cool but civil, and he shared with her the content of any calls he received from the police. The latest news was that Amelia and the neurologist were not found in the ambulance that had taken her from the care facility. The ambulance itself was on fire. The police believed Amelia and Dr. Conway had escaped the burning vehicle.

Kim didn't know what to do or what to say. She was even hesitant to ask questions. All she could think of was how heartless she must have sounded when the lawyer first called her. She wanted this man's trust. He'd been in charge of Amelia's life for six years. And he actually seemed to care. She could tell on the phone, and even more so in person, that this attorney was committed to taking care of the young woman who'd been put in his charge.

Kim wanted him to wipe away whatever negative opinion he had of her. She wanted him to believe that she cared for her daughter.

A member of the staff poked her head inside the room and told them that there was fresh coffee in the kitchen if they wanted it. Viera wearily got to his feet to go get a cup.

Kim decided to say what was on her mind.

"I know I didn't make a good impression on you the first time we spoke," she said quickly. "I'm honest enough to admit I wasn't a model mother for my daughters, especially for Amelia, before she ran away. But things have changed. I am—"

"I don't need any explanations, Ms. Brown," he interrupted. "I'm the court-appointed conservator. My responsibility is to see that Amelia's care is—"

"Please listen to what I have to say," she pleaded. "I need to say this…not for you or me, but for Amelia."

He looked at her for a long moment before sitting back down at the table across from her.

Kim nodded in gratitude. She tried to think through what she was going to say.

"I…you…"

She cleared her throat and closed her eyes for a second, trying to focus on what was important.

"You're right in not wanting to hear my life story. And it would be selfish of me to try to excuse my actions because of how disappointed I was with my life." Kim looked across the table, holding his gaze. "What's important for you to know is that during this past week, I've received two blows regarding my daughters. I don't remember exactly what I said or how I acted in each case. One thing I do know is that I didn't come across right. I know I sounded indifferent and cold."

It was easy to get emotional. Just saying these words made her want to cry. She tried to keep her voice steady.

"I've done a lot of thinking this past twenty-four

hours. I've been given a second chance at life with Amelia...possibly even with Marion. I'm not going to make the same mistakes. I'm not the person I was twenty years ago, ten years ago, or even a week ago. I am here to try to help Amelia and not make life more difficult for anyone, especially her. Please understand that I'll do whatever is necessary, whatever her doctors and you think is best to help her recovery. I'll do my best to be a help, not a burden."

He was silent for a moment, then looked down at a legal pad and a pen sitting on the table. On it she could see the notes he'd taken whenever someone called.

Viera nodded and looked up. "I appreciate your honesty, Ms. Brown, and I'm relieved to know that we're on the same team. One thing you should know is that we have absolutely nothing that confirms your other daughter Marion is alive, other than Amelia's claim."

"Then I believe it," Kim said. "Those two girls are connected to each other in ways that are totally unexplainable. And that's been true for all their lives. If Amelia says her sister is alive, Mr. Viera, then you can believe Marion is alive."

70

Connecticut

Five minutes after they started back toward the ambulance, Sid and Amelia ran smack into a search party.

State police, the local volunteer firefighters, plain citizens. When he first saw them through the woods, his first impulse was to run. Regardless of their badges and their obvious relief at finding them, Sid was not quite ready to trust anyone. But with so many of them out there looking for them, he had to give an inch.

"Where are we?" he asked one of the state police officers in the first group that reached them.

"White's Woods," the man told him.

"Wait a minute." Sid thought about it. "In Wickfield? We're up in the northwest part of the state?"

"That's right. Where did you think you were?"

Sid knew exactly where they were. There were dirt roads and trails that snaked all through these woods. Even a wooden boardwalk that ran across acres of marshland.

Two police cars and an ambulance were brought in close to where they were found. Amelia was carefully placed on a gurney and carried to the ambulance, where her vitals were being checked. Sid didn't go more than two steps away from the open doors of the vehicle.

"What happened to the two men who were in the front of the ambulance?" he asked the same state trooper.

"One didn't make it. The other is in intensive care in Torrington." The trooper shook his head, letting him know the second one didn't have much of a chance. "We need to get you on the road. There are reports that need to be filed, but we can complete those once your patient is transferred to Gaylord."

"Will I be charged for what I did to them and to the ambulance?"

"I very much doubt it. We've already established that they were kidnapping you and your patient. You acted in self-defense against killers."

"What do you mean?" Sid asked. "Do you know who the men were?"

"We haven't positively ID'd them yet. But Waterbury police *have* found the bodies of the real drivers who were dispatched to the care facility."

"And what about that other ambulance that the police were following by mistake?"

"Whoever's behind all this had somehow arranged for that ambulance to go off to Gaylord at just the right time for what the drivers thought was a pick-up. They were pretty surprised when the cops pulled them over on the highway."

Sid rubbed his neck. *What were they in the middle of?*

"She's ready to go," the person checking on Amelia announced, stepping down from back of the ambulance.

"Is anyone from Waterbury on their way here?" Sid asked, wanting to eradicate the last seed of doubt. After what they'd been through, he wasn't going to take any chances, even when it came to trusting people in uniform.

"Two detectives from Waterbury should be here any-time now," the officer told him. "We're going to meet them at the Conservation Center out on Route 202."

It was completely dark outside now. The wind was picking up and it was considerably colder.

"I think she's trying to say something," another officer standing nearby told them.

Sid looked inside and saw Amelia trying to lift her head off the bed. Immediately, he climbed in.

"We hang around here a couple of more hours, and you'll be well enough to drive the ambulance to the hospital yourself."

The hint of a smile broke on her lips. She looked pale. The EMT personnel's recommendation was to connect her to an IV, but Sid hadn't allowed it. Not yet.

He had to be a hundred percent sure that nothing here was tainted. He knew that wouldn't happen until he saw a familiar face. Even at that, he didn't think his mind would rest until she was safely settled in at Gaylord.

He saw the movement under the blanket and drew her hand out. Her fingers were moving.

"We are getting good at this, aren't we?" Sid asked, placing his hand under hers. *M…A…*

"Marion," he said aloud. He remembered what he'd promised her about calling Mark.

Sid poked his head out of the ambulance and asked if he could use someone's cell phone. One of the officers handed him his.

"Damn it," Sid said, sitting down. "I had Mark's num-ber in my cell phone. Let me see if I can remember…"

He saw her hand move. She was giving him the number.

"You were still MCS when you gave us his phone number," he said. "But you remember it."

She nodded.

It might be days or months, but Sid couldn't wait until she regained the use of her vocal cords. He had hundreds of questions for her, perhaps thousands. She was truly a phenomenon.

If Sid was happy when Mark answered, the man at the other end was absolutely ecstatic to hear his voice. Mark had spoken to different people in Waterbury and he knew that the ambulance carrying Amelia and Sid had been hijacked. Sid assured him that they were both fine and got to the reason he'd called.

"Amelia has been insistent on wanting you to know that Marion is in danger. She's stressing the name of the same facility again and again."

Mark sounded frustrated. He explained to Sid that they were waiting for search warrants and had yet to identify an area where Marion and her group could have been working.

Before ending the call, Mark had one last suggestion.

"Listen, this might sound stupid, but I don't know what else to do."

"What?" Sid asked.

"If you could just ask Amelia to get her sister to send me a message…a text message on my cell…something. If she could give me a clue where she is…"

That *was* a long shot, Sid thought. But stranger things had happened. After hanging up, he told Amelia what Mark had requested, word for word.

She simply stared at him, giving no indication whether it could be done or not.

71

Nuclear Fusion Test Facility

"How much time?"

Marion looked down at the watch. "Five hours and forty-two minutes."

"Why haven't they called back?" the man asked, pacing back and forth in the hall.

Marion sat with her back against the wall. He'd pulled her up out of the elevator shaft, but sitting next to the open door was as far as she'd been permitted to go.

Nothing was settled. She wasn't any better off here than down in the hole. A dozen steps away lay the decomposing body of Andrew Bonn, a grim reminder that death was looking at her right in the face.

"Why aren't they coming down?" the man muttered aloud.

Marion decided to answer. "Because the danger is real. There's a very real possibility that there are airborne radioactive particles in this area now. Your friends don't want to expose themselves to the hazard."

"Who told you to talk?" he snapped at her.

Marion shut her mouth and leaned her head against the wall. She wondered if getting killed could possibly hurt more than all the pain she'd been enduring these past few days. Death didn't scare her. On the other hand, a generation of children born with serious birth defects caused by a nuclear disaster was a tragedy that tore at her insides. The clock was ticking.

"How much time?" he asked again.

"Five hours, twenty-nine minutes," she said.

He continued to pace. Marion looked around the hall. Precious time was being lost. She didn't want to wait for someone else's decision on this. She feared what that decision might be, anyway.

She wished she had the crowbar now. When he'd dragged her up out of the elevator shaft, he'd kicked it back in and let the doors slide shut. There was no way to get it.

He paced fifteen steps one way. Fifteen steps back. There were times when his back was completely turned.

She looked down at her swollen ankle and wondered if she had enough strength to somehow get away from him. Marion looked up at his back. He was twice her size and easily three times as athletic.

"How much time?" he asked on his way back.

She held the watch up. "Why don't you just take it?"

His obsession with the ticking clock gave her a perverse satisfaction. She'd successfully planted the truth inside his head. He could kill her and walk away, but she didn't think he wanted to be responsible for a nuclear holocaust.

He waved her off and turned his back to her again. Marion looked around. A glass-front emergency fire cabinet like the one by the maintenance closet was bolted to the wall three steps away from her. She eyed the ax. Right above it, she could see the surveillance camera. The light was blinking.

She'd thought everything was being taped to reduce their record keeping. It was a lie. She suspected there was a live feed on every camera to a security monitor upstairs. The camera was stationary, incapable of panning across the area. She tried to guess what portion of this hall the film captured. It seemed to be directed at Andrew Bonn's feet.

A phone rang down the hallway inside the control room. It was the line that she'd heard him using to talk to his partners at the surface. That line only went to the security office in the building at the top of the elevator shaft. During their first days in the facility, they would get a call whenever the elevator was being sent down. The day of the attack there'd been no calls, though, and no one had thought to question it.

"You don't move," the man ordered, stepping over the scientist's dead body and striding down the hall.

Looking battered and weak, Marion was no threat in his eyes. As soon as the killer disappeared, she pushed herself to her feet and, ignoring the excruciating pain in her ankle, hobbled over to the cabinet containing the ax.

"What?" she heard the man snap in disbelief.

Marion tried to pry open the glass door, but it wouldn't budge.

"She's *not* crazy. You saw all the 'radioactive' signs down here! It doesn't take a fucking genius…"

Marion hit the window with her elbow and the glass splintered inward. The man was now yelling into the phone. He obviously hadn't heard her. Carefully pulling the ax from its cradle, she moved over next to the hall leading to the control room.

"I can still take her out. But *first* I should let her shut this stuff down."

Marion adjusted her grip on the handle of the ax. She looked up at the camera. There was no way she could be in view.

"How can the order be *no?* You went into that lab. Didn't you see all kinds of stuff set up?"

It was obvious that the orders were clear. Whoever was behind this didn't want anything shut down. Marion had always been of the belief that even hard-core criminals had some basic good in them, just waiting for the right moment to blossom up. Circumstances of desperation made people do wrong. Hearing that someone was willing to risk killing or maiming an entire generation of people blew her mind.

"I'm just saying I don't like it," the man bellowed into the phone. "I know she's not lying."

There was a pause. It took all her strength to lift the ax over one shoulder.

"Yes. I've got it." Pause. "Right…whatever. Send the elevator down." Pause. "I said I've *got* it. Send it down."

Marion held her breath. She saw the tip of the machine gun come through the door before she saw the rest of the man. She aimed for his head and the ax came down hard. The blow was a glancing one, of metal off bone. Involuntarily, she shut her eyes as she swung.

She opened them just in time to see him go down. The gun clattered to the floor, and she heard him groan as he sprawled out on the tile.

She couldn't hit him again. He moved his arms and legs as if he was trying to crawl, and then lay still. She could hear his labored breathing. At least he wasn't dead.

Marion glanced up at the camera. She was certain the man's body hadn't landed within view of it, but she wasn't sure about the machine gun.

Dropping onto all fours she reached one hand out and quickly pulled the gun along the floor to her. The weapon was heavier than she expected it to be, and as she looked at it, she wondered if she could actually point it at someone and pull the trigger.

"I can't," she murmured. "I know I can't."

Picking up the ax in the other hand, she started down the hallway toward the lab, pausing only to throw the gun into a trash room.

She had just one thing now she needed to do…seal the sample containers.

In a minute she was standing at the door of the test lab. She punched in her code, and the lab doors opened. Going in and closing them behind her, she activated the locks and assessed the situation.

Inside the first room of the lab area, two cameras were mounted high on the walls. She managed to smash them both with the ax. Next, she moved to the computer and started bringing up the security parameters for the test lab.

The people who'd been sent down here had detailed knowledge of the facility. They had the codes to get in and out of every room. They knew the layout of the facility better than she did.

The first thing she had to do was change every password and access code.

While waiting for the files to upload, she checked her connection to the New Mexico Power R & D group. There was no live help online.

"Of course not."

She opened a new e-mail message.

I am in the URL adjacent to Test Drift facility at WIPP. Killers on site. Please help. Marion.

She addressed it to her department head at the College of Engineering, UC Davis. She had to tell someone that she was still alive.

With her finger on the send button, Marion paused.

She didn't know where the idea came from. But all of the sudden, it made sense.

She opened her cell phone and turned it on. The battery was nearly dead. Pulling up Mark's cell phone number, she sent the e-mail to his number, as well. Wherever he was, he'd get it as a text message.

Marion didn't have time to try to remember anyone else's e-mail. The security screens had come up. She tried resetting the passwords. A dialogue box immediately popped up. She didn't have authorization to make the change.

"No," she moaned aloud. She had forgotten that she was only a peon in this project.

Her next priority was to start the cementation steps. She turned on the equipment.

She then looked around her in growing panic. They might think she had a machine gun, but that wouldn't stop them forever. Clearly, they were experienced killers who'd faced weapons before.

The walls of the test labs were layered concrete, lead and steel. The doors were lead and steel, as well. But she had no way of locking them out, short of knocking out the power. And if she did that, she wouldn't be able to complete the cementation process.

As lame as it seemed, moving furniture in front of the door appeared to be the only possible way she could think of to slow them down.

Marion knew they were going to get to her eventually. But before that happened, she would secure these test samples…or die trying.

72

Legal or criminal.

Nellie Johnson knew how laws were made. She'd seen firsthand how the power company coaxed and lobbied and bribed legislators into passing laws that favored their self-interest. She knew how it all worked. Right and wrong had very little to do with legal and criminal in the real world.

So long as Nellie felt there was a justifiable motivation behind an action, she didn't bother with the formality of how that action was perceived under the law.

Even killing Fred Adrian was justifiable. Young people were sent to war to die every day. And not just in America's defense, but in defense of America's business interests. Maybe this was the same thing, she reasoned. Killing and dying in the interest of business. That was the real world.

They would never have been able to buy Fred's approval to kill the nuclear project. He had to be taken out of the picture. The same applied to the R & D people in the plane. Nellie was even okay with Cynthia's accident, despite the fact that she liked her personally.

This latest decision regarding the elimination of

Marion Kagan before the experiment could be made secure…that she couldn't understand.

Martin Durr sat in his mansion back East without a care in the world. It wouldn't bother him if New Mexico disappeared off the face of the earth. He had nothing to lose. Nothing at stake. He just didn't care.

But Nellie cared.

There were three suitcases open on her bed. She'd already called a limo service and booked her seats on a flight out.

She called her mother in Albuquerque. Angela Johnson's answering machine picked up. Nellie tried her cell phone next. When there was no answer, she tried the home number again, this time instructing her mother to pick up.

Angela didn't bother to answer her phone whenever one of her favorite television shows was on. A second call and Nellie's voice bellowing into the answering machine always worked like a charm, though.

Angela answered.

"I'm picking you up in two hours, and we're heading to the airport," Nellie said into the phone.

"Who died?"

"No one, not yet. But if you're not ready to leave with me by the time I get there, you will die."

The first suitcase was jammed full. Nellie pushed the top down and sat on the edge, closing the locks.

"Stop with the dramatics," Angela told her.

Nellie could hear the TV blasting in the background. "Turn the darn thing off, Mother."

The sound seemed to go up rather than down.

"I'm giving you time to pack some of your stuff," she said into the phone. "But if you're not ready when I get there, I'm taking you with only the clothes on your back."

Nellie started filling up a second suitcase. Other than the sound of the television set, she could hear nothing else on the other end.

"Mother, did you hear me?" Nellie asked.

There was nothing.

"Mother?" she screamed.

The sound of the TV died. "I was waiting for the commercial to mute the sound," Angela told her. "So what were you saying?"

The doorbell rang. Nellie figured it had to be the limo service. Tucking the phone between her neck and shoulder, she closed the second suitcase and pulled them off the bed.

"I'm picking you up in two hours. We are getting on a flight to New York City," she said into the phone.

"What for?"

"It doesn't matter what for," Nellie told her. "I'm just telling you to pack and be ready. I'll tell you more when I get there. Please pay attention. This is very important, Mother."

The doorbell sounded again.

"How long do I pack for?" Angela wanted to know.

Nellie started pulling the suitcases toward the front door. "I don't know. Two weeks, three weeks…maybe more."

"That's way too long. I can't go away for that long and not tell…"

Nellie dropped the phone on a table as she reached the front door. She knew how her mother was. She was a chatterbox and had a zillion friends. If she knew what was going on, half the fifty-five-and-over population in Albuquerque would know in a matter of minutes. With the resulting traffic, Nellie and her mother would never get to the airport in time.

She looked out the security peephole. A man in a driver's uniform was in the hallway. She opened the door.

"You can take these two bags to the car. I have one more suitcase that will be ready in a sec—" Nellie stopped, looking at the silencer of the gun aimed at her heart.

She didn't have time even to turn around.

Angela Johnson's voice could be heard on the phone.

"...can't just get up and go like that. Seriously, Nellie. Who died?"

73

Dealing with the Department of Energy was giving Mark Shaw a colossal headache...and he was only a listener on the field conference calls. Special Agents Harvey and Botello had spoken to four different people within the DOE bureaucracy, and they still didn't have the right person who could tell them what they were looking for.

The good news was that the message was getting across. Everyone was trying to help. Finding the right person, however, was the challenge.

The way Mark understood it, the underground facility dated back to the early 1980s, and there were numerous engineering groups who'd been involved with it over the years. To obtain the official copy of the facility drawing, they were initially told they'd need to wait until tomorrow morning, during business hours. To get what they were looking for any sooner, they would have to find one of the engineering project directors who'd actually been involved in the latest stages of the site development.

No one, however, seemed to be able to come up with a name, and there seemed to be no quick answer.

Agents Harvey and Botello were trying to convince the current person on the phone to authorize overtime and bring someone into the print room to pull the files of the WIPP facility. As the agents were playing their best good cop–bad cop routine, Mark felt his cell phone vibrate.

He looked down at the display. He had a text message.

Mark opened the phone to read it.

"Marion," he said aloud, forgetting the other conversation. "She's alive."

Both FBI agents stared up at him.

"I have a text message from Marion Kagan. It's right here. It was sent only a minute ago from a New Mexico Power Company e-mail address."

Harvey was telling the DOE engineering director to hold the line.

"What does it say?" Botello asked.

He read it aloud. "'I am in the URL adjacent to Test Drift facility at WIPP. Killers on site. Please help. Marion.'" Adrenaline surged through him. He had to do something right now.

"What's URL?" he asked the DOE engineer they had on the phone.

"Underground Research Lab."

"Is there an underground lab attached to the Test Drift facility?" he asked in a rush. "How do I get there? Where's an entrance? How do I get down?"

"I don't know if there *is* an underground lab next to that facility," the person on the phone said.

"Then you better find out," Agent Harvey barked into the phone. "And if there is one, find out how we can get into it. We'll call back in five minutes. See what you can find out."

They ended the call.

"I know you need to wait for a search warrant," Mark told the agents. "But I'm a private citizen. I'm going to WIPP right now. I'll break into the place if I have to, and you can arrest me later. But I can't wait around anymore. We have reason to go in there. She needs help."

No one argued with him. Botello was the one who spoke up.

"Come with me. I'll arrange for your transportation."

"He should be armed," Harvey recommended.

"I'll make those arrangements, too."

Mark looked at the two agents, surprised that they were taking a chance of being named as accessories to what he was doing.

Harvey stood in front of him. "Raise your right hand. I am hereby deputizing you as a federal agent. Your assignment is to maintain surveillance of that WIPP facility until the search warrant arrives."

"As for what you do when you're there…" Botello shrugged. "If you determine that you need to go in because a crime is being committed, well, you do what you need to do. You're a trained law enforcement officer."

"But we need to keep a direct line of communication open," Harvey ordered.

Mark knew that the agents understood what he was going to do. FBI procedures would not allow them to storm that facility without a plan worked out for going in and coming back out. And that wouldn't happen until they had complete authorization for their actions. It was understood that, officially, they hadn't heard him say what he was going to do. That part of the conversation had never taken place.

74

Nuclear Fusion Test Facility

Four hours and ten minutes.

The process was extremely slow. Marion didn't know if she had enough time to finish cementation sealing of all the containers. All this effort would be for nothing if someone busted into the lab and killed her before she was finished, anyway.

Still, Marion argued with herself, each container sealed would lessen the risk of explosion and, even if it all went up, reduce some fraction of the long years of nuclear contamination.

Step by step, she told herself. Just keep going.

Nonetheless, she was surprised the killers had not stormed the lab yet.

"Don't think about them," she told herself. "Think about what you're doing."

She looked through the special layered glass window of the test housing of the sample containers. The cementation process was primarily used for casting the inside of a hazardous material shipping container. Using the overhead lifts, Marion maneuvered all the supplies she needed into place, including a number of larger containers, and started the mixing.

The entire process was fairly straightforward. The cementlike homogeneous aggregate material was prepared by combining inorganic compounds with water. The mixture was then poured into the space between an inner storage containment vessel—in this case, the individual test samples—and a larger outer container. Once the test samples were encased, she needed to vibrate the mixture inside the larger container to fill any spaces, and then begin the subsequent process of curing, baking and cooling to solidify the material. This solidified material formed a protective enclosure around the test-sample containers. That would stop them from emitting the hydrogen gases that would start the chain reaction of explosions.

Because of the size of the fixtures and the ovens, Marion knew she could only go through the process one container at the time. She had done the calculations and knew which of the nine test samples was most critical. That was the one she started with.

Marion put on the gloves and protective clothing. As much as the chance of ever getting out of this facility alive was nearly nonexistent, she had enough fear built in not to skip any safety steps.

She checked the watch right before she took the first container out of the case. Three hours, fifty-five minutes.

The cement mixture was ready. She placed the first test sample in the larger container and started the pouring process.

The computer beeped. *An e-mail.* Elbow-deep in the project, Marion looked over. She couldn't leave what she was in the middle of, but her hopes buoyed tremendously.

Someone had answered her.

75

Nuclear Fusion Test Facility
Ground Level

Even in the daylight, anyone wandering through the Chihuahuan Desert—that vast, arid land of red sand and clay, dotted with the daggerlike clumps of lechuguilla, prickly-pear cactus, honey mesquite and ubiquitous desert scrub—would think the two-story concrete building was just a deserted relic of another era. A line of rusted garage doors faced a square patch of cracked tarmac that one might assume had once, long ago, been used as a landing pad. A broken-down barbed-wire fence identified the boundaries of the facility. On the roof, an old crane sat, barely visible from the ground.

Behind the building, out of sight of the dirt road, an SUV was parked, the driver standing beside it. The tip of the cigarette glowed as the man smoked.

Night had fallen quickly, and darkness had swept across the desert before his very eyes. Nearly an hour ago, he'd been told to come out and have the car ready. The rest of them were supposed to be out in minutes. Nothing had happened since.

The man turned to the building as one of the garage doors opened, spilling light into the darkness.

"What's the holdup?" he asked.

"Jay is still not up."

"Has anyone called him?"

"He's not answering," the one who'd come out of the building explained.

"How about the cameras?"

"Something went wrong. The rest of us are going down."

The driver knew he wasn't being told everything, but that suited him just fine.

"I'll stay here," he said quickly.

He'd seen the greenish color in the faces of the two who'd first come up. Those dead bodies must be stinking the place up down there.

"I want you to wait inside so you can hear the phone. In case we need you."

The driver pocketed the car keys and followed the other man in. He didn't care where he waited, so long as he didn't have to go down into that facility.

76

Waste Isolation Pilot Plan

Chain-link fence with rolls of barbed wire on top. A security post and a gate. Dozens of buildings were spread out over a few acres. Spotlights illuminated every corner, making the facility shine like the moon in a dark sky.

Parked behind a low rise next to the other FBI vehicles that had set up surveillance on the facility, Mark Shaw was feeling a bit overwhelmed. He had no idea where to even start looking for Marion. He checked his phone to see if there'd been any other messages from her. None.

He looked down at the drawings that they'd received from TMC Corp. They'd gone through it with a fine-tooth comb, and there wasn't a single area where they could pinpoint any research lab.

Mark decided he had to get past the security gates. Once inside, he hoped that Harvey and Botello would have more specific information for him from the DOE.

He got out of the car and joined the other agents who were waiting in the darkness. He already knew everyone here was expecting to have a search warrant in hand by eight o'clock tomorrow morning. To Mark, though, that was a lifetime away. *Killers on site.*

"There's only one person working security in the booth by the gate," one of the agents told him. "We've received permission to tap into the phone lines. We can create a distraction…"

Mark reached for the phone vibrating at his belt. It was Harvey.

"We just had a sketch faxed to us from DOE," the agent said.

"What have you got?" Mark asked, moving away from the others.

"There's another facility. It's a nuclear lab. Underground. It butts up against the WIPP facility, but DOE's documents show the facility was shut down back in the nineties."

"Where is it? How do I get in there?" Mark asked.

"If you come back here, we're putting a team together now. Technically, it's still a government facility. We don't need a search warrant."

"How do I get there from here?" Mark asked, impatient.

"You won't find any street signs out there. Get behind the wheel and I'll have one of my men here direct you to it via GPS."

77

Nuclear Fusion Test Facility

Marion had the first four test containers working, though each was at a different stage of the procedure. She couldn't get another one started, though, until the first came out of the oven.

She glanced at her watch. Two hours, forty minutes.

Sweat beaded on her brow. Her skin was crawling, and a feeling of pins and needles had spread across her shoulders and back. Lack of food, drink and sleep meant nothing. Fear was driving her. Her gaze kept darting uncontrollably to the door.

By now the attackers had to have realized something had happened to their partner.

This was her first chance to take a step away from the samples. She removed the gloves and went to the computer to read the e-mail she received.

Her heart kicked. She stared at the e-mail in disbelief. It was from Mark's cell phone number.

I'm in Roswell, NM. I know where WIPP is. But where are you exactly?

She didn't know how complicated it was to get through the Test Drift to reach where she was. She had to tell him that there was another elevator shaft. A different entrance.

But what about the killers? He'd run right into them.

Before she could type anything, there was the sound of another e-mail. This one was from Mark, too.

I found where the lab is. I'm coming.

Marion wanted to jump up and down in joy. This wasn't a figment of her imagination. He was really coming.

Her fingers started flying on the keyboard. There are at least two armed people at the top. Here to kill me. Everyone else dead. One killer below badly injured. She looked at the watch. Only two hours nine minutes left till disaster.

The lights on the door lock keypad lit up. They were here.

She pressed the send button.

78

"The building looks deserted," Mark said into the phone. The headlights from his car shone on the two-story building. He was parked in an opening in the fence where, at some point, the entrance to the facility must have been.

"Are you sure?" the agent on the phone asked him. "The drawings in front of me pinpoint the entrance of the lab as right where you're sitting."

There was a click on his phone. "Wait a minute. I'm getting a call or a message. I have to check this. I'll call you back."

Mark ended the call. He had a text message. It was from the same e-mail address Marion had contacted him from before. He read the text.

"She's here," he murmured, immediately turning off the headlights of the car. He called the agent back.

"We have the right place." Mark told him exactly what the message read. "I don't know what two hours and nine minutes means, but it doesn't sound good. I'm going in."

"Wait for backup. It should be less than ten minutes before the first team reaches you."

"I can't wait."

Mark ended the call and got out of the car. Drawing the FBI standard-issue Glock 9mm from its holster, he started running toward the building.

He didn't know what the chances were that they hadn't seen his headlights. There was nothing he could do about that now.

What was left of the driveway circled around the structure to the back. Trying to stay low, he followed the path until he reached the back corner of the building. Peering around the corner, he saw the SUV parked by the line of garage doors. Mark looked around. The only way to get into the building seemed to be through one of those garage doors. The building looked like a fortress.

He decided he had to find a way to draw them out. His options were limited. He ran toward the car. There was no one inside and the doors were locked. He saw the red blinking light on the dash.

"Thank God for security," he whispered under his breath.

He slammed the driver's window with the butt of the pistol and backed quickly away as the SUV's lights started flashing and the alarms started blaring.

79

Nuclear Fusion Test Facility

They were either having trouble with the door code or they were worried that she might be armed.

Torn between continuing with the cementation process or standing by the door with her ax in hand, Marion finally laid the ax down on the table she'd moved in front of the door. She had to keep going.

The first container was now through the cycle. Marion had to keep moving all the rest through the steps and start the process on the fifth one.

She put the protective gloves back on and went to work. Her gaze never wavered too far from the door, though. They were out there, but they were hesitating. She'd moved a heavy cabinet and a table in front of the door, but she knew that wouldn't hold them for long—if at all.

She had the first in the series out of the oven when there was a loud bang against the door. She put the sample down and ran toward the door as the second bang moved everything an inch. The door was unlocked.

Marion looked around her for anything she could use as a weapon—anything that she could use to slow them down. She'd have a hard time swinging that ax more than once.

The torch caught her eye. The portable rig was there for welding containers in certain test setups. She'd learned to use it in a lab two summers ago, but she never thought she'd be using it for this. She discarded the gloves, turned on the gas at the tank, and unrolled the torch's rubber hoses. Quickly, she moved with the torch and striker to the side of the door.

Marion jumped at the next smash to the door. This time everything moved a couple of inches. She spotted the man's hand slip through the crack. He was trying to wedge his arm in for leverage.

She fired up the torch and leaned over the table.

He screamed in pain, yanking his arm and hands out.

Marion slammed her body up against the table and shoved the door shut.

The sound of the machine gun outside startled her, but the door only vibrated with the shower of bullets. Nothing came through.

"Steel and lead layers, you bastards," she murmured.

She didn't know how long she could keep them out. She could only slow them down. At least she was giving them reason to pause.

She glanced down at the watch again.

One hour and thirty-five minutes left.

She couldn't wait. Marion put the gloves on and went back to her emergency assembly line.

80

Nuclear Fusion Test Facility
Ground Level

As the garage door opened, Mark pressed himself flat against the building.

Taking the butt of Mark's revolver to the back of the head, the man inside crumpled against the vehicle and slid to the ground.

Mark swept the pistol around, peering into the open bay of the building. The place looked empty. Keeping one eye on the open door, Mark patted down the unconscious man. He found a well-used HK pistol inside the man's jacket and put it in his own empty shoulder holster. That was the only weapon the man was carrying. No wallet or ID, but he took the keys to the SUV and tossed them away into the darkness.

Leaving him on the ground, Mark moved inside the building.

The garage doors opened onto what looked to be a large shipping area. Other than stacks of folded cardboard boxes in a Dumpster against one wall, there was nothing else there. Straight ahead, he saw an elevator set in a cinder-block island in the center of the building. A lit, glassed-in office was next to it and a set of stairs went up one side of the structure.

Moving across the open space, he could see the stairs led to a door on a small landing a flight up. The elevator machinery, Mark decided. A steel ladder continued to a door to the roof. Access to the crane.

Mark ran quickly to the empty glass office and slipped in. To his right, there was a line of computers and screens. The area was set up as a surveillance office. There were images on the screen. He moved closer. One view showed what looked like the feet of a corpse. His gaze swept grimly across the other screens. Dead bodies, scattered in a number of rooms, were visible on a few. Several screens were not functioning. Movement in one of them caught his attention. Two men were using a rolling table to try to shove open a door. They were both armed.

"Marion," he whispered. That was where she had to be.

He ran to the elevator doors. On the way here, the agent had told him that the lab was more than two thousand feet below the surface.

His finger hovered over the elevator button. If he pressed it, he might alert the two armed intruders. They or another member of their group could be waiting for him at the bottom.

He forced open the elevator door. A gaping hole greeted him. He looked at the cables disappearing into the darkness below.

Leaning into the shaft, he looked up. Above him, half the space was open to the crane on the roof. He could see the hook in the dim light. The other half of the space was taken up by the platform holding the huge elevator wheel and the electric motor that turned it. The cables, looped around the wheel, would begin to move as soon as the elevator started its ascent. If he was on the way down and someone started coming up, he was in trouble.

On the side of the shaft, a ladder ran down into the darkness. It would take him too long to climb down that ladder.

Mark made up his mind.

Going back into the surveillance room, he looked at the screen where he'd seen the men. One of them was crouched in the corner, holding his hand and arm. The other was staring at the door, gripping an Uzi.

In the corner of the room, a box of old maintenance tools sat, half-hidden under a greasy tarp. Yanking the tarp away, Mark found a pair of gloves. Digging deeper, he found something he could use. Pulling the chain wrench from the box, he slipped his pistol into his belt, donned the gloves and went back to the open elevator door.

It was going to be a long way to the bottom, but this was his best chance.

Wrapping the chain wrench around the elevator cable, Mark ratcheted it until it was nearly tight. It would need to work like a brake. He just hoped it was strong enough to hold his weight.

Holding the handle of the wrench in one hand, he grabbed the cable with the other and swung out into the open space. His legs wrapped around the cable and he began to slide.

By the time he had descended what he thought must be halfway, the muscles in his arms and back were screaming. The chain wrench helped Mark control his downward speed to some extent, but the friction on his other gloved hand and on his legs still burned right through the protective covering.

But Marion was at the bottom, he told himself.

Close to the bottom, his grip on the cable grew weaker and he felt himself starting to slip faster. Leaning more heavily on the handle of the wrench, he realized he was not more than twenty feet away from his destination and coming down too fast. Ten feet above the roof of the elevator, Mark put all his weight on the handle. The chain snapped. Clutching desperately for the cable, he tried to slow himself, but he couldn't. The pulley apparatus was just beneath him when he let go, and he hit the roof hard.

Even as the loud bang of his landing reverberated in the shaft, Mark shook off his gloves and drew his pistol from his belt. He stayed on one knee on top of the elevator for a long moment, flexing his hands and listening for any sound in the elevator or outside the shaft. Nothing.

It took him only a moment to find the emergency access door on the top of the elevator. Pulling it open, he ducked his head through the opening. Seeing no one, he quickly dropped down into the elevator and moved through the open doors into the research lab.

The putrid smell of the body in the open area hit him like a slab of bad meat. In front of a hallway leading into the facility, the body of a man in gray overalls lay face-down in a pool of blood. Moving to him, Mark started to check for a pulse, but stopped. The bullet wound in the man's temple told him all he needed to know.

Mark looked around him, deciding which direction he should go.

And then, the sound of gunfire sent him quickly down the hallway in front of him.

81

Nuclear Fusion Test Facility

One hour, fifteen minutes.

All nine containers were out of the test fixture. Two had gone completely through the cementation steps. Another one was ready to come out.

There were repeated blows against the door. Marion tried to shut out all other sound and focus on what she had to do. Minutes ticked by and she continued to work steadily.

She knew the time left was under an hour now, but she didn't want to look at her watch.

Suddenly, the wall just above her head exploded, showering splintered fragments of concrete around her. She looked up at the hole in the wall and then back at the door. The bullet had missed her head by two inches.

"Close," she snapped. One of the men had an entire arm inside the door. In his hand, he was waving a gun.

She threw the gloves aside and grabbed the torch again.

"I'm trying to save your miserable life—your children's lives," she screamed, not knowing where this energy was coming from.

The man squeezed the side of his head in and fired

another shot that clipped the sleeve of her shirt. Not giving ground, her eyes focused on the torch as she lit it. Marion saw his eyes widen and she rushed toward the door. Instead of firing again, he backed away.

Marion didn't slow up, hitting the table again with her hip and driving the cabinet hard against the door, shutting it. Extinguishing the torch, she dropped it on the floor and moved back to the samples.

The third one was ready to come out of the oven. Using the overhead lift, she carefully took it out and began to move the others along in the process.

Suddenly, there was another shot. She glanced over as three more shots were fired in rapid succession. They were outside the door.

"Mark?" she asked under her breath.

Marion looked down at her watch. She had only fifty-six minutes left. She had to finish pouring the cement into the last container and get it at least to the curing stage before time ran out.

The sound of more gunfire outside drew her attention. It sounded like it was farther away, in another part of the facility.

Marion kept working.

There was more gunfire, somewhere nearby again… and then nothing. It was this silence that almost killed her.

A knock came at the door.

"Marion?"

It was Mark's voice. Her heart began to race.

"Marion, are you all right?"

"Mark! I'm here! I'm fine," she cried out. "Don't come in. I need to finish sealing these containers. Forty-nine minutes…that's all I have left. Please…go up. Wait for me up there…"

"No," he called through the door. "I'll be waiting for you here."

He had come for her. He was waiting for her.

With tears of relief and happiness streaming down her face, Marion turned and went back to her work.

82

Nuclear Fusion Test Facility

Mark Shaw was a seasoned cop. He'd been to war. He'd seen death in every form. But nothing he'd ever seen or experienced matched up with what Marion had lived through in the past five days down here. The bodies of her fellow scientists were scattered throughout the facility, every one of them bloated and decomposing. The stench was horrific.

The three others that were not in such an advanced stage were equally dead, nonetheless, two by his hand.

A phone rang in the Control Room, and he answered it. It was Special Agents Harvey and Botello. He told them briefly what had happened and what they were going to face down here. He also told them that Marion was apparently continuing to work on stopping some kind of radioactive leakage.

Harvey told him that they'd already contacted the NRC and the DOE. They were bringing in emergency teams from Los Alamos, and a team from Roswell was on its way.

Mark sent the elevator up and went back to his place by the door of the lab where Marion was working.

He looked at his watch. He'd been keeping track of

the time since the text message he'd received from Marion. She had less than two minutes left.

He leaned against the wall across from the door. He had a million things that he wanted to tell her. He glanced down at his watch again, wondering vaguely if he was going to have the opportunity.

"One minute," he whispered, looking up at the door again.

The muffled sound of furniture scraping across the floor came to him.

He stood up straight.

The door opened slightly. "I can't do this. I can't move them."

"Back up," he said.

Mark threw his weight against the door and it opened a few inches. Putting his shoulder to it, he pushed, feeling it move again. He could hear her pulling at the furniture, trying to help him from the inside.

And then the door was open.

At first, Mark didn't recognize the battered shape that limped toward him. Dried blood, dirt, drawn eyes, chapped and bloodied lips.

"You waited," she said through her tears.

He gathered her into his arms. He knew who she was.

"Too long. I've been waiting for you way too long."

83

"I just came from speech therapy and she's not there yet," Sid said accusingly to the nurse on the floor where Amelia was situated.

He didn't have to mention the patient by name. They all knew who he was and why he came here seven days a week. The study that Sid and his partners from UCONN were doing was a topic of interest to everyone. But of more interest to the staff was the fact that they all believed there was a romance blooming between a certain patient and a certain doctor.

"She has a very special visitor today," the nurse told him with a smile. "I thought it was more important for the family to spend some time together. Don't you agree?"

"Family?" Sid asked, just as he saw Mark come out of Amelia's room.

He forgot about the nurse and went to the other man, shaking his hand happily.

"I didn't expect you back on the East Coast until tomorrow."

"They couldn't keep Marion in the hospital for another day. She was threatening the doctors and nurses with violence."

Sid had been talking to Mark every day. They had hospitalized Marion because of the bullet that was still lodged in her skull and because of the radiation she'd been exposed to while working in the lab during the last hours before being rescued. Mark seemed happy for now to stay with Marion. As far as what he planned to do in the future, he'd told Sid that it all depended on which part of the country Marion ended up settling in. Because of her involvement in the research in New Mexico, she would have options, that was for sure.

"How is she doing, physically?"

"Good, for now. As you know, she's being operated on here in New Haven next week to get that bullet out, but the doctors that we talked to yesterday sound confident that they'll have no problem with it. Recovery will take a while, but they all say she'll mend just fine. She couldn't wait to come East and see Amelia."

And see their mother in the bargain, Sid thought.

Kim Brown was far from perfect, but he had to give her credit, she was trying hard. He could see a dramatic change in Amelia, knowing that Kim was there and that she cared. Most surprising was the friendship that had sprung up between Kim and Jennifer Sullivan, who'd stopped in almost every day to check on Amelia.

"Where are they now?" Sid asked.

"I think I heard something about a solarium? Someplace Kim said Amelia likes to be taken to?"

Sid knew exactly where that was. He'd already spent many hours there with Amelia. And he was happy to say that the two of them had no problem communicating.

As far as Amelia's memory, there were gaps in what she could remember. She had no memory at all of being dumped on a highway on a winter night. Sid hoped that whenever the time came that she remembered that, he'd be there with her and help her through it.

Amelia's rate of recovery was something for the record books. She'd already given up the feeding tube. Her speech was progressing. She could sit upright in the wheelchair and had a much greater range of motion with her arms. The physical therapists were now working on building her leg strength. Mark knew all of this, as Sid had been giving a daily report over the phone to Marion.

The two men started for the solarium.

"Any more news about the investigation?" Sid asked.

"That's why I stayed behind just now. I was on the phone with the FBI in Albuquerque."

"What's going on?"

"Apparently, they're tracking a number of criminal activities across the country that all seem to be related. They think there's a single figure behind it all, and they have a good idea who it is, but they've been frustrated in nailing him."

"They have no leads?" Sid asked.

"Leads?" Mark repeated. "They have leads. Like the secretary to the director of R & D at New Mexico Power, who was found dead in her apartment the same night that Marion was found. There were packed suitcases next to her body. She was obviously going somewhere, but hadn't given any notice of it to her employer. Also, that same night she'd spoken to a member of the company's board of directors on the phone. Now, that guy claims that he'd been speaking with Nellie Johnson regularly because of the reshuffling of staff at the company."

They went through a set of double doors.

"And that's not the end of it," Mark continued. "The assistant to this same board member was killed that same night in his apartment building in Washington, D.C., the victim of an apparent robbery. It's just too co-incidental that the two homicides, Nellie Johnson and Joseph Ricker, were in contact with each other almost constantly during the days before their deaths."

"So the suspect is the board member," Sid said.

"Suspect, yes. But they have nothing solid on him," Mark said. "I'm glad that I'm not working on the investigation. These guys feel like they're chasing their tails."

Sid forgot what they were talking about the moment they came around the corner into a sitting area, where large glass windows let in golden shafts of warm after-noon sunlight. Sitting in a wheelchair facing him was Amelia. Her gaze immediately lit up when she saw him. She smiled and he felt that familiar tightening in his chest that he'd been getting lately.

The two women sitting with Amelia stood up.

Sid said hello to Kim before turning to Marion.

"Finally, we meet in person," the young woman said, taking his hand warmly in hers.

The resemblance between the two sisters was as-tounding. He could now better understand Mark's re-action the first time he walked into Amelia's room.

"I can't thank you enough for everything you've done for my sister," Marion said.

Sid smiled at Amelia and put his hand on the arm of the wheelchair. "I didn't do a thing. It was the two of you, working together."

"We needed a lot of help," Marion corrected him.

"They couldn't have done it if you hadn't been able to decode what Amelia was trying to tell everyone," Kim told him.

"Dr. Future Hotshot," Mark teased him. "Take the credit."

They all knew he hated to take credit for anything this special. Sid believed the bond between the two sisters would triumph over any difficulty.

Thankfully, the conversation moved on. Kim started saying something about how incredible it was to have both her daughters here, together. She also told them that, next week, the girl's grandfather was flying to Connecticut to see them. Dr. Baer, Amelia's physician in Waterbury, had even arranged for the older man to get outpatient therapy at Gaylord while he was here.

Sid felt Amelia's fingers move over his. He took her hand and looked down. Her lips were moving. He brought his ear down to her lips and heard the slight murmur.

"Thanks," she whispered, pressing her lips lightly against his cheek.

84

Rancho Bernardo, California
Three weeks later

"Are you sure you're ready for this?" Shawn asked.

Sitting in the passenger seat of her fiancé's car, Cynthia looked up at her condo. This was her first time back here since the day of her accident. She'd been released from the hospital last week and had moved to Shawn's apartment. She was selling the condo. The real estate agents were supposed to go through next week. Shawn had already spoken to a moving company that was going to take care of what she wanted to keep. She was leaving behind some of the big furniture.

The police had found Helen's body in a Dumpster behind a grocery store twenty miles away. The reports confirmed that she'd been taken by force from the condo. She was strangled, they told her.

Cynthia had lost both her parents in a matter of weeks. Both of them murdered, she knew now. Everything was related. The death of the scientists in the research lab, the plane crash, her parents' homicides. It went on and on.

The authorities knew that the destruction of the platform in the Gulf had been a cover-up for the killing of the researchers, but there were so many unanswered questions. They still didn't know who was responsible for it all.

Cynthia knew the answer lay with the report she'd held in her hands the day of the accident. The same report that her neighbor had handed to Helen the morning her mother was taken from here and killed. The same report that undoubtedly was destroyed.

"Honey?"

Cynthia realized Shawn was waiting for an answer.

"I'm ready. I really want to go through this place one last time before I get rid of it."

He came around the car and helped her get out. She would be on crutches for another three weeks, at least. Shawn opened the front door and helped her in. She knew the condo had been dusted for prints after her mother's body was found. Shawn had told her that the police had done a clean job. There had been no damage to her personal things at all.

At this point, Cynthia didn't care. What was important to her was gone. Her parents were gone.

It was a challenge to climb the steps, but—as he'd been the entire time—Shawn was an angel, helping her along.

In the kitchen she had to sit down to catch her breath. One of the injuries she'd sustained in the accident was a perforated lung. The doctors said she would eventually get back to normal. For now, though, she was easily winded.

"I called Karen Newman this afternoon and told her we'd pick up Shadow tonight. Do you want me to go get her?"

Cynthia nodded. She'd been so grateful that her neighbors had held on to her cat for all this time. She missed the little monster.

"I'll be right back," Shawn said, trotting down the stairs.

Sitting on the chair, Cynthia looked around the place. From the police reports, she knew this was where her mother had been taken from. Her eyes burned with tears as she imagined Helen's horror during the last minutes of her life.

For once, Cynthia hoped that her mother had been completely drunk.

Pushing herself to her feet, she walked toward the cabinet where she kept her liquor. In a way, it was ridiculous to even look, but she needed to know. Perhaps, knowing for sure would somehow lessen the guilt she was feeling.

Cynthia leaned against the counter, reached up, and opened the cabinet doors. She moved one of the bottles of wine and smiled.

The vodka was gone.

Looking up at the bottles of wine, she thought that now was as good a time as any to take them to Shawn's. As she dragged down the first bottle, however, the corner of a sheet of paper appeared. Curious, she reached for it.

"What are you doing?" Shawn asked, startling her.

He was standing at the top of the steps, trying to hold the squirming animal. Cynthia immediately reached out, and as Shawn came closer, Shadow jumped right into her arms.

"I thought we could bring some of this wine to your house," she said.

"But you couldn't wait for me to get it, I see."

She smiled and hugged her pet as she sat down. She looked up at the triangle of white paper peeking out from the cabinet.

"There's a piece of paper up there. I don't know, maybe it's an IOU from my mother," she said, trying to sound cheerful. "Could you get it for me?"

Shadow was snuggling in against her, lifting her chin to be stroked. Cynthia thought this was the most warmth Shadow had ever shown in seeing her.

Shawn reached up for the piece of paper and took it down. As he glanced at it, his expression grew serious.

"What is it?" she asked.

"It's a page from a New Mexico Power Company classified document." He shook his head in disbelief. "It's from the file that your father sent you. He has a note written in the margin."

Helen must have put the sheet up there. No one else could have done it.

"What did he write?" Cynthia asked.

Shawn stared at it for a long time before looking at her.

"He's written the name of the person who arranged for the change of test facilities. It was Martin Durr."

Author Note

There are so many people that we are grateful to for helping us research this book.

Dr. Steve Holland of St. Mary's Hospital in Waterbury, Connecticut. Steve, your help and research with information on area trauma centers and Title 19 patients fed our imagination and opened the floodgates. Thank you. Thank you. Thank you.

Gobakwe Montshiwa, the new member of our family from Botswana. Thank you, GK, for expanding our knowledge of a beautiful culture and a beautiful part of the world. Thank you for being the loving and affectionate *you*.

Gaylord Hospital in Wallingford, Connecticut. One of the best long-term acute-care hospitals in the nation. Our knowledge of the facility comes from a good friend's stay there. Thank you to the doctors and staff for your dedication.

Once again, we can't finish a book without thanking our sons, Cyrus and Sam, for their support and collaboration. We are waiting for *your* books to hit the bookstores!

As always, we love hearing from our readers:

Jan Coffey
c/o Nikoo & Jim McGoldrick
P.O. Box 665
Watertown, CT 06795
or
JanCoffey@JanCoffey.com
www.JanCoffey.com

International Bestselling Author

RICK MOFINA

VENGEANCE ROAD

The body of Bernice Hogan, a former nursing student with a tragic past, is found in a shallow grave near a forest creek. While searching for Bernice, struggling single mom Jolene Peller vanishes.

Hero cop Karl Styebeck is beloved by his community but privately police wonder about the answers he gives to protect the life—and the lie—he's lived.

Jack Gannon, a gritty, blue-collar reporter whose sister ran away from their family years ago, risks more than his job, pursuing the story behind Styebeck's dark secret, his link to the women and the mysterious big rig roaming America's loneliest highways on its descent into eternal darkness.

"Vengeance Road is a thriller with no speed limit! It's a great read."
—Michael Connelly, #1 *New York Times* bestselling author

Available now wherever books are sold!

MIRA®

www.MIRABooks.com

MRM2638

New York Times Bestselling Author

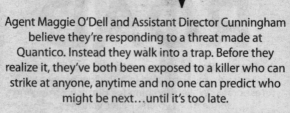

Agent Maggie O'Dell and Assistant Director Cunningham
believe they're responding to a threat made at
Quantico. Instead they walk into a trap. Before they
realize it, they've both been exposed to a killer who can
strike at anyone, anytime and no one can predict who
might be next…until it's too late.

The killer's weapon is a deadly virus, virtually invisible
and totally unexpected. His victims appear to be random
but, in fact, they are chosen with a vengeful precision.
Now Maggie and Cunningham must profile the
deadliest and most intelligent killer they could imagine.

"A killer read."
—*The Lincoln Journal Star* on *One False Move*

Available now wherever books are sold!

www.MIRABooks.com   MAK2640

New York Times **bestselling author**

BRENDA NOVAK

**continues her Last Stand series
with three suspenseful new novels.**

On sale July 28! On sale August 25! On sale September 29!

**"Brenda Novak expertly blends realistically
gritty danger, excellent characterization
and a generous dash of romance."**
—*Chicago Tribune*

**Available wherever
books are sold!**

MIRA®

www.MIRABooks.com

MBNTR09

Emmy Award–winning television reporter

HANK PHILLIPPI RYAN

**brings readers into the world behind prime time news,
where you're only as good as your last story,
and everyone's watching....**

Available now wherever books are sold!

www.MIRABooks.com

It's going to be a

RED HOT SUMMER

LAURA CALDWELL

All available now
wherever books are sold!

MIRA®

www.MIRABooks.com

MLCTR109R

REQUEST YOUR FREE BOOKS!

2 FREE NOVELS
FROM THE ROMANCE/SUSPENSE
COLLECTION PLUS 2 FREE GIFTS!

YES! Please send me 2 FREE novels from the Romance/Suspense Collection and my 2 FREE gifts (gifts are worth about $10). After receiving them, if I don't wish to receive any more books, I can return the shipping statement marked "cancel." If I don't cancel, I will receive 4 brand-new novels every month and be billed just $5.74 per book in the U.S. or $6.24 per book in Canada. That's a savings of at least 28% off the cover price. It's quite a bargain! Shipping and handling is just 50¢ per book.* I understand that accepting the 2 free books and gifts places me under no obligation to buy anything. I can always return a shipment and cancel at any time. Even if I never buy another book from the Reader Service, the two free books and gifts are mine to keep forever.

185 MDN EYNQ   385 MDN EYN2

Name _____ (PLEASE PRINT) _____

Address _____ Apt. # _____

City _____ State/Prov. _____ Zip/Postal Code _____

Signature (if under 18, a parent or guardian must sign) _____

Mail to **The Reader Service:**
IN U.S.A.: P.O. Box 1867, Buffalo, NY 14240-1867
IN CANADA: P.O. Box 609, Fort Erie, Ontario L2A 5X3

Not valid to current subscribers of the Romance Collection,
the Suspense Collection or the Romance/Suspense Collection.

Want to try two free books from another line?
Call 1-800-873-8635 or visit www.morefreebooks.com.

* Terms and prices subject to change without notice. Prices do not include applicable taxes. Sales tax applicable in N.Y. Canadian residents will be charged applicable provincial taxes and GST. Offer not valid in Quebec. This offer is limited to one order per household. All orders subject to approval. Credit or debit balances in a customer's account(s) may be offset by any other outstanding balance owed by or to the customer. Please allow 4 to 6 weeks for delivery. Offer available while quantities last.

Your Privacy: Harlequin is committed to protecting your privacy. Our Privacy Policy is available online at www.eHarlequin.com or upon request from the Reader Service. From time to time we make our lists of customers available to reputable third parties who may have a product or service of interest to you. If you would prefer we not share your name and address, please check here. ☐

BOB09

In 2009 Harlequin celebrates
60 years of pure reading pleasure!

We're marking this occasion by offering
16 **FREE** full books to download and read.

Visit

www.HarlequinCelebrates.com

to choose from a variety of
great romance stories
that are absolutely **FREE!**

(Total approximate retail value of $60)

We invite you to visit and share the Web site
with your friends, family
and anyone who enjoys reading.

SMP60WEB1

JAN COFFEY

32458	THE DEADLIEST STRAIN	___$6.99 U.S.	___$8.50 CAN.
32610	THE PUPPET MASTER	___$6.99 U.S.	___$6.99 CAN.

(limited quantities available)

TOTAL AMOUNT	$ _____
POSTAGE & HANDLING	$ _____
($1.00 for 1 book, 50¢ for each additional)	
APPLICABLE TAXES*	$ _____
TOTAL PAYABLE	$ _____

(check or money order—please do not send cash)

To order, complete this form and send it, along with a check or money order for the total above, payable to MIRA Books, to: **In the U.S.:** 3010 Walden Avenue, P.O. Box 9077, Buffalo, NY 14269-9077; **In Canada:** P.O. Box 636, Fort Erie, Ontario, L2A 5X3.

Name: _____

Address: _____ City: _____

State/Prov.: _____ Zip/Postal Code: _____

Account Number (if applicable): _____

075 CSAS

*New York residents remit applicable sales taxes.
*Canadian residents remit applicable GST and provincial taxes.

MIRA®

www.MIRABooks.com

MJC0909BL